A Daughter's a Daughter

Irene Vartanoff

Formatting by Polgarus Studio
Copyright © 2016 by Irene Vartanoff All rights reserved.

Published by Irene Vartanoff
www.irenevartanoff.com
P.O. Box 27
Gerrardstown, WV 25420

ISBN 978-0-9968403-2-3
ISBN 978-0-9968403-3-0 (ebook)

To Robert Freedman,
a gentle soul gone too soon

A Daughter's
a Daughter

Chapter 1

September, 2008
Pam, 8:30 a.m., Wall Street

Pam Ridgeway picked up the ringing phone on her desk and started to recite, "Document Retention—"

Her daughter burst out with, "What's happening over there?"

"Linley? Is everything all right?"

"Is it true Menahl is going under?"

"I'm fine. You don't have to worry about me," Pam replied.

"I'm asking about Menahl, not you. What's happening?" The anger in her voice came through clearly.

Pam's chest hurt as her breath caught in her lungs. Her daughter didn't want to know about her. She only wanted information she could use to promote her career. The same pattern Linley had followed for years now, brushing aside Pam and her feelings as unimportant.

She looked around the Document Retention Department, where her coworkers were quietly placing their personal possessions into tote bags and plastic grocery sacks and a few cardboard cartons. Trying to process the shock of the mass layoff by doing something.

"I'm sorry. We've all lost our jobs. I can't talk now, Linley." She put the phone handset gently back on the receiver.

The rock she'd clung to since Jeff's death had crumbled. Bankruptcy had been declared this morning. Pam felt adrift in a sea of dread. What would her life be now?

#

Linley, Times Square

Linley Ridgeway fought the desire to throw her cell phone against the wall. Her mother wasn't helping at all. Damn her.

Only minutes ago, Linley's morning had been normal. As usual, she'd stridden in hours early to the WFWF news network studio, well-prepared for her day of being a featured expert on cable television. On the way to her dinky cubicle, she'd tried to make sense of a new tweet. The tweet was garbled. Something about Menahl, the venerable Wall Street investment banking firm. A huge volume of financial transactions passed through Menahl. What could it be? Damn tweets for being only one hundred and forty characters.

Walking by the offices with windows that employees with more status occupied, she had promised herself she'd soon rate one. Why not? She looked the part of the successful news anchor, from her carefully styled blonde hair to her fashionable journalist suits to her designer shoes. She was a hard worker and made sure everyone knew it. She had featured spots on three finance-oriented shows, but she wanted more.

As soon as she'd thrown her fashionable messenger bag under her desk, she'd flipped on the desktop computer and started the television feed with access to all the competing networks. She began looking for news about Menahl. Then she saw the flash from the AP wire.

"Oh, my god!" Unbelievable. She leaped out of her chair.

"Jason!" she shrieked. "Did you see this about Menahl?" She ran around the cubicle barrier and down to Jason Egan's office.

Jason moderated the afternoon show on which she was a panelist, and he always came to the station early too. He wasn't her boss, but he outranked her. She found him studying the same flash she'd seen. His office had a window, but the room was small and stuffed with tapes, DVDs, papers, and all kinds of accessories to the job. The windowsill was being used as another shelf.

Jason sat at his computer, his tall, fit body immaculately turned out in a well-tailored suit and tie as always. He was concentrating hard, tapping in multiple URLs to find confirmations and details.

She moved to his side. As usual, she had to hide an intake of breath from the impact of seeing him. Jason was a handsome man. His brilliant dark eyes were intelligent, piercing, and ringed with thick eyelashes. His strong nose was set off by an even stronger chin. His mouth was full and could curve with humor. He exuded the self-confidence of a mature male. She was no teenage virgin, so the strong virility he radiated didn't frighten her. Instead, it tantalized.

"Unreal. Menahl is the lynchpin of investment banking.

How could the Fed let it die?" Jason muttered. "This could cause the entire U.S. financial system to crash."

He checked out the source. Then he grabbed his office phone.

"Who are you calling?" she asked.

"I know a few traders at Menahl. They'll have details."

Then he paused in the act of punching in the speed dial command. He raised his handsome head and looked up at her.

"Doesn't your mother work for Menahl?"

"Yes," she admitted. Her mother's mundane, low-level job was embarrassing. Linley tried never to mention it. Today, however, her mother was a potential news source.

"I'll call her," she conceded. She turned away to make the call to her mother's office number. Pam Ridgeway toiled in a large room filled with low-level worker bees. She didn't even rate a cubicle.

Yet her mother had hung up on Linley.

#

The sounds of sobbing came from behind Pam in the large room, along with low, muttered curses, but she heard them from a distance, shielded by a wall of silence. The blood rushing inside her own head was much louder. She tried to catch her breath and failed.

Her job was no more. Her life as she had known it was over. Again.

Her heart seemed to shrink, trying to absorb the pain and smother the fear. A huge chasm had suddenly opened up in front of her.

The shock had numbed her. Slowly, the numbness wore off.

Magda, who had been in the same office with Pam for five years and had a son just starting college, began sobbing, too.

Stan was the first to openly rebel. "I've worked at this lousy company for twenty-eight years. Twenty-eight years. No severance, but they want me to wrap up my projects and go quietly? Screw them!" he cried. His mostly bald pate seemed to glow red to match the fury in his face, and his lumpy body lurched as he leaped up. "I'm outta here. I'm never going to staple a document again." He grabbed the stapler from his desk and tossed it in the trash can. Then he stalked out.

Magda still sobbed as she made a pile of the documents on her desk. "Calca che vacca! Du-te dracului!" She either cursed or prayed in her native Romanian as she clicked her lighter to set the papers on fire.

The smoke curled upwards lazily.

"Are you crazy?" Pam grabbed the glass vase from her desk and threw the water from it onto the fire. Then she knocked the papers to the floor and stamped on them.

Magda watched without attempting to fight. Her eyes glowed with a frenzied light.

"I hate them! I hate them!" Magda cried, her face contorted with rage. "In one month, tuition payment is due. One month. What shall I do? How shall I pay?"

"Destroying legal documents won't help," Pam said, although Magda's anger was justified.

Magda kept repeating, "How will Marc stay in university?"

Pam moved closer to the younger woman and put a hand on her arm. "Go home now. I'll call you. We'll figure this out."

Pam would give her the money if necessary.

Magda sniffled and then straightened her spine. "You are right. I must leave this accursed place."

Magda began packing up.

Pam returned to her desk, found her tote bag, and threw her possessions into it. Family photos, odds and ends from ten years of pushing papers. She kept packing. When the bag was full, she stopped. Whatever was left would have to stay. She picked up her purse and her sweater. "I'll call you," she said again to Magda.

Pam nodded at other former coworkers and then walked out of the records room the back way. She didn't wait to witness more tears and lamentations. She was trying hard to stifle her own. Going through the motions, her lifelong method of coping.

When she exited the elevator into the main lobby, she saw half-a-dozen security guards through the glass doors to the building. They held back a pushing, shoving crowd of people. Mostly reporters with cameras. Her mother, the activist Dorothy Duncan, would have swaggered up to them and held an on-the-spot press conference.

Pam shuddered. She'd never had the courage to face such open scrutiny. Keeping her face averted, she hurried past them and the gantlet of gawkers as they battened on others who'd been in the elevator with her. She left the building, knowing she would never return.

#

"My mother said they were all fired. Then we got cut off." No way would she admit to Jason that her own mother had hung up before Linley had gotten what she wanted. How dare she? Didn't Pam know how important getting insider news was to Linley?

Jason said, "I can't get through at all. Management might have shut off the phones." He consulted the list on his phone and hit a different number.

"I'll try her cell." She was already tapping the buttons. No answer. Her mother must have the phone turned off. If she was even carrying it. Pam Ridgeway was old-fashioned. Not like Grandma Dorothy. Grandma would be on her phone right now if she was still in the game. She'd be telling media connections her side of the story. Dorothy knew the secret to shaping news in her favor.

Jason had better luck with his contacts, but nothing concrete yet. Linley hastened to start down her own list. Within a few minutes, they had more details.

Jason had hardly put down his cell phone before he picked up the office landline to call their boss, Marty.

"You heard about Menahl? When do we air our special? Who do you want on it? No, not many details yet. Only Linley's here."

He looked up at Linley, and spoke to her on the side, "Hustle up whatever you can find out. Keep calling everyone you know. Especially your mother." Then he waved her off and got back to Marty.

Linley could hardly hold in her elation. Her strategy of coming in hours early had finally paid off. She had a jump on the other guys. If they were here, they'd each be pushing to get airtime on this hot situation. Now she had the inside track.

She needed something useful, or Marty and Jason wouldn't put her on the air. Why didn't her mother keep her cell phone on?

#

"Pam! Over here!"

She looked toward the sound and there was Sarah, her best friend, at the edge of the crowd outside the Menahl building. Far enough away from the reporters a shout didn't alert them.

Sarah held out her arms. Pam changed course and walked into the comforting embrace.

"Oh, you poor thing. Come on, let's get out of here."

Sarah walked her briskly away from the crowd, where any open emotion could become camera fodder. Sarah grabbed the stuffed tote bag. Its weight pulled her arm down. "What's in here, gold bricks?"

"Just my stuff. Not including a final paycheck."

"Severance?"

"None." No need to explain more. Sarah worked in finance at an executive level.

"Bastards," Sarah said. "Of course the traders and the execs will still get their bonus money and golden parachutes."

Pam nodded. "Support staff gets nothing."

"Too bad you didn't take my advice and retire."

"Not that again. You've got a one-track mind," she said. "I need a new job."

"In this job market? At your age? Get real."

"I have to work. I need a regular paycheck."

By now, Sarah had steered her into a mostly empty coffee

shop. Once they were seated in a booth, Sarah went on the attack. "Didn't Jeff leave you set?"

Pam made a small grimace. "I used up all the life insurance."

"In only four years? What did you do with all that money?"

"I paid off the children's college loans and my mortgage. Then I bought each of them a home."

Sarah stopped her coffee cup in midair. "You didn't tell me."

"You would have said not to."

"You got that right." Sarah banged the cup on the saucer. "Jeff left that money to you, for your future. Steve and Linley are adults who can pay their own bills."

Without giving Pam a chance to comment, Sarah continued. "Linley earns big bucks working for that cable network."

Sarah's expression showed her irritation. "Plus, she treats you like crap. I'm sorry, but it's the truth. You yourself told me she never calls or visits. She doesn't make time to lunch with you once in a while, like Steve. Did she even thank you for buying her that fancy condo?"

"I didn't require thanks, not exactly." At Sarah's silence, she continued, recalling the loving impulse that had urged her to help her grieving daughter deal with the shock of Jeff's sudden death. "I wanted to reach out to Linley."

"It didn't work," Sarah commented.

"She took it as an inheritance from Jeff, not my gift to her," Pam sighed. She made a helpless gesture with her hands. "I guess I was trying to buy back her love."

"You were being a generous mother." Sarah patted her hand. "But you have to look out for yourself."

"I'll be okay for a year or two. I have rainy day savings."

"You're too young to qualify for your pension or Social Security, of course." Sarah gave a half-laugh. "Imagine being too young for anything at fifty-eight."

Pam didn't feel young, but she didn't feel old, either. She felt blank, as she had for four years. She drew an abstract pattern on the Formica tabletop with her fork. Then she shrugged and looked up. "I'll find a new job. I can't sit around the house and do nothing all day."

"You should take the layoff as a gift. You were on automatic. Now you have time to examine your life and improve it."

"No way. I like my life as it is."

"We've had this conversation before," Sarah said, drumming her restless fingers on the table. "You're stubborn, but fate has outsmarted you. Don't you see? Your comfortable rut has disappeared."

#

Sarah's harsh words about the emptiness in Pam's life echoed in her head a few minutes later as she walked to her train station. Sarah had an office to return to. Sarah's law degree, coupled with her finance degree and her years of experience, would keep her employable. Unfortunately, she had told the unvarnished truth about Pam's chances. A middle-aged clerical worker was likely to face age discrimination and diminishing employment opportunities. Plus, thousands of her former coworkers would be competing for the same jobs. What a mess.

Pam was sure she could eventually find a new job. She still had a youthful figure and her face was unlined. Hair color never had to be grey as long as there was Clairol.

Her duties at Menahl had not been challenging. At first, the job was something to do once the children were in college. Jeff also worked in the city, so they drove to the train together, met up for lunch often, and commuted home together. It was cozy. After Jeff died, she continued the same routine, trying to keep her mind off how lonely she was without him.

Pam turned on her cell to call Steve and noticed a series of calls from Linley. No messages, though. She pressed Send.

"Linley? You called several times. I'm fine. You don't have to worry about me."

"I want details about the Menahl collapse." Linley's crisp tone showed her impatience, her barely leashed contempt.

Pam absorbed the slap contained in Linley's hard accents. Linley didn't care that her mother was standing on the sidewalk with no job anymore. Pam took a deep breath, fighting down her hurt. "It's a huge company. It was, anyway. I'm not privy to the big picture."

Linley said, "We have a special coming up in one hour, and I can be on it if you tell me what happened."

For once, she could help Linley. She sighed. "What do you need to know?"

"How did they tell you? What did they say? Are you being paid for time worked? What about severance?"

Pam recited everything that had happened, everything she knew.

"Thanks, Mom. Gotta go."

Linley clicked off.

Pam was left staring at the silent phone. Linley had actually thanked her. Called her Mom. That hadn't happened in years.

If only there was some way to continue this friendlier contact instead of returning to the cold distance Linley usually kept between them.

Her phone rang again, surprising her. She was still standing on a downtown city sidewalk, jostled by fast-moving people. Seeing a bench nearby, she sat.

It was her son, Steve. A half hour later, as she started walking again, she contrasted the one minute Linley spared for her to Steve's lengthy, concerned call. He had wanted to know how she felt. He'd invited her to stay with him and his wife Callie and the grandchildren for a while. He'd asked if she had enough money and offered some of his own. What a wonderful son he was. But he had a wife and children to think of. Pam did not want to impose on them. She could fend for herself.

She made her commute back to Ardsley, her green suburb north of the city, in a daze, returning to consciousness only when she walked in the door of her home. She put her keys on the polished brass key rack she had installed inside the kitchen door. She gazed across at the beautiful yellow granite countertops, which she had highlighted with the occasional pop of a red accent. She had carefully and lovingly decorated each room of this typical suburban house to be the perfect nest for her husband and children. All of whom were gone. A family's life had been centered here. No more. Had she been living in the past, like a ghost wandering the rooms of an abandoned house?

If so, it was over. Time to get on with her life.

#

Dorothy, Suffolk County, Long Island

Dorothy Duncan took her morning stroll along the beach near the house that had been her home for over thirty years. She'd always loved the south shore of Long Island. When she and Malcolm had saved enough, they had built a lovely place right on the water. By then, the children were off to college or launched as adults. Malcolm was about to retire early from the advertising business. They had planned to spend many long years walking on the sand, enjoying the play of the tides.

Of course, it was not to be. Malcolm was of the generation of American men who smoked a couple of packs of unfiltered cigarettes a day, drank a couple of martinis at lunch, and had a couple of highballs at a bar near the office before coming home via the Long Island Railroad. Those men died years earlier than anybody expected.

She had loved the life they led together. He had been in charge of earning the money and she had been responsible for raising their four children and making a home. It had worked fine throughout the 1940s and 1950s, and even into the 1960s. She was an organized and energetic person and her children were all healthy. She had a weekly maid at first, and then a housekeeper. Even before all the children were out of diapers, she had thrown herself into community activism and political causes. She'd marched in many protests, painted many signs, and knocked on many doors.

She'd never spent much time in Manhattan, except on ladies' lunches with her girlfriends. Once a month, they'd dress in their best and go to Schrafft's down on 5th Avenue near the arch where Greenwich Village began. Or the Russian Tea Room on 57th Street next to Carnegie Hall. Or the Women's Exchange on Madison Avenue at 59th Street. After lunch, they'd attend a matinee on Broadway, with intermission cocktails for spice. When the play ended, they would split up and return to their suburban lives.

In their younger days, the lunches had been less lavish but more frequent. They'd gone to Horn and Hardart, the Automat. Or the Chock Full of Nuts coffee house. That was when they briefly were working girls, first in the war effort and later in clerical jobs or teaching until they found husbands. Once they were married and the babies came, they were busy being homemakers.

She had filled many long, happy days painting and sewing for the home she had made for her family. Plus carting the children around to their activities. She had easily moved into running the PTA and organizing local fund drives, and more.

It had been a lovely life. She missed it. She missed her oldest friends too, but one by one, they had died. Ethel Bush had dropped dead of a stroke twenty years ago, which shocked them all. Ethel had never seemed the high blood pressure type. In fact, she had been the quietest of their group. For good reason.

Colleen Murphy, a hearty Irish girl from Queens, had developed Alzheimer's and been locked up in a nursing home for years before she finally died. Dorothy had visited her long past the point when Colleen recognized anyone. A protracted travail for the family.

And Greta, dear Greta. She had died so young. Over fifty years ago now. Dorothy had never forgotten her. Lately, she thought about Greta often. How wrong it was Greta died as she did.

Greta's tragedy had changed Dorothy. After Greta died, no vulnerable, oppressed group lacked a spokesperson if Dorothy could help it. She had thrown herself into countless causes that helped the abused, the forgotten, and the poor. Malcolm had tolerated it without understanding exactly why she was so driven. He was proud of her achievements in the community.

Malcolm. He'd not lived to enjoy the beach house for long. All the years of work stress, the cigarettes, and the alcohol had caught up with him. She had found him dead in the bathroom one morning. A heart attack in his fifties.

Ah, well, it was a long time ago now. Over thirty years already. Her life was simple here at the beach. The children had grown up. All four were self-supporting, even her little shy one, Pamela. When their children were young, they made many family visits during summer vacations. They still visited, but not often anymore.

How odd that she thought about Greta so much lately. Perhaps it was part of getting old, truly old, at last. She took a walk each morning, down the beach and back, to keep herself from falling apart. Maybe it wasn't working. Her thoughts kept returning to the past, to Greta.

She had reached the old stone pier, built a long time ago, when fishing had been important in a tiny village that no longer existed. It was warm on the beach, but she was getting hungry. Time to turn back and have her morning tea. She began to retrace her steps.

What lovely homes these were. Weathered clapboard,

painted grey or white. A few newer homes had vinyl siding, although that was a mistake. The winds could be fierce in winter. They could blow such light siding right off a house. The newcomers would soon learn.

The grey house was attractive, but it looked empty. All the shades were drawn. Probably the people only lived there in summer. It was late season, already September. The Smiths, that was their name.

The white house showed signs of life. There was a car in the driveway and a little dog running around the small fenced side yard, barking. A wire-haired fox terrier. Like Asta from the Thin Man movies. Wire hairs were popular in the 1930s because of those movies. She'd had one as a girl. Later she bought one for Greta's boy. A very long time ago. Now she didn't have a dog. Maybe she should get one. It was a bit lonely out here sometimes.

A tall man came outside to stop the dog barking.

"Hello, Mrs. Duncan," he called, and sent a casual wave her way.

"Good morning," she replied, but she did not linger to chat. It was time to be getting home.

She had always liked a yellow house and there was a beautiful one coming up. Two stories, with a slate roof, and a sunroom running the length of the back of the house with French doors leading out to an old-fashioned flagstone patio. It connected to a path and steps leading down to the beach. A little white wooden gate at the top of the path politely reminded beach walkers that although the beach was public, the homes were private property.

She liked a yellow house. She approved of this one. Silvery dusty miller and pink petunias bloomed along the path and steps. Above, on the patio, large planters held orange gerbera daisies, deep blue lobelias, and contrasting greenery. A charming old-fashioned iron patio set, painted white, with an umbrella, was perfect for sitting outside and enjoying the air without too much direct sun. Lovely. The black shutters and white trim lent a crisp air to the home. How pretty it was.

Her steps had slowed to a stop. Of course. It was her house.

#

Bruce

"Calm down, Yappie," Bruce Wicklow spoke quietly to his wire-hair fox terrier as he watched Dorothy Duncan slowly make her way up her beach steps and into her house. The little dog loved to bark.

"We want to be friends, boy," Bruce said, giving the dog a consoling pat as he picked him up and carried him inside.

Bruce was a writer, although he was quick to point out to new acquaintances that he was the unglamorous kind. He didn't pen daring thrillers or hard-boiled detective novels. He made his living synthesizing information about global economic trends and science. Dry stuff to some, but he'd had reasonable success, mostly in magazines and newspapers, and lately in books.

Renting this big beach house in the off season was something new for him. The people living in these fine homes along the shore liked to pretend it was an exclusive enclave. Take old Dorothy Duncan next door. Bruce had of course introduced himself to her when he'd moved in. She had been gracious but regal and somewhat aloof.

Yet in the town she had the reputation of being a tireless activist and do-gooder. When he mentioned her, people praised her to the skies. Maybe his lack of appeal to her was his self-sufficiency. He was well launched in his book writing career. Doing fine. He didn't need anything or anyone.

What a lie. He needed the truth from Dorothy Duncan. She was the entire reason he'd come here.

Chapter 2

As the news special ended and the credits rolled, Jason turned to Linley. His smile was triumphant.

"We won. Our report aired first."

Before she could think of a reply, he stacked his notes, closed his laptop, unhooked his microphone, and stood.

"We'll be airing at our regular time, but mostly to talk more about the Menahl collapse. See you then."

After he left, Linley slowly removed her clipped-on mic and walked back to the cubicles, trying not to let her frustration show. The special news hour had gone well. She'd been a key part of it because of all the details she'd gotten from her mother. She should be happy she had received the extra air time.

Jason had been meticulously polite and even friendly on air. Off air, he kept it strictly impersonal. Completely professional. Jason acted impervious to her as a woman.

It should be enough for Linley that being around Jason advanced her career. He was a rising cable star with an ambitious eye on a late-night talk show gig. Powerful people kept checking out their regular show, and she sat right next to Jason, looking good and saying all the right things. She was being noticed, too.

Yet, Jason ignored her personal appeal. Being an attractive blonde was one of her major assets. She expected men to react, to grant her favors. Not that she hadn't worked hard to get this far in a super-competitive field. She'd put in the long hours, the extra effort. The other men on their daily show, Ernie, Mike, and Ralph, were softened by her classic blondness. Only Jason showed no sign he felt the same. He didn't address flirtatious comments to her. He didn't favor her during the show. In fact, he called on the guys more often, and he looked at them most of the time. Even his posture leaned away from her.

She didn't like feeling this way. Most men were interested in her. She could have her pick of dates and hookups. She didn't need Jason. Marty had hired her. She appeared on several lifestyle and consumer-oriented programs each weekday for the cable network. Why should she care that Jason didn't act interested?

In spite of her feelings, she behaved like a complete professional. At least, she hoped so. Maybe some of the other sharp men or women at the station noticed how girly she felt around Jason. She fought not to show it, but she might not be succeeding. She hoped Jason had no clue, either. Each time he looked at her, she held her breath, hoping he saw nothing of her interest in him.

#

Pam dreaded telling her mother she had lost her job, but couldn't put it off any longer. Dorothy Duncan was retired now but she still watched television news and would surely find out about Menahl soon.

Would Dorothy be sympathetic to Pam's situation? Right now, Pam felt bruised. She could use a hug. Few of her friends or relatives were the hugging type, certainly not her mother. Instead, Dorothy would say something to make the bankruptcy of a huge multinational corporation a result of Pam's lack of spine. Dorothy Duncan was a fighter who had never understood Pam's retiring nature.

Taking a deep breath, Pam tapped in the familiar numbers. "Hello, Mom?"

"Speak up. Don't be tentative, Pamela. You're a grown woman."

"Uh…I have some news." She paused, then pushed on in a hurry. "Everybody at my company was laid off today. Including me."

"You're not going to accept that, are you? This is why you should have unionized. Is anyone picketing? Speaking out to the media? What about hiring an employment lawyer to fight wrongful termination?"

"Mom, the entire company has gone belly up," she said, stopping Dorothy's rapid-fire strategic questions in mid-flow. "Bankrupt. It can't satisfy its major creditors, let alone what it owes its employees."

"Then you and the other employees should start a class action suit as creditors. Get in at the head of the line."

"I—I can't."

"I still know people," Dorothy continued. "They'd help you organize a protest and find you the right lawyers."

"I don't want to—"

"Immediate action works best."

"Uh…I'm going to have lunch now," Pam finally said in a strangled voice.

"Pamela." Her mother's voice was stern, but also resigned. "Call me when you're ready to fight for yourself."

"Thanks for your support, Mom. Bye." Pam clicked off.

Pam had not expected her mother to offer any consolation. Dorothy Duncan was made of such stern stuff it didn't occur to her that her daughter's feelings were fragile.

Pam sighed as she prepared a simple lunch. A sandwich was enough. Two years ago, Dorothy had given up her leadership of the local civic group out on Long Island where she lived, but she was still the same as she'd always been. Eager to right wrongs, to charge in and demand the big guy make it right for the little guy. Pam felt small by comparison.

She was proud of her mother's activism, but Dorothy was exhausting to be around. Pam usually ended their conversations feeling she had failed, that she was lacking somehow, and Dorothy knew it.

Still, her mother's disappointment was better than the open scorn her own daughter dished up. Linley disdained Pam's housewife career. It bothered Linley that her mother had "gone along with the program," as she put it, instead of breaking free of mid-twentieth century social norms and pursuing a career outside the home. Pam hadn't even kept her own last name, but had taken Jeff's, a complaint Linley had voiced during her school years. Linley wanted a hyphenated last name like the other kids. In vain, Pam had argued she liked Jeff's last name. She was happy not to be associated with Dorothy Duncan's vociferous activism that had often brought Pam unwelcome notoriety while growing up. Linley even was embarrassed because her mother had the free time to make cupcakes for the class.

Enough wallowing. Pam sat up straighter. What could she do with the rest of her day, and with the rest of her life?

First, she should file for unemployment benefits. That was likely to be the only money she ever saw from Menahl in the future. How unfair not to pay the last paychecks.

She spared a thought for her former coworkers. Most of them were not the only breadwinners in their family. Probably they would be okay. But what about poor Magda? She was on her own in her new country. Her son's tuition bill was due soon. Maybe Pam could help with that. She had savings. She could make a private loan, perhaps. Although she needed to live on her savings from now on. Maybe it would be better to find a way for Magda to get the loan, to spare her pride.

Filing for unemployment benefits should take fifteen minutes, and calling Magda to arrange a meeting would take another five. That still left Pam with far too much time on her hands for the rest of her life.

Her house did not need cleaning, but her closets were filled with Jeff's things. After he'd died, she hadn't felt up to dealing with them. She had simply packed them away into the spare bedrooms. She was overdue to confront the relics of her married life. Now that her situation had changed again, surely she could face her past?

#

A few hours later, Pam had bagged a huge pile of clothing up to give to charity. She'd boxed up Jeff's accounting books and his adventure novels to go to the public library. She'd also set aside odds and ends she'd pass by the children in case they wanted them. Done.

She had kept a favorite shirt, and a casual jacket of Jeff's she often wore to get the mail or take out the trash. She had shed a few tears over his clothing, but she had finished. Why had it taken four years to face up to this cleanout?

Now she had nothing left to do. The huge empty spot in her life was very obvious. For four years she had been in a total rut, with nothing in her life except useless routines. She had settled for her clerical job because it was easy. Now it was gone, and she already missed the big space it had occupied in her otherwise empty days.

She heated water for tea in the microwave and sat uncomfortably on the edge of a massive easy chair, Jeff's favorite, in the living room. The floor was now jammed with the boxes she'd run out and bought this afternoon to complete the clearing-out task. Her house was filled with memories of her life with Jeff and their children. Did she want to spend more years living in a shrine to the past? Or did she have the courage to make a serious change?

She got a pad from a drawer and started writing down things she liked, things she wanted to do, things she was good at. Places she'd like to visit, too. As for places she never wanted to see again, Wall Street would go on the top of that list. She wasn't bitter, but it had chewed her up and spit her out, and now she wanted to go in a different direction.

Sarah would be pleased.

#

Linley was seated in her usual position on the panel, waiting for the regular afternoon program, *Hot Tracks,* to begin.

"Linley, I've got a special role for you today." Jason's voice broke into her thoughts.

She looked up. He loomed over her, holding out a piece of paper. She took it.

"What's this?"

He smirked and took his seat. Then he swiveled in her direction, waiting for her to read it.

"I get to interview the moron who drove Menahl into the ground. Yes!" she nearly screamed.

"Oh, tell us what you really think," Ralph jeered.

"Yeah, we know you love those big, dangerous investment bankers," Mike chimed in.

"You're what's called a motivated interviewer," Jason said. "Hang the bastard out to dry on national television. That's all the revenge I can offer you."

"What's he talking about?" Ernie asked.

"My mother lost her job with everybody else at Menahl today. The rank and file received no severance," she explained.

The guys looked surprised and concerned.

"Is she okay?" Ralph asked.

"Sure. Thanks." She didn't say a dead-end job as a paper pusher was no big loss. Anyway, it was the principle of the thing. The top dogs at Menahl had screwed up, but the low-level workers ended up paying for it.

"We're going to set Linley on this guy like a junkyard dog?

That's the strategy?" Ernie asked.

"Yes," Jason weighed in again, taking them all in with his sweeping gaze. "This man ran the company into the ground, and now he's giving interviews trying to justify his golden parachute."

They followed the plan, first carefully disclosing Linley had a personal interest because her mother had been laid off by Menahl today with no severance. Charles Saunders sat in a remote studio when Linley asked her questions. Although he started to complain about how the Federal Reserve had not stepped in to rescue the company, she broke in and asked,

"Why isn't Menahl paying the rank and file severance and wages to date?"

"We're doing our best to ensure all our loyal employees get a fair deal," he claimed, trying to look concerned. His ten thousand dollar custom suit told a different tale.

"Isn't it true, Mr. Saunders, your company let go all the non-trading staff without any promise of severance? Or even their final paychecks?"

He visibly calculated how much it would cost him to act as if he cared. Finally he said, "We're still looking into the possibility. Our assets are very much in question right now."

"If there's no money for the rank and file, why are you accepting thirty-five million dollars in deferred compensation? Isn't that money meant to be paid for performing your job correctly? And wouldn't you agree that leading your company into bankruptcy is exactly the opposite of doing a good job for the shareholders?"

His eyes hardened. His cloying attempt at playing the caring leader crumbled. Saunders couldn't deny the facts behind Linley's accusation. "There's a difference between leadership and rank and file."

Linley said nothing. She let his reply sit there and stink. Saunders's arrogance and self-satisfaction and his signal failure were on view for all to see.

"Thanks for talking with *Hot Tracks*," Jason said formally, ending the interview. His cold tone fooled no one. They'd pinned Saunders to the wall.

Once the video feed was cut, she could contain herself no longer. "That has to be the most hypocritical and smug appearance we've had on this program," she said, surprised at how angry she felt. They were still on the air.

"Looks as if self-interested thinking is still happening in the nearly empty boardroom at Menahl," Ralph said, speaking more professionally than she could at the moment.

Jason nodded. "Can New York's crusading D.A. take Menahl on? Ideas, Ernie?"

"Doesn't state law require a company to have cash reserves to cover payroll?"

"Probably, but they're bankrupt now," Jason dismissed.

"They still have assets to be sold off to satisfy creditors, don't they?" Ralph rejoined.

"Of course, but that's the meat of the problem," Jason said. "The credit default swaps are mere insurance contracts, totally unregulated. No one actually knows what any of them are worth. Not having sufficient cash reserves after they spurned the Japanese deal and couldn't get the Russians to play ball is what sent Menahl into bankruptcy."

"The Fed refused to help, let's not forget," Linley said.

"Bad move. Crazy move," Ernie said. The others nodded.

"The ripples of Menahl's bankruptcy are spreading across the entire economic structure," Jason warned. "Get ready for a bumpy ride."

Then Jason brought it back to the personal, asking Linley, "What's your mom thinking?"

"I don't know," she admitted. "But she's not happy about losing her job."

Although Linley wasn't sure. Her mother had never seemed attached to the work itself, only the routine. A place to go each day. It kept her from getting weird and keeping a lot of cats, or something.

Pam had no ambition, unlike Linley, who was determined to grab fame for herself. She'd seen how people looked up to Grandma Dorothy, how they crowded around her wherever she went. People respected Dorothy Duncan. They asked for her help and advice. Linley wasn't as public-spirited as her grandmother, but she was equally determined to be a force. This on-air financial expert gig was only the beginning for her.

#

Dorothy wandered into her living room, where a pile of mail was stacked on the table next to the couch. She ought to take another look at it soon. She had sorted the incoming pieces, hadn't she? Mostly charitable appeals and activist newsletters.

She must remind these groups to stop wasting trees with paper newsletters. Let them send their information via email. Not that she had anything to do with computers. Linley had given her a computer, a notebook, she called it, and shown her how it worked. Impressive, but Dorothy found herself confused when she was alone with it. When she was a younger woman, she would have taught herself mastery of a new machine. Lately, it all seemed too complicated. She was an old woman now. Surely she did not have to keep up with every new technology?

She leafed through some of the photographs on the dark mahogany dining room table. A pile of photos had accumulated on the polished surface. Oh, that's right. She'd been going through some old boxes of photographs and old albums, intending to separate them out for the children.

Ah, there was her photo of Greta, taken when they both were young girls working in the war effort in the 1940s. Greta was smiling, wearing a beautiful white linen suit and matching big-brimmed hat. Greta had long hair that she had refused to cut despite the war admonitions that it wasn't safe in a factory. Her clerical job in the factory office didn't put her hair in jeopardy, she insisted. Anyway, Greta said she had to keep her long hair so her husband would recognize her when he came back from the war. Such a beautiful deep red color her hair had been.

Of course, the photo was black and white. That's all they had back then, but it was crisp and sharp. Greta was smiling that lovely smile she'd had, the one that said she was the most daring girl in their circle. It was true. Greta was the one who had the courage to marry a soldier before he shipped out. She had written him throughout the war, and finally Roger had returned alive. Then they'd set up housekeeping, gotten to know each other, and had a baby.

Dorothy hadn't thought about Greta, dear Greta, in years.

Oh, she'd remembered the good times, the ladies' lunches and the teas. The rest Dorothy had put firmly behind her. Greta was dead and it was over. Lately, thoughts of Greta had come to her frequently. She wondered if at this age she was developing a sense of guilt, finally. She examined her conscience. No.

How ironic. Her own daughter, Pamela, feared and admired her because she was a do-gooder. If she only knew what a truly bad person her mother could be. Dorothy's actions back then had hardly been moral or legal. She had meted out justice, and she had never been sorry.

The dog was barking next door. He'd been barking ever since she returned from her morning walk, hours ago now. She would go over and meet the annoying little thing. Maybe it would bark less if they were introduced.

She walked next door and started petting and playing with the dog.

"What's your name, boy? Oh, yes, you're a good boy, aren't you?" she cooed as she patted the springy fur on his spine. The little dog practically danced from the attention. He kept yipping.

"It's Yappie," said the man who came onto the deck. He was wearing jeans and a dark tee shirt, the hallmark of the baby boomer generation.

She straightened a bit, not at all discomposed to have been caught on her neighbor's property petting his dog. "He certainly is yappie."

"No, I mean, his name is Yappie," the man said, smiling. He looked healthy and in good shape, about Pamela's age. He was home in the daytime so he must be retired.

"Because he yaps a lot."

She straightened up completely at his words, frowning. "Do you mean to say you allow this dog to bark all day?"

"Uh…" His face took on a guilty expression.

Before he had time for a reply, she swept on. "Because that's very ill-mannered, and he ought to be trained to behave. It's a wonder you haven't been evicted from where you lived previously. Or were you?" She stared down her nose at him.

"Are you volunteering to train Yappie out of his sole hobby?" he asked. His smile was in evidence again.

What a pleasant young man. So reasonable. She smiled back. "I'd be happy to help you make Yappie a model citizen. That will make you more popular with your neighbors. Shall we agree on once-daily sessions?"

Looking a little surprised at how quickly she moved, he soon agreed to allow her a half-hour of training Yappie each morning. Then he would join her for a walk on the beach afterwards to solidify Yappie's progress.

"Excellent. My name is Dorothy Duncan, by the way. Welcome to the neighborhood. What's your name?"

#

After he'd waved a polite goodbye to Dorothy Duncan, who reentered her house, Bruce stood on the deck a while. He looked at the ocean. Technically, it was a bay or something, but to him it was the ocean.

He had introduced himself again to his neighbor. Perhaps she had forgotten they had introduced themselves a few days ago. Yet, he had hailed her by name as she returned from her daily beach walk this morning. He hadn't taken into account the forgetfulness common in old age. That could be a problem.

Yappie sat by his feet, silent for once. "Yappie, you're a regular babe magnet."

Yappie had barked endlessly at the pound where Bruce found him. Bruce could not resist the hopeful, crazy little dog. He'd had a wire-hair fox terrier puppy when he was a boy. He remembered being given the dog on his fourth birthday.

His father got angry. "It's hard enough to make my paycheck stretch to you two without adding another mouth to feed," he'd said on coming home and finding Bruce petting his new friend. His father was always angry. Bruce did not understand, but he saw little of his father. His mother always put him to bed soon after his father came home each night.

This night, Bruce was too excited to want to go to bed, but his mother had insisted he only rated an extra ten minutes after his bath. He was already in his jammies, playing with his new puppy, when his father got home and started yelling about the cost of feeding a dog.

"You make enough money, Roger, if you don't spend it at the track," his mother said. Bruce heard a *smack*. When he looked up, his mother was holding her cheek as if it hurt. Had his father hit his mother?

"Oh, Roger, don't—" his mother said, in a shaken voice.

"I want a beer," his father ordered. She hesitated, then turned and left the living room to go into the small kitchen. She came back with a tray with a brown bottle, an opener, and a glass, and put it on the table next to his father. Bruce still played with his puppy in the corner.

"Get the kid outta here. And that mutt."

"Okay. It's bedtime, anyway. Come on, honey."

His mother had whispered softly to Bruce then, and he had gone to kiss his father, who was sitting in a big upholstered chair, holding a beer bottle and looking at nothing.

"G'night, Daddy," he'd said.

His father had suffered the kiss and muttered something, then pushed him away. Bruce was relieved. His father was an intimidating figure. Then the excitement of his new puppy took over. His mother had made up a box in Bruce's bedroom for the puppy, right next to his bed.

"You two may keep each other company," his mother said after kissing him and pulling his covers up around him. "Now go to sleep." She turned out the overhead light but left the night light on. Bruce remembered not being able to sleep for a long time. He kept looking at the puppy in the bed on the floor. Each time he did, the puppy stirred and whined a little. Finally, the puppy crawled up onto the bed and nuzzled into Bruce. Then they slept.

That day had stood out in his young life. Even now, nearly sixty years later, he could still remember it vividly. How pretty his mother had been. How surly his father.

Sometimes, he dreamed he remembered more, screaming and yelling, but it was unlikely. Human brain development wiped out early childhood memories. He'd researched the phenomenon for one of his long magazine articles.

Within two months of his fourth birthday, both his parents were dead. Aunt Nora had taken him in. Bruce and his puppy became part of a big, boisterous Irish family. Bruce remembered missing his mother, but surrounded by cousins to play with and with two loving new parents, he'd recovered. He hardly thought of those early years. Only lately had he tried to remember.

The time had come to confront the past. If it was possible.

#

Back at her cubicle, Linley stretched her arms over her head to relieve her tension. Jason was driving her crazy. On camera, he smiled at her, he called on her, and he deferred to her opinions in a collegial manner. Contrast that with before and after the broadcast when he joked with the other panelists and usually left her alone. Somehow, he managed to make it seem completely natural. He wasn't interested in getting to know her on a personal level.

Why was she carrying on about this anyway? She hadn't taken this job to be near Jason, but to further her career. She should be looking around, capitalizing on whatever push being on Jason's show gave her, and looking for her next opportunity. Screw Jason.

She raised the phone. Time to call everyone she knew and ask them what they'd heard lately about movement in the cable news and talk world.

"You're at ground zero," her college pal Tamara insisted. "Jason Egan is the hottest of the info hunks. He's coming up fast. Stick close to him."

"What have you heard?"

"Girl, a lot of people are talking about how fine he is. You're lucky to be with him every day."

Tamara liked to exaggerate, but two other media contacts

confirmed Jason was on the fast track for up-and-coming cable television personalities. If he got tapped for a new opportunity, should she angle to take over the show? Was it too soon? Or should she create an exit plan? She had to carve out a niche for herself, brand herself, so the execs would think of her when considering a replacement.

For now, she had a brainstorm. Why not use her own mother's job loss as a dramatic example of ordinary people being thrown out of work? She could even get Pam on the air. Viewers loved slice-of-life stuff, loved criticizing the average citizen's clothing and hairstyle choices. Not to mention their bad luck. Schadenfreude.

Linley quickly fired off email queries and made calls to some managers and producers. She hit gold. A gig on the *Today Show*. Now all she had to do was convince her mother to appear on television.

#

When the phone rang, Pam expected it would be Sarah, checking up on her. Instead, for the third time in one day, she heard her daughter's voice. Pam eagerly rushed into speech.

"Hello, dear. It's sweet of you to call me again, but I'm fine, you know. No need to worry about me."

"I wasn't worrying."

"Oh."

"I got us a great opportunity. A spot on the *Today Show* tomorrow morning. They want to interview you about how it feels to have been laid off from Menahl."

Pam grimaced. Those jackals outside the building this

morning had wanted fresh blood, too. "Thousands were let go. Why talk to me?"

"Because I called them and pitched it."

There was great satisfaction in Linley's tone. Her daughter was triumphant at having arranged an opportunity for Pam to be an object of pity on national television.

"You wouldn't believe how many news agencies are interested," Linley continued. "The *Today Show* is the big deal."

"That's nice, dear. Couldn't you do it by yourself?" She'd never been comfortable as the center of attention.

"Of course not. They want the story from the person directly involved. From you."

The impatience was in her daughter's voice again, the undertone that said Pam knew nothing.

The moment stretched out silently.

"You'll do it, right?" Linley prodded.

Pam cringed at the idea of exposing herself in public. She'd like to help Linley, of course, but she did not want to be on television. "Why not interview Magda instead? She has a more dramatic story. Magda works with—" she corrected herself, stumbling over her words, "she worked with me. She has a son she's putting through college. Tuition is due in a month and she has no way of making payments if she doesn't have a job."

"The interview is with you and me, not with Magda."

"I'd rather not be on television," Pam said.

"Say yes."

"I'd freeze up."

"I promised you'd be on. Don't make me a liar."

"I hate being the center of attention. I can't."

"How can you be so selfish?" Lindsay wailed. "You're ruining my day."

Linley clicked off.

Pam stared at the phone. Linley had hung up on her. Oh, technically, Linley could not hang up a telephone she carried in her pocket, but it was the same thing.

Her daughter had hung up on her.

Useless tears trickled down Pam's cheeks. Why was she so weak? So afraid of being in the public eye?

She and Linley hardly communicated anymore. Unlike her, Linley was ambitious. Linley's quick success in her glamour career had reinforced her opinion that she was far superior to her mother. An adolescent attitude that hadn't changed in a decade.

Ten minutes later, the phone rang again.

"It's me," Linley said, her voice hard. "You've got to do the *Today Show*. Otherwise, I'll lose the spot."

"I—I…"

"If you don't do this for me, I'll never speak to you again."

Pam gasped.

"I mean it," Linley said.

"You'll be interviewed, too?" Pam choked out the question.

"Yes."

"I won't have to be alone?"

"Yes," was the impatient reply. Linley didn't bother to coax.

Pam knew what hung in the balance. "It will help your career?" Pam asked, anyway.

"Are you kidding?" Linley named the time and the address. "Be there. Or I'll never speak to you again. Never."

She clicked off.

Pam hung up the landline and stared into space. Linley had not asked her for anything in years. Now suddenly, she demanded this from her mother.

What if she made a fool of herself? Being on live television was exactly the kind of public exposure from which she had always shrunk. What if she started crying? Would Linley feel guilty? Would she care?

No use going there. All Linley thought about was the publicity for herself.

Was there a chance that caving would revive their old mother-daughter closeness? In case there was, Pam would go on the *Today Show*. But how could she keep from making an utter fool of herself or breaking down?

She picked up the phone again. When Dorothy answered, Pam said, "Mom, I need your help."

Chapter 3

Before they convened for their weekly planning meeting, Linley couldn't resist telling Jason about her coup. Though broadcast network television was kind of passé, the decades-old *Today Show* still averaged nearly five million viewers. An impressive difference in magnitude from their cable show's audience.

"Good move, Lin," Jason said, "your appearance might pull in a crossover audience for us later in the day. We could use it."

"You're unsatisfied with our paltry half-million viewers?" she asked.

Jason smiled. "I love each and every one to death, but I've got enough love to go around if we could attract more. Remember, our contracts have escalator clauses." He cocked his head inquiringly. "Or are you above such petty considerations as mere money?"

Since their boss, Marty, had just walked into the cramped meeting room, Linley wasn't about to say that money didn't matter. She wanted to ensure she was being paid on a par with the men. Although she didn't much care about money. She only used it to keep score.

"I'm not doing this out of the sheer goodness of my heart," she replied.

"Here I always thought you were an angel, come down from heaven to show us the error of our money-grubbing ways," Ernie quipped, coming into the room.

Marty started laughing, if one could call his hoarse croak a laugh. It was the signal to shift the topic. She hugged to herself the excitement that tomorrow she'd be doing a star turn on the *Today Show*. Maybe this would be her big break.

#

Dorothy turned off the television once Linley's afternoon show ended. Somehow, her youngest grandchild would find a way to make that show her own. Linley was a fighter.

Heredity was strange. None of her children were go-getters. Pamela was the meekest of them all. Among four children and nine grandchildren, all the rest were like Malcolm, the embodiment of the conformist "man in the grey flannel suit" typical of men in the 1950s. They were solid, but they lacked daring. Yet Linley had it in spades.

Dorothy had high hopes for that girl. This was only Linley's second television network, but she was already very visible and only twenty-eight years old. With each move, Linley achieved more airtime and prominence. She was building recognition as a personal finance expert, making herself a hot commodity in this era of financial chaos.

Linley hadn't let herself get distracted by men, either. Things were different for young women today. They didn't see marriage as their ultimate career. Dorothy had enjoyed that life, herself, but times had changed. Young women like Linley wanted to make their mark on the world with business careers.

Did Linley have any idea how much her old grandmother was rooting for her? Probably not. It didn't matter. Linley would succeed on her own. She did not need Dorothy's help.

As for poor Pamela, Dorothy had given her some sensible advice when she phoned earlier, whining about being forced to go on television for a few minutes. Pamela needed to toughen up.

#

As the evening hours wore on, Pam's initial determination faded. She paced through the house, picking up objects and setting them down restlessly. How could she face those cameras? Why had she been stupid enough to agree? She'd freeze up, she knew it. She would not be able to utter even a single word. Linley would be mortified.

Pacing had brought her in front of the liquor cabinet. Why did she even have one? She didn't drink, although right now she wished she did. She was going to bomb out on national television tomorrow morning.

Oh, think of something else. What to wear. Linley would be in the usual newscaster's garb of a man-tailored blue or white shirt under a severe suit, and discreet accessories, probably plain gold earrings and a thin gold necklace. Pam should look what she was, a suburban housewife. A camera-shy, terrified, middle-aged widow.

Pam's next stop was the bathroom medicine cabinet, but there was nothing in it to take away her growing panic. A few pills for headaches wouldn't calm her.

How did her mother do it? Dorothy gave interviews on the spot when she was leading protests. She eagerly sought air time on television and radio during her frequent community campaigns. Linley had inherited Dorothy's love of the limelight, but the gene had skipped Pam. She had spent much of her youth cringing from the public attention her mother's activist lifestyle had brought. Dorothy thrived on it, used it to her advantage. Linley was following in her grandmother's footsteps. Pam was proud of her daughter and her mother, but she was not like them. This would be a disaster.

After stewing for what seemed like hours, Pam forced herself to go to bed. There she lay rigid, unable to connect with her soft mattress and relax. She was miserable with stage fright. She even allowed herself a few tears in the dark.

She could call Linley and cancel, but that would make her daughter furious. Besides, it was the coward's way out. No, she had to see it through.

Perhaps she could take Linley out to lunch or brunch afterwards. Maybe Linley would show her where she did her own job. Yes, and maybe the sun would rise in the west for a change.

She sighed. Linley had been such a sweet little girl. That ended when Linley had hit her late teens and ambition became her god. She had looked around at the snug domestic life Pam had created and disdained it. This little adventure wasn't going to change Linley's attitude. As soon as Linley had gotten what she wanted from Pam, she'd walk away.

Or perhaps not. Maybe if Pam did this thing right, she could get her little girl back. That was her last thought before the exhaustion of the day finally claimed her.

Chapter 4

Linley held in her excitement as the appearance on the *Today Show* proceeded. Pam was tastefully dressed and made up, looking like the ordinary housewife she was. Linley naturally wore a power suit softened with simple gold jewelry. The interviewer was Matt Lauer, who was a winning choice for big exposure because TV executives liked to keep an eye on him, as did the housewife viewers. More eyes would be on the screen than when the women anchors were interviewing.

"The Wall Street collapse isn't about executives earning millions. Here in New York, it strikes close to home. You may already know Linley Ridgeway, a regular on our sister cable company, WFWF. Linley Ridgeway keeps track of personal finance concerns for Jason Egan's show, *Hot Tracks*. Today, Linley has a very personal story to tell, right?"

"Yes, I do, Matt. My mother, Pam, worked for Menahl for ten years. Yesterday, she and all thirty thousand of her coworkers were laid off."

At that, the camera moved to show Pam, seated on the couch next to Linley. Matt turned to Pam and spoke in his most sympathetic tone.

"How did it feel to be laid off abruptly after many years of loyal service, Pam?"

"I was in shock, Matt," Pam said.

"Why is that?" he prompted.

Pam continued, "It was hard to grasp that such a big, important company had fallen apart overnight. We were told to leave immediately, too."

Linley interjected, "Matt, Menahl announced it wasn't paying any severance or even a final paycheck."

Matt turned to Pam again. "How did that make you feel?"

"Stunned. Is it even legal?" Pam's confusion showed on her face.

Linley said, "The D.A. has moved to freeze Menahl's remaining assets, pending payment of wages to the former employees."

Matt nodded. "That's a step in the right direction. But Pam, how did you and your coworkers take the layoff?"

Pam sighed. "We were all upset. Some of us more visibly than others. Most of us packed up our personal items silently. Many of us were in tears."

"What did you do?"

"I—uh…I put out a fire someone had started on a desk," Pam said, stumbling slightly over her words. Linley had made sure she'd shared that in the briefing session earlier.

Matt expressed suitable amazement, and the interview proceeded along the lines they'd predetermined. On cue, Pam described her coworker, Magda. "She's a new citizen from Eastern Europe. Because we all lost our jobs, she has no way of paying her son's college tuition."

Then it was Linley's turn again. "Matt, here are some simple steps for workers caught in a mass layoff. They can attempt to negotiate better severance terms, or ask for use of the office to look for work, or for outsourcing assistance."

"Good advice. Unfortunately, these services are unlikely to be available to the thousands left high and dry when Menahl went bankrupt. What are you going to do next, Pam?" Matt asked. "How will you rebuild your life?"

She smiled tentatively. "I don't know. This has been a blow."

Linley leaned in protectively, and Matt finished the spot. "Good luck, Pam. At least your daughter has a job. Linley Ridgeway can be seen regularly on our sister cable network show, *Hot Tracks.*"

He turned away and wrapped up the segment before they went to commercial.

Then he pivoted to face Pam again and offered his hand graciously. "Shocking story, Pam. I hope everything works out for you. Thanks for bringing it, Linley." After he and Linley shook hands, Matt moved to another part of the set and they were hustled off by an assistant.

"Great job, Mom!" Linley said.

"I did okay? What a relief. Now, do you have time for a cup of coffee or something?" Pam asked.

"I'm due at my studio."

"Oh."

Linley didn't usually feel sorry for her mother. Pam had chosen to lead a small, useless life. Although now, after hearing the pain in her mother's voice during the interview, Linley felt a tug of something.

"Why don't you come with me? We've got coffee and maybe a bagel."

"Oh, that would be wonderful!" Now Pam was smiling broadly. "If you're sure I wouldn't be in the way?"

Did her mother always have to be needy? Didn't she have a life?

"No, Mom. Let's go."

#

An hour later, Pam watched Linley on another television show. She herself had been tucked away in a viewing room, because this was a small studio without seats for an audience. Linley stood by and then was called to sit at the anchor's desk for one short segment of the program. The viewing room was a small box to one side of the studio entrance. Next to Pam was a larger box with all the production equipment and people in it. Except for the cameras and operators, of course.

Pam was still amazed at herself. She had lived through being interviewed on network television without falling apart. She had answered Matt Lauer's questions in complete sentences, with poise. She hadn't stuttered much, or frozen up. She had even remembered to mention Magda's difficult situation.

The *Today Show* set had been cozy, with couches and greenery like someone's living room. She had felt comfortable. She had never been in danger of losing her composure. Why had she been so frightened beforehand? Why had she thought this was so difficult? Had she been such a mouse when she was young? She was a grown woman now who had suffered tragedy yet lived through it. Was that the reason she had not fallen apart on camera? She must think about this amazing experience, but not now. It was Linley's turn to speak.

Linley's daily appearances were on what they called "talking heads" shows because they usually featured people sitting at desks and sometimes only from the shoulders up. She had shown Pam quickly through the studio where Jason Egan's daily program was broadcast. On that show, the panel of men and her daughter yelled at each other. Pam already knew some of these details because she recorded the show for later viewing daily, not because Linley had invited her to stay and watch it. She didn't tell Linley she watched her on television regularly. As interested as she was in Linley's life, she had to give her daughter space.

On this current program, Linley made deft professional comments, but was not the prominent contributor she was on the show with Jason Egan. Pam had noticed something between Linley and the host, Jason Egan. He had been introduced to Pam briefly at the studio as Linley had dragged her quickly through, and she'd marveled at his conventional handsomeness. He looked like the heroes of her romance novels.

Not that she said such a thing. Linley might think Pam was unsophisticated, but it wasn't true. Linley had hardly spent any time with her once she had become an adult, so how would Linley know? Oh, no need to think about that at this moment. There was her baby, at ease on the second television show in one morning. Quite an accomplishment.

Did Linley have a secret crush on Jason? She had looked at him the way she'd looked at that boy in seventh grade. Now she hid it better, but Pam was not fooled. She could always recognize the signs of interest on Linley's face. They were clearly visible when Linley looked at Jason.

#

Later, during a solitary lunch, Pam thought about Magda. It was less painful than considering Linley's casual parting from her earlier. Pam's reward for doing the *Today Show*, at emotional cost to herself, had been a grudging extra hour, and then a quick goodbye. She should stop hoping that Linley would come around.

How to help Magda? There was a chance that people would send money for Magda to the *Today Show*. That nice assistant had explained that it often happened if a story touched people. Unfortunately, Magda needed more than a one-time gift. College tuition cost many thousands of dollars, even after all the scholarship money Marc merited, and the government loans. Other loans Magda had obtained didn't qualify for forbearance because she'd lost her job. As it was, unemployment compensation would hardly support Magda. Without vacation pay, current pay, or severance, Magda would struggle merely to make her usual household expenses.

That damned corporation. It made Pam angry to think about how hard they had worked all those years, only to be kicked to the curb. There ought to be a way to even things out. The D.A.'s actions against Menahl could take years to complete and might result in nothing more than a little back pay. If that.

Linley handed out nice-sounding clichés when she did her personal finance expert thing, such as, "Keep six months of living expenses in savings." Single mothers like Magda had too many day-to-day calls on their income. Yet Magda had come far in the years Pam had known her, conquering English and supporting herself and her son. Magda was proud of that boy, determined to ensure he had a better shot at life than she'd had as a single mother. There must be something that Pam could do to help.

Although at first she had thought about offering a large financial gift, she knew that wouldn't be the right way. Magda had her pride and needed to keep it. Pam also had her pride, and if she wasn't careful with her money, she could be in financial trouble, too. The whole economic system had turned scary shaky overnight. Menahl's collapse had started a domino effect that threatened everything. What had been a hefty retirement account a few days ago had lost half its value.

Maybe a loan of some sort? That was the downside of living in an industrialized nation. If this were Africa, South America, or Asia, Pam could make a micro loan of a hundred dollars, and Magda would buy two sheep and four chickens, or ten pounds of yarn or rattan, and go into business. Soon, Magda's entire extended family and her village—the women, anyway—would be self-sufficient profit centers.

Why couldn't Pam seek something similar for Magda? There were Internet micro loan sites. She was sure that she'd read about them in the *New York Times*. Hadn't there been that crazy girl who maxed out her credit cards on frivolous junk, and then asked everybody to send her money? And they did?

Maybe she could arrange to broker a micro loan for Magda. Pam herself wasn't all that Internet savvy, but now she had plenty of time to learn.

Or perhaps she could find venture capital. Why not? Magda's son was brilliant and a hard worker, set on a profitable professional career. He could repay a loan eventually, from wherever it originated. Not that Pam had the first clue about how to find venture capital, but she wasn't stupid. She could teach herself what she needed to know.

#

Later that day, Linley's frustration added to the vehemence of her on-air disagreement with Jason.

"You're all wrong about the cause of the Wall Street meltdown," she insisted.

Jason merely raised an eyebrow, even as Ernie asked, "How so?"

"Look at the subprime mortgage home foreclosure rate," she insisted. She pulled up a chart on her desktop computer, which appeared to the other panelists and the viewers full screen. "See how it rose dramatically in 2002, long before any Wall Street firms were affected? Homeowners precipitated this mess. Not the other way around," she said.

"I don't agree, Lin," Jason said. "Who convinced people to buy houses as investments, instead of as homes? It was the banks and brokers, that's who."

"The banks didn't force individuals to buy houses they couldn't possibly afford." She pulled up another visual. "Look at these statistics. Prior to the housing bubble, most people bought modest homes. During the bubble, the number of people who bought huge houses with big price tags was substantial. Most of those people are the ones in trouble now."

"A family ought to be able to find affordable housing, but speculators kept forcing the prices up," Jason said.

The other men on the panel stared at them. Linley and Jason seldom argued.

The guys weren't jumping in, so she kept going. "Many homeowners knew it was a scam. They bought houses they couldn't afford in collusion with dishonest appraisers and mortgage brokers. Then they either resold the houses immediately for a huge profit, because demand was pushing home prices up, or they refinanced and took out equity from the houses—equity that had supposedly doubled overnight."

Jason shook his head. "This is worth debating further, but we're out of time for today. We'll have to leave it at me thinking the little guy got conned, and you believing he was complicit in his own fleecing."

Jason did the usual sign off, and the program went to credits. He turned to her as the other men were standing up to leave. "Why are you against the little guy?"

"What makes you think I am?" she replied, trying to keep defensiveness out of her voice.

"Oh, come on." He threw his pen on his desk in a rare show of disgust. He stood. "Every day you say it's their fault our entire economy is facing collapse."

She stood, too, meeting the aggression of his stance. "I refuse to pander to greedy fools by pretending sympathy for them the way you do."

Jason listened calmly, but out of the corner of her eye, she could see Ralph looked taken aback by the rancor in her voice. Which reminded her how inappropriately she was acting.

Yelling at Jason. She backed off.

"Sorry. We should be able to hold opposing views without me accusing you of hypocrisy."

Jason waved away her apology, frowning. "You have a low opinion of the average person. Why?"

"Maybe because the more I learn about how people handle their finances, the more I realize how irrational and self-deluding they are," she said.

"That's a pretty tough accusation to make."

By now she'd taken off her microphone clip and closed her laptop. "You forget that personal finance is my specialty. I don't think much of people who try to con their way into the good life instead of earning the right to it."

Ernie came around the desk and stood between them. "I like seeing you two duking it out. You make us all sound more interesting."

Jason looked amused. "What? Yelling about stocks isn't exciting enough?"

"Sure, Jase, but you two shouting at each other makes it personal," Ernie replied.

As the two men continued to trade remarks, Linley slipped away to the safety of the hallway outside the studio. She hadn't done a good job of hiding how riled up she was. It wasn't only about the average consumer, who could go into bankruptcy for all she cared. She'd simply report the trend.

No, the reason she'd blown up at Jason was the same as always. She needed a break from sitting next to him. She needed an escape from the chemistry bubbling between them that pushed her over the edge into irritability.

There was so much under the surface, so much they weren't saying. She'd been a fool to take this job.

At the end of her job interview three months ago, Jason had reached his hand across the conference table and shaken hers. A tingle had run up her arm from the contact. It was all she could do to maintain her self-control and smile politely as her new boss, Marty, nodded in approval. Jason hadn't seemed to notice the electricity. Maybe it was one-sided. Was that even possible? How could he have forgotten?

It had happened a year ago. She'd met Jason at a media party when he was still writing news copy and hadn't yet penetrated the cable talk shows. He'd been trying. Linley had known he was interested in her initially because she worked for CNN at the time. Jason was more impressed with her job than her looks or personality. Although they had clicked on that level, too.

They'd gone to the hotel bar after the media event. At that point, it still could have been considered a business thing. They worked for competing media outlets and were networking, getting a feel for the lay of the land about a potential employer of the future. Jason was honest about his curiosity. Linley answered his questions about her employer only after she made Jason answer hers, though. For every one he'd lobbed at her, she'd smashed back with one or two of her own. After a half-hour of give and take, Jason had gazed at her with admiration.

"You're a tough one, Linley." He'd smiled. Something inside her had melted at that smile, a smile that had seemed to encompass who she was under her professionally groomed presentation and her cagey banter.

"I aim to get what I want," she'd acknowledged. Then she'd

allowed herself to smile her first real smile with him.

An hour later, they were upstairs in a hotel room having sex. No single Manhattan guy would bring a woman to his own apartment unless he wanted a relationship. Renting a hotel room was a declaration of lack of intention. Linley knew and didn't care. Sex with Jason was just for a giggle. They'd been having fun at the bar. Why not continue the fun in private? They had laughed their way to the room he'd gotten and smiled as they'd tossed off their clothes. There had been shrieks and chuckles as they had thrown themselves on the bed.

Then everything had changed. With a touch, the casual hookup had turned into lovemaking. Sighs and groans had replaced the laughter. What was supposed to be mere pleasure became more. She'd felt as if this sex was different.

Jason obviously had not felt the same. As she was drifting off afterwards, he literally sprang out of the bed. He quickly dressed, then leaned down to give her a light kiss and a lame excuse.

"Sorry, but I've got an early call." As the glib words passed his lips, his eyes looked into hers. Was he searching for something from her? By now, any feelings she might have had for him had been shut behind her self-controlled façade. She gazed at him silently. He found nothing, nothing except her cynical acceptance that their hookup was over.

She had secretly been angry at Jason ever since. Marty's offer to be on the panel show had been too good to turn down, but it was accompanied by the constant danger Jason was to her equilibrium. Over the months, her unrequited ire over how he had left her that first night came out over and over again in her adamant opposition to whatever position he took on a topic. If he said the market was up, she'd find a way to say it was down. Probably if he'd said the sun was shining, she would have claimed it wasn't.

She knew her attitude was irrational. It had just been a hookup. She'd done enough of them in college it shouldn't have bothered her. This time, her emotions got involved despite herself. She'd tried to be philosophical about it. Nothing much came of hookups with strangers, although she had consoled enough girlfriends to know sometimes people hoped. Especially women. She had no intention of being so foolish herself, yet emotions she could not tamp down told her she had been exactly that dumb over Jason.

For a few minutes, she had felt something between her and Jason. She knew he'd felt it, too, but he had denied it and run from it. She could do no less herself. Fronting, laughing at being emo, while hiding how drawn she was to him.

Here they were, a year later, working on the same news talk program. Jason had come up with the idea for the show and sold it to the cable management, becoming the moderator but not the ultimate boss. That was Marty. When one of their original panelists had moved on, they'd done a search and found her, also searching. Since Jason said nothing at their first interview about knowing her from before, she had never referred to it herself.

It ate at her constantly. She kept wishing for something more between them and at the same time dreading it. The more she knew Jason, the more attracted to him she was. That hair, his broad shoulders, his eyes. She remembered how he tasted. She wanted him.

She needed to calm down. She had more shows to do with Jason, and she intended to handle them with consummate professionalism. She was strong. Enough of this endless girlish yearning.

#

Dorothy was sitting on her patio. She had not taken her morning walk today. She would wait until later, when she went with Yappie and the new neighbor. Bruce, that was his name. Nice young fellow. About the right age for Pam, and no sign of a wife or a girlfriend. Maybe she should invite Pam for visit, since the poor girl had lost her job. Seeing how Pam took to Bruce would be entertaining. That girl needed to re-start her life. Why not with a new man?

As the sun swung around, it was very pleasant to be protected by the umbrella. She watched the waves and wondered how much longer she had to live. A curious thing to wonder, some might say. Eventually, when you got old, you did think of it directly instead of pretending death would never happen. She was already eighty-seven, not a great age compared to some people, but her family only lived into their eighties. Her elder brother and sister were already dead. She probably had only a few years left, if that. Just as well. Life wasn't as interesting now as it used to be. She simply did not have the stamina, let alone the razor-sharp memory, for the crusades she'd led in the past. Oh, she knew dimming memory wasn't unusual as one got older. But it was damned annoying.

At least she could still drive her car, although lately she hadn't felt comfortable doing it much. More and more, she simply called the local shops and ordered what she needed, and paid for delivery.

Not getting out in the car did leave her feeling a bit cut off sometimes. She had a regular card game on Wednesdays, and there was a luncheon out at the club on Fridays, but during the rest of the week, there wasn't any reason to leave the house. Since giving up her committee leadership positions, she'd somehow lost interest in their doings, too. Although she studied and signed petitions that came around, of course. She didn't attend the meetings she used to run herself. She didn't interfere. She had retired.

Was she waiting to die? Perhaps.

That boy next door reminded her of someone. She didn't know whom it was, but she'd remember eventually. During a long life, she had seen many faces. She supposed there were some characteristics that repeated. No, he reminded her of a particular person. Was it someone she had liked? Or disliked? It might be easier to remember who it was if she divided her mental list into people she'd liked and those whom she had wished the earth would swallow up.

Occasionally, her wishes had been granted. Pamela would be scandalized to know how satisfied her mother was when an enemy fell. Pamela was always a goody two-shoes. A sweet-hearted girl, far too sensitive and easily hurt. It was a blessing she'd married Jeff. He wasn't the hurting kind; the boy hadn't had a cruel bone in his body. Dorothy had known cruel men, but she had been smart enough to avoid or get around them. She'd known how to spike their guns if they got in the way of her campaigns. Many men had been bullies in the old days, but she'd refused to tolerate them. In fact, she had made it a point to bring them down when she could. She wasn't the type to wait for the Lord's vengeance the Bible promised.

Ah, well, but that was a long time ago.

#

That afternoon, Pam called Magda. "How are you, dear?"

"I am well, Pamma." Magda said. She had never quite gotten her mind around the nuances of American nicknames.

"Did you by any chance see me on television this morning?"

"No…it was important?"

Pam explained she had been told there was a chance that viewers would send checks.

"This is—what you say—amazing," Magda sputtered. When she got excited, she lost some of her English.

"I don't want to get ahead of myself and give you false hope," Pam stressed. "It might only be a few hundred dollars."

"Oh."

She was lying, of course. She planned to ensure Magda would have enough cash to make several tuition payments, even if she had to donate it herself under a false name via a U.S. Postal Money Order. There ought to be some system to help people like Magda, people who were in a temporary jam and needed a short-term hand. "I have thought of another possibility. Would you like to hear what it is?"

"Yes. Of course."

She explained her fledgling idea of securing a loan through an online micro-credit lender.

"I would be grateful. You are my blessed friend," Magda

declared, sounding very excited.

Perhaps she should have researched the micro-loan idea before suggesting it to Magda. She tried to back off a little.

"Anyway, that's a possibility. I will go on the Internet and find out everything I can, right away," she promised.

Oh, Pam, what have you done? she thought as she hung up. She wasn't the expert on helping people. She should call her mother and ask if she was doing the right thing. Although she already knew that her mother would say Pam was doing it all wrong. As she always did.

#

Jason surprised Linley by coming to her cubicle between segments of the other shows they both contributed to.

"Did you take your mom to lunch after the *Today Show*?"

Linley stared at him. Why on earth did he want to know? On the other hand, it was actual conversation unrelated to the job, a first for Jason.

"I had work to do. She went home," she said. Why did it suddenly sound selfish of her? She could have spared the time to be nicer to her mother. Pam had come all the way into the city at such an early hour on Linley's behalf, not her own. Her mother hadn't asked for public sympathy for herself. Linley had used her mother's bad luck to further her career.

Jason said, "She's a classy lady. If she comes into town again, we should take her out and invite Marty. He's single, too."

He couldn't be serious. Wanting to fix up her mother with a new man? He had to be jerking her chain.

"Was there something you wanted, Jason, or are you just

trying to annoy me?"

"Go out with me Friday night. We should get to know each other," he said, in an offhand manner.

She searched his eyes, not seeing the irony she expected. Had he forgotten the night they'd ended up in bed? Was it possible? No, his eyes showed he remembered.

"Been there, done that." She didn't make any attempt to soften the refusal. She kept her voice too low for others nearby to hear.

"I don't recall us talking much," he countered, leaning closer, his voice challenging. "It's only dinner. Hands on the table at all times." He spread his hands out palms up, indicating his pure intentions. Then he spoiled the innocent gesture by smiling at her and dazzling her with his raw animal appeal. She wanted to melt.

Was he serious? Was he pretending he didn't feel the chemistry that still sizzled between them? Day after day, she could barely restrain herself from staring at him inappropriately. Drinking in his features, laughing like a fool at his witticisms, lusting after his powerful, well-shaped body she'd memorized that one night last year. Professional protocol forbade any random touching because of sexual harassment issues, which was all that saved her. That one handshake when she got the job had been electric. If they ever touched again, she would go up in flames.

She refused to take the risk.

"Thanks for the invitation. Some other year." If only she felt as coolly indifferent as she sounded. He was very tempting. He could hardly look any more handsome. His dark tailored suit was a perfect foil for the shocking pink shirt and tie he wore, and both emphasized his regular features, skillfully trimmed hair, and piercing dark eyes. He was an attractive, virile man and he was smiling at her and wanted to spend time with her. She wanted to make love to him. She wanted to have time to explore his face, kiss every indentation and crease. His body. She wanted to press the skin of his naked chest with her own, and feel the heat of their flesh mingling.

She couldn't take this another moment. She stood abruptly, and swiftly walked around Jason. Then she picked up speed and headed for the safety of the ladies room. It was definitely a retreat. She'd soak her neck and wrists in cold water until he went to his next program appearance. Or until she had regained some semblance of her usual poise.

Wasn't this what she wanted? After all these months, he had made a move. She was a wreck. How was she going to tough out sitting next to him on the panel in a few minutes?

#

That went well. She ran away from him.

Jason looked after Linley's disappearing figure. Linley disliked him. He'd been a jerk that night last year. It had started out as just another hookup, exciting for the moment, but meant to be meaningless in his life. Then, he didn't know how, it had changed. After they'd finished, he'd wanted to stay close to her, to hold her. Something he hadn't wanted to do since he'd been a naïve teenager. The mere idea had galvanized him to leap up and dress in a hurry.

Linley must have thought he was a pig. A gentleman softens

the inevitable goodbye. He'd always tried to act like one, even with women he was bored with as soon as he'd gotten off. With Linley, his unexpected emotion had made him act like a boor. He'd seen it in her eyes when he'd finally looked at her again as he was about to leave.

He had seen that same expression in Linley's eyes often in the three months since they'd been working together. An expression that judged him and found him wanting. It made him want to crash through her defenses, prove he was more than she took him for. One kiss would do it, he was convinced, but he resisted the urge to touch her at the studio and commit career suicide at the same moment. Daily, he fought to keep a poker face, to act in a calm, professional, and distant manner, especially when they were on the air. He had to keep it formal. Sometimes, he turned in the other direction so he didn't have to look at her.

When would she forgive him? Why did he even want her to forgive him? He didn't deal with women on those terms. He was careful to keep things cool and equal. With Linley, he felt as if he was on an uphill quest. Her aloof demeanor rolled him down to the bottom again and again.

She'd had her nose stuck up in the air ever since that night. He didn't intend to sit next to her any longer, day in and day out, and take it. It was a struggle to keep his mind on his job when she was getting under his skin. She affected his concentration.

She didn't put much of her terrific body on display. She was a lady. It was enough to see the delicate skin of her neck. A thin gold chain often rested gently on her flesh. Nothing flashy for her. At the oddest moments, he found himself wanting to reach over and pull her chain off. With his teeth. Then put his lips on that neck, that white, long neck, and kiss his way down into the secrets hidden by her conservatively buttoned blouse.

He cursed silently. This had to stop. He was going crazy from lust. He had to get her to bed again. This time, he'd spend the whole night. He'd luxuriate in Linley until he'd had his fill. Maybe, if the sex was as great as he remembered and anticipated, they'd even date for a while. Until he got tired of her. It had been years since any woman had held his interest for more than a month, if that. A month should do it.

First, he had to convince her to even speak to him outside the studio. She'd made it clear she wasn't going to cross professional lines. How to lure her to take that step?

He walked to his office, automatically glancing at the calendar on his phone. There was his answer. A day away from the studio, that's what he needed to crack Linley's shell. A joint project for extra credit. It had worked in high school when he'd been hot for a girl in his class. All he had to do was come up with a project that played on Linley's naked ambition. Then get her naked.

Chapter 5

Pam had spent a week shilly-shallying. There was no other way to describe her lack of action. She'd had such a great idea and then gone nowhere with it.

During her first, optimistic check on the Internet for micro loans, she'd discovered a serious hitch. The major company that did them in the U.S. was suspending all capital investments. With Wall Street and the American banking system in chaos, chances were that an iffy new loan program would not receive regulatory approval. Meanwhile, the Internet loan storefront had effectively been shut down.

She'd tried other sites, but there wasn't any significant feedback about whether they were working. With the country in financial upheaval, everything was changing. Certainly her life was. And Magda's.

How could she have messed up so badly? She was in over her head. She had no clue how to help Magda as she had offered. Peer-to-peer lending was all over the Internet and in theory it was no big deal, except that with no job, Magda wouldn't have the regular income to repay a loan. Pam had been combing

Internet sites, but she couldn't figure out how to help a person with no income. Magda would need her unemployment compensation to pay her rent and put food on the table.

This was making a mountain out of a molehill. She had spent several days at the library reading about loans and grants. She had trolled the Internet for hours. Now she had to put her money where her mouth was. Come up with a plan that would work. She was afraid, afraid she couldn't do it.

Finally, she bit the bullet and called her mother. As she explained the problem and all the side issues, she could hear herself get more frantic.

"Pamela, calm down," Dorothy's voice came through the line in her typical admonishing tone. "You are making this too complicated. Now, do you have any information about the tuition obligation? Do you know the total? When it's due? What the interest rate is? If it's a secured loan? A balloon loan? A government loan?"

Dorothy finally paused, and Pam answered in a low tone, "No. I don't know any of it."

"Call your friend and find out, dear, and while you're at it, ask if she has any other source of income available to make repayments—even tiny ones—on a loan."

Hearing nothing in reply, Dorothy continued, "Pamela, did you hear me?"

"Yes," she sighed. "I can't. I can't do it, Mom. I'll mess it up and embarrass her. And myself."

"Have you contacted any lending sites to find out what their rates and repayment plans are?"

"Yes, but…"

Her mother made a sound of disgust. "What's your problem?"

"I don't know, Mom," she wailed. "I had this great idea, and now the easy options have vanished. And I can't follow through. I feel blocked. I know Magda is depending on me. She's looking to me with a lot of hope because I spoke thoughtlessly."

"Why don't you just give her the money?" her mother asked, impatience in her voice.

"I don't have it. The value of my 401k has dropped drastically in the last week because of the ongoing financial crisis. Oh, maybe I could borrow it against the house, but I suspect getting a loan when I am unemployed wouldn't be very easy. The mess on Wall Street has sent every financial institution into a panic. Banks are freezing credit. Even my credit cards suddenly have tiny cash limits."

"I've been following the news. Do you have enough for yourself?"

"I'm okay, but I can't spare the many thousands Magda needs. Plus, that would change my relationship with her. Wreck it."

"What do you think raising false hopes will do?"

"I know, I know." She swallowed the bile in her throat to confess, "I'm mad at myself. I'm all talk and no action."

"We can fix that, dear," her mother said. A new briskness had entered her voice. "Pack some clothes and come out to my house and we will brainstorm how to help your friend obtain some money."

Relief flooded Pam. Her mother could fix it all. Dorothy knew what to do. What would she do without her mother?

#

Dorothy hung up the phone. How had she come to raise a girl with so little gumption? Her other children were capable types who had managed complex careers and large families, but Pamela still needed direction and reassurance. Good lord, the child was nearly sixty. It was time she got her act together.

Although she was a dear, affectionate girl, Dorothy reminded herself. She must be fair. Pamela was also the warmest of her children. Now that Alexander had retired to North Carolina, Pamela was the child who lived the closest.

Alexander had lived in Queens County for many years. Then he announced that he was done with northern winters, and he and his wife were heading south to retire.

She was getting distracted. She could have organized Pamela's silly little charitable project easily in the past. She did not have the energy anymore. She wasn't quite willing to admit that, though. Anyway, it was high time Pamela learned to stand on her own two feet. Good thing the child was coming for a visit. Together, they would figure out what to do.

#

As Pam drove the Long Island Expressway toward her mother's house on the south shore, she still was angry at herself for her impulsiveness. First, she had gotten the big idea that helping Magda was going to give new purpose to her own life. Then she'd stupidly told Magda too much too soon, raising hopes she might not be able to fulfill. To make matters worse, she'd dragged her feet for a whole week, trying not to complete the very task she herself had initiated. Why was she such a wimp? What was she afraid of?

Why was she clutching? There must be many ways to obtain money for a good cause. Her mother certainly never gave up after a mere initial setback. Dorothy always had ideas. Unlike Pam. Here she was, running to her mother for help, and at her age.

Glenvale Village, way out on Long Island, was a pleasant place to visit, and her mother's house on the beach was more than charming, yet Pam dreaded how their talk would go. Dorothy Duncan's plans usually worked, but they often involved some very showy, media-noisy tactics. Tactics that made Pam cringe. Dorothy had the knack, the secret to making publicity work for her. Pam didn't. It was a miracle she hadn't been a wreck when she appeared on national television last week.

The reward had been a precious extra hour with her daughter. Not much, but more than Linley had allowed her all year. Linley was punctilious about visits for Thanksgiving and Christmas, and that was it. Sometimes, the only other time Pam saw her in a year was when the entire family was visiting Dorothy at the beach. It was not enough.

She might as well stop rehashing her reasons to be miserable, and enjoy the scenery and the good weather. She'd been making this drive now for nearly forty years, and in that time, her mother's country retreat had turned into a suburb, even though it was far out on the island. The roads had gotten better, at least, and the signs. The simple country village her mother had retired to was now part of an exclusive enclave whose homes had increased exponentially in value and priced the middle class out.

How ironic that her mother, for whom the rich were a natural enemy, now lived as one of them.

Her father had left her mother comfortably off. Dorothy had always managed her own affairs and had never mentioned any money issues. Of course, Dorothy lived a simple life. Her only real expense in the past had been her activism. Now she had retired from that at last. Pam's brother, Alexander, had been influential in getting their mother to call it quits once traveling to protest sites became burdensome.

During Dorothy's last years on the activist circuit, she had worked the angle of shaming her opponents by being a newsworthy elderly lady whom they in their greed or intransigence had arrested. It made for excellent TV and sound bites, too. She had milked it for all it was worth, even carefully choosing her hairstyle and wardrobe to get the maximum effect out of the indignity to which she had been subjected. Pam admired her mother's shrewdness, though she often felt immature and foolish around her.

Feelings of insecurity were not what kept Linley away from her own mother. More like a belief in her own superiority to Pam.

Chapter 6

Linley's shaken retreat from Jason yesterday still played on her interior monitor, mocking her. She had totally lost her cool. Running away from him had probably encouraged him. Which was confusing. She was a sharp observer, especially of men she'd been to bed with. She knew damn well he'd backed away from the something more that could have developed between them that night last year. Why was he trying to rekindle it now?

On her side, being apart had done nothing to change the strong chemical attraction. Months of sitting next to him every weekday for an hour had intensified her desire. She wanted him. Lack of interest wasn't her problem.

She refused to play games with her career. She had no intention of risking her burgeoning television presence for a mere hookup. Or even for a fling. Something about Jason told her he was the fling type. If they had worked for competing networks or even on different television shows, she wouldn't have any compunction in having it on with him. He was handsome, well-mannered, and smart. Hot in bed. He had a brilliant future. She was drawn to the complete package.

One session in bed wasn't much. Call it an introduction. Since they'd started working together, she had learned how his mind worked when addressing a financial or political issue. She couldn't infer from that how he felt about her, or any number of personal issues. Too many women leaped to unfounded conclusions about men, especially the ones who took after her mother's excessively passive, sentimental femininity. They assumed emotion that wasn't present. Linley was too smart to fool herself that way. Maybe Jason had some feelings for her. Maybe not.

Every day, when the show was over, she waved a pleasant farewell to the others and left the studio quickly, stopping only at her cubicle to pick up her personal possessions. She was careful to do her networking early in the day, not at night when men were more likely to get drunk or proposition her. The downside of being an attractive blonde. The studio in the evening was no place to linger. At this hour, she wanted to relax. Since her last appearance for the day was done, and the stock market was closed for the day, she could wind down a bit before heading home. She went up the street to her favorite coffee shop and found her usual quiet corner in the back. She checked her phone for the latest news, but then her thoughts drifted to Jason.

What would she do when he made another move? After last week's scare, she needed some armor. For all his talk of it just being dinner, she wasn't naïve. Blondes got hit on all the time. She usually knew when a man wanted her. Both Ralph and Ernie had shown signs of interest when she first was hired. Then she'd made her position clear, and they were content to settle for a comradely professional relationship.

Why now, after several months of playing it cool, was Jason actively pursuing her? She would not be surprised if he drew encouragement from her recent show of weakness. He could be very persistent. She'd seen it on the air when he'd worked on getting answers from stubborn guests. She felt a new vibe from him now. It excited her.

She was in control of her sexuality. Her body wasn't going to betray her if he touched her. She wouldn't melt in his arms. Anything that happened between them would be her decision, not his. She wouldn't let him crowd her into a corner.

Did she even have time for a relationship? She was super busy, not only researching her role on the show but looking for ways to maximize her career momentum. The *Today Show* was the big win, but she also had a couple of radio talk shows to do, and a cable guest appearance. Her excuse for not inviting her mother to these was that the poor dear was in shock. Now that Pam had told her story once on a major network show, all Linley had to do was refer to it. Anyone interested in her mother could watch it on YouTube or elsewhere. Meanwhile, she would push herself as the person deserving a hearing, even if it was secondhand sympathy. She would use the opportunity to show off her expertise in personal finance. To give some desperately needed, sound financial advice. Maybe someday she could topple Suze Orman from her perch. It wasn't easy to get attention with all the competition, but Linley was in it to win it.

She had to be careful not to overplay her ambition. She hadn't hired a publicist yet. For now, it was up to her. She already had a slice of the *Today Show* video linked on her website, which linked automatically to social networking sites like Facebook and Twitter. It was on YouTube, of course. That was last week, and now she needed new content.

Seeking fame and fortune via the net could be very complicated and time-consuming. It made her television ambitions seem quite doable by comparison. How ironic. No pressure here.

#

Her mother called. "Linley, hi, it's Mom."

"I know. All cell phones have caller ID." Duh.

"Oh. Of course. You're right. Anyway, I didn't want you to worry in case you called the house. I'm going to Long Island and staying with Grandma for a few days."

"Is she okay?" Grandma Dorothy was her favorite relative. What a fireball she had been when she was younger. Linley was proud to be related to her and sometimes even boasted to people about her activist grandma. A shame Dorothy had gotten too old to continue her campaigning. She was way out on the Island so Linley hardly ever saw her now that her mother wasn't dragging her there for the summers or for family events. Thanksgiving at Uncle Alex's house wasn't quite the same, and anyway, he had moved out of state.

"She's fine, dear. I needed to consult her about something, and she invited me out. Since it's nearly a hundred miles from our house, I'm staying here for a bit."

Okay. You said that already. Don't you have anything else to do but bug me? You know I don't care.

After a moment of silence, her mother continued.

"I'll let you go now, dear."

"Say hi to Grandma for me."

"Of course."

She clicked off, wondering when her mother would stop bothering her. Pam kept trying to have a relationship with her, but Linley didn't need a mother anymore. She was perfectly happy living on her own, having her own friends as her social life. It was okay to see the family at Thanksgiving, but the dutiful Christmas appearance happened too soon after. She was always bored and restless, wishing herself elsewhere.

At least Mom had gotten the message about making suggestions. Linley knew how to run her own life, and she did not need her homebody mom giving her career advice. Pam had never taken a career seriously, despite all the years she had worked. She had nothing useful to say about careers.

Her dad hadn't talked much about careers either, because becoming an accountant like he had been was a straight shot: accounting degree, apprenticeship, take the exam, get your certification, get hired or put out your own shingle. Not like media, where everything was changing super fast right now. What she'd learned in college was already out of date. She'd never had to take the classic journalism first job in a tiny market, for instance. Instead, her audition tape had been a YouTube video. She'd started on cable, and not as a behind-the-scenes apprentice producer, another classic foot in the door she'd skipped. She was headed for the big time. She knew it.

Her mom had done nothing. Nothing in her life was relevant to Linley's life today. Mom didn't understand the career Linley was trying to build. She didn't even understand why Linley wanted a career because she came from an era when most women had to choose between a family or a career. Her mom had chosen to stay at home and be a nothing.

#

"Why did you run off? I wanted to talk to you."

Linley looked up to find Jason looming above her, blocking her view of the rest of the café. He had a smile on his face and a cup of coffee in one hand. He looked entirely too handsome and confident. He had the kind of broad-chested body that did justice to a well-tailored suit. She knew exactly what he looked like stripped, which was even more intimidating and exciting.

Rein it in, girl.

When she merely eyed him without responding, Jason invited himself to sit next to her on the bench seat that stretched the length of the corner she was tucked into. He sat too close. His long, well-muscled leg touched hers.

"Ah, this is cozy," he remarked, setting his cup on her table and making himself very much at home.

"What are you doing?" she asked impatience evident in her voice.

"Getting comfortable. How was your day?"

His blandly delivered question nearly drove her to say something foolish, but she maintained her control. "Jason, I'm not doing this," she warned.

"What?" he asked, all innocence.

"Spending personal time with you. It's not happening." She knew her last words had risen in volume.

"I get it when no means no. I merely came by to tell you

about our field trip." Despite his denial, there was mischief in his eyes.

"Field trip?" What had he dreamed up now?

"We're taking our show on the road. Marty approved it."

"What? When?" She hoped it wouldn't interfere with everything else she had lined up.

Jason seemed pleased with throwing her off balance.

"Next week. You and I are taking the show to DC, where the regulatory action is. I've already got some great guests lined up." He named several government figures they hadn't been able to lure onto the show previously.

"Impressive. How did you land them?"

"By promising them more air time and less hostility."

"How will you keep Ernie in check?" He was their most combative panelist. "He's very hostile to government officials."

"He won't be there. I'm not taking the whole group. It'll be just you and me." He repeated that phrase as if he savored it. He made it sound very intimate. What was Jason up to?

"Why me?"

He glanced down at her, still smiling. As if this whole discussion amused him for some reason. He was a big man, and his shoulders seemed to press into her space. She was trapped in the corner.

"As the personal finance expert, you're there to kick butt about what Washington is doing for Main Street."

Nice to be called an expert, but was he sincere? She suspected he had a secret agenda. "Flattering. Your idea?"

He smirked. "Yeah. Marty liked it."

Jason was warning her there was no point in complaining to

Marty or trying to get her part in the road trip changed. Why was Jason so pleased?

"We're there for an afternoon and then come home?"

"Nope. We've got an invitation to the press club reception that night. We can rub shoulders with even more valuable contacts. It's a dressy affair. We're staying in DC overnight."

Ah, now she got it. Jason was happy because he had maneuvered her into being his date for the evening. Probably he also hoped they'd hook up later. Made easier by adjoining or connecting hotel rooms, or the like.

Huge temptation. They would be alone, no scrutiny from coworkers. They could spend the whole night in bed. Get to know each other's bodies intimately all over again.

Then what?

"No way," she said.

"Marty's orders."

"Sure, blame Marty," she said, barely veiling her anger.

"I want to spend time with you, Lin," he said. His dark eyes sized her up, lingering at her lips and her breasts appreciatively. "You're elusive at the station. You won't see me outside of work. Can you blame me for arranging for us to be together?"

She shivered. It had been difficult to hold back her desire when she'd thought she was alone in it. Now Jason was openly declaring his determination to have her again. How was she going to resist him?

"We won't be together," she insisted.

"Yes, we will, Lin." He gave her his patented, direct stare that held the camera on his face for a long fade out. "Count on it."

He calmly got up and left, content to let her freak over the possibility he would make a move on her during their business trip.

Did she want him to? Hadn't she been fretting daily because he'd played it cool all these months? Then why all of a sudden did she feel hunted?

Chapter 7

"I'm almost there. I'm driving through the village right now," Pam told Sarah. She wore the hands-free cell phone setup Steve had given her. "I should have asked you for help before I called her, I guess."

Her thoughts had gone around and around for the entire drive. Only as she drove down the short main street with its deliberately quaint storefronts did she remember she hadn't told Sarah anything.

"It's okay. I forgive you," Sarah's cheery voice came through. She knew Pam often got into a tizzy when dealing with her mother. "Listen, I can probably help you, too. You didn't have to get out your sackcloth and ashes and go do penance with your mother."

Pam choked on her laughter. Sarah had a way with words. Sarah also had plenty of financial knowledge. Why hadn't she consulted Sarah first? Because Dorothy was the family expert on helping people.

"Now don't get stuck out there," Sarah warned. "You've got decisions to make about your future."

Pam listened to Sarah's admonishments about relaunching her Wall Street career with a sense of weariness. She wasn't cut out for the networking efforts Sarah was suggesting. Right now, the thought made her cringe.

"Could I postpone all that until I come home? Please?"

"Sure, kid. Meanwhile, try not to kill your mother."

"She's more likely to do me in," Pam muttered. Sarah laughed. They made plans to see each other soon and clicked off.

This was silly. She had been competent and effective as a mother and as a housewife. She had pulled her weight in the document retention department. She shouldn't be down on herself because she didn't instantly understand all the ins and outs of finding Magda some money. There was a learning curve to everything. The trouble was, she had a vivid mental image of how high the spike was on the classic learning curve and she felt stuck at the bottom of it.

There was the house. It looked crisp and well cared for. Her mother was keeping up with the maintenance. The large pots of petunias and dusty miller flanking the front door were obvious recent seasonal additions, too.

A car was parked next door. Someone was living in the house this summer. That was good. The previous owners had only been occasional residents. Although Alexander used to visit Dorothy every week without fail, he and Edie had moved south three months ago. In fact, as the only one of the four siblings now living within driving distance of their mother, Pam was overdue for a check-up visit to Dorothy.

As she parked the car in the curved driveway, it occurred to her for the first time that none of them had made any plans for when Dorothy got too old and feeble to live out here alone. How irresponsible. Jeff's death should have proved to her that all good things come to an end. Still, there was plenty of time. Dorothy was in perfect health.

#

Bruce saw the tidy Toyota Camry drive up and park next door. A slender woman emerged and pulled a travel bag from the trunk. A relative? Granddaughter? No, not young. In great shape, though. Nice behind. A daughter? Looked like she'd be staying awhile. Good. That made it more like a fair fight.

#

Dorothy loved all her children equally, but she had always worried about Pamela. Pamela was the most vulnerable and kind-hearted of her four children. Pamela constantly needed reassurance and guidance. As a girl, she had wanted someone strong to lean on. Jeff had been her rock. Since his death, Pamela had simply been going through the motions. Dorothy had not interfered. It was her life.

Now Pamela had asked her mother for help because she couldn't manage a simple thing like gathering some money for her friend. At first, Dorothy had given Pamela advice via the phone. Then it became obvious Pamela couldn't absorb it all quickly, and further, could not see herself actually following through. That was when Dorothy changed tactics and told her to come for a visit. There would be time over a few days for the lessons to sink in. If Pamela actually had the gumption at last to do anything on her own. Which her mother, much as she loved the child, sincerely doubted.

#

"Ah, here you are at last," Dorothy greeted her daughter. "What took you so long?"

"I had to close up the house and get gas—" Pam started to explain. Then she shut her mouth. She wasn't late. There was no appointed hour. Dorothy always wanted Pam to move faster.

Dorothy looked well. Her shortish white hair was nicely kept. She maintained a regular appointment at a hair salon. Of course, she never went in for finicky fashions or manicures. They weren't her style, just the usual wash, set, dry. Still, she had the well-maintained look of a woman of means who comfortably wore the same conservative garments year in and year out.

It was part of Dorothy's camouflage. She'd never been the conservative matron whose style she affected, but she had figured out a long time ago it was easier to impress some people if she wore a string of pearls. Obtained at a deep discount, of course.

Pam knew her mother's tactics, but had never herself thought to use style as a social tool. If anything, she had spent her life trying to avoid being noticed. Her mother's notoriety had deeply embarrassed her as a child.

Pam quickly settled in to her usual room. Then she wandered down to the living room. She was surprised at the piles of mail on several surfaces.

"What's all this? A new campaign?"

Dorothy shrugged it aside. "Junk mail I should have torn up by now."

Pam cast a casual glance at the stack nearest her, and realized that the top envelope was from a bank. It looked like a statement. She picked it up and found it hadn't been opened.

"Don't you want to look at your bank statement?"

Dorothy looked briefly puzzled. "Oh, is that what it is? Of course. I'll take care of it." She held her hand out for the envelope and Pam passed it over.

They went to sit in the sunroom, the room the family spent the most time in here because it had a panoramic view of the beach and received direct sunlight all day.

"Ah, this is nice," Pam said. "You have the best view here."

"I've always liked it. I don't know why Alexander didn't buy here. Instead, he insisted on going all the way to North Carolina for a piece of beach."

"Maybe he wanted to get away from New York. Many New Yorkers are moving south, and not to Florida. It must be nice down there."

Dorothy changed the subject to more family catch up. Later, they went out to dinner. Pam drove. The restaurant was an elegant little place, not crowded tonight because the busy summer season was over. The maitre d' made quite a fuss over Dorothy, and seated them at a comfortable banquette.

The menu had a lot of modern options which seemed to baffle Dorothy.

"What is jerk chicken?" Dorothy asked.

They found out from the waiter, and then continued looking at the menus. Then Dorothy asked the same question again.

Pam smiled. How funny. Her mother was losing a bit of her short-term memory, she guessed. She herself hardly remembered the waiter's explanation. She hadn't been listening closely. Something to do with jerking the chicken apart instead of slicing it.

They had a pleasant evening. Pam was grateful that Dorothy didn't immediately push about the reason for the visit.

#

The next morning, Pam ducked out for a quick trip to the local grocery store to buy milk and fruit. Dorothy had begged off. She wasn't interested in shopping, she'd said. She usually had her groceries delivered.

On her return, Pam brought in the mail, which seemed to have accumulated in the mailbox for a couple of days. "Where would you like the mail, Mom?"

"Oh, over there's fine." Dorothy pointed to the dining room, which they had not yet used. The fine old mahogany table was covered with newspapers, magazines, and stacks of mail.

"Here? At your place at the table?" She made to put the mail on top of a stack near the end of the table usually reserved for Dorothy when they all ate together. After Jeff died, the big family celebrations switched to Alexander's home so Pam didn't have to travel a long distance alone. By now she was used to doing things alone, but as a new widow, she had been a timid driver. Dorothy had thought nothing of driving into Queens for Thanksgiving, and so the family tradition changed. It modified again after she retired. Alexander had arranged to have his son,

James, swing by her home and pick Dorothy up.

How sad that the table was now a mere repository of papers. This house had seen a lot of good family times over the years, even though her dad had died young. Like Jeff. Now that Alexander was gone, they'd have to find a new family member to host Thanksgiving.

Dorothy waved an okay to Pam. She obviously had no interest in the mail.

"Come sit with me, Pamela. Let's talk about your money issue."

She obliged, seating herself in one of the comfortably cushioned wicker couches in the sunroom. She could see up the beach from there. Dorothy was in a wicker chair that she had angled to view the full length of the beach. The deep cushions were in a bright floral print, and coupled with the potted palms in the corners, they gave the sunroom a definite tropical feel.

"Oh, this is nice, Mom. You're lucky to live here."

Dorothy gave a snort. "It's pleasant enough, but I won't be enjoying it much longer."

"What do you mean? You're not sick, are you?"

"Of course not. In this family we drop dead without warning."

Dorothy said it with trenchant glee, but seeing Pam's flinch, went on in a no-nonsense tone. "Oh, come now, Pamela, you're surely not being sensitive because of Jeff? After all, I lost my own husband in the same manner. I didn't fall apart."

Her feelings weren't the same as her mother's. She had ached for many months after Jeff's sudden death. Even thinking about his final moments pained her now. She'd never had a callous approach to life. Why didn't Dorothy understand?

"Pamela." There was censure in Dorothy's tone.

"I can't—" she struggled to get it out, "I can't see life as you do. I don't think personal tragedy is a good source of amusing quips."

Dorothy practically rolled her eyes. "Where did I get such a child? If I hadn't given birth to you naturally and seen you born—quite a rebellious decision back in the day—I would swear the hospital gave me the wrong baby."

Her mother's words mocked Pam's sensitive nature. They lived nearly one hundred miles apart for a good reason. She couldn't take a lot of this.

Pam took a breath and let it out. "If you're not ill, then why did you say you might not be here much longer? Are you thinking of moving to a retirement home?"

"Bah, they're prisons," Dorothy said. "Remember that no one in my family lives to be ninety, and I'm eighty-seven already. You'd better face reality. I have at most three more years to live."

"You don't know for sure."

"Of course I do. My brother died last year, and my sister the year before. Do you think that's coincidence? No, it's genetics. We Lanes don't have the gene for exceptionally long life spans."

"You're healthy. You're not going to—to…" Her words trailed off.

"Die. I'm going to die, Pamela. Don't be so wishy-washy about saying the word."

Not only was her mother ragging on her again, but this conversation was becoming surreal. Pam gazed around the room, which looked completely normal, with sunshine pouring in through the many windows. The beach was empty and beautiful. Yet they were arguing about dying. "Why are you thinking about death?"

"It's an interesting topic to someone of my age," her mother responded. "My brother died last year, and my sister the year before. No one in my family lives to be ninety."

She'd just said that. Why was she telling Pam what she already knew? Not that Pam wanted to hear talk about death. There had been too much death already in their family.

"Enough." Dorothy waved the topic away. "Let's talk about your sudden onset of do-gooderism."

Pam explained about Magda, ending with, "She's proud of her son's achievement. She'd do anything to make it happen. If she can't pay her share, he'll have to give up his scholarship."

"Would that be so terrible? Many young people work their way through college."

"The scholarship is for Harvard. Pretty much a once-in-a-lifetime opportunity."

"I see," Dorothy said. "This boy must be something special."

"Oh, he is. I've met him. He's a good kid, too," she couldn't help adding. Marc's demonstrative love for his mother counted for a lot with her.

"Remind me why the family is here, not home in Romania."

"Magda was an orphan. She married an American, and came over here when she was pregnant. Then it fell apart, but she stayed and is now a citizen. Marc—his real name is Mircea—was born here."

She went on, "Marc is a brilliant student. He deserves help."

Dorothy raised her palm, signaling Pam should stop. "All right. I'll accept this is a worthy young man. Why can't you just give him the money?"

"At first I thought I could. The stock market's massive dip has cut my 401k in half, and for all I know, it will fall farther. I have to conserve what little I have left, make it last."

Dorothy's eyebrows went up. "Jeff left insurance, didn't he?"

"I spent most of it." When she explained what she'd done, her mother reacted differently from Sarah. Dorothy approved.

"Security for your children is good. You used the insurance money wisely."

After asking more questions, Dorothy finally conceded giving Magda the money would not be a good move.

"You have to protect yourself first, although when I go, you'll inherit something." Dorothy cackled a little. "Don't worry. It's not in the stock market." She asked a few more questions, then gave her verdict.

"This will be a piece of cake, Pamela. We'll call my lawyer and have him set up a simple nonprofit. He knows how to fast track it. You can be the president and do the publicity and the fund raising."

"Oh, no, I couldn't," she began.

"Don't start, Pamela," Dorothy said. She continued, "This was your idea. Of course you will see it through. Don't be a coward."

"I'm not."

"Oh? Then why did you come out here? You've already done the research on loans and concluded they aren't a viable solution at this time. You know what you want to accomplish. A nonprofit charity will be the easiest method of achieving your goal."

Didn't her mother understand? "I can't be the public face of an organization." Pam squirmed restlessly.

"Why not?"

"I don't…I can't…" She became all tangled up trying to express herself. "I fall apart in public."

"I watched you on the *Today Show* mere days ago. You were fine."

"I was?"

"You were eloquent on your friend's behalf." Dorothy replied. "I taped it. I still have a working VCR. You should listen to yourself. You were good."

This was high praise indeed from her mother. Could it be true? Anyway, the *Today Show* appearance was a one-off, all for Linley's sake. Pam couldn't count on having that level of poise under pressure again.

"No, I can't be a fund raiser." It was safer to refuse. "I'm not the type."

"Of course you can. Anybody can." Dorothy's voice showed her exasperation. "All you have to do is present your case and never accept no for an answer."

"I can't." Pam felt herself trembling under the force of Dorothy's insistence. Her mother always did this to her. Dorothy expected everyone to be as strong as she was. Oh, why was it so hard to explain?

Pam rose, agitated. She couldn't keep talking to her mother now.

"I—I need to go for a walk." She bolted out the door to the patio, hearing her mother's cry after her. She didn't stop until she was far enough up the beach she couldn't hear her anymore.

Chapter 8

Such adult behavior. This was exactly what she'd been afraid of. She always acted like she was a pouting six-year-old with her mother. Overwhelmed, overawed, and reluctant. What came naturally to Dorothy was painful for her.

After a few minutes of walking along the beach, Pam calmed. How silly she had been. She wasn't a child anymore. Why had she run away? Her mother's idea was sound. Was it a knee-jerk reaction to Dorothy's past efforts to recruit her daughter to her many causes? Pam had hated that. She'd been dragged into some of them, and she'd always felt awkward and incompetent.

Was having to face being in the public eye such a high price to pay to help a friend? She'd been okay on television last week. She could do this, if she didn't let herself panic. Her mother's brisk efficiency made her feel inadequate by comparison, but she could overcome it. She clenched her fists at her sides as she turned around to walk back and face the music.

A man headed in her direction, walking a small dog. The wire-hair fox terrier ran up to her joyously, leaped on her, then sniffed at her in confusion. The dog's owner caught up and attached his collar to a leash.

"Sorry. I'm usually the only one walking here. Yappie thought he recognized a friend."

He smiled. He was tall and lean, about her age. His hair was grey and his face was time-weathered under his baseball cap. He was dressed casually in blue jeans and a navy T-shirt that showed off nicely muscled arms. She was struck by how attractive he was.

Attractive? How long had it been since she had noticed a man was attractive?

She hid her face as she leaned down to pat the dog, who was panting hopefully. "That's okay. He's a cutie."

Yappie took that opportunity to butt at her in a friendly fashion.

"Good boy," she said.

"He needs to learn some manners," the man said, pulling his dog back as she straightened up. "My neighbor is teaching him. I think you're staying with her? Dorothy Duncan?"

"That's my mother. She's very good at training dogs. Or anything else," she couldn't help adding. Although whether that was good or bad was a question in her mind.

"I'm Bruce Wicklow. I'm renting the house next door to yours."

"Pam Ridgeway." Although it wasn't her usual custom to ask personal questions, this man made it easy to continue. "Are you on vacation?"

He smiled. "Working. What about you?"

"Oh, well, I just lost my job. You probably heard about Menahl going bankrupt? Thirty thousand of us were laid off."

"That's got to be tough," he said.

"It is."

"Are you staying for the summer?" he asked.

A horrified look must have come into her eyes for he immediately added, "Just wondering. I was surprised to learn Dorothy lives here all year by herself."

"It's her home."

"She's pretty old to be alone."

"Oh, that's not a problem. She's very strong and self-reliant." When her confident words didn't seem to convince him, she added, "She has many friends here." Although come to think of it, none had been at the restaurant last night.

Bruce turned to walk in the direction she was headed. The water lapped a few feet away as they proceeded down the sandy beach. Yappie danced at his side. "Do you have a future care plan in place?"

"Why are you interested?" she asked. Should there be a plan?

"Sorry to scare you. There's probably no hurry. Your mother appears very healthy."

"Are you concerned because of your own parents?"

"My mom's living alone also, but two of my sisters are within five minutes of her."

"You've given me a lot to think about," she said.

The beach ahead of them appeared endless, but that was an illusion. Perhaps her mother was right to talk about the end of life before it happened.

"I'm sorry," he said. He stopped, and she automatically stopped too. She looked at his concerned, life-worn face. Despite his grey hair, a still-dark, unruly curl fell on his forehead. His mother must think it was darling.

He said, "You're probably here to relax, and I've spoiled it."

"I…it's already been a tough week."

She almost told him details, but then she stopped herself. They had met only ten minutes ago. Bruce Wicklow certainly had a way about him.

The little dog leaned his head against her leg. She looked down at his sympathetic pose and burst out laughing. "I love your dog."

"Yappie's a fun guy," Bruce said, smiling. They started walking once more. She had the warm feeling he was interested in her worries. It was nice to think someone was concerned.

When they arrived where the path to his house began, Bruce said a pleasant farewell and turned off, with his little dog at his side. She made herself move on briskly, even though she wanted to linger. Bruce Wicklow was so self-confident, so assured. He was at the same stage in life she was, but he seemed a lot calmer about it.

She had to face her mother again after having bolted like a teenager. When would she ever grow up?

#

Dorothy was a little dismayed when Pamela ran away. All these years, and she still panicked and got tongue-tied. Dorothy had hoped she had broken Pamela of that bad habit. Apparently not.

She picked up one of her crossword puzzles from the white wicker table next to her chair. She only did the hardest days of the *New York Times* puzzle. Her favorite was the Saturday, a killer even to an experienced solver such as herself. They said doing tough puzzles helped keep your brain working. Now, where was her pen? Ah, there. She always did them in pen. It was hard to see pencil on a newspaper page. Too much glare.

After a few minutes, she laid her pen down. She wasn't enjoying doing her crossword after all. For some reason, she couldn't think of easy answers like the name of that lake in Asia. It began with an A. Irritating.

Many little areas of her life were getting harder. Things she used to handle quickly and easily took much more time now. She simply did not have the energy. Take those pots of flowers outside. She'd asked that nice girl who owned the nursery to come and get the pots and put a showy selection of annuals in them. The workers had returned the pots filled with flowers and positioned them as Dorothy had asked. Now some of the annuals would benefit from deadheading, and she didn't have the energy. She looked out at them and saw that the yellow ones—oh, what was their name now?—the yellow ones needed deadheading. Maybe today she would get to it, after lunch.

If her errant daughter ever returned. That girl needed a keeper. It was a shame Jeff had dropped dead so young. An aneurism nobody had suspected had felled him in his prime and left her youngest girl adrift. Pamela's grief had subsided by now, but the girl still acted as if she was newly widowed. She worked and she went home. She didn't date. She looked it, too. She had that abandoned aspect women got when they lived without men.

Dorothy supposed she had it herself. She was just another old widow. Back when she was still young enough for her appearance to matter, she'd had her causes to keep her interesting and fresh. She met new men all the time during her campaigns. There had even been a few discreet flings. She hadn't needed a second husband.

Pamela was a different kettle of fish. Pamela's life was empty. The girl was drifting. She needed a new romance.

Oh, good. Here was Pamela now. She'd met up with that handsome young man from next door, Bruce something. And the dear dog. They were walking together, coming closer. They made a nice picture. They'd probably make a good couple. They were the right age for each other. She suspected Bruce was divorced. She'd have to ask him. Pamela needed a new husband. Perhaps nature would take its course if Dorothy threw them together a time or two.

#

After Pam returned from her walk—which had been a flight—she apologized to her mother. They had a much calmer discussion about the charitable organization.

Dorothy exerted herself to soothe Pam about the publicity aspect. "You can do this, Pamela. All you have to do is set your mind to it."

She got out a pad and a pen, and urged Pam to copy down the strategies she would dictate. As the afternoon wore on, Pam began to gain some confidence that maybe she could.

Then Bruce Wicklow arrived to walk with Dorothy. "Won't you come with us?" he invited.

Pam felt shy now. "I wouldn't want to interfere with your routine," she demurred.

She watched them slowly stroll along the beach. When her

mother was around, Pam hardly knew where she was. She only focused on her. Now, alone, Pam sat in the sunroom and enjoyed the feeling of relaxing in someone else's home, where she wasn't required to do a thing. This house never felt empty. It was spacious and welcoming. Pam could get comfortable in a place like this.

On their return, Dorothy announced, "Bruce is coming to lunch tomorrow." She cast him a reproving glance. "He says he's too busy to go to the yacht club with us tonight."

"I need to complete the chapter I'm working on," he explained. "I'm a science writer, and I've got a book contract to fulfill this summer."

The two women dined at the yacht club by themselves later, although they were hardly ever alone. Everyone recognized and spoke to Dorothy. She practically held court. Pam breathed an inward sigh of relief. Dorothy still had plenty of local friends, and they weren't all elderly.

#

The next day, Dorothy insisted on taking her usual solitary morning walk. Pam practiced some of the dialogues her mother had her copy down. She tried to visualize herself outsmarting a clever CEO, and getting a large donation for her charity. The vision did not come easily.

Pam didn't have to do anything about lunch. Of course Dorothy didn't cook. She never had. When Pam arrived, she had been surprised at how well stocked the kitchen was with basic food. Then this morning, a delivery girl knocked on the door with a beautifully arranged platter of cold cuts and other sandwich fixings, and one of fruits.

"Mom, did you order some food?" she called into the living room. Dorothy entered the kitchen briskly.

"Oh, good, now we're set," she said, and tipped the girl who had placed the platters in the fridge.

"Now we won't have to go out for every meal, and you're not stuck cooking, either." Dorothy was proud of herself for arranging their food. Pam didn't have the heart to say she would have welcomed the opportunity to cook their meals. She hadn't cooked for anyone but herself in four years. Solitary meals for one were the bane of widowhood. Maybe she could make a meal from scratch for her mother another day.

Bruce showed up promptly at one, and they ate on the patio since it was a beautiful day. As well, since the dining room table was still buried in papers. She should offer to help her mother sort through them tonight.

The patio table was protected by an umbrella, and the iron chairs she covered with plush, gay red-and-blue cushions. She had found some colorful rainbow-striped placemats in the server in the dining room. She had balked at using the plastic flatware and plates the deli had delivered, instead pulling out a perfectly good stainless steel set and some brightly colored casual china. It all looked very festive, and Bruce commented approvingly as they sat down to eat.

"What a spread. Thanks for inviting me. I tend to live on pb & js when I'm working on a draft."

"You can order in easily enough," Dorothy said, dismissing the store-bought food and Pam's effort in setting a beautiful table. Dorothy had never cared much about gracious living.

"By the way, if you hear Yappie barking, don't think he's miserable," he warned. "I gave him a special snack before I left."

"Once he learns better manners, he'd be welcome as a guest," Dorothy said.

Bruce turned to Pam. "Did your mother tell you she's schooling Yappie?"

"No. He seemed well-behaved yesterday," she said. Seeing Bruce giving her a disbelieving look, she continued more truthfully, "That is, except for the leaping."

"Exactly." They both smiled.

"I'll train him not to do that anymore," Dorothy promised. Pam believed her. Dorothy could make any human or animal obey.

Bruce explained about the training sessions and how when he was writing, he had little time for Yappie. "He's probably bored and lonely out here. He's used to a smaller suburban neighborhood with lots of dogs to bark at and sniff."

"Don't you feel the same?" She stumbled over her words, "I mean, isn't all this isolation lonely?"

"Oh, nonsense, Pamela," Dorothy interjected. "This is an inspiring setting, perfect for a writer."

Bruce smiled. "With all due respect, Dorothy, I'm not an oversensitive creative artist who can't write unless he communes with nature in isolation."

He turned to Pam again and explained. "My work is nonfiction. Mostly I do a lot of Internet research and phone interviews with scientists. No glamorous beach locale required."

"Too bad," Dorothy said with a twinkle in her eye. "But it doesn't have to go to waste. Tomorrow, why don't the two of you take a picnic with today's leftovers and explore the beach? I've got my regular date playing cards with the girls. Pam could tell you all about the history of this area."

Pam was discomfited. Why was her mother throwing them together so obviously? She tried to decline politely without seeming to. "If you'd like to hear about it, we don't have to go on a picnic."

"A picnic sounds like a great idea," Bruce said, smiling at Pam as if he found her attractive.

She gulped. Now there was no way to gracefully refuse.

Dorothy continued to dominate the chat, boldly asking Bruce where he grew up and about his parents.

"I actually was born here on Long Island in a town that was way out in the country then—Ronkonkoma."

"It's still way out," Dorothy said. She'd never been afraid to voice a trenchant opinion.

"Anyway, I grew up in Queens, went to Hofstra, and got lucky. I went straight into writing science material for magazines. I've been doing it ever since. A simple story."

Dorothy gave him a straight look. "Nobody's life is simple. Do you have a wife? Children? Grandchildren?"

"Mom," Pam remonstrated, horribly embarrassed. "Maybe he doesn't want to talk about his personal life." Her mother had no sense of people's privacy. People did not move out to solitary homes on the beach to become bosom buddies with the neighbors. Yet, Dorothy was barreling ahead in her usual fashion, insisting on making a friend of Bruce merely because he lived next door.

"I don't mind," Bruce said. He took a sip from his water. "I was married for over twenty-five years, but we broke up after the kids were out of college. It was an amicable divorce. My wife—ex-wife, I should say—has remarried happily. We have a boy and a girl, who are thirty-four and thirty-two. Nobody is married yet, although I'm wondering if my son has found the girl. He's living with someone, but he hasn't indicated yet it's for keeps."

"What about your daughter?" Pam asked. She might as well play a part in the conversation.

"My daughter is gay." He said it calmly as if his daughter's sexual orientation hadn't been a crisis in their family that had caused the divorce. As if he could handle it fine.

Pam wondered if that was the truth, but didn't dare ask. She was mortified enough that her nosiness had led to this confession.

Dorothy however had taken Bruce's announcement in stride. "You're sure she's not a lipstick lesbian?" Dorothy asked, seeming interested but not disapproving. Pam wasn't even sure what that meant, but trust her mother to be up on all the latest terms.

"We went through a period of wondering. Hoping, too, if I am honest. It's not an easy situation to accept. She's the real deal." Bruce was calm about it.

"When I was younger, there weren't many women who dared to live an openly lesbian life," Dorothy said, "Most were very secretive. A friend of mine was a lesbian, and I found out in a very shocking way."

Pam stared at her mother.

Dorothy seemed to realize they might be assuming the

wrong thing, for she continued. "Oh, nothing nasty. I happened to walk into a store and a natty, formally dressed man I passed on the way out was my friend in full drag. It was a stunner."

"You never told me that, Mom."

Dorothy gave Pam a sharp look. "You never asked if I knew any lesbians. You were too mealy-mouthed to talk of such things."

"I—well—I," she tried to reply.

Bruce came to her rescue. "It used to be a lot more under wraps, as I am sure you remember, Dorothy. Even in my generation, which Pam is probably at the tail end of, people didn't talk about homosexuality when we were growing up."

Dorothy inclined her head in agreement. "Yes, that's true. Ethel never even acknowledged to me that I had seen her dressed as a man. I never mentioned it, either. Of course by then we were both married. It hardly mattered to our friendship."

"She married?" Pam asked, surprised.

"Of course. Most gays and lesbians through history have," Dorothy said, as if it was a matter of common knowledge that Pam should have realized.

"What about your friend's husband?" Bruce asked.

Dorothy replied, "I really have no idea. Ethel might not have known the truth about herself until after she became intimate with her husband. Young girls back then were not encouraged to discover their sexuality before they took the wedding vows."

"Good point," Bruce said.

"Wasn't Cole Porter gay? And married? And his wife knew?" Pam threw in.

"That's fairly well established. The jury is still out on Cary

Grant, though." Bruce smiled.

"The man married four times," Dorothy said. "He must have wanted to be straight."

It sounded so strange to Pam to hear her mother use jargon. Especially when she herself didn't feel comfortable with those terms.

"Movie stars," Dorothy harrumphed. "We've moved from a weighty modern issue to gossip."

Bruce shrugged his shoulders a little. "It helps to be reminded that having a gay daughter isn't unusual."

"It's not the end of the world," Dorothy averred staunchly. "She may provide you with some grandchildren yet. A daughter-in-law, too," she added, ever the optimist.

"Decent of you to say," Bruce replied.

They soon finished their lunch. Bruce thanked them and said he must get back to work.

"I do have a deadline." He made to pick up his dishes and bus them inside, but Dorothy waved him off.

"Let us deal with the dishes, and you go on. Yappie's afternoon walk will come soon enough."

After reiterating his thanks, he departed for his house. Pam started the cleanup. Dorothy did some, but then sat. Pam suspected that her mother's thoughts had reverted to the long ago past and that friend who had a secret lesbian life. Ethel? Had she ever come to their home? Pam didn't remember.

Pam hadn't thought much about such things. Dating boys had been difficult enough, with both her shyness and her boisterous, well-known mother as deterrents. Only when Pam went to college did she get out from under the oppressive public spotlight. There she met Jeff, who was perfect for her.

That was over. She had decades yet to live. Would she follow Sarah's advice and look for a new love? Or try to launch herself in a new direction? This charity idea was daunting and she'd hardly taken even the first step. What was wrong with her that she was frightened of making a few phone calls? Or writing a press release? How hard could they be?

She'd start later today. Not the phone calls, but at least the press release. That didn't require talking to anybody.

By now she had the few dishes washed and drying in the rack she suspected her mother never used. Her mother preferred paper plates and plastic forks to washing anything. It was amazing that she had raised four children without any of them succumbing to malnutrition, obesity, or high blood pressure, considering how much takeout food they had eaten as children before the housekeeper was hired. Dorothy's lack of interest in cooking healthy meals couldn't have helped her father's health, either, but she mustn't blame her mother. They all knew Daddy smoked like a chimney and drank too many cocktails. He was a meat-and-potatoes man, too. No vegetables for him.

It was a long time ago now. She still remembered going with her mother to pick Daddy up at the Long Island Railroad station, before they'd gotten a second car. How eager she had been to see her father emerge from the train, wearing a suit and a hat and carrying a trenchcoat and the newspaper. With a cigarette in his hand, of course. How she had run to him, and how he had caught her up in his arms and given her a kiss and hug. He'd say, "Who's my best girl?" in that hearty voice of his.

Oh, dear. As she stood in the pristine, seldom-used kitchen, the tears flowed down her cheeks. She hadn't cried for her father in many years, although she had broken down in sobs for months after the surprise heart attack killed him. There hadn't been enough time, time to say goodbye, time to get used to the idea that he would pass from her life.

As with Jeff. It wasn't fair. Mindful of her father's early death, Pam had insisted that Jeff get regular yearly physicals. She had done her best to feed her family healthy meals. The fluctuating USDA guidelines had not helped, not that it had mattered. Jeff died from an unsuspected aneurism, something that only would have been picked up from a scan. The kind of scan he had never needed because his doctor each year declared him healthy.

She wiped the tears from under her eyes, thankful she had no mascara on, and hung up her dish towel. Enough of this. She would make a dent in the dining room piles. Her mother surely did not need so many newspaper or magazine back issues.

#

Dorothy was sitting outside. Her mind was on the past. How strange it had been to have recognized her dear friend, Ethel Bush, wearing a three-piece tailored man's suit and a man's hat. No makeup, of course. Although maybe there had been a hint of a five o'clock shadow? Perhaps some deliberate attempt to highlight hair on her upper lip?

Back then, in the 1940s, men's clothing had been as generous as it was again today. Men could hide their bodies in very loose pants, full shirts over undershirts, and wide-cut suit jackets. Then there were the hats. None of those little fedoras

Frank Sinatra affected when he was balding. No, the hats in the 1940s had been big with wide brims. Men could hide under them. Women could bundle up their hair and conceal it under hats, too. It wasn't unusual for a man to wear leather gloves in winter, either. The delicate fingers of a woman could be easily hidden in man's gloves.

Women's clothing and makeup was frankly feminine back then. The makeup colors were very stark and red. Most women wore dresses and skirts, not slacks. Yes, of course, Marlene Dietrich and Katherine Hepburn had famously worn slacks in the 1930s. Some women had worn slacks to do their factory jobs during the war effort. Greta had. Most grown women didn't wear slacks regularly until the skirts became immodest in the 1960s. Then, many women switched to slacks merely to look less old-fashioned while still retaining some coverage. The fashions were awful for a while. One couldn't lean over or sit down safely in a skirt from 1966 on.

Ah, but those were exciting times. It was more pleasant to think about them than to dwell on the distant past. She didn't want to think about Ethel right now. Ethel was dead.

She decided to get up and see what Pamela was doing. She found her daughter in the dining room, leafing through newspapers.

"Hi, Mom," Pamela looked up. "Do we need to keep any of these newspapers? Can we recycle them?"

"Of course. I meant to put them out last week."

Pamela gave her an odd look, as if to say that these newspapers had been here for more than a week. She gathered a batch and headed for the kitchen door, calling over her shoulder. "Is there a recycle box, or do we have to bag or tie them?"

"A blue box. It's by the trash cans."

Dorothy leafed through the stacks of magazines. Some were as much as a year old. She'd gotten very behind. She looked at one or two, but nothing about them interested her. Why on earth was she keeping these?

Pamela returned for a second batch of newspapers and noticed what Dorothy was doing.

"Are you done with those magazines?"

"Yes. I don't know why they've been hanging around so long."

"Okay, I'll grab them, too." Pamela removed a stack.

It was nice her daughter had the energy, because Dorothy didn't right now. She wandered out to the sunroom again to look at the water. It was always full of motion.

"Where'd you go?" her daughter called.

"I'm out here," she replied. Pamela came out to the sunroom with a stack of magazines. "How about these?"

"What about them?"

"May I recycle them?" Pamela's tone of voice suggested she'd asked the question before. Perhaps she had. Dorothy was paying attention to watching the tide. She didn't want to think about dealing with papers.

"We can decide on that another day. I'm a little lacking in ambition right now."

#

At least her mother had allowed her to toss several stacks of newspapers and magazines before telling her to leave the rest.

Dorothy obviously tired much quicker these days, because there were telltale signs all over the house that she was not keeping up with her housekeeping. That was just an expression, as now that Dorothy no longer had a housekeeper, she had a regular cleaning service. The cleaners probably were responsible for the many stacks neatly piled on the dining room table.

None of the papers or magazines looked as if they had been read. Maybe it was time to stop the newspapers, even though they were getting thinner anyway because advertising had fled to the Internet. Dorothy had devoured newspapers in previous years, searching for any little bit of information to help her current campaign, or spark a new one. There had been no end to the numbers and types of quests her mother signed up for and then pressed friends and acquaintances into joining. Pam always found it exhausting, but her mother had done a lot of good in the community. Pam was proud of her mother.

As a child, Pam had wished Dorothy had had more time for her. Pam was the youngest of the four. She always suspected she was the afterthought, the unplanned baby no one was enthusiastic about having. She'd never asked her mother about it. When had they ever sat down just to talk? Dorothy was always busy, continuously in motion.

In the old days, Dorothy was constantly on the phone, harassing and haranguing, or on her way to a meeting or protest. She'd organized and participated in numerous sit-ins. She routinely dragged all the kids, including Pam, to swell the numbers at protest marches. Daddy had to bail Dorothy out of jail several times. After he died, Alexander took over the bailing job. He even had a bail bond company on retainer at one time.

Dorothy had been especially active in the 1970s and 1980s.

Even their hobbies were dramatically different. Pam liked to sew, especially to crochet. Dorothy couldn't bear to sit still long enough to do hand work. Did Dorothy even have a hobby, come to think of it? Oh, of course. Her crossword puzzles. She played with them during odd moments, but Dorothy's real hobby was people. When they went out anywhere, she was hyper alert to the other people they encountered. She noticed if someone looked poor or unhappy. She was fearless about approaching them and asking if there was any way she could help. Many times, Dorothy had improved people's lives.

What was the story on the pile of mail? It ought to be dealt with. Maybe after a little while, she could suggest to Dorothy that they could add more to the recycling bin.

Meanwhile, she would make a few homemade goodies for the leftovers picnic with the attractive man next door. She would have squirmed in mortification at the blatant matchmaking, but Dorothy's forthright actions had embarrassed her many times in the past. She had grown a little numb to it. If Bruce made any moves, she'd deal with them. He probably would not, since he wouldn't want to risk arousing Dorothy's ire.

She wondered if Bruce had a sweet tooth. It had been years since she'd made any cookies. Maybe she would tonight. It would be fun.

#

Bruce was pleased with his progress getting to know Dorothy Duncan. Meeting Pam was a bonus. Obviously, Dorothy was trying play matchmaker by sending them on a picnic, which in turn accelerated his neighborly relationship with Dorothy. He was excited about Pam for different reasons, though there was always the chance she knew something to help him move forward on his quest.

Aunt Nora had sent him here, but he'd been the one to decide on the oblique approach. Although perhaps he needn't have bothered. Dorothy seemed like a forthright old girl. Still, getting her to admit to murder would be an effort. She had to know there was no statute of limitations on the crime, if indeed a crime had been committed. He wanted her to let her guard down and confide in him. Then he'd know what to do.

He was somewhat regretful his friendliness with the family would eventually be revealed as self-interest. But he was willing to take that rap to learn the truth.

#

Pam sat in the sunroom. She'd hauled out her crocheting, which she always found soothing. She had donated many blankets to charitable drives over the years. Dorothy had gone into her first-floor bedroom a half hour ago. It was a relief to be alone for a while. Pam wasn't used to being with people constantly, at least, not at home.

Dorothy came out of her bedroom and walked over to the sunroom. She held a framed photo, which she looked at searchingly in the strong light.

Neither of them said anything for a while. Dorothy looked at the photo over and over, sometimes touching the glass as if to caress the face of the woman in the picture, sometimes staring at it. Pam didn't recall ever seeing that photo around the house before. Finally, her curiosity overcame her desire for peace and quiet.

"Who's that?"

"My oldest friend, Greta. You never met her. We volunteered at the same USO canteen."

"The USO? That was the organization that entertained servicemen during the war, right? I didn't know you ever did anything like that. Wasn't it kind of creepy, dancing with all those men you didn't know?"

Dorothy smiled, remembering. "It was considered a bit fast of a girl to dance with strangers, but also patriotic. I enjoyed it. They were flattering, eager. I even kissed my share of them."

"Really?"

"That was nothing. We got marriage proposals. Back then, most boys would have been ashamed to ask a decent girl for relations unless there was marriage involved. Some of them would soon die in combat and this was their last chance to touch or kiss a girl. We all knew it could happen to this boy or that boy. Would happen. Some girls married soldiers they hardly knew."

"I've heard about wartime marriages. Don't they mostly fail?"

"Perhaps that was why the military rules made it hard for soldiers to spontaneously marry, because the boys were fueled by alcohol, lust, and fear of dying. Yet despite the obstacles, many couples found a way."

"Marrying a boy you'd merely danced with a couple of times sounds like a recipe for disaster. Did you know anyone who did that?"

"Greta. She married Roger Dietrich after they met at a USO dance early in the war. He was shipped overseas and didn't come back 'til after the war was over."

"Did their marriage break up once they got to know each other?"

"She had a baby right away, and I know she was happy about it. I'm not sure Roger cared about the child, although back then most men weren't interested in their babies until they learned to talk. Your father wasn't, either."

Reacting to Pam's shocked expression, Dorothy laughed. "Oh, don't give me that look. I'm not criticizing Malcolm. Times were different then. Women did all the nurturing while the men supported the family."

"Jeff was always interested in our babies," Pam said.

"Decades later, when being a touchy-feely dad became fashionable. Caring for infants was not the manly thing to do in the 1940s and 1950s. Malcolm never changed a diaper. I was pregnant a lot then, too. I could have used his help. Let's see. Christine was born in 1944. Neil in 1946. Alexander was 1948. Then you came in 1950. Then I'd had enough."

Pam had heard this part before. Although she waited for her mother to say her last child was an unwelcome afterthought, Dorothy didn't. Instead she gazed at the picture again.

"Did your friend Greta have a lot of babies, too?"

"No." There was sadness in her expression. "That boy next door reminds me of Greta. Take a look at her photo and tell me what you think."

It was black and white, as photographs from that period all were. A slender young woman with a broad smile was wearing

111

one of those light-colored, knee-length linen suits with big shoulders that women wore during World War II. She sported a large hat with a wide brim, like the one Ilsa wore in *Casablanca.* Jaunty and romantic looking. Greta wore the harsh makeup of the period. Her eyebrows were very dramatic and dark, as were her lips. She had a cloud of shoulder-length dark hair. A pretty woman who knew it and was happy about it.

Bruce's hair was mostly grey and his features didn't contrast strongly with it. That's what happened to people as they aged. They dimmed. Oh, he was a good-looking man, but this young woman had been a stunner. It was hard to see any similarity. Maybe the nose? Her hairline was hidden by her hat. It was no use. Many people shared similar facial characteristics. Perhaps Bruce did resemble Greta, but Pam couldn't see it.

"I can't tell." She handed the photo back, and picked up her crocheting again.

Dorothy stared some more at Greta's photo, then put it carefully upright on a small table. She took her usual seat and looked out at the water.

Pam wanted to ask what happened to Greta, but then the landline phone rang. Dorothy gestured for her to answer it.

It was Sarah. "You didn't pick up your cell. I've found a job prospect for you, but you'll have to act fast. Have you updated your résumé? I want to send it to my contact right away."

"Uh, no." Her thoughts had been focused on helping Magda.

"Then jump on it. Get the résumé done today. Do you have a computer you can use out there in snobland? One that does the Internet?"

"Linley gave my mother a laptop for her last birthday. I assume it's still here."

"Good. After you write the résumé, take the laptop to your local coffee house with wifi and email me with the document as an attachment. Now copy down my email address."

She dutifully did because of course she hadn't brought any notes with her.

"I need the résumé by four today. Got that?"

She felt like saluting. Sarah didn't have children, but in running a division at her corporation, Sarah had developed her version of the mommy voice quite well.

"Yes. Thanks, Sarah. I'll get right on it."

She asked and received Dorothy's permission to use her laptop, which as expected was still in its original box and showed no signs of ever having been used. Dorothy was simply too old to care about this new medium of communication. For her a landline telephone was good enough.

Pam cobbled together a résumé that was vague about her education dates and thus protected her age. Unfortunately, she didn't have a lot of accomplishments to list, but it would have to do. She ran into town to a wifi spot. Despite the cutesy old-fashioned village charm, it was completely modern, as befitted a shopping Mecca for the wealthy local inhabitants.

Sarah called her right away to complain about how modest the résumé sounded.

"I'll have to punch it up," she said.

"What's the point? I'm not exactly a career go-getter." Was that hopelessness in her voice?

"This is a competitive world, and you need to fight for what you want. You're not working merely to pass the hours."

"I used to be," she sighed.

"That was before, my friend. You're living in a new era." Sarah hung up, never the type to waste time.

Sarah didn't need to mention that the collapse of Pam's firm was merely the tip of the iceberg. The Wall Street downturn was all over the media. Like many others, Pam had gone overnight from someone who was financially secure to one who could be in danger. At least she had retired the mortgage on the family home. With the housing market in chaos, it was good not to worry about foreclosure, but she was now land rich and cash poor. It wasn't fair. Jeff had saved for decades, and she had saved for many years, too. There ought to be more security to show for their efforts.

Enough repining. She did far too much of it these days. She locked the laptop in the trunk of her car and nipped into a nearby drugstore for a few odds and ends, including a cute doggie toy for Yappie. He might come on their picnic. She was looking forward to her date with Bruce. Walking on the beach with someone was more fun than walking alone.

Chapter 9

The hike and picnic started smoothly. Bruce got Yappie on a leash, and went next door and knocked soon after he saw Dorothy being picked up in a cab.

"Should we have done this some other time so you could drive your mother to her appointment?"

Pam was looking quite fresh and pretty in a bright yellow striped slacks outfit. She shook her head as she motioned him in.

"Thanks for asking. I already lost that battle. She insists on her independence. She takes a cab so she can have a drink with lunch."

He'd come to the kitchen door. Yappie wasn't dirtying any fancy rugs as he pranced around and sniffed in corners. She gathered up a large wicker picnic basket covered with a checked tablecloth. She shrugged.

"I couldn't resist this classic, although I guess a Styrofoam cooler would be lighter."

Bruce took the basket and handed her the leash. "This'll work."

She smiled her thanks, and they took off.

The walk down the beach was about what he had expected. Pam was a restful companion. She didn't talk too much, although she dutifully pointed out and identified local landmarks, and told short tales about them. He pretended to pay attention.

She appeared to be bothered by something. He wondered what it could be.

They found a good spot for a picnic, laid down the blanket, and soon were relaxed under a sheltering outcropping of rocks. Yappie ran around nearby, sniffing at everything while they sorted through the large selection of leftovers. She had turned the cold cuts into several kinds of sandwiches. There was bottled water, and what looked like homemade cookies, too.

Bruce felt relaxed. Perhaps now he could learn more about her. She had been discreet about her personal life in their previous encounters.

"Why were you running away from Dorothy yesterday?"

"I wasn't."

"It looked that way to me." He was taking a gamble by pushing her, but in his experience, women wanted to talk about their problems and their feelings. Most men never bothered to listen. He smiled at Pam reassuringly, and she sighed.

"I want to help a coworker—former coworker, I should say. She and many other people have lost their jobs and need financial help. My mother thinks I should start a charity. It's a good idea, but she also wants me to be the public spokesperson."

"I thought it was something personal."

"To me it is." She took a deep breath. "You know about my

mother being a retired community activist?"

He nodded.

"She always courted publicity to help her various causes. But I've never liked being in the public eye."

"So if you start this charity, you'd be fighting your natural impulse to stay out of it?"

"Exactly." She moved restlessly on the blanket. "I hate the idea of putting myself out there, but how else can I get people to contribute to a new charity?"

"Tell me more."

She talked about her friend who needed money. He nodded at appropriate moments, noticing how bright her expression was as she spoke. Pam was a sweet woman, unselfconscious about her womanly appeal. He felt a tug of attraction, something he'd not felt for any woman in a long time. Too long.

He decided he liked her ears. They were small, set tight to her head, and had soft lobes with no holes in them. He found himself reaching out to touch one. Her flesh was incredibly soft under his thumb and forefinger.

Pam was so shocked she stopped speaking.

"Why don't you have pierced ears?" he wondered out loud.

"I…my mother wouldn't let me," she replied, stuttering. He was still admiring her earlobe. He leaned in.

"What are you do—?"

He hushed her with his lips on hers. Her lips were soft, and tasted of surprise. His hand cradled the back of her head as he kissed her more thoroughly.

Hesitantly, Pam's lips opened under his. Her stiff body softened. He gathered her closer and let his tongue penetrate her mouth. She sighed and put her arms around him, finally returning his kisses with her lips and tongue, and pushing her soft breasts against his chest.

A while later, they were recalled to reality when Yappie wedged between them, whining.

Pam held the dog to her chest, stroking him while she stared at Bruce with wide eyes.

"Don't think Yappie's going to protect you. He's my dog." He couldn't help smiling as he made the threat. She was so clearly, sweetly overcome. He wanted to kiss her again.

She put up a hand to stop his forward motion. "I hardly know you."

He shrugged. "I'm willing to work on that." He fed Yappie a scrap and sent the dog away.

The interruption had allowed Pam to gather her protective barriers. She shrank away from him.

"No?" He cocked his head.

She shook hers, not looking at him. She started feverishly gathering the picnic things. He put a hand out and covered hers. She froze, but still refused to look in his direction.

"What are you afraid of?" he asked. "I won't hurt you."

Her head bowed.

"Talk to me. What's the problem?"

She finally looked at him. Her eyes were filled with tears. "I haven't kissed a man in four years."

"Since your husband?"

"Yes." The topic obviously upset her, but why? He could see she was trying not to explain, but her emotions were working against her. He waited.

"I—People keep telling me to date. I haven't. I guess I'm shocked at myself."

"Because we kissed and you liked it?" He didn't want her to slide away into denying her enthusiastic response. She gulped and wiped the unshed tears away. Then she gave him a frank look.

"Bruce, I need time to process what just happened."

"Speaking of time, how long are you staying?"

She looked suddenly rueful. "I might have a job interview later this week. I'll have to leave in a day or two. Then I have to work on starting the nonprofit."

She would be back. He could tell. He had managed to forge a bond between them, and she would find reasons to return. He wasn't being a conceited fool. By his age, he knew women, some of them, quite well. Pam was transparent, unlike his ex, who had shown an amazing capacity for deviousness once they were divorcing. What you saw was what you got with Pam. It was very soothing.

He hoped she would return soon. Meanwhile, they had the walk home to enjoy. He'd hold her hand and they could pretend they were teenagers with their whole lives ahead of them.

Chapter 10

Dorothy was a little lonely with Pamela in the city for a job interview. Surprising how pleasant it had been to have her daughter here. She had always been a sweet little child. Possibly she hadn't gotten as much attention as the older children, but what was done was done. Pamela had seemed happy with the life she had made for herself. She still owned the home she'd bought with Jeff in Ardsley. A nice suburb. Perhaps Pamela would get this job she was interviewing for, and her quiet life would resume without a hitch.

Dorothy had never liked that kind of existence for herself. She despised inactivity, although these days she was not as able as she had been. Not only had she lost the fire, but also she could not keep all the facts she needed in her head when on a campaign. The key to her success had always been her ability to marshal the data and present them when she could make the opportunities to be heard. No longer. She'd had to pass the torch to the younger generation of activists. Her brain had gotten old, like her body. It had succumbed to the inevitable ravages of time. Her skin was thin, wrinkled, and fragile. Her hair had passed through gray to white, which she made no attempt to hide with color out of a bottle. She suspected she wasn't hearing quite as well as she used to. She knew her sense of smell had dimmed. She made a special effort to wash every day. She didn't want to get the old woman stink that came with diminished sense of smell. She had a system for keeping her clothes clean. Once she wore them, even if only for an hour in town, off they went to be laundered.

What she hated most was the dozing off while she was trying to do something. She couldn't count the number of times it had happened while she was working the crossword. As a result, she was still trying to finish a book of crosswords she'd had around for months.

At least she was better off than her friends whose grown children had taken away their driving privileges. She could still drive. Although the last time she had driven the car, it had taken forever to get home. On the whole, it was easier and safer to take a cab if she wanted to go somewhere.

#

Pam was afraid to pursue the charity idea, but also drawn to it. If total strangers might send Magda money merely from hearing about her on television for a few minutes, why shouldn't rich executives want to contribute? Perhaps some of those men might have genuine charitable impulses. The rest would only give with ulterior motives, wanting fame or glory along with a tax deduction. Could she work on their vanity successfully?

She hadn't tried to do anything difficult in years. Perhaps the charity idea, outlandish as it seemed, was the answer to the questions plaguing her about her future. Helping displaced workers was a worthwhile goal. Occupying herself with building a new charity would give her a reason to wake up in the morning. Although, so would looking forward to seeing Bruce.

Did she want to get involved with a man again? Have a romance? Have sex again with a live human? Her attitude might be prudish, but she'd never been one of the flower children in the 1960s, talking about free love and sleeping with multiple partners. She had stayed a virgin until she had met Jeff. They'd learned about sex with each other, and that had been enough for both of them for all their years together.

She wasn't naïve, another reason she hadn't jumped into dating once widowed. Every younger woman would be a potential rival. Older men wanted a nurse, or a sexpot. What if she suffered bad health? How could she ever trust any man she met in the future to want to take care of her? She couldn't. She didn't intend to.

Then there were the body issues. It was a cliché, but she didn't much want to expose her sagging, crepey flesh to a stranger's eyes. Bruce had been married, too. He'd obviously experienced how bodies changed over time. Why had his marriage ended? What was his attitude toward a woman aging? Did she even care to find out?

More questions surfaced. Why have a relationship with a man again? What was in it for her? Why not concentrate on trying to build the nonprofit charity idea into a viable structure? Wasn't helping Magda and other distressed, displaced workers more important than kisses or sex?

Chapter 11

Linley managed to avoid talking directly to Jason all week except when they were on the air. She also made herself absent for the briefings before the DC trip.

She had kept busy, doing her guest radio segments and blogging. She had worked her mother's job loss as far as she could take it and had met with some success. An area university had invited her to give a talk on personal finance. There was no real money involved, but it was a prestige gig. Another new contact had suggested Linley teach an adult education course at one of the many local colleges. She didn't need academic credentials to teach those classes, and teaching at the college level was a cerebral touch to add to her resume. She didn't want anyone to mistake her for an empty-headed television personality. Bad enough she was a blonde.

She'd ridden as far as she could ride on her personal connection to the Wall Street crisis. Now what could she do about Jason? This situation was becoming untenable. She refused to let him force her into a hookup. Even though she was desperate for him. Sitting next to him now on the train down to

Washington, it was all she could do to ignore him.

Jason had been surprisingly circumspect. After declaring his intentions, he'd backed off. He'd let her run away at the studio. He hadn't bugged her all week. Even now, although they were entirely alone because the production crew would be picked up from the DC branch of the network, he wasn't pushing his advantage. He wasn't trying to talk to her. Not pressuring her in any way.

He probably thought he didn't need to. They would do their broadcast, go to the press club bash, and one thing would lead to another. Jason was depending on her to behave the same way with him this time as she had the first night they had met.

Her feelings were completely different now. She knew Jason. She worked with him. Hooking up with him was not on her agenda. Instead, she was thinking seriously about starting an affair with him. If he didn't want more than a hookup, too bad for him. Whatever happened between them tonight would be on her terms.

She shifted in her seat. She could feel the heat of his body next to her. They were physically closer than they had been in months except for three nights ago at the café when he had crowded her into the corner. At no other time had they been this near to touching beyond the formal handshake that had almost slain her three months ago when she'd been hired.

Their bodies were within mere inches, from head to toe, for the first time in a year. They had always maintained a careful distance of several feet between them at production meetings, and of course her spot on the panel was separate by a couple of feet, for the camera's convenience. Not today.

She could save herself a lot of angst if she simply turned in his direction right now and put the moves on him. Then they'd miss their broadcast for sure. They might even be thrown off the train, because if she started something, she wasn't sure if she could stop. No, it was better to build up the anticipation. Let him suffer as long as possible. She shifted again in the seat, trying to dispel some of her sexual frustration. Who was suffering here?

Jason spoke quietly, so he wouldn't be overheard by the other Amtrak passengers. "If you don't stop squirming, I'm going to march you into the bathroom and we can renew our acquaintance there."

That brought her head up in wonder. Jason's desire was plain on his face. He nodded, acknowledging the pulse between them. "First we work, then we play."

Linley raised an eyebrow. Jason thought he'd made the winning move. He thought he was in charge, that being on assignment away from their normal work restraints would annihilate her resistance to a hookup. He didn't know how strong she was, but he'd soon find out.

His self-assurance should have angered her. Instead, she felt half relieved. She was tired of fighting herself, tired of guessing at Jason's intentions.

Only half relieved.

"I'm not going to make it easy for you," she vowed in an equally discreet whisper. "You have a lot of explaining to do. I'm not planning on doing any drinking tonight. You'll need a super sales job to convince me."

She smiled, the kind of smile that should have daunted him. Instead, Jason looked eager to fight for the privilege of going to bed with her again.

"I've been ready for three months," he said. He smiled, too. His self-assurance shook her, yet excited her even more.

The rest of the ride, they did not speak. It had all been said.

#

After the tense moments on the train, Linley and Jason shifted to professional mode, and neither even blinked inappropriately. Their show went smoothly. Later, they met in the hotel lobby for the press club dinner. Jason was in a tux, and he looked fabulous. He could be a movie star. He simply had the regular features and broad shoulders that looked best in formal menswear. As for Linley, she was wearing a short red cocktail dress that showed off her long, slender legs. The sleekly muscled arms and shoulders of the modern woman who works out were apparent in the strapless, sleeveless design of the dress. In case Linley's youth and beauty weren't emphasized enough, the bodice was boned and pushed her breasts up and held them firmly. Good thing she didn't feel cold easily because this dress didn't cover much. Yet it wasn't outrageous, either. She carried a light wrap, but it was for show, not to wear. While she had the assets of youth and a good body she intended to use them. She attracted male attention in red, the color research had shown men now approved of the most. Today's statistics said men liked a woman empowered in red. She used her power.

Jason eyed her appreciatively, then took her arm to lead her to the cab rank. "You look sensational. I'll be fighting them off."

She gave him an incredulous look. "We need to act like professionals tonight, remember. There are some important people at this reception."

"You have no sense of humor, do you? I was trying to pay you a compliment."

"I take my career seriously," she said. She shivered at the image of him pushing aside the men who would crowd around her tonight and boldly declaring she belonged to him. She could not allow that to happen.

The press club was in a little old building on its very own block in the city. It actually had gardens around it and an iron fence. How quaint. Jason helped her out of the cab and they entered the gate and presented their invitations. Inside, the place had the air of an old, old club, with a hint of it being ready to collapse.

As they made their way into the party rooms, a strange thing happened. Men did not gravitate to Linley. They surrounded several different middle-aged women.

"That's Cokie Roberts," Jason whispered, seeing her discreetly eyeing a well-preserved lady who wouldn't see sixty again. "And there's Lesley Stahl." She looked even older.

They strolled around, and again there was a much older woman holding forth, surrounded by interested, even admiring men.

"I recognize Andrea Mitchell," she said. "She's married to Allen Greenspan, the retired Fed chairman."

"She had a longtime career as a news reporter before they tied the knot, and she's still in the game. That's why she's a big deal in this crowd," he reminded her. He pointed to another, somewhat younger woman, tastefully but very conservatively garbed in a business suit. "Gwen Ifill. Have you seen her on *Meet the Press* or *Washington Week in Review?*"

Linley shook her head. Oops.

Jason got them drinks and then they separated as they each started talking to some of the media people they already knew. The evening continued to be surreal for Linley. Despite her red dress, and her youth and beauty, she never became the center of a group of men vying for her attention. In fact, when she did offer a comment, the men shied away.

The other women were dressed in a frankly dowdy manner. A really old woman in her sixties shouldn't show lots of skin, of course. But the young women, the local anchors, were all in very conservative garb, too. Finally, Linley started talking with a girl her age who looked bored enough to be approachable. One who wasn't totally dressed like a maiden aunt.

Linley introduced herself, then asked, "What's with the women here? Is there some Washington dress code? As in, dress badly?"

The other girl, Beth, choked on her laughter. "Never been to DC before?"

"No." She shook her head.

"This is the one city in the U.S. where brains and power are considered more glamorous than looks or money. Women dress not to make waves."

"You mean like the First Lady or a Senator's wife?"

"All of us. It's a formal kind of town, what with all the foreign dignitaries and consulates and embassies," Beth said. "Plus, this club is famous for insisting on old-fashioned formal wear." She nodded in the direction of the others. "Look at all the men in tuxes."

Linley glanced down at her red dress, her favorite. "When I put this on tonight, I thought of it as acceptable," she said.

Beth eyed it consideringly. "There are other Washington parties where it wouldn't raise an eyebrow. Not this one. Anyway, being young and hot doesn't mean much in DC. Contacts and experience count here. That's why the guys hang around the older women." She sipped at her drink.

"I'll remember for next time," Linley said. They talked for a while about their jobs. Beth hadn't heard of Linley, which was disappointing. Linley didn't know much about Washington, DC, television. A mistake. She should know more about the field in which she hoped to rise. About print journalism, too, even though it was dying because of the Internet and she personally didn't want to be involved with print. It was sobering to discover that she had a blind spot in her knowledge of her profession.

She kept circulating, trying to talk to more partiers, but this go round she was careful only to approach groups with women in them, so she wouldn't be perceived as some bimbo. Her pleasure in the evening had fled once she'd understood she was dressed completely wrong. She was unlikely to find any good career lifts in this situation. Retrieving her evening wrap from the coat check would look odd in such a hot, crowded room.

Finally, she found Jason, surrounded by a group of youngish men. They were all laughing. She sauntered closer, and Jason drew her into the circle, but did not touch her or make his move seem proprietary. They were still being professional, thank goodness.

"Lin, we're talking about that CEO we had on the show

yesterday, the commodities guy."

She picked up on his lead and played her part smoothly. She was careful not to act flirtatious in the slightest. The men at first eyed her oddly and tended to ignore her. All because of the damn red dress.

After what seemed like years, her torture was finally over. Linley was silent as they returned to their hotel in a cab. Jason crowed about finding several influential and well-connected Washington insiders who were eager to be on the show. "A good night," he concluded.

"It was horrible," she said, practically shuddering.

"What?" He sounded confused.

"Didn't you see what a fool I made of myself in this awful rag? It's a designer model, but no one at the party cared. Doris Kearns Godwin was wearing a day dress she'd merely thrown a silk scarf across. Plus a string of pearls. Pearls! Me, I'm dressed in hooker red, ready to perform a lap dance."

"You look like a lady to me," he said, casting an admiring glance at her heaving bosom in the revealing dress. Right. That kind of male admiration she could do without. She'd been so caught up in the lust drama with Jason, she hadn't done basic research about the trip. She'd skipped the briefing sessions to stay away from him. This was all his fault.

"Why didn't you warn me Washington could be like this?" She turned on him.

"Huh?"

"You're the one who planned the trip. You should have prepped me for the peculiarity of that press club's dress code." She didn't even try to keep her voice from rising. "The men all thought I was a bimbo."

"If you'd come to the briefing sessions, you could have asked."

"How the hell was I supposed to know? You've been around, Jason. You knew. You set me up."

By now, she was nearly ready to shriek at him. "I've never been so humiliated."

When they arrived at the hotel, she tore out of the cab, stalking angrily ahead as Jason paid. He caught up to her at the elevator. "Lin—"

She rounded on him.

"Don't say another word." She practically hissed at him. "I'm going to my room. Alone."

"You can't be serious—"

Her voice rose. "You're damn right I'm serious." She jabbed the elevator button fiercely. "You ruined my evening. You let me look like a hooker at a classy party. No, we won't be having sex tonight, is that clear enough for you?" She was screaming.

Jason's expression, which a few seconds ago had been confused, hardened into a poker player's careful lack of expression.

She pushed by him into the elevator, anger in every movement. "Now get out of my way!"

As the doors closed, she kept muttering, "Damn you! It's all your fault."

Chapter 12

Pam dressed in her best and went into the city for the job interview at a Wall Street firm, but it was a disaster. The hiring manager was a young know-it-all who nevertheless acted clueless about dealing with an older person as a potential hire. Because of his youthful insecurities, she wouldn't get this job. Probably the young person he'd end up hiring would not have the patience older people did for the mind-numbing work involved, but there was no polite or appropriate way to warn him of his error in the making. Instead, convention dictated she must go through the motions of listening to him attentively and thanking him for his time, knowing all the while he would not hire her. She recounted the tale to Sarah when they met later, ending with, "What a frustrating waste."

"At least you had your brain switched on," Sarah pointed out. "You analyzed the situation and decanted its essence."

They were lunching at an upscale Chinese restaurant. Sarah was wearing a dashing three-piece pinstripe pantsuit. The third piece was a vest that outlined her shapely figure. She looked nearly thirty years younger than her real age. Pam was more conservatively clothed in a skirted grey suit with a white silk blouse and gold earrings. Standard interview uniform, but perhaps old-fashioned for today's world, and revealing her age too clearly.

"You're right. There will be another job," Pam said.

"That's the spirit. Anyway, you weren't interviewing for a senior enough position. One that a senior should be hired for. Get it? A senior?" Sarah grinned, pleased with her awful pun.

Pam dutifully chuckled. "Let's talk about something else." She'd had enough of feeling frustrated for one day.

"Sure," Sarah shrugged. "You never told me. Did your TV show appearance with Linley break the ice between you?"

Sarah must have seen how her face fell, for her expression softened into open sympathy. "No, huh?"

Pam shook her head, fighting stupid tears. "I'm not giving up. She can't see yet that our family tie is important. Eventually, she'll realize."

"You hope," Sarah muttered, taking a quick sip of water, obviously to stifle her angry reaction.

"I have to believe it'll get better. I have to." She hoped she didn't sound desperate and weak.

"I'm sorry I asked. I also apologize for dragging you all the way into the city for a bad job interview. Are you still working on how to help your friend, Magda?"

Pam stifled a small giggle. "Last week, I was feeling negative about that, too, if you recall."

Chagrinned, Sarah mimed banging her head with the palm of her hand.

"Am I zero for three? Should I go home and eat worms?"

With a hint of the cat in the cream, Pam announced, "I am launching a nonprofit foundation."

"What?"

"My mother talked me into it."

Sarah looked shocked. "What do you know about running a charity?"

"Not a whole lot." She paused to take a sip of her iced tea. "If anyone can teach me, it's my mother."

"That's true enough," Sarah muttered, "I'm finding your sudden switch into rampant social activism hard to believe, though. You're serious?"

"Yes, even though she scared me at first." Pam grimaced. "My mother is so publicity-oriented. She pushed that angle."

"Whereupon you, the one who likes to sit in the corner unnoticed, ran away screaming," Sarah nodded.

"You don't know how close to the literal truth that is." She sighed, still ashamed of her flight down the beach to escape her mother's advice. "Anyway, even though I'm not thrilled about having to be the PR person for the nonprofit, I'm the logical choice until it becomes big enough to hire one."

"In this economic climate, what makes you think you can shake loose charitable giving?"

"It's always a good time for some people, even when it's a bad time for others," she replied. "What about all those stockbrokers and other traders who walked away from the Wall Street mess with millions in bonuses and commissions?"

"They spent it all on Lamborghinis and gated estates."

"Maybe."

"Or on cocaine and call girls."

Pam shrugged. "I only need to find a few traders or executives who didn't." She gained volume and enthusiasm as she continued. "Then there are the corporations themselves. They're all in a guilty position because they've laid off thousands of workers. If I can leverage that guilt, I can get substantial contributions they can deduct off their corporate taxes."

Sarah nodded slowly. "That approach could pay off. Your idea or your mom's?"

"Mine," she said with justifiable pride.

"You've thought this through."

"I have. I've already gone ahead and hired a website designer. I'm meeting him later today to plan it, although I have to wait until the incorporation papers are filed before I can start the site."

"So I shouldn't line up any job interviews for you next week?" Sarah's inquiry was only half humorous.

"Tomorrow, I'm driving out to Long Island again to meet with my mother's attorney and draw up the papers."

"You're moving fast," Sarah said, approval in her voice. "Let me know how I can help."

"Thanks for offering. I may need your contacts to get me in to see certain highly guarded people."

"How about going back on television to give it a push? Shows like to do follow ups on human interest stories."

"True," Pam said, struck. "Linley could probably broker it."

"Even if she can't, she'd love the opportunity to try. That girl is a go-getter." It was the closest Sarah had come to a compliment about Linley in years. Pam's heart swelled. Perhaps Sarah was beginning to see Linley's admirable qualities.

Not once during their lunch had Sarah urged her to get a life, or to date. Probably because she was finally doing both, although she hadn't told Sarah about Bruce yet. How ironic.

Three hours later, her head was spinning with all the possibilities before her, but she had taken the plunge. The basic website would start operating immediately, complete with a click through to a secure donation site. A fancier design would debut next week. Depending on the traffic her publicity efforts generated, she could access more powerful servers and even more complex design.

She had written an earnest money check to the designer, with more to come on delivery. She had paid the web hosting company for a year in advance.

The foundation could afford to be in the red for a while. The nonprofit might be able to pay her a small salary by the time her unemployment benefits ran out. For now she could fulfill the letter of the law and look for a new job, and at the same time hit up every possible employer as a potential donor, too. There was no reason a human resources employee couldn't be coaxed to help garner donations.

She deliberately had forgotten to tell Sarah about her picnic with Bruce. About the kiss. She wasn't ready to withstand bawdy girlfriend teasing. Her feelings were mixed up. Guilt over Jeff, even though she knew he would want her to be happy. Confusion about what she wanted from a relationship and what Bruce wanted.

They had arranged to go to a local park Dorothy had been instrumental in creating many years ago. Dorothy's name was even on a plaque at the entrance. They'd probably take his dog and walk around. She had no idea how adults courted these days. She and Jeff had met when they were both very young and inexperienced. They had gone on inexpensive dates at first, spending time in parks, and—oh, no. Was she unconsciously trying to duplicate the past?

If she was, so be it. She wasn't comfortable with what she had heard recently—that men expected sex on the third date. Or sooner. No way would she want to do that. She should ask Linley if it was true. Linley dated, so she would know. No. Linley and she didn't have that kind of relationship. They didn't swap girlish confidences. Not at all.

Chapter 13

"American consumers are like sheep," Linley said, unable to keep the disgust out of her voice. *Hot Tracks* was on the air again, and the topic was the debt load of the average American.

"Linley, that's harsh," Ernie said.

"They're all about following fashions trends, and spending money they don't have. Getting rich is the American dream, but nobody knows how to hold onto their money. People are pitiful," she insisted.

"You're being tough on them," Jason said.

"There's no point sugarcoating the truth. These are the same people we the taxpayers are supposed to bail out from their insane mortgage debt."

"That's socialism," Ralph frowned. He was the one who always worried the most about indications the government was trying to take care of citizens.

"Even if—and let's suppose you're right, Ralph and Lin, and the average American consumer is incompetent at managing his or her money—even if it's true, we've still got a desperate situation on a national scale," Jason said, using one of his patented portmanteau sentences that tried to encompass everything they'd touched on at once.

"True, but Linley here has no sympathy for these people caught in the clutches of the credit card companies and their usurious rates." That was Ernie again.

"I do sympathize," Linley insisted, "but a personal finance bailout doesn't build character. All it does is teach the average citizen that there are no consequences to his or her foolish actions. That kind of federal policy will cripple people." She shook her head.

"You're worried about creating a moral hazard?" Jason asked.

"People only want to get debt relief so they can run out and spend some more."

"Why do you think that is? Ideas?" Jason asked. He turned to Ernie and Ralph.

They offered opinions and argued more. Linley was content to have had her say.

After the Washington disaster, she'd pulled herself together and started ignoring Jason's sex appeal. She concentrated on building her career, not messing it up. Her degree was not in journalism. She had a hole in her knowledge about her field. Too late, she had Googled all the distinguished women she had seen at the DC press party. Some had hard lives before the feminist movement gave them more opportunities. Others were bona fide media stars. Had Ariana Huffington been there, and Linley hadn't noticed?

Knowing her core subject, statistics, was not enough. Nor was being young and attractive, although for television how she looked was important. Maybe less than in the past? A lot of the women who had significant television shows were so old they were long past the pretty stage. Barbara Walters was ancient, although she dolled up to pretend otherwise. Of course, there were plenty of ugly guys on television. Not Jason. He was a stunner. She loved the way his curly hair looked as if it was a total wig, it was that perfect. Oh, damn, she was thinking about him again.

She'd allowed her temper to deep six any possible hookup after the press club event. Now she thought of it as a close escape. She had no business doing the horizontal mambo with a man she almost worked for. Sure, Marty was their boss, but Jason ran the show.

She'd avoided trouble, but try telling her body. Her breasts ached for Jason to fondle them. Her thighs wanted to be entangled with his. And that was just for starters.

The mess-up in DC had changed her somehow. She started interrupting the guys and yelling her opinions across the room. She'd learned if she used a low-pitched tone but high volume, she could cut them off successfully. They'd run on long enough about the poor pitiful consumers. She opened her mouth to re-enter the fray with a zinger.

#

With another show over, Linley retreated to her cubicle and sent an email to Beth, the girl she'd met at the DC press club party. She would keep in touch with her, to network.

She knocked on Marty's open office door a few minutes later.

"What's up?" he asked.

"I'd like your advice about what I should study to make myself more valuable as a journalist," she said.

"You mean like a course?"

"I don't know," she said. "Whatever."

He leaned back in his plush office chair and gave her an appraising look. Something in her face must have convinced him that she was sincere and not merely currying favor. He nodded and stood up. He walked to his stuffed floor-to-ceiling bookcase and hauled out a couple of books.

"Try reading these first," he said, putting them into her hands. "Until you learn where this business came from, you won't understand it. These will give you a good start."

"Thanks. I appreciate this," she said.

He stared at her, again visibly weighing whether she was in earnest. Then he shrugged as if the answer was up to her. "Happy reading."

She retreated from his office, knowing herself judged and wanting. Evidently, her discovery of her ignorance at the press club party wasn't news to more senior people at this network. She would read all these books, and take notes, too. She had to become more than a talking head with an empty brain.

She and Jason seemed to have a truce going at the moment. It was not an easy one, at least on her part. He called on her even less during the program, although she'd been fighting back effectively with her increasingly incendiary comments.

He hadn't asked her out again. She'd tried not to dwell on sexual issues when her mind should be on business. It was hard to keep Jason out of her dreams. She wondered why.

She also wondered what his intentions were. He had been

crowding her before the DC trip. On the train down, he had acted extremely confident. Yet he had made no effort to talk her out of her snit that night when she'd yelled at him. He had tried nothing sexual then, either. Of course she had made it clear she blamed him for the whole fiasco, but he hadn't argued with her or tried to get her to calm down. During their train trip back to New York, he had spent most of his time in the bar car, avoiding her.

She was angry at herself. Although she had lashed out at Jason, she knew her mistake was entirely her own responsibility. Maybe the reason Jason backed off was he'd decided he didn't want her and her temper after all. She supposed she owed him an apology. They worked together and needed to have a civil relationship.

The next day when she arrived she saw Jason heading toward his office. No time like the present for eating crow.

"Jason!" He turned at her call and gave her an inquiring glance.

"What's up?" he asked.

No big smile. No attempt to charm. She had an uphill slog ahead of her. She might as well start.

"I wanted to apologize to you. My behavior after the press club dinner was way out of line. I'm sorry it took me a while to say so."

He searched her face, something she'd never noticed him do before. She had given him evidence of the caustic side of her personality, and he clearly had paid attention. She held her breath as he thought it over.

"Accepted. We all have our off nights."

"That's very gracious of you." In her relief, she couldn't help confiding, "I shouldn't have yelled at you. I wasn't mad at you. I was mad at myself."

Jason didn't seem inclined to linger. He only nodded. "See you later." He continued on his way.

She had been dismissed. Jason wasn't interested. Her outrageous behavior had scuttled their personal relationship far more effectively than had all her previous efforts to remain coolly professional.

Why was she upset? It would be dangerous to her ambitions to fall for him. Others would view her as a mere adjunct to Jason, and some managers didn't want to employ people who were involved with each other. Marty might disapprove. Which meant she'd get fired, not Jason.

Plus, she'd get distracted, and she'd end up like his other girls who swooned over him and who got used up and tossed away when he got bored with them. She didn't want anyone to think of her as Jason's discard. She had Googled Jason and read all the talk about his relationships with women. The reports weren't good. He apparently wasn't a cheater, but he never stuck around with any woman for long. He was already in his early thirties, a bit old not to have been engaged at least once, or lived with someone long term. No hint of a serious relationship among all the dishy Google remarks.

This was why it was best not to talk to the object of a hookup or a booty call. Do the sex, and leave. Jason had followed the unwritten rules, yet she had felt unsatisfied and angry because he had. Yet there had been times she'd told guys not to talk, just get to the sex. With Jason, she had felt differently but resisted her feelings. She had wanted Jason to stay and talk and even, ohmigod, cuddle. She was messed up for sure.

Forget the sex thing. Who cared about sex, anyway? She had to convince Jason she was a likable human being. She didn't want him going around telling people she was a stone bitch. It would be bad for her career. How ironic. She thought she was so smart. She hadn't slept with the boss. Instead, she'd yelled at him. Brilliant.

What had she been thinking? She had presumed a relationship where there had been only a hookup. She could make all kinds of excuses, claim Jason was pressing her too much sexually, both earlier in the week and on the train. She could even blame his aggression as the real reason she had lashed out at him. It didn't compute. She wasn't afraid of her sexuality or of his, only of making a wrong move in her career. She had a fierce temper and she blew it. In one single minute, she'd made a total failure of the entire trip.

How to repair the damage? Think, Linley. What else could she do?

Of course. She could bring Jason opportunities to push his own agenda—that of becoming a popular media personality like Stephen Colbert. If she could work her connections to present Jason with a chance to shine on another, more popular television show, maybe he'd revise his low opinion of her.

She would be especially careful from now on. She would research new studies and stats every day. She would be an added value to the show.

She should be more collegial with the panelists. She shouldn't be waiting like a princess to be called on. She should comment actively on what the men said. Even Jason, though that would be hard. She should become a familiar voice in the background, if nothing else.

She should stop looking like a bimbo when she attended industry social events. Her too-blonde habit of dressing provocatively was the reason she and Jason had hooked up in the first place. She'd been broadcasting that she was available. Nice job, Linley. What a fool she had been. She was lucky Jason had even considered her for this position after that introduction. No matter how much people wanted to say that it was who you screwed that got you ahead, that wasn't true. Hookups got you nowhere. Having a relationship, living together, even being married, that got you on the inside. Not that she and Jason had a relationship anymore. Okay. She'd start all over again. She would earn his respect as a professional.

Chapter 14

There went that boy again. The one who looked like Greta.
How strange to see her likeness in an older person. He even
walked like her, that long, loping stride Greta had even in high
heels. That's what they'd called them then. High heels. Now
they called them something very explicit. Times had changed.

Dorothy finished her morning tea and collected a
windbreaker. Time for Yappie's morning training session. They
were almost at her door. Last week, she had missed a session. It
had slipped her mind. On hearing that, Bruce had offered to
come pick her up for each session. To be a kind of human
appointment book. She liked that arrangement. The more
regular and routine her life was, the easier it was for her to keep
track of her responsibilities.

Returning from training Yappie, Dorothy noticed the stacks
of papers in the dining room. She should roll up her sleeves and
get going on them. First, she needed to sit down for a while. She
didn't have the energy she once had.

A few minutes later, she roused herself from a doze. Darn it.
She'd fallen asleep in the middle of the day again. She consulted

her wristwatch, a dainty gold one Malcolm had given her on their tenth anniversary. Only fifteen minutes had passed. Not a tremendous long nap. But a nap. Bah. She was getting to be an old woman.

She went to the front door to collect the mail. Bills, ads, nothing interesting. She put them on a table in the dining room. She looked for the newspaper she'd retrieved from the doormat this morning. Oh, of course. It was on a console table in the front hall. She took it out of its plastic bag and went back to the sunroom to sit down and read the paper.

She skimmed the headlines. The president was talking to foreign leaders. When wasn't he? She looked out at the water. It was more interesting than the headlines. Look at that wave for instance, going up and down, up and down.

#

Linley continued her efforts to make up for her outrageous folly in DC. She'd gone out of her way to gain knowledge of a new but obscure financial study that shed some light on how the ordinary consumer behaved regarding credit card debt. It made more sense if she revealed the data on the earlier shows today where she had her own tiny segments. Instead, she waited to put out the information on Jason's program while they were debating what the government bailout of a huge credit card company would mean for the consumers.

"Unfortunately, the government isn't handing them a new usury cap along with the money. This is going to mean huge profits and more consumer debt," she said.

"That's good for the company's health and for people buying

147

the company's stock," Ernie said.

"At a certain fixed point, consumers simply stop. They stop spending. They stop paying their bills." She pulled up a graphic to highlight the new study, and explained the study parameters briefly, including what a large study it was.

"If the government doesn't affix usury cap conditions to their bailout of Towncorp, customers will bail?" Mike asked.

"Yes, they'll walk away. The higher delinquency rate would undo all the government efforts to shore up the company," she replied.

"Behavioral economics hoodoo," Ralph said. He tended to get grumpy when actual consumers were mentioned instead of stock traders.

"Maybe, but what if it's correct?" she replied. "The markets operate on confidence and gossip. Why shouldn't consumers?" she replied. "We have a major crisis of confidence right now that can spread to all financial sectors."

"A lot to think about. Thanks, Linley," Jason said and wrapped up to go to commercial.

During the break, they argued some more about her data. All the men seemed interested. She had added value to the show.

The next day, she presented more data about how non-traders behaved.

"This is important why?" Mike questioned.

"Because the stock market's big highs until recently were buoyed by the vast investor pool contributing to 401(k)s," she argued. "These people don't have any idea how their funds are being managed, or any real control over them. The fund managers are the ones who control the buying and selling of individual stocks."

"Panic selling is within their power," Jason pointed out, "as recent weeks have shown."

He turned to Ernie to ask the obvious. "Given the recent debacle, how is the market going to lure back these investors whose 401(k)s took such a hit? Ideas?"

Ernie answered with his usual air of sarcasm. "They're not coming back and good riddance. Their naïve panic has undone Wall Street."

"You don't think it was Wall Street itself panicking?" Jason asked. "Based on big investment banks failing for instance?"

Ernie bridled. "No. Give me some professionals and we can run this right. The stock market shouldn't be influenced by amateurs."

"Then I guess you don't mind that all the amateurs' money has left the market?" Jason asked.

"Of course I do." Ernie was indignant, but not terribly serious. "They should give Wall Street their money and butt out."

Jason merely said, "It's their money."

The silly debate ended. Linley had contributed her bit, but the men had run with it. She wasn't sure if she was winning any points with Jason. She hoped so, but there had been nothing personal about the exchange. Nothing passionate, if she discounted the passion the men all had for money. Did she? Good question. Her family had always been solidly middle class, comfortable enough but not living in ostentatious style. She didn't have the typical girl vice of expensive shoe shopping or spending thousands on purses or handbags. Gucci, Prada,

Manolo, and Louboutin were familiar names, but not because she bought their wares compulsively. Her girlfriends did, which was why she was solvent and they were all in debt, despite some of them earning much more than her. She didn't care about getting rich, because what would she do with the money? Buy a bigger condo, sure. Otherwise? Not important. Ironic that she talked about money every workday.

#

A few days ago, Jason had thought he'd had a close escape. Seeing how immaturely Linley behaved when she wasn't the center of attention in DC had made him wary of getting intimate with her. A hookup wasn't intimate, of course. In her fit of anger, she'd changed her mind. To tell the truth, so had he. Hooking up again would be unprofessional.

Now he wasn't so sure.

Should he avoid Linley completely because she had revealed she had a bad temper and would take it out on the nearest person? Probably. Her temperamental freak-out was too close to the psycho girlfriend profile.

But there was something about her. Something kept him interested in her. He still sensed she was interested in him and not only for the sex.

She had been fantastic on the show lately, coming up great added-value contributions. It wasn't that she hadn't been trying in the past, but now she was firing on all cylinders, making her time on his show count by enhancing the show's punch. He had to admire that. If she was attempting to make up for being such a bitch, she'd found the perfect way to do it. Leaving out what she could do for him sexually, that is.

Sex didn't matter. He could get that from other women, and not have to worry about professional complications, or set himself up for some kind of off-the-wall sexual harassment charge. That was the problem. Linley had revealed that she might be crazy, although perhaps it had just been a one-off, a never-to-be-repeated freak-out. He'd have to think about that. Maybe she was. Maybe she wasn't. Or maybe she was his kind of crazy. She had the same fiery ambition he had.

#

Linley watched as Jason aggressively questioned the expert guest who was on the president's team. He didn't usually go for the throat like that. Of course the expert was giving the usual party line. She guessed Jason didn't like hearing that. It took up too much space on the show and didn't add any facts. Their program was all about facts—and speculations about the facts to come.

Her campaign wasn't working. Jason acknowledged her hard work on the show, but he hadn't made a single new effort to personalize their relationship. No asking her out. No suggesting they have a casual lunch. No dropping by her cubicle to say a kind word. She'd have to find a way to bring him back, panting for her.

Although, maybe she should let it alone.

No. There was something still unexplored between them. She'd behaved like a prima donna in DC, so he was being cautious. Fine. She would lure him closer.

A college friend of hers had become an actress and had

offered her tickets to an exclusive awards show. She would not do the obvious and invite Jason to go with her. She would offer the second ticket to Ernie, who was a film buff. Jason would learn about her connection to a rising star when Ernie started raving about all the famous people he met that night, thanks to her. Ernie was very predictable. Jason was ambitious, like her. Linley's connections to famous people would mean something to him.

Right now, she needed to call her *Today Show* buddy and set up a thank you lunch for getting her and her mother on the program. Then she should work all the other new contacts her mother's job misfortune had created.

The mess with Jason was just a hiccup. Life was good.

#

"What an amazing night. I actually talked to Brad Pitt," Ernie said, a couple of days later as they were all sitting in the planning meeting before the show. He turned to Jason, next to him, explaining their evening out. "I couldn't believe it. Hugh Jackman was a row away, and…"

Jason gave Linley a sharp, questioning look, then quickly muffled it and bent his attention to Ernie's ravings about the star-studded night.

She could tell Jason was wondering if she was starting a thing with Ernie, or if they had hooked up, or what. Good. Most men didn't like competition. Knowing they had it made them more eager.

#

Jason got home from the job around eight p.m., out of sorts, knowing he wanted something. He made a booty call. He knew it was a risk, but so what.

When Linley answered, he said, "You want to hook up tonight?"

He could hear her shocked intake of breath. A beat later, she said, "That is not a smart idea, Jason. Goodbye."

She clicked off.

A minute later, she called him back.

"Want to go get some pizza?"

Pizza instead of sex? Guess he'd take what was being offered.

"Sure." He ripped off his tie and dress shirt, tossed his undershirt in the hamper after them, and threw on his khaki carpenter pants and a fresh black tee shirt. He gave the apartment a visual once over before leaving. In case he got lucky with Linley after all.

Half an hour later, they were wolfing down slices of Sicilian pizza in a hole-in-corner joint in Chelsea.

"Know what I like about Sicilian?" she asked, talking as she licked sauce off her fingers. He'd like the opportunity to lick her. He shook his head. He'd better pay attention to what she was saying.

"No, what?"

"You can't order a whole pie."

"Sure you can."

"Can't. No one eats a whole Sicilian. No one."

"Three lonely college boys do," he said, remembering one night when he and his friends had indulged in entirely too much of everything.

Linley was insistent. "Look at that one on the counter. There are twelve slices. No one who comes in here ever orders the whole thing. They order one or two slices."

"I never realized you were an expert on pizza."

"I'm a statistician by trade. Of course I count everything around me."

"Here I thought you were just a pretty face." He meant it to be funny, but she obviously didn't take it that way.

"Did you?" Her expression was displeased. "That's the problem with television. If you're a girl, you have to be pretty. If you are pretty, you have to fight to make people believe you're qualified, intelligent, educated, the rest of it."

Girls always complained. He couldn't help a semi-exasperated rejoinder. "Oh, lighten up. You know what I meant. You know what the game is all about."

"I'm not complaining." She pointed at him with her piece of pizza for emphasis. "I'm stating a fact. Because I have a pretty face, you don't look at me and think 'expert analyst.'"

"No, I think 'babe,'" he smirked. She rolled her eyes, but he could tell she was pleased. For all her talk of professionalism, she was a woman, and women liked men to compliment their looks.

He wondered what the hell he was doing.

He'd called her on an impulse. He should stay away from her. He hadn't called so they could have a date. Yet Linley had turned the evening into a typical boy-girl dinner out.

An hour later, back at his apartment, alone, he was still wondering. They'd shared some laughs and parted casually. Without any mention of his booty call. Or any mention of hooking up. He hadn't even tried to kiss her. He had wanted to.

154

He'd been wanting to for weeks. He must be losing his touch.

Women had never been mysterious to him because of his two older sisters. He'd watched them and listened to them and even spied on them as a kid. He'd scoped out boy-girl relationships early as a result. Most important, he'd learned how to talk to girls. He'd been lucky because girls had liked his looks. From then on, he'd cruised. Now, after two decades of pursuing girls and women, he thought he understood them. He didn't understand Linley. At work, she acted like a girl scout. Outside of work, she was a hottie who liked to enjoy herself to the fullest. Tonight, she'd been the kind of girl he'd hung with in college, a gal pal. He'd hooked up with his gal pals, at least occasionally. Did that mean she'd be amenable to a hookup at some later date?

Bottom line, he thought he knew the rules, but Linley was not playing by them. She was an asset on the show, and that should be enough. Anything she did to help the show helped him. She was ambitious and was developing her contacts as fiercely as he was working on his.

If her goal had been the same as his, he'd see her as competition. Linley wasn't bucking for a late night talk show as he was. She wasn't trying to be a comedian slash entertainer slash political commentator as he was. She might want his current job. Not a problem unless she wanted to take it before he was ready to give it up. He'd never sensed any aggression of that sort from her, and he would have. That guy who'd been on the show the first couple of weeks had been bucking for a bigger spot at the table. A talk with Marty had gotten him paid off. It was Jason's show. He was the moderator and he didn't want anyone else trying to run the table. He didn't care who management brought in to replace him when he had to take a day off because he was augmenting his rise by appearing on other television shows. Appearing on *The View* had been a coup. He wanted to hit *Rachel Maddow* and all the rest.

#

Linley was happy to go home alone. That had been a close one. When Jason had made his booty call, she'd been horribly tempted. No need to talk, no need to care. The opportunity to touch him all over and get some, too. Very tempting. No. Been there, done that. She wasn't so hard up that she needed to accept all invitations, even though it had been a long time since she had bothered to hook up with anyone. She used to have a casual arrangement with an old pal from grad school, but since that night with Jason, she hadn't been interested. Something about their one time together had ruined her for sex-only screwing. At least temporarily, she hoped. She shouldn't let herself dry up like an old virgin.

She hadn't been able to resist at least trying to get a relationship going tonight. Her ploy had worked. A casual pizza meal and some talk. That was a lot more than they'd had for a while. Maybe they could build on it. It had been exciting being with him. Difficult, too, because she'd been distracted by her desire to sex him up. She wanted to straddle his waist with her legs, hold tight, and feed him pizza with her mouth. Then more.

Sex between them wasn't in her game plan. Finally, she'd been paying attention to her own best interests and following her plan. Tonight she'd behaved like a pure little convent girl. No touchy.

What else could she do to encourage Jason to pursue her, to want to date her, to show her his emotions? She wanted all that from him. She could admit it to herself even if she was too savvy to even hint at it to him at this stage. Guys were dense. They loved being the chasers. She would let him be the big macho man, let him think he was in charge of creating this relationship, when in reality, she was calling the shots.

How different their little dance was from the relationship her parents had. Her dad ran the family, and her mother kowtowed to his every whim. She built her life around him. She rushed to the door when he came home from work. She pampered and spoiled him. Linley had loved her dad, but her mother's subservience had been sickening once Linley had noticed her friends' mothers did not behave that way.

Although, come to think of it, her mother had not been sly. She hadn't kept secrets from her father, or spent money behind his back and hidden purchases until she could coax him into a good mood, making herself a child to his daddy figure. Guess her mother wasn't a total throwback to the bad old days Grandma had described. Grandma hadn't suffered them, either. According to everyone, Grandma had ruled her home and the family life entirely, with never a peep of protest from her husband. Linley never met her grandfather because he died before she was born. Everybody said he had been a workaholic, a man's man who smoked and drank because that was how men behaved back then. He had his sphere at his office, and his wife ran the house. Linley had no interest in being a housewife, but she liked to think she had inherited Grandma's groundbreaking self-confidence. She did not intend to be bound to a man in some limiting relationship. She wanted to grab for success and achieve it. Eventually, she'd like to be with a man who respected and admired her for her success and her drive. Who wouldn't feel threatened by her. Who would have drive himself.

Jason had drive. That's why he was so tempting. It wasn't just the sex. It was the entire package. Unfortunately, the package was not on offer. She supposed they were acting out clichés of being Generation Whatever. They didn't have any urgency to marry or nest. Living together wasn't even something her crowd bothered with unless for economic purposes, and then it was smarter just to have a roommate with some sex privileges. Career success and having a good time along the way was the plan. Oh, sure, she knew some girls who went the Bridezilla and Cute Young Couples route. They all took up the same habits in lockstep. What about knitting? Boring. Her mother crocheted. Linley had no intention of ever sewing anything. That's what the person behind the sewing machine at the dry cleaners was for.

Linley let Jason stew for a while. She was busy showing off her statistician chops on the show and earning points with Marty by reading the books he had lent her. When she returned them, she asked questions about the old-time journalists he had known.

Of course Marty wasn't fooled into thinking Linley merely had an historical interest in the field.

"You're trying to find a way to put your name in these books, aren't you?" he said, giving her his gimlet look.

Why lie? She nodded. "Of course. I want to succeed. I've been too focused on recent radio and television."

"As I recall, you got your undergraduate degree in radio and television, not journalism," he said. Marty remembered everything. Better keep that in mind.

"That's right. My MA is in statistics. I have a lot more to learn about journalism." She tried to say it with sincerity without being saccharine. Marty had shown a keen sensitivity to the phony. Maybe in the past she had coasted a little on her promise as a pretty young thing who also was bright. This wasn't a prom queen contest she could win by being a smiling, attractive blonde. She must concentrate on improving herself, on becoming a valuable asset to the network. There were younger pretty faces from good schools arriving in the city every day, and she did not want to be easily replaced.

"Thanks again," she said, and left Marty's office quickly. As daring as she had been to engage her boss in discussions about journalism, she felt far safer out of his presence. She didn't want to put a foot wrong accidentally. Her automatic youthful arrogance, which she had finally caught onto and was actively trying to tone down, irritated him. This wasn't a game; this was her career. She couldn't play with Marty, and she couldn't manipulate him. He was far too savvy.

Jason was a different story. Not only was there the sexual undercurrent between them, but she had an advantage over Jason. He was a moderator, not an expert. She was a trained analyst who could offer both information and expertise to boost his program. From now on, that was what she would do, day in and day out.

#

Bruce was more than ready for his first real date with Pam. He hadn't come to this beach town to start a romantic relationship, but there was no denying that spontaneously kissing a pretty woman and wanting to spend more time with her meant something. He'd moved on since the breakup with Carol, but he hadn't been looking for a replacement for a wife in his world. Wife. Now there was a loaded word. No need to think about it now.

Or was there? He wanted to be with Pam, absorb the peaceful femininity of her personality. He should find out about her past, about the kind of woman she was in a relationship. Something told him it was important to know how she dealt with a man's inevitable mistakes. Toward the end, Carol had enjoyed being a bitch to him.

Did people entering into late-in-life relationships have more tolerance for each other's frailties? Did they have the same high expectations as when they'd been young? The same delusions about how perfect life together would be?

Why was he thinking about these things? Was he another of those men who knew at first sight? Who simply knew he'd found the woman? It hadn't been that way with Carol, had it?

He looked at himself in the mirror next to the closet. Not something he'd have installed, but the house was rented fully furnished. He patted his stomach. Still lean, thank god. Somehow he'd sidestepped the gut most men got. His hair was grey, no getting around it, although having hair at his age was a triumph. Women liked men who had still had hair on their heads. He'd heard they weren't so crazy about the body hair men developed late in life, but his wasn't terribly heavy. You wouldn't mistake him for a chimpanzee if he took his shirt off. Not that he would. That had never been his thing. He'd never been the Italian Stallion type, although he'd grown up around plenty of them, and Irishmen in love with their own blarney. His brothers were like that, macho guys. He'd always been more the intellectual type. He liked baseball, not football, because it was a non-contact sport if played correctly. He'd been plenty shrimpy as a young boy, only gaining height and the muscle to go with it late in his teens. He had appreciated playing a sport that didn't give the bigger boys many opportunities to run him over.

Youthful experiences shaped one. His dislike of physical bullies had sent him into a career in which quickness of wit and nimbleness with the written word were the hallmarks of success. He'd done well for himself, considering his fixation on the sciences. They'd only recently become more sexy—that was the word his literary agent used—to the ordinary reader. For a long time, he had labored in relative obscurity. In the past five years though, his books had become real sellers. Talking about the technical whys and wherefores of the world suddenly appealed to a public worried about global warming and about running out of oil and other natural resources.

His latest book had been a best seller and he'd been interviewed on television and radio to promote it. Book tours sponsored by a publisher were rare these days, so he was fully conscious of having arrived at a position of being, finally, a successful author. It felt good. He'd taken the few television moments with a grain of salt, letting himself relax and enjoy himself, not trying too hard to sell his books. He must have been doing something right. As a result of a few minutes on a popular morning show, sales had tripled.

The big push for that book was over. He was tasked now with the follow-up, which was a killer. Follow-ups always were tough. The audience suddenly had big expectations. The publisher, his editor, and his agent all had a lot riding on his ability to hit a home run the second time out. There was plenty of pressure. He'd never minded pressure if there was something he could do about it.

The only possible stumbling block was the other reason he had taken this beach house. Dorothy Duncan. The secrets she kept. If she kept secrets as Aunt Nora thought. If he allowed himself to get too distracted by that quest, it could show up in his writing. He wasn't worried about being distracted by Pam. She could only make his writing happier.

It took time to court a woman. Time he needed to write, time he needed to discover what Dorothy knew about the past. Pam was another potential threat to achieving his goals for the summer.

He'd cross that bridge when he came to it. First, to see Pam again, and, definitely to find an opportunity to kiss her soft lips once more.

Chapter 15

Marty called Linley and Jason into his office.

"You can shut the door," he said to Jason, gesturing for them to sit in front of his desk. His expression gave nothing away, which Linley took to be ominous.

They sat. The chairs looked comfortable but they weren't. Linley strove to project polite eagerness, but inwardly she was quaking. Whatever Marty had to say was going to change her life. Was he about to fire her?

"I hear you two have been mixing it up on the show lately." An understatement, since Marty undoubtedly watched every second of every show.

Oh, crap, he was going to fire her. Maybe Jason, too?

"Merely proposing differing points of view," Jason replied, obviously trying to put a good face on it, plus feeling his way about why Marty was inquiring.

"Is that all it is?" Marty asked her.

Don't show a weakness. If she was about to be axed, she'd go down swinging.

"We don't always agree on who the bad guys are," she finally said.

"Is this a genuine philosophical divide, or something you each put on for the cameras?" Marty enquired.

Jason answered this time. "I tend to think anti-corporate. I'm pro the little guy."

"Nobody is forcing these idiots to buy $5,000 televisions instead of paying off their debts," she snapped before she thought. Every time Jason took a stand for the little guy, it burned her up.

"You're ignoring the profound effect Wall Street manipulators have on the economy's stability," Jason said, but more calmly than she had spoken.

Marty inclined his head, taking note of Linley's instant heat. "Sounds like a television show. How would you two like to do an extra half an hour per day of airing your differing points of view?"

Linley's jaw dropped. This was it. Her big break. *Don't screw this up.* She glanced briefly out of the corner of her eye at Jason. He looked surprised, but not as shocked as she felt. "When?" she asked, having trouble keeping her voice from squeaking in excitement.

"Right after Jason's show. You'd take one topic per day and chew on it. I don't want mere opposing opinions. You each have to bring facts to the fight."

Marty turned to Jason. "Are you up for this? Your background is more general than Linley's."

Jason gave his patented moderator look, the one that said he was serious, he was paying attention, and he understood. "I can handle it."

"All right," Marty said. "Now this is a team show, you two."

Then he went into details on compensation, which he said would be the same for each of them to promote fairness and collegiality despite the acrimony the show might produce. He asked them to come up with a list of topics and some format input for a planning meeting. Then he dismissed them. "Remember, you're to be friendly adversaries."

She left Marty's office in a daze. After all these years, she'd finally arrived. A show of her own. Oh, wow. Okay, so she'd be sharing the spotlight with Jason. Still, her name would be on the show, wouldn't it? Would it? She couldn't remember if Marty had said the title of the show.

Jason, who had been walking beside her, suddenly grabbed her arm and pulled her into the file room. It was a room with no windows because it held part of the old tape library. Now the digital library. People used it all the time, so the door was always kept open. Jason shut it, pushed her up against it with his big body, and kissed her hard on the lips.

"We did it, girl," he exulted.

She felt the impact of his touch down to her toes. Her raging excitement abruptly shifted to focus on Jason, Jason, Jason.

He kissed her again. This time, she opened her mouth and kissed him back just as fiercely. They grabbed kisses all over, and groped each other feverishly. Her skirt was quickly hiked up around her hips as Jason's big hands touched her everywhere.

Then someone tried the door.

It broke them apart. She immediately wiped her smudged lips, and straightened her dress. She didn't look at him directly. She could tell he was adjusting his tie, and re-tucking the shirt she had ripped nearly out of his pants. Oh, god. She had to get

165

herself under control.

She went to the wall of tapes and grabbed one at random. Jason went to a different wall and did the same. Then he flung open the door. The person had left. They didn't have to use their thin alibis.

"Dump the tapes. We might as well leave together," Jason said.

She re-shelved the cassette carefully and walked out of the file room in a daze far different yet as profound as the one she'd been in before.

She suddenly came to herself. She had walked all the way to the entrance of her cubicle without noticing. Jason was walking next to her, obviously equally thoughtful.

"Don't say anything," she said in a low, dangerous voice. "Don't you dare say a word." She struggled to keep her words from gaining volume. She wanted to shriek at him. Their big chance, and he'd almost screwed it up totally by grabbing her. Didn't he have any control?

She took a deep breath and let it out, conscious Jason was staring at her. His expression was impossible to fathom.

"Did Marty say the name of the show?" she asked, forcing herself to speak in a quiet, well-modulated tone. They had to get back to what was important. This was business.

"No. How does 'Jason and Linley Duke it Out' sound?" he asked, obviously not serious. His thoughts were clearly elsewhere. As were hers.

"Lousy. 'Linley versus Jason' is better. We should think of some dignified and exciting possible titles to propose to Marty."

He shook his head as if to clear it. He obviously was

brimming with disparate, conflicting thoughts, just as she was. Was he regretting his impulsive action? He damn well should be.

He nodded. "This is big. A personality-driven show instead of news driven. It's the next rung of the ladder." He looked down at her with a determined expression. "Let's make sure we don't screw it up."

"I'm not planning to," she replied, a frosty edge in her tone. "Maybe you'd better watch yourself." She raised an eyebrow in emphasis.

Jason eyed her carefully. "I won't mess up. See that you don't, either," he said before walking off.

Egotistical bastard. It was okay for him to have sex with her in the file room—and they would have if someone hadn't tried the door—but she needed a warning to behave? Or was he now only thinking about the money program? Did he think she would get lazy now, and sabotage her big chance? No way. Success was so near she could taste it. From here, she could get her own solo show. She'd be a somebody from now on.

She sat at her desk and started feverishly brainstorming show topics and possible show titles, ways in which they would introduce each day's topic, and more. Oh, lord, what would she wear? Should she dress more in anchorwoman mode for this program? For Jason, it was simple. He wore a suit all day, on every show to which he contributed. He always looked correct and handsome, too. She had almost ripped his shirt buttons off trying to get at his skin five minutes ago. That would have messed up his polished look. Although doubtless he kept substitute shirts for emergencies in his office. All the on-air people did, including her. He would have had to button his suit jacket to cover his skin. Oh, god. His skin. It had been a year since she had touched the firm flesh of his belly, and now her fingers tingled from the memory. She'd felt the rough hairs there, the skin covering his hard muscles. She wanted Jason.

He wanted her, too. Maybe he even liked her. After all, he had pulled her in there to celebrate their new show. He had kissed her to share their triumph on a nonverbal level. It had felt good. Too good. Her thoughts were in a tailspin once more. She should concentrate on shaping the show.

Her more business-oriented ruminations were interrupted a few minutes later by a call from her mother. What did she want now? Couldn't she leave Linley alone? Did she have to be in her business all the time? Still, she picked up. There might be an emergency.

"Linley, dear, how are you? It's Mom."

"I'm good. What's up?" she said, trying to get her mother to the point before she started screaming.

"I had an idea. I have a project, and actually, it was Sarah's idea to call you, and…" the nervousness in her mother's voice was obvious.

Linley didn't have time for her mother's endless hesitation. "What?" Spit it out, will you?

"Could you help me with the nonprofit I'm setting up?" her mother said in a rush.

"You mean, donate to it?"

"No, no, dear. I'm not asking for your money."

Would her mother ever get to the point? "Then what? I'm busy working."

Finally, it all came out in a rush. "I'm sorry to interrupt, dear, but I need your expertise. You knew how to get us on that TV show. This nonprofit I'm creating is meant to help people who suffer catastrophic job losses. I was thinking maybe you could contact some people and see if they were interested in a follow-up interview, to talk about my charity?"

Not a bad idea. She was busy right now. Her mother's project could wait a little. No. Maybe the publicity phone calls could serve a dual purpose by also leaking an announcement about her new show. Start building her some free buzz.

"You're actually starting a charity?"

"Yes, I'm getting it incorporated next week. There's lots to arrange and—"

Linley cut through her mother's endless babbling.

"Call me when it's a done deal and you have a website and a mission statement you can recite if Matt Lauer interviews you again. Once you're ready, I'll talk to my contact at the *Today Show*."

"Oh. Oh, I see. Yes, you're right, dear. I'll get working on a mission statement immediately. Thank you so much, sweetie. You have a lovely day, you hear?" Her mother was practically gobbling, she was so grateful.

"You, too, Mom." She said it reluctantly, knowing it was the right thing to say and the kind thing, too. Knowing she didn't actually care if her mother had a lovely day. Because her mother's days were all the same, boring and useless.

A surprise that her mother had this idea for a nonprofit. She must care a lot about her friend Magda. Which was strange, because she didn't recall her mother ever mentioning Magda before they all got laid off two weeks ago. Not that she talked much to her mother.

Oh, wow. Once again, she'd forgotten to ask her mother if she was okay financially. Maybe she should call back or call Steve. Her brother probably knew. He and Mom were close. Or at least as close as his cold bitch of a wife let them be. Callie was such a typical upper middle class snob. Linley had no patience with her. None. She was spoiling her children, raising them with obsessive attention, like veal. Bet she scrapbooked every drawing they did in preschool. Poser.

#

Pam would not have described her daughter-in-law in such negative terms, although she also felt a little breath of cool air every time she met Callie. She always had to remind herself that Callie was a good woman who loved Steve and their two children.

Pam was surprised to receive a call from Callie, who seldom spoke to her directly. Not that Pam was keeping score or anything, but Callie's immediate family unit was strong and there wasn't much room in Steve and Callie's life together for Pam to play a part. She saw her grandchildren less often than she liked. Given all the changes she was experiencing in her life, maybe this phone call was the harbinger of a new era in this relationship, too.

"How are you, dear? How are the children?"

"We're good, Mother Ridgeway."

She wished Callie would relax enough to call her by her name. Callie always stood on ceremony. She was an exceedingly proper young woman. She led Pam through a polite description of everybody's doings. Pleasant as that was, Pam decided she'd had enough roundabout talking.

"What's exciting at your house these days?"

"Actually, Steve and I were wondering if you could do us a large favor. We wouldn't ask it of you except that we know that you don't have a job—that is, that you have a little more free time right now than in the past."

How tactful. "Of course. What can I do for you?"

"We've been offered a wonderful opportunity. Steve's employer wants to reward him with a bonus that includes a luxury trip to Tahiti. Wives go free. I want to go, but we can't unless you can babysit the children."

Callie explained why her own mother, who usually did quite a bit of babysitting because she lived near them in Roslyn, could not oblige this time. She had broken her leg and would be recovering in her own home for the next six weeks. Callie's sister was moving in to nurse her. Of course Callie would not consider hiring a stranger to care for her children. Callie apologized profusely for asking Pam.

"No need to apologize. I would be delighted. When is this trip?"

"That's the big problem, Mother Ridgeway, it's the week after next."

"Oh, you poor thing. I'll bet you already have new swim suits and snorkeling gear packed."

"I do."

"Grandma to the rescue. I'll be happy to help." Within a few minutes, they had ironed out the details and arranged which day

Pam would arrive. Callie was very organized, sometimes excessively organized. Having obtained what she wanted, she ended the phone call with further ritual protestations of gratitude.

Now this was more like it. No more hanging around in an empty house. She'd go to Steve and Callie's a day before they left to observe and learn their routines. Callie was big on routines. Then they'd take off for their week in the South Seas. Then, on their return, she would debrief and leave. What a wonderful week they all would have.

She must think of some presents to bring the children. Grandmas had that privilege and responsibility. They were the dispensers of gifts. How much fun that would be? Something for Steve and Callie, too.

She called her mother to tell her.

Dorothy said, "You ought to bring those children out here to stay for the week. Let them run wild on the beach. The water's too cold for swimming, but that won't matter."

Pam controlled a shudder. "I don't think so. They have school."

"It's only elementary school. They can skip a week," Dorothy said.

Pam was quite sure Callie would not want her two little ones pulled out of school to be near the dangerous ocean for a week. She was the type of woman who valued safety over adventure. Even though she and Steve were about to have a little adventure of their own. Pam wondered idly if Steve would use Tahiti to convince Callie they should have a third child? There had been a hint that he would like one the last time they'd had lunch.

Maybe, amid all that beauty, Callie would relax a little. She always seemed so driven despite being a stay-at-home mom.

Her mother was speaking again. "Talk to Steve about letting the children come here to the beach for the weekend, at least."

"That might be acceptable. They're biddable children, but the promise of a big treat will help make them more so." If Callie didn't object to what she might view as a bribe. Many times, Pam's attempts to encourage the children to do something had been criticized as bribery, something Callie was set against. Pam didn't think it harmed a child to be rewarded for good behavior, but she yielded to Callie's rules. Being in charge of the children on her own would be relaxing.

Seeing Steve before and after the trip would be a bonus. He was an affectionate, if busy, son. He always had made a place in his schedule to lunch with her at least once or twice a month since they both worked in Manhattan. That would change now. Or perhaps not, if Pam made the effort to go into town often enough. Steve was worth the effort.

After Pam and her mother hung up, she puttered around, organizing clothing for the time away. It would be a different kind of visit from her stay at the beach with her mother. Strange, her recent visit had not been as awful as she'd expected. True, she and her mother had argued and she'd run away to walk on the beach. Afterwards, they'd managed not to rub each other the wrong way. Or more specifically, she had not gotten upset at her mother's usual highhandedness and assurance that her way was the only method by which anything could be achieved. Or maybe it was because Pam had secretly enjoyed Dorothy stage-managing lunch with Bruce and then throwing them together on a picnic date. Only her mother could do that.

Bruce. Oh, Bruce. There was so much possibility. If she dared to follow through. They already had a date set up for her return on Thursday. The visit to that lovely botanical garden farther out on the island. Bruce had never been there, and she'd gone only once, many years ago. Walking around the garden would give them the opportunity to talk, or to be silent, and didn't push them into a cliché, pressured dating situation. Which she simply could not bear the thought of doing again. She had not liked dating when she was young. Why go through those rigid, uncomfortable scenes all over again?

When Pam called Sarah to talk about how she disliked dating, Sarah disagreed.

"The good aspect to a dinner or movie date with a new guy is that you can ditch him with ease. All you need is a friend to call your cell with a coded emergency. If you don't like the guy after knowing him for an hour, you claim you must leave, make your apologies, and scram."

"That's harsh."

"No, it's not. The loser gets to keep his pride even if he suspects you of pulling a con. Pride is everything to men. If he's deluded enough to call and ask you for a date some other time, you can say no thanks and not have to face him when you do it."

"What if you like him or can't make up your mind?"

"Then you say the call was no big deal and you continue the date." Sarah's offhand manner indicated she had ended dates both ways, many times.

"Why are we talking about dating?" Sarah asked suspiciously.

"Because I met a man."

"When? Where?" Sarah practically shrieked.

"He lives next door to my mother at the beach."

"Oh, you dog. You had lunch with me three days ago and you didn't let any of this drop. Shame on you."

"I was shocked. I had to think about it." She defended herself weakly.

"What was shocking? Tell me everything."

She could picture the mischievous look on Sarah's face. Pam poured it all out, ending with the kiss that had so surprised and discomposed her. She heard Sarah sigh.

"You must immediately go back there and have sex with that man. He'll be good at it, I guarantee you."

"No way. I hate dating."

"Did I say anything about dating? Knock on his door, ask to borrow a cup of sugar and jump his bones in the kitchen. Sex on the counter can be fun. Put a dishtowel under your butt."

The image was far too vivid for Pam's comfort. She could see herself making love with Bruce, but in a kind of misty romantic haze.

"It sounds delightful, but that's not me. I'm more the slow burn in a comfortable bed type."

At which Sarah said something so filthy that Pam immediately blocked it from her mind.

"Sarah. Don't."

"Okay, my prudish friend. You know you will eventually."

"Maybe. That's my business. I won't be sharing any details with you." Telling Sarah that Bruce had kissed her was different. It was the proof that he was interested in a romance with her.

Or sex. Or something. Sarah was certainly assuming the sex, since the next words out of her mouth were a safe sex lecture.

"Remember you'll still have to use condoms, even though you don't have to worry about pregnancy anymore."

"Yes, Mother," she said.

"Your mom would say exactly the same and you know it."

Sarah was right. Dorothy would. Time to change the subject. Pam told Sarah all about her coming adventure with grandchildren.

"You're sounding almost as excited about that as about Bruce," Sarah groused. Not being the grandchildren type herself, she often didn't see the need to pay attention to them. Sarah had been happily childless and was equally happily grandchildless, too. Or if not, she never expressed any regrets.

"I'm very excited. I don't get to see them as much as I would like, you know. Everybody is so busy."

"See? Another reason it's good you don't have that stinking job anymore."

"Considering that you're the person who helped me get it, I've never understood why you were so down on it."

"Because it became a waste of your intelligence, and we both know it. I was okay with you working there as a stepping stone to better things. But you never stepped."

"I'm trying now. Better late than never."

"Where do you get these clichés, anyway?"

"My mother. She's originally from the Midwest where they have great big bowls of clean-cut clichés in everybody's entry hall."

"Ha, ha."

"I've lived a long time tossing out non-obscene clichés instead of swearing. Life is more pleasant that way," Pam said.

They joked around some more and then hung up. Sarah was her best friend, always there, always with a point of view that challenged her yet accepted who she was. Although Sarah was pushy about what she believed in. Her last instruction was that she wanted to meet Bruce. "I'll size him up for you," Sarah had promised. "Tell you if he's a keeper."

Whether that was a good thing or not, Pam was not sure.

Next week, Pam would have her first test of her ability to do anything concrete for her new nonprofit. Through patient and persistent effort, many calls to many people, she had obtained an appointment for an interview with Charles Saunders, the former CEO of Menahl. The man who had brought the company to bankruptcy, and sent her and Magda and so many others out into the street without even their last paychecks. She was already losing sleep over how she would handle their meeting.

Meanwhile, there was work to be done. She was meeting with a realtor this afternoon. Although she probably would not lease an expensive rented office, she intended to investigate what was available. For now, she had opted for the Internet as the foundation's major presence, with a post office box for mail. Snail mail, it was called now. She might as well get into the twenty-first century and use current terminology.

She would provide much of the foundation's physical reality. She planned to personally visit as many financial executives as she could, and get as much press as possible. She was writing her first press release for later this week. She would use every contact

Linley gave her, and build her Internet and physical mailing list. A friend from college had promised to help fine tune the mission statement. Magda insisted she would be office clerical help.

Pam still wasn't wild about seeking the spotlight, but she wouldn't do it Dorothy's way. Her mother had made a major success out of causing controversy that resulted in news coverage. The free publicity helped her various causes. Pam couldn't tread that same path, but would adapt the bargaining procedures Dorothy had frequently described at the dinner table and recently reviewed. Pam had seen the game played all her life and she knew every step. She would make this foundation a success.

Only a few weeks ago, she had thought her work at Menahl was all that could keep her safe and sane. Jeff was gone, and she would be adrift unless she clung to the rock of her routine. She'd finally woken up.

Her impulse to help Magda had motivated her, despite her initial panic. Imagine at her age running to her mother for advice. Dorothy had pushed Pam to think bigger and do even more. Now she was on the road to try something very difficult.

Approaching arrogant, outwardly charming executives would not be easy. Even getting in to see them was a challenge. She did have some resources. Her friend Harper had been born with a silver spoon in her mouth and she knew lots of people. Sarah, of course, had connections. Secretaries, assistants, and other lower-echelon workers would have fellow feeling for what Pam was attempting. Some of them helped her gain access because they too feared job loss without a golden parachute. Or had experienced it. That was her wedge. Soon, there would be

Linley's contacts to draw on, too.

She was thinking like her mother. Strategizing. Planning her campaign.

She was a bundle of nerves. She'd even written a script, and then practiced her speech in front of her mirror. She had called Dorothy and practiced and amended it. Her mother claimed that even though Charles Saunders was seriously persona non grata right now, he would act as if he was terribly busy and could only spare Pam a few minutes. He'd pretend he was still the boss of the universe. Dorothy had warned her. That's why Pam was practicing carefully.

Linley had seemed interested in helping with the nonprofit. That was good. She still showed impatience with Pam for daring to interrupt her day. That was bad. It made Pam nervous and then she talked in a silly fashion. She knew it, but she couldn't stop herself. She always got flustered and acted down to the expectations of people she felt despised her.

She had a mission statement to create. The nonprofit was important. Her issues with her daughter would have to wait. She gathered a legal pad and a pen and walked into the generous-sized living room to write. She could have written at the spacious kitchen counter. It was completely empty. The house was too big for one person. She didn't need all this unused space to remind her she was alone. She ought to sell this house and move. To where? Into the city? Linley's condo in Manhattan had been incredibly expensive. Pam would have to give up her car or spend a fortune to garage it in the city. Must she live in Manhattan? Although she enjoyed cultural events, she wasn't compulsive about them. Neither she nor her new foundation had to have a Manhattan address.

Should she move into a retirement community? She didn't feel ready for that, not with this new project on her plate. Did she want another house with a yard, or a condo or co-op? City or suburban setting?

Would her future be as a single woman or with someone else?

Chapter 16

Jason had hardly returned to his office—yes, he was visibly higher up the totem pole than Linley was now, but perhaps Marty had in mind to change that too—when he was stopped short by a thought. What the hell was he supposed to tell his buddies on the *Hot Tracks* show? Sorry, you're not ready for prime time? When he'd been listening to Marty describe the opportunity, he frankly hadn't been thinking about anyone but himself. Oh, Lin a little, of course. She'd make a pretty foil for him, and the show would come across as sexy, and that would draw new viewers. All to the good. Lin didn't want to be a night-time talk show host. She wanted her own daytime money show. As she kept telling him, trying to prove her merit beyond being a blonde, she also had a profession as a statistician. That and a buck might buy a cup of coffee somewhere. She was deluded if she thought her promotions were because of her brains. People liked to see a pretty woman talk.

As for him, he wanted to ascend the ranks to host his own show. Not about money or politics, even if that was the conventional way up. No, he wanted to go straight for knocking

Jay Leno off his perch. He didn't have twenty years to do it anymore. He'd already been climbing for ten.

Marty was giving him a shot. If he and Lin could turn their bickering about socialism versus knee-jerk liberal democracy into something hot and sexy, they could get the audience to tune in, even the non-financially-fixated audience.

No more crazy grabbing her and kissing her. In the office, for God's sake. Did he have a death wish? Although it was hot. She felt so good under his hands. No more. He had to be a monk around her. No booty calls. No more attempts to reduce the pressure. No other women. Let the sexual tension build. Let it seep through their every move. They needed to become the hot couple of cable talk, seething with repressed sexuality. He wanted the fantasy stock market predictors to take bets on if and when he and Lin finally did it.

Marty said they'd have an initial ten weeks. If they made good numbers, they could have ten more. That was enough for a start.

He stopped pacing his small office and shrugged out of his suit jacket, which he still had to wear for three more shows today. After unbuttoning the tight shirt cuffs and rolling up his sleeves, he got to work on the computer. Possible topics. Possible ways to enrage Lin. Possible ways to calm her down again but leave the pot visibly simmering. He loved how she took those deep breaths when she was angry, and those luscious breasts of hers rose. He wanted to make that happen on every episode. Maybe he could even get away with staring at them. He smiled. This would be good. Torture. But good.

Ernie phoned. "I saw you two get herded into Marty's office.

What's up?"

Good thing Ernie had seen nothing else. "I can't spill yet." Marty had sworn them to secrecy.

"C'mom, Jase, I'm your bud. If I need to find a new gig, tell me now."

That one was easy. "As far as I know, nothing's changing with the show."

"Something's up."

"Yeah. Sorry I can't give you the details. Soon." He made a mental note to be sure to call on Ernie plenty during today's show, to make Ernie feel more secure. Owning his own brokerage should make a guy confident. Not Ernie. Maybe it was the constant ups and downs of the stock market. Ernie should have chosen a different line of work.

Time to go over the notes for today's show. Every day, the show rode on what the stock market had been doing that day in comparison to that week. Linley's recent forays into heavily researched segments had helped increase their solidity, made them all seem less gossipy. She should keep it up. She'd better not slack off now that she'd gotten what she wanted. Ernie had told him last week he'd seen her going into Marty's office and coming out with books. She'd been buttering up the boss, probably. He didn't care. Whatever worked, as long as she wasn't trying to stab him in the back. She was the type who might, but Marty was no fool.

Why was he wasting his time thinking about Linley again? Man, he had her on the brain. Ernie had also let on about how sexy she'd looked in her killer red dress at that movie awards show he'd attended with her. That was Ernie yanking his chain.

Ernie knew he had marked Linley as his. Maybe he hadn't scooped her up yet, but the guys knew, all of them, not to mess with her. Linley belonged to him. The new monk on the block.

#

Linley was in a fury of working and thinking. In her element. She had no time for further ploys to ensnare Jason's interest in her. The way he had behaved in the file room was proof enough he was interested. Maybe even too interested. They'd both gotten crazy.

She didn't have time for that. She was planning their brand new program, the show that would launch her as a media star. To that end, she was researching every possible competitor, the successes and the failures. Being a network employee gave her access to all kinds of old tapes and other media records as well as current. Of course, the feed they received showed their sister stations owned by the same company, and their competitor networks' offerings, too.

Her reading about media figures had helped. She was not as ignorant as she had been only a few weeks ago. Now she understood why Ernie had called Jason and her the James Carville and Mary Matalin of financial television. They were a famous married couple who met while they were working for opposing presidential campaigns. They fell in love and married while continuing in their separate opinions. Unlike in Hollywood, Washington marriages seemed to last a long time. Funny, when she considered that in both towns, power was probably the major aphrodisiac.

What made her so hot for Jason? Could she isolate it and use it to make their show as exciting as watching Angelina Jolie making Brad Pitt fall in love with her in that movie, *Mr. & Mrs. Smith*? The movie had been part of Linley's research, too. She'd watched it and several other movies famous for real-life off-screen love affairs, including old timey movies such as *Cleopatra*, during which stars Elizabeth Taylor and Richard Burton had begun a super-scandalous affair. She remembered Grandma talking about how notorious they were. All this research was not because she was interested in affairs. She wanted to see what people showed on camera when they were hot for each other.

As she was hot for Jason. Oh, lordy. When he'd pulled her into the file room and kissed her, she'd been desperate to do the deed completely. She'd even begun to plot out how they could jam the lock and get a few minutes of privacy. Although a few seconds was all either of them would have needed. Her desire for him had reached the hair-trigger stage.

What good did it do her to be so achingly aware of her sexuality when she couldn't do anything about it? Or rather, when she shouldn't? Too bad she wasn't some innocent virgin from a hundred years ago. Or a nun.

Chapter 17

Dorothy hung up the phone in the hall. It had been the hair salon. She had missed her appointment. She was losing track of the days, despite all her efforts. Despite the calendar in her bedroom with the dates crossed off, and the note attached to it to cross it off every night and write down the time. Despite her other calendars with reminders on them. Despite the reminder on the refrigerator—well, that one made sense, because she hardly ever entered the kitchen, and she never cooked if she could help it. A little microwaving went a long way. She did not get hungry much these days, because she didn't do much.

She had forgotten her hair appointment. The girl at the salon said she had called to remind her this morning. It must have slipped her mind.

How would she remember things in the future? She could order a cab to pick her up at a certain time, of course, and keep it waiting if she discovered she had forgotten her appointment. She only had two regular appointments per week. Why was she having so much trouble remembering a simple salon visit?

She was losing track of the days despite all her efforts. Despite the calendar in her bedroom with all the days crossed off. What to do? Have the television on all the time, giving the day and date? No. She wouldn't become like those helpless victims in nursing homes. She wasn't going to live the rest of her life in front of a television.

She moved into the sunroom and sat in her favorite chair. The waves were hypnotic, as usual. Calming. She wondered when that man next door would walk by with his little dog. He reminded her of Greta so much. So much. Poor Greta. Ah, well, but there had been justice at the end.

After a few minutes, she realized she had fallen into a doze again. This was getting ridiculous. She should see her doctor, find out why she kept napping. Dr. Ong would know. No, Dr. Ong had retired ten years ago, and died soon after. She had a new doctor now. A young man. A sassy fellow who thought he knew everything, as young people always did. Life would teach him differently soon enough. She didn't need to see a doctor. She felt fine. There was nothing wrong with her. She merely got a little absent-minded from time to time.

She should call Alexander, see how he was doing in his new home. He had given her the number for his new place in Carolina. North Carolina? South Carolina? She couldn't remember right now. Where was his new number? Surely he had given it to her? It was probably in her desk, or by her bed. She'd go get it in a few minutes. For now, it was restful to sit and look out at the waves. She had always loved living by the water.

\#

Bruce contemplated the water, standing with a mug of coffee as he took a break from his writing. His contact with Dorothy sometimes was the only human connection he had in a day. He didn't count emails and phone calls, because most of those were business related. Dorothy was turning into a friend. He wondered if she suffered from incipient dementia because she repeated herself often. Although she was far sharper than the average old lady was reputed to be. Come to think of it, so was Aunt Nora. Maybe old ladies had been getting a bad rap all these years.

Aunt Nora could be stubbornly tunnel-visioned. That day he visited her, a couple of months after Uncle Joe's death, had been strange.

They had both been missing Joe, of course. Both of them sitting in the den but conspicuously not sitting in Uncle Joe's favorite easy chair. Then Aunt Nora said,

"I'm sorry you never had a father to take care of you."

"Huh? Joe was my father." Her words were distracting, but not enough to pull him out of his grief for the old man who had made him a full member of the family and been a father to him his whole life. The cancer had eaten at Joe until his death became a release.

His mother spoke again. "Joe was the best. Not like your real father. He was a...a prick."

Bruce had been surprised, but amused, too. He'd never heard Aunt Nora use that word. She was always too ladylike to curse. He'd had to learn all his bad words from Uncle Joe and his adoptive brothers, Ned and Billy.

Aunt Nora was trying to tell him something. "Roger

188

Dietrich, your real father, was a queer duck. He never seemed to have any friends of his own. He disliked all of Greta's friends, and her relatives. He refused to attend family events, and he didn't want my sister Greta to come to them, either. That was a problem, especially after you were born. Our parents wanted to know their grandchild. Greta was always making excuses for why she couldn't visit or have any of us over. At first, we each thought we were being personally snubbed. Then, we compared notes and realized she told everyone the same thing. We understood. Her life with Roger was busy. She had a little baby and a new household to cope with. But it was more. One time I happened to be in the area and I dropped in on her."

Bruce doubted it was accidental. His adoptive mother was nothing if not a manipulator.

"Roger behaved oddly. Greta acted nervous. She kept trying to get me to leave in a big hurry. I hardly had a chance to see you. Roger drank a beer and glowered at me. When Greta was going to show me something upstairs, he forbade her. He made her go get it. It was as if he didn't want her to be alone with me."

Bruce was suddenly more alert.

"Aunt Nora, you know what you're describing don't you?" he asked, trying to be gentle about it. She was already twisting her fingers together. She was obviously getting more and more upset.

She nodded. "I don't like telling you this, Bruce. He was your father after all. We began to suspect Roger abused Greta."

"Did you ever see him act violent toward her?"

"No, but it was obvious he had her under his control. She

had always been such a lively, spirited girl. The difference in her behavior and attitude was very marked to anyone who had known her before Roger entered her life."

"You always said it was an impulsive wartime marriage. Lots of people probably repented of those. War can change a man, make him more likely to act out violently." He was thinking out loud, but it sounded as if he was condoning abuse, which wasn't the case.

She made a dismissive gesture. "We knew. It wasn't called Post Traumatic Stress Syndrome, but after the Great War, World War I, many men had mental problems. It was ascribed to having been gassed, but the truth was they had seen horrors. There was a man who lived down the street from us when we were growing up who had it. Sometimes we'd hear him shouting in the middle of the night."

"You think my father had it?"

"Possibly. None of us knew him before he returned from the war. Not even Greta. She met him at a USO dance and married him fast. We never met any of his people."

He stirred restlessly in his chair. Everything was the same in this room as it had been his whole life. He could remember playing hide and seek behind the back of the couch. What was Nora driving at with this talk of the past?

"Why are you telling me this? What's the point after all these years?"

"I would have told you a long time ago, but Joe forbade me. He didn't want you to be burdened with our suspicions. Now that he has passed, I feel I simply must tell you."

Still, she hesitated. She struggled to get up from her chair, and took a couple of shaky steps closer to him, assisted by her wooden cane. He took her other arm, to support her. She wasn't strong anymore. He stood before his adoptive mother in a stance he'd taken as a boy when he wanted to face a punishment head on. Only now, his mother was much shorter than he was, and none too steady on her feet.

"Why did you stand up? Do you need something?" he asked.

Nora was as stubborn and determined as she'd always been. She continued into the kitchen, and pulled down the cookie jar. It was filled with cookies. She gave him a questioning look.

"I'll have a few," he said.

She put cookies on plates for both of them and then set water to boil. "French press?"

"Sure, Mom. What's this all about?"

Nora's earlier haste had been replaced with an obvious reluctance to go through with whatever she had planned to say to him. She was stalling.

They had French press coffee, a hangover from her family's Norwegian heritage. They ate cookies. He had procured beautifully ironed napkins, too, from the breakfront.

"Oatmeal raisin. These are great."

"Too bad your former wife wasn't interested in the recipe. She might have done a better job of keeping you."

Nora said it with a tart edge. She hadn't been a fan of Carol's, but oddly, usually blamed Bruce for the divorce. Even though it had been Carol's idea.

"Past history," he said.

"I'm in the past today, boy. Don't get wise with me."

"Come on, Mom, don't keep me in suspense. What did you

want to tell me about my parents? Although it's a little too late to warn me my father was an abuser and I could become one, too. My kids are grown and gone without a mark between them."

Bruce slouched in the wooden kitchen chair, wolfing down cookies as he'd done countless times in his youth. He still felt like a boy when he was around the woman who had been a second mother to him. He suspected she knew it.

"I don't believe any of that inheritance nonsense, do you?" Aunt Nora asked.

"No, but I have inherited Dad's tendency to get annoyed when you beat around the bush like this," he said, smiling. Gently kidding Mom was a pleasure. He picked up their dishes and put them in the sink and turned on the water. Aunt Nora would insist on doing them by hand. He grabbed a sponge and got to work.

"I trained you well," she remarked, pleased. He felt a smile creeping into his heart. She was so familiar, so openly loving. When Carol left, he'd missed the familiarity and implied love of being part of a family. He'd managed his newly single life okay, but it wasn't the same. Maybe that was one reason she'd ended their marriage. With the kids grown, she'd wanted a deeper relationship, and she and he simply had worn theirs out. It had never been much more than a convenience, anyway. He had married too young, and had paid the price for his lack of discrimination. So had Carol. When she had finally called a halt to the empty show of a marriage that remained, he had been relieved.

Nora took the fragile coffee cup from his hand. "You've been rinsing for a whole minute. You're wasting water, boy." She gave him a sharp look.

He turned off the water and dried his hands. Nora had set the cup in the drainer and was slowly leading the way back to the den. She never used the front parlor, it was reserved for company. She always called it the parlor, stubbornly clinging to the terms and habits of her parents' generation.

She dropped to her chair again. Bruce was too restless now to sit.

Nora seemed to gather her strength. Finally, she burst out with it. "We always believed Roger was the cause of Greta's death."

"What do you mean?" He hadn't expected this. "I thought she had an accident. She fell down the stairs."

At his mother's silence, he made the obvious connection. "You think he pushed her?"

She nodded. "Joe disagreed with me. Since Roger was dead soon after, there was no way of proving anything. That's why Joe made me promise not to tell you."

"What made you believe it wasn't an accident? Many people are injured or killed in simple home accidents."

"Don't show off with me, boy. Statistics mean nothing. Greta was like the rest of us Hagens. Big, thick bones. A mere trip down the stairs should not have killed her. As children, we learned how to fall. Go limp, our father always told us."

"You're making a lot of assumptions." He wasn't sure he wanted to be led where she was taking him, but now she would not be diverted. Her aged face, lined and crepey, took on the semblance of a younger woman as the anger showed. Her deep grey eyes still had snap in them.

"You listen to me, young man. My sister was not killed by an accidental fall. Her husband either pushed her or threw her down those stairs. He probably hit her first."

"Why are you so sure?"

"Both her arms were bruised, she had broken ribs, and one leg was broken. What killed her was a broken neck."

Aunt Nora had painted a horrifying picture. The thought that his blood father had murdered his birth mother was a jolt, but somehow not as unbelievable as it should have been. He didn't know why.

"You saw her like that?"

She looked at him straightly. "Joe didn't want me to, but I insisted on seeing her body before the embalmers could touch it. I talked to them and to the police. Her body had sustained tremendous damage."

She struck the floor with her cane. "Back then, people took the attitude that what was done was done. I sensed that the police and the embalmers had their suspicions, but she was dead and it was too late. Roger acted broken up about it, and you were a little boy needing Roger's care. The police decided there was no point in being involved further."

"Didn't anybody know about abuse in those days?"

"Of course. They called it wife beating. It was considered a private matter. Something low-class people did. The police didn't order an autopsy on Greta's body and Roger would not permit one. There was no opportunity to find evidence of previous injuries she hid from us. We could have raised a ruckus, sued to demand an autopsy, but Greta was dead. We had you to consider. We didn't want you to grow up branded the son of a killer."

"If he was one. What happened next?"

"We suffered through Greta's funeral. Roger had to put a decent face on it and allow her family and friends to attend, not to draw suspicion on himself."

"That was it?" he asked.

"No, boy. Of course not. I made a huge scene at the funeral, accusing him of killing Greta and warning him I would be watching his treatment of you carefully. I told him he'd better not try to deny me if I wanted to visit you."

"Bet that went over like a lead balloon."

She smiled a little, remembering. "My open accusation shook him. Then Dorothy spoke up."

"Dorothy?"

"Greta's best friend from when she had been working in the war effort. Dorothy disliked Roger intensely and she wasn't afraid to say so. She told him she knew he had killed Greta and she was going to make sure he paid for it."

"Whoa. You two didn't pull any punches. I'll bet Uncle Joe was trying to shut you up and drag you away."

Nora smirked. "Of course. It made a dramatic picture. I was trying to claw Roger's eyes out, and Joe was protecting the wretch. Pitiful." Her wrinkled hands, soft from a lifetime of housework, smoothed the fabric of her dress. Nora always wore a dress and hose, even at home. She had never taken to what she excoriated as the ugly newfangled fashion of pants.

"Afterwards, Dorothy and I talked. We pooled everything we knew about Greta's life with Roger. Dorothy told me not to worry. To get ready to take you in once you were orphaned."

"You're kidding."

"That's what she told me." Nora smiled in satisfaction. "It wasn't two weeks later that Roger died in a car crash, leaving you to us to raise."

"Another accident that wasn't one?" This was sounding melodramatic and unbelievable. Was Nora losing it? Nora was all alone in this big house now. She could be getting fanciful.

"You don't believe me?" She sounded outraged.

"How can I? You tell me this crazy story, accuse my own father of murdering my mother. Then you claim a friend of yours killed my father out of revenge?"

"It's all true." She shook her head, sighing. She winced slightly at some random pain. "Now I understand why Joe didn't want me to tell you."

"Do you have any evidence? Any proof?" His voice sounded angry, and he softened it. He should not take out his frustration on his mother.

"Nothing. Perhaps Dorothy does." Nora folded her hands in her lap. "I've agonized over this for years. I could have let it go, but it sticks in my craw. It always has. Roger got away with murder."

The fire returned to her eyes. "You don't know what Greta was like. She was beautiful, but more than that, she was always the life of the party, the funny girl who turned every chore into a game. Roger smashed it all to bits. She lost her smiles. Then she died. It wasn't right. If Dorothy did something to make him pay, I am glad."

Nora ended her tirade, and the life drained out of her. She

looked old and tired.

He felt old himself. By now he was pacing the length of the room. It was hard to get his mind around all she had told him.

"My father murdered my mother and then some woman I have never heard of killed my father out of revenge? This is complete bull—"

"Don't swear in my house," came the stern warning.

"It's okay if this woman murdered my father, but not if I say a bad word? Aunt Nora, you're impossible."

"I don't believe in an eye for an eye, son. Don't mistake me. You were our concern."

"Why did you tell me this?" he asked, exasperated.

"Because I thought you had a right to know. Dorothy is still alive. You might be able to find out from her if she truly did cause Roger's death. If he admitted anything about Greta before he died. I've never been brave enough to ask."

"Why not? Why have I never heard of this Dorothy before today?"

"She's older than me. She was Greta's friend, not mine. She changed after Greta died. Got very fierce. Maybe we all did. I concentrated on the children, determined to raise you up right and help you have good lives. Dorothy took the other route. She started her causes. I'd hear about this protest or that protest she was leading. Or some petition drive she was spearheading. She went up against some powerful people in politics around here, and she was absolutely fearless. I always assumed that was connected somehow to Greta and Roger. I was afraid to look in Dorothy's eyes and see the truth of what she might have done to Roger. Even though he deserved it. I know he deserved it."

One of her hands trembled visibly.

She was an old woman. Sometimes he forgot. He was not young anymore himself. He should have been paying more attention to this beloved woman who had raised him.

"Joe's role in this?"

"He told me to let it alone."

"Papa Joe was right, as usual." He said it with a certain bitterness. Just when his life had gotten simple. When he was ready to goof off for a while. His dear adoptive mother was sending him on a quest. Oh, she hadn't said it in so many words, but his duty was clear. He was to meet this Dorothy and find out the truth from her. Mom Nora probably had it all worked out and knew where Dorothy was living and how to contact her.

Which was why Bruce Wicklow, born Bruce Dietrich, was living next to Dorothy Duncan, born Dorothy Lane. To scrape up an acquaintance and learn whatever secrets she knew of his family's tragedy. Talk about a messed-up reason to rent a house on an exclusive beach. This topped anything.

He'd made remarkable progress on his quest. He'd insinuated himself into Dorothy's daily life by using Yappie, a dog he had searched for and adopted deliberately to soften Dorothy up because Yappie was the same breed as his childhood puppy. Supposedly, she had been the one who gave him his puppy when he was four. He thought he remembered a tall, dark-haired lady. Perhaps he didn't. Aunt Nora had given him an old photo of Dorothy from that period, and she had not looked familiar. The photo had also included his mother, Greta. He hadn't looked at her picture in a long while. She was a beautiful woman, as Nora had claimed. A beautiful woman who died long before her time.

Did Dorothy know if it had been an accident after all, or had she discovered it was murder? Had she possibly, somehow, taken revenge and caused his father's death? His father had supposedly died in a one-vehicle car crash. He had been drinking. It was night, and a country road. He could have wrecked simply because he'd tried to avoid a deer. Although the police report said there had not been any skid marks indicating he'd braked suddenly. Yes, Bruce had checked the old records. Research was his longtime passion.

Time to go over and roust Dorothy for their daily beach stroll. He was convinced she was having trouble with her memory. Which wasn't good for the success of his quest.

He should ask her before her memory got worse, but he was finding he didn't want to barge in and rudely burst out with his questions. He needed some softer lead in. To get her to reveal the truth might be difficult. If she even remembered the truth by now. Although they said that memory of the newest parts of life left first. He'd been checking it out on the Internet. Memories of older events stayed the longest. He should be okay for a while at least.

Bruce whistled for Yappie, who rose from his mat and obediently came to have his leash snapped on.

"You're a good boy. Thanks for going along with this little game, fellow." He patted the well-trained dog. After he had found Yappie, he'd attended dog obedience school with him. The teacher and he had quickly realized Yappie already knew the basics. Bruce was the one who had to learn how to behave around a domestic animal again. It had been a long time since there had been a family pet in his home. They'd had a dog when the kids were young. Not in the later years, when everyone was busy. It was another instance of the sterility of their home. No one had the love to spare even for a dog. How he and Carol had come to make such a wrong turn, he still didn't know. He didn't intend to make that kind of mistake ever again.

"Come on, Yappie. Time to play with Dorothy." They walked next door, and as was his habit, he knocked at the entrance to the sunroom. She was sitting in her usual seat, but got up when he tapped on the pane.

"Hello, Dorothy, how are you this afternoon?"

"Very well, thank you," she smiled and nodded, but had a slightly puzzled look on her face.

"I've brought Yappie so you can reinforce your morning obedience lesson as we walk along the beach."

"Oh, of course. It's that time already? How quickly the day passes." She opened the door and leaned down to pat the little dog.

"He's been behaving well since you took him in hand," Bruce remarked.

"He's a good dog. It doesn't take a good dog long to learn."

Had he not been looking for signs of faltering memory, he wouldn't have noticed anything amiss. Dorothy's manners were refined and automatic. She had carefully responded to his prompts, never giving a hint she might not recognize him, or know his dog, or even know how long she had been giving the dog lessons or taking afternoon walks with Bruce.

Even though the first time he had met Pam, he had given her a strong warning, she hadn't listened. Nor had she seemed to pick up on any of it during her visit. Was Dorothy deteriorating suddenly, or was it because he was a newcomer in her life that he noticed? Pam was her daughter, after all, and was deeply familiar. Dorothy was probably on autopilot with her.

What if he introduced himself to Dorothy one day as Greta's son? Would she recognize him then?

Chapter 18

Pam hauled out her car again and made the long drive to Long Island to see her mother's attorney in his office in Port Jefferson. He was even farther out on the island than Dorothy.

Signing the documents only took half an hour. The emails they had exchanged in the past week had saved them precious face time. She had come prepared. The attorney knew exactly how to handle the filings and promised he'd expedite them as much as possible. After shaking hands again, she'd walked out a bit poorer but happy to have taken the first big step to solving Magda's money problem. Luckily, the law allowed Pam to partially fund the nonprofit. She had cashed in a CD, and used the proceeds to start the ball rolling.

Now it was time to visit her mother again. The beach community was all the way south across the island, but not terribly far. When she had driven most of the way, she stopped at a grocery and picked up a prepared meal, the kind Dorothy preferred, and a few other things.

An hour after she left the lawyer's office, she was turning her car into the drive at the beach house. The houses were far enough apart that some of the beach was visible behind and between them. Dorothy and Bruce were returning from their daily beach walk with his dog.

"Hello," she called from the driveway.

They waved, and Bruce left Dorothy with his dog and sprinted over to help Pam, whose arms were filled with groceries.

"Pam. Glad you're back."

The words were conventional, but the expression on Bruce's face said he meant them. He wasn't exactly smiling. That would be too revealing. By his age a man knew how to keep a poker face. There was a lightness to his expression. His eyes looked happy.

She had no such hesitation. She smiled, a big goofy smile.

"Yes, I'm back."

They stared at each other for a second, taking each other in. Then they both started, as Dorothy came up behind him.

"Now don't stand there gawking, Pamela. The man is holding your packages. Open the door." Dorothy chided her.

Pam sprang into action and opened the door, which as usual was unlocked. In other times, her mother's words would have mortified her. With Bruce, it didn't seem to matter.

"You don't keep your front door locked, Dorothy?" Bruce asked. It was obvious he disapproved of unlocked front doors.

"Of course not. Who would bother me way out here?"

"You're not in the sparsely populated countryside anymore," Pam reminded Dorothy. "The New York suburbs have spread all the way out here. Maybe you should."

"Oh, nonsense. After all these years of living in an unlocked house, it's more likely I'd forget the keys and lock myself out than somebody would bother me." Dorothy said it in her usual take-no-prisoners manner.

Pam said no more, but Bruce didn't know Dorothy well enough to stop. He frowned. "I'd be happy to keep a set of keys for you. If ever you got locked out, you could come to me. I'm here all the time."

"No, thank you. I'm not planning to change my habits," Dorothy replied in a crisp tone of voice. Her mother would never be so rude as to tell off a neighbor, but she made it clear she would not take his advice or his assistance.

Pam held her breath.

Bruce smiled ruefully, "Have it your way, Dorothy."

He set the grocery sacks, reusable mesh that Pam kept in her car, on the kitchen counter. Then he took back Yappie's leash and turned to Pam. "Are we still on for our trip to the park tomorrow?"

She smiled. "Yes. You're doing a lot of walking with my family."

"The rest of the day, I sit and write. It's the perfect balance."

Tomorrow, they would go to the arboretum. She could hardly wait.

Before she could say anything more, Bruce spoke up again. "Would you like to go out for a drink later this evening?"

"Why don't you have dinner with us?" Dorothy offered.

"I've got to finish a chapter." He replied."It'll take me about three hours."

By now, Dorothy had gotten the lay of the land. Bruce and Pam were interested in each other. She didn't press him. "I don't like going out at night anymore. You and Pamela go."

Pam looked at her mother, ready to argue. They'd gone out to dinner last week and Dorothy hadn't said one word about not liking going out at night. Dorothy winked at her, then said blandly, "I'm a little tired. I'm going to sit down."

She left them alone in the kitchen, staring at each other. They were only three feet apart. Pam felt her breathing accelerate.

Bruce broke the silence. "I like your mother. She's the anti-chaperone."

She laughed. "You're right. She might as well put an 'Available' sign on me."

"Are you?"

"What?"

"Available?" he asked softly.

She squirmed. Suddenly she felt defenseless, as if everything she was feeling was being revealed to him through her eyes and her body language. He put a hand on her shoulder, gently.

"Don't be shy. Tell me."

"Yes. Maybe. Yes," she said more definitely.

Bruce leaned down and kissed her lips.

"Is eight o'clock okay?" He kissed her again. "Pam? Eight o'clock?"

"Yes…"

He kissed her once more, this time clasping her in a close embrace. She could feel him from her shoulders to her knees. Inside, she could feel him everywhere. Her blood sang. She kissed him back. Her arms raised and wrapped around him, too.

Suddenly, she felt something around her ankles, pulling tight.

They broke the kiss and looked down.

"Yappie, no."

Yappie had wound himself and his leash around their legs and was straining toward the door.

Bruce grinned. "Guess he's telling me it's time to go." He carefully reeled in his anxious pooch and untangled the leash from their ankles. Then he grabbed another swift kiss and headed for the door. "See you later."

As Bruce and Yappie let themselves out, Pam stood by the counter, turned to stone. How did he do that? How did one little kiss become many? Why did she cooperate enthusiastically? It was crazy. She was crazy. She had never been like this before in her life. She felt buoyant, carried away like a bright balloon. Exhilarated.

They ate dinner in the sunroom. Her mother would never eat in the kitchen, but the dining room was still cluttered. In fact, the piles looked a little higher. When Pam made to do something about them, her mother waved her away.

"They'll wait. Now that we're done with dinner, let's discuss how you go about getting substantial contributions for your charity. You should push for big money, Pamela. Go talk to the richest executives you can find, and ask each man for at least several million dollars."

Pam gasped. "That much?"

"These men have it. Remember, they think in millions. You must show you're in their league by speaking in millions yourself," Dorothy said in her most didactic voice.

"Why would they be personally willing to donate millions of dollars?"

"Because you're going to let them in on the ground floor with this new charity. They can be the big names for it."

At Pam's puzzled look, Dorothy explained. "Well-established charities already have a hierarchy of big names attached to them. A newcomer trying to make a name for himself as a charitable giver would merely be an also-ran. Despite his millions."

"I'd be offering these men a chance to be the first major contributors?"

"Exactly," Dorothy nodded. "Appeal to their raging egos. Make sure you come across as if you are upper class.

"In fact," she paused, "I've got some suitable clothing for you in my closet. If you want to convince executives and corporate big shots to part with big money for your new foundation, you should dress the part."

"I have clothes, Mom," she protested.

Her mother wasn't listening. Dorothy led the way to her ground floor suite, and then into her walk-in closet. She started rifling through the garment bags that lined one side.

"Ah. There it is," she said. She unzipped the bag and carefully pulled out a pale pink suit. Even Pam, who normally paid no attention to fashion, recognized what it was.

"Chanel? You have a vintage Chanel suit?"

Dorothy inclined her head at the words, and then gently opened the suit jacket to show the hexagonal label that simply said "Chanel" on it.

"It's the real thing, Pamela. Look at this." She used a fingertip to lift the label and under it was another label with a code printed on it. "The certificate of authenticity."

Then she lifted the jacket hem and had Pam hold it. "Feel that."

"Why is it so heavy?"

"A couture suit is always weighted so it hangs right. Chanel suits all have chain inserted between the lining and the fabric, along the hem."

"It's beautiful, Mom, but why are you showing it to me?"

"This is what you should wear when you're bearding self-important men in their offices. They'll be in twelve thousand dollar, hand-tailored suits. You should wear something equally impressive."

"Did you wear this suit to visit the mayor or the governor?"

Dorothy smiled a reminiscent smile. "I did indeed. Not for the public protests. For them, I always dressed like a suburban housewife, the way you do." She gave Pam a stern look. "That will not work with these executive types. Don't try to dress down. You must dress up, way up."

"I don't think I could wear something this valuable. Or antique," she demurred. "Anyway, it probably wouldn't fit."

"Don't be silly, Pamela. It's Chanel. It never goes out of style. Here, put it on right now. Let's see if it fits."

She couldn't well protest. Her mother wouldn't pay any attention. Pam stripped off her nondescript slacks and blouse and carefully lowered the skirt over her head. Then she buttoned herself into the jacket. To her surprise, it fit well. It felt wonderful, soft and luxurious. She ran a gentle hand over the fabric of the skirt.

"Ah, it's perfect. Look in the mirror," her mother said.

Pam gazed at herself. The cut was amazing. She looked taller.

She felt stronger. "I feel different."

"That's what couture does, dear."

Pam twisted a little, to admire her backside. It looked good.

"Make sure you get some designer shoes. You won't need a handbag since you'll be carrying a briefcase."

Her mother was in her element, citing rules for jewelry, hairstyle, and more. It all became too much.

Who was Pam kidding? She couldn't pull this off in a million years. She changed out of the suit quickly.

Dorothy hadn't noticed her sudden shrinking away. She bustled about, carefully re-hanging the Chanel suit in its garment bag.

"Take it to your bedroom so you won't forget it." She rezipped the garment bag and thrust it into Pam's hands.

Dorothy shooed her off. "Come down quickly. We must find you something to wear tonight."

Pam dutifully placed the garment bag in the closet of the upstairs guest bedroom she used. Her mother was always so sure of herself. She must have moved mountains while wearing this suit. Not that Pam remembered it from the old days, but then she'd hardly paid attention. Her mother couldn't be right about such an old piece, could she? Even if it was Chanel? If she was, could Pam muster up enough presence to get the same effect?

She ran downstairs to her mother's suite. Dorothy had pulled out several bright print sundresses.

"One of these might do for cocktails tonight."

"But it's already October."

"The weather hasn't turned yet. Add a cardigan and you'll be warm enough," Dorothy said.

"In that case…"

Pam was drawn to the gay colors in spite of herself. She picked out one with a large red pattern on white. It had wide halter straps and a full skirt.

"That will go well with your pale skin and dark hair," Dorothy approved.

Pam put it on, whirling in front on the three-way mirror her mother had at the far end of the closet. This dress didn't ask her to grow in presence or be someone she wasn't. The red flowers contrasted with her still-dark hair. It was a dress fit for an evening in a beach town. Even when the season was over. She liked it.

"It looks good on you."

"You're sure you don't mind if I wear it tonight?" she asked her mother.

"Of course not. I'll never wear it again," her mother said. "In fact, we should clear out this closet sometime. Most of the clothes could be given to charity or to vintage re-sale shops."

"Should we sort things now?"

"I've had enough for a while. I want to sit down. Bruce will be here soon."

Bruce arrived a few minutes later. He wore khakis and a nicely pressed long-sleeved cotton shirt. He whistled when he saw her coming down the stairs carrying her purse. "You look fantastic. I should go back home and put on a tux."

She couldn't help a delighted smile.

He turned to Dorothy, standing at the bottom of the stairs. "Why don't you throw on your glad rags and join us?"

Dorothy declined. Earlier she might have been faking being

tired. Now, the time spent standing and rummaging through her closet had clearly worn her out.

Bruce drove them to the pier, where the yacht club bar overlooked the busy marina. The bar was a quiet place on this weeknight, conducive to talking. They sat at a candlelit table next to a large window, where they could watch the boat lights and the occasional departure or arrival.

Bruce said, "Your mother seems to be throwing us together. Is she always like that?"

Pam reddened. "No, this is new. Embarrassing. Of course, I was married for twenty-seven years. She didn't have to play matchmaker then."

"That's a long marriage. What was he like?"

"Most men wouldn't want to hear about the previous, er, well, you know," she stuttered to a stop.

"Would I sound conceited if I said I'm not most men?" he asked. "You spent half your life with him. Were you happy?"

"Yes," she said. She paused. "Yes, we were, although we had our moments. Jeff was…he took care of me, and that's what I needed when I was young. He took charge, and I molded myself to him."

"But? You outgrew him?"

"I never tried to grow at all," she admitted. "I submerged myself into being a wife and mother. Then he died, and I was lost."

She shook her head, looking out over the water. She had wasted years in the futile effort to pretend her life had not changed.

"You still haven't told me what he was like." Bruce's

comment drew her back to focus on his question.

"It's hard to remember now. He was a good man who would have wanted me to do more with my widowed life than I have." She wanted to take the spotlight off herself. "How about you and your wife, or is that a sore subject?"

Bruce answered readily. "No. Carol and I looked around once the kids were grown, and realized we had lost touch with each other. Sadly, neither of us cared enough to reestablish our relationship."

"You fell out of love?"

"I guess so." He shrugged. "We split up two years ago. She's happier with her new husband."

"What about you?" She gave him a concerned look.

"Better now that we've met." He bent a soul-searching gaze on her.

She flushed with pleased embarrassment. "Oh." She couldn't think of anything else to say.

He said, "You have a quality of womanliness, of femininity, that is rare these days."

She frowned a little. "Do you dislike women who have careers?"

"Nothing to do with that." He smiled a little ruefully. "If I was a fiction writer, I'd have smooth phrases to explain why I find myself so relaxed and happy when I'm around you."

"I understand," she replied, relieved. "I feel the same. As if I don't have to pretend or be on my best behavior. I can be myself with you."

Bruce picked up her right hand and kissed the back of it softly. She shivered with delight, feeling a thread of electricity coursing through her body.

After dinner, still in a haze of happy discovery, they drove back to Bruce's house. He invited her inside. She knew what he wanted. He didn't bother making any excuses. He wanted her. Was she ready for this step?

They could continue talking and learn more about each other, but why stretch things out? Must she carefully weigh the merits of Bruce's long-term intentions? Must she ponder her own? Why not go with her feelings and let the romantic evening end in lovemaking? Enjoy herself without considering lifelong plans? She wasn't an ingénue anymore, even though Bruce had made her feel like one.

Yes, she was ready. She wasn't interested in beating around the bush, either. It had been a long time.

They went upstairs to his bedroom. The lovemaking was swift and satisfying. There was no substitute for a real, live man. She was a little uncomfortable at first, but Bruce took care of her, and soon she was taking care of him. Still, she could sense each of them had held back. Their emotions, if they had them, were not on display. They made no confessions of love.

Afterwards, she lay next to Bruce and wondered silently what came next. So she asked him.

"More," he said and drew her into his arms again. She went willingly.

Finally, it was late. "I have to get home," she said.

Bruce helped her dress, kissing body parts as she covered them up. That was sweet.

"I wish you could stay," he said. Perhaps he meant those words, but he didn't try to convince her further when she shook her head in refusal.

She slipped into Dorothy's house, which of course was unlocked, and found her mother had gone to bed but left a few lights on. She turned off all but one on the ground floor and went upstairs to her own room.

Then she lay in her bed, only a few dozen feet from Bruce, but with many walls between them. How strange. She'd had sex for the first time since her husband died, and she hadn't felt a thing. Nothing. Oh, Bruce knew how to please a woman in bed. Somehow she'd lost the spark of excitement she'd had about him before. Even earlier today. Or rather, she had scratched the itch? Sex had been enough. Being comfortable with Bruce was enough. She would see him again, but romance didn't have to be the biggest thing in her life, not as it had been when she was young.

What occupied her thoughts right now was the Chanel suit hanging on the door of her closet. It signaled an exciting new life direction for her. It symbolized danger, and risk, and trying to become a bigger person. Even though Bruce was new in her life, having sex with him, being his lover, was not an adventure on the same level.

Neither of them had spoken words of affection to tie each other to a commitment. Even if they had, she had no clue about how to integrate a new love and a new life. Of the two, the new life seemed the more important right now.

Which didn't mean she would refuse to have sex with Bruce on her next visit. No vibrator was a satisfying substitute for a man, and she had enjoyed their time in bed. She had responded physically. That's all it was. Sex. Not love. When she was younger, she had confused the two, but not anymore.

Their big date at the arboretum the next day was pleasant, but a letdown now they had become lovers. It had been planned as an opportunity to talk and get to know each other, but they'd already said all they needed to say. They cut it short and managed another hour in his bedroom. Bruce surprised her with some inventive and playful sex she enjoyed. Her body was satisfied but her emotions were no different. It was an empty emotional experience. Maybe that was a good thing. They had fun but nobody was likely to get hurt.

As before, she didn't linger in bed with Bruce. She dressed and they said goodbye. Then she went next door to wrap up her visit and return to the city.

In line with the oddness of this short stay, she was feeling clingy about her mother. For the first time, Pam had the thought that moments with her mother were precious and limited. When she had packed her car and they were standing by it in the driveway, she said, "I'll be back here soon, Mom."

Dorothy radiated self-assurance as always. "To see me, or your young man next door?" her mother asked, raising an eyebrow.

"You, Mom. I'll come back to see you." She gave Dorothy an impulsive hug.

Dorothy looked surprised. As they let go, Dorothy stared at her searchingly, then smiled as if she was finally seeing something in Pam's face she'd been hoping for and never saw before.

"You mean that, child."

"I do," she said solemnly.

"Then I'll look forward to it." Her mother patted her a little and then pushed her toward the car. "Get going now. You don't want to hit the traffic."

Chapter 19

Linley was at her desk when she got an excited call from her friend at NBC. "This is amazing considering the economy. We've received stacks of checks and envelopes with cash in them. All for your mom's friend, this Magda. How do we get her the money?"

"I'll call my mom and have her contact you."

"Would you explain to her we can't release the money to her? Only to Magda?"

Linley assented and then hinted she'd have some news about her own career soon. Her contact perked up her ears, begging to be the first to know. Excellent. A little more chitchat, and this contact would be someone she could count on to call her when the *Today Show* needed a substitute expert. It was a long shot, of course. They already had a batch of well-known people, but there would always be that holiday weekend or summer vacation week when Linley might be the only game in town. She made sure her contact knew she was free to be interviewed on financial topics at any time.

She should call all the other stations she'd been on, to ask if they'd received money for Magda. Any excuse to talk to her contacts and improve on them.

Three had. She'd have to call her mom. That could wait. Right now, she had a show in a few minutes with Jason and the guys. She downloaded a couple of charts to her laptop, and posted her notes on the desktop so she could easily refer to them.

She hoped Jason would have settled down from earlier today. The more she thought about it, the crazier he had behaved. Kissing her at ten-thirty in the morning? In the office? He didn't show his emotions much so he must have kissed her because he was thrilled at getting the new show. That's what his first kiss was all about, anyway. The rest were about sex. Yum. She was hungry for more of him. Too bad she was on a no-Jason diet.

The show went off smoothly. As she was packing up for the day, she realized no one had asked them why they had been in Marty's office. Television stations were hotbeds of gossip. Someone would have seen them. Someone probably saw them in enter the file room, too. At least Jason had closed the door. She hoped she and Jason weren't unconsciously beaming, telegraphing their secret. Or if they were, perhaps their coworkers would think the secret was only about the new show. Not about how hot they were for each other.

"Good night, Ernie," she said, as she headed for the elevator.

"Wait up, Lin," Jason called, as he sprinted down the hall carrying his leather messenger bag. She held the elevator door.

"Thanks." He bolted inside as the doors closed.

They were alone in the elevator, as he quickly noticed with one comprehensive look. Without hesitation, he swooped her into his arms and planted an enthusiastic kiss on her lips. She felt his warmth all over. She began to heat up.

He released her. "Great day today," he smiled. The doors opened and he strode out, tossing words behind him. "See you tomorrow."

Hit-and-run bastard. She'd need the girl equivalent of a cold shower now. He'd revved up her engines and then left her spinning her wheels.

Car analogies. Bah. She hauled out her cell phone and texted her longtime pal, Caitlin.

R U up 4 dinner

A few seconds later, she got a ping back.

Call me

"Whassup, girl?" Caitlin answered. She only texted when she was in meetings or on conference calls. Caitlin hated typing of any sort.

"Want to meet me at Dutch's in five?" Linley asked.

"You're upset about something. I can hear it in your voice."

"You got that right. Coming?"

"Yup. Make it ten minutes."

Caitlin worked nearby, farther up Sixth in one of the sterile, gleaming towers built by an oil company. Linley's studio, closer to 42nd Street, looked about the same from the outside, all chrome and glass. It had been a famous cable entertainment headquarters years before. When she was a teenager she used to go there with her girlfriends, including Caitlin, and wait outside, hoping to see rock stars. Now an entire floor was rented to her cable news network. Ironic that a major network or its corporate overlord was willing to rent to anyone, especially its competition. Further proof that old-style television was losing out and the corporate owners were grasping for income wherever they could get it. Broadcast television was far from dead. It still had major hit shows watched by millions even though the many cable stations offered strong competition. She intended to get famous on television, although she didn't much care in which kind, broadcast or cable. So far, she'd only worked for cable.

She was in the café section at Dutch's restaurant and bar, seated in a booth when Caitlin came in. Her neat dark pants suit and pulled-back hair signaled she was a serious career woman.

"I didn't order you anything. You still on the wagon?" Linley asked. In the past year, Caitlin had been frank about struggling with her drinking.

"For the moment. At least I haven't had a binge in seven months."

"You're looking good." Caitlin was back to looking ethereal and very Celtic. She'd lost that little alcohol pooch to her tummy. Linley complimented her new slenderness.

"Yeah, no more puffy face, either," Caitlin said. She ordered a latte when the waitress came around.

"Or weird adventures in bed?"

Caitlin grimaced.

"Oh, come on. You have to admit it was funny to wake up with two completely strange guys in your bed and no memory of what happened," Linley said.

"Har har. I never knew I was the threesome type until then."

"If it wasn't roofies." Linley still thought it was hilarious. Although it had been tacky of her to bring it up. Maybe she ought to give it a rest.

"The truth is, when I'm drunk, I'm a slut," Caitlin said. She shrugged.

"Not any more," Linley raised her coffee cup in salute.

"Yesterday's excitement. So tell me your news."

Linley explained what had been going on, from beginning to end, leaving nothing out. By the end, Caitlin looked amused.

"Ambush kisses? That's so cute." She got a devilish look on her face. "Maybe next he'll bring you flowers."

"Or chocolates in a heart-shaped box," Linley said to show she thought it was funny. Although she didn't.

"Or...I know. A balloon bouquet."

"No, no. An edible bouquet with chocolate-covered strawberries." Linley was giggling by now.

"Or...a diamond engagement ring." Suddenly, Caitlin was serious. "You wouldn't laugh at a ring, would you?"

"No way would that happen," she replied. "Jason is playing. He's not serious. We don't even have a relationship."

"Forget the phony diffidence." Caitlin could be hard line when she wanted to be. "You've already done the sex. He's asked you out on a date. He even made a booty call, and now he's kissing you whenever he feels like it." She ticked off the incidents with her fingers. "I'd say at least one of you thinks you're involved."

"Maybe," Linley admitted. Which was confusing because despite all her recent efforts to ensnare his interest, she kept waffling about how she felt about having it.

"How do you feel about Jason? I've seen the show, remember, I know he's a prime hunk."

"That's the problem. I thought I knew."

"What do you mean?"

"I guess I've succeed in getting Jason interested in me as a person. Now what do I do with him?"

Caitlin's answer was pithy and obscene. Then she relented. "Oh, okay, serious answer. What do you want from Jason?"

"I'm not sure," she replied. Why hadn't she asked herself this before? "I know what I want in a man," she continued. "I want someone who won't get in my way. Who will help me get famous and let me enjoy every ounce of it. Who won't be jealous when I hit the big time."

"Fine, but will you get jealous if he does better than you? Because face it, girl, most of the time this is a man's world and women are still supporting players."

"Jason wants to be a major late night talk show host. A household name. My ambition isn't quite that grandiose."

"Why not?" Caitlin was logical when she was sober.

"Good question. Something to ponder." Linley had never thought about her own ambition as limited. Not until she'd met Jason, who wanted to be even more famous and rich than she did. "My dreams are modest and conventional compared to his, aren't they? No big leaps or twists in style. A straight shot up to have my own TV show and dispense good financial advice."

"Don't put yourself down. You want a lot, girlfriend. You want to win out over every other blonde clawing her way onto a TV screen."

"That's how I've been looking at it." Linley sighed. "From Jason's perspective, I want mere peanuts."

"You can think about why some other time. Let's get it back to the personal." Caitlin sipped her latte. "Either you'll be a power couple, or you won't have time for anything but a convenience relationship. Which is only one step away from hooking up or booty calls."

"Do I even want a boyfriend right now when I have to concentrate on not screwing up my big break? Then again, Jason might be the only man who'd understand and not get in my way."

After dinner, Caitlin went to the evening knitting class that was part of her no-drinking regimen. Linley returned to her condo to collapse.

It had been a relief to talk it all out with someone who understood. Caitlin's ambitions lay in a different sphere, but she sympathized with Linley's determination to reach the top of the heap she'd chosen.

Pam would not relate to Linley's ambitions at all. She would be confused by Linley's drive to be a television success. Pam would get hung up on the sex part, wincing away from it, no doubt and pushing her toward convention and getting married. Maybe her grandmother would understand. Maybe not. She'd been a suburban warrior. She became a somebody without taking over a man's role as a wage earner. Although she did invade offices to make her activist goals. There had been a sit-in at the mayor's, for instance.

Once Linley was home and comfortable, she called her mother to report on the contributions the media outlets had received.

Pam got excited. "There's money for Magda? Oh, wonderful. How do we get it to her?"

Linley relayed what her *Today Show* contact had said, which had been echoed by the other media outlets.

"Dear, do you know how much money it is? I don't want to raise Magda's hopes over small amounts. She needs a lot of cash to pay her son's tuition."

"No. The rep from the *Today Show* was pretty excited though. It's likely to be in the hundreds of dollars at least."

"What a godsend. We owe it all to you, Linley, for arranging the publicity. You have done a good thing, dear."

She was surprised to feel a warm glow at her mother's words. Since when did her mother's praise matter to her? She quickly banished that thought and gave Pam details on how to contact the various media reps. Her mother's voice turned uncertain, as it usually did. "Would it be all right if I tell them now about the foundation I've started? Or should I wait? Do you think there will be more donations? I do want to publicize the new foundation."

"You actually went ahead with it?"

"I had to. Magda is very deserving, and there are so many other people who have suffered catastrophic job loss. I want to help everyone I can."

"You're beginning to sound like Grandma."

"Is that good or bad? Oh, don't answer. Anyway, I visited her lawyer and he's filing all the paperwork for me."

"Mo-om. You should have gone online to do it. There are companies that provide legal services cheaply."

"Oh? You didn't tell me before."

"Yes." When would her mother catch up with the twenty-first century? Probably never.

Pam said, "I guess I could have saved some money but I'm used to the personal touch, dear."

"This is the cyber world, Mom. You've got to get with the program." Her mother was so quaint. Sweet, really, but clueless about how the world had changed since she was young.

"Do I have to?" Her mother's voice sounded wistful. "Human contact is so important. I wouldn't want to lose it."

That was unanswerable. Okay, enough time wasted with her mother. Except…maybe there was some publicity they could create over picking up the checks.

"Mom, I'll arrange the *Today Show* pickup. Maybe they'll want to do a minute on you and Magda receiving the checks. As a follow up." Maybe with Linley coming on to explain the exclusive footage, which she would shoot herself with her iPhone if necessary. Yes, that would work nicely to give her more air time.

"I want to talk about my foundation, don't forget."

"Right. We can work that in."

"It's called the Bright Side."

"Why that name?"

"Because the purpose of the foundation is to find a bright side to catastrophic job loss by providing interim economic assistance."

"Not a bad mission statement. I'll get right on presenting the idea to my contact at the *Today Show*." Her mother had gotten it together after all. Surprising. Impressive, even.

"Thank you, dear. You always did have a way with words."

Again that warm glow. What the heck? How long had it been since she cared how her mother made her feel? Since she had tried to help her mother do anything?

What a surprising reaction to her mother's praise. Linley was still thinking about it later. How unusual it was for her mother to be active in a cause. What was it about Magda that had galvanized Pam to act? She was normally a shrinking violet.

Jason called. She didn't give him a chance to open his mouth.

"Jason, don't you dare ask—"

"Chill, babe. I got the word on something important. Why don't you meet me at Benny's, and we can talk about it?"

"Why don't you jump off a cliff?" She wasn't going to be suckered into a hookup. Being near him was dangerous.

"What's wrong with Benny's? You like pizza. They've got pizza."

She swore she could hear him smiling. "Don't be dense. You went crazy on me today."

"Crazy?"

"You know. In the file room."

"If you didn't like it, why did you kiss me back, feel me up and practically rip my shirt out of my pants?"

"I'm about to click off," she said, not wanting to be tempted by remembering the details of their hot minute in the file room. Her body was heating up all over again.

"Okay, okay. Listen, Marty sent me an email. We need to talk about it."

"Just forward his email. I'll buzz you back if I have any comment."

She could hear his exasperation. "Have it your way. Forwarding right now. Stay on the phone, dammit."

She opened her computer, which she'd had in sleep mode while talking to her mom. She didn't bother to fill the dead air on the phone while she waited for the message to come in. Then it did, and she read it quickly. Oh, my god.

Jason,

It would help build interest in the new show if you and Linley were seen together socially. Curiosity about your personal relationship will boost the ratings.

Tell Linley about this idea.

Marty

"No. No way." She couldn't believe it. What a lame idea. "Marty's being an idiot. We could sue him over this. It's harassment, creating an uncomfortable workplace environment."

"I think we'd be very comfortable together," his voice came over seductively. Memories of how well they fit together earlier today arose, but she fought them off.

"That's not the point. We see enough of each other already."

"Come on, it's not a big deal. We'd go to a couple of media parties and hang."

"Why does that sound familiar?" she wondered out loud, sarcasm in every syllable. "Oh, I remember. Because that's how we met last year. And ended up in a hotel room, banging our brains out."

"Not that there's anything wrong with it," he put in.

"Whatever."

"Marty may be skirting the political correctness line here, but would it be such a bad thing to try to stir up advance interest in our new show?" Jason was using his "fair-minded moderator" voice.

"Marty is suggesting boring crap that'll eat into our time and produce nothing but media chatter, not the big buzz we need," she said. "I respect and admire Marty, at least I did until he came up with this trashy scheme, but he is old. He doesn't get how word spreads today."

"So let's do some social media. Whatever's newest and hottest."

She said, "The problem with that is the core audience of WFWF. It skews too old for social media to be the main info source. What about a video?"

"One that goes viral. That could work."

"We can't make a video go viral," she reminded him. "It happens or doesn't on its own."

"Plus, videos aren't exactly cutting edge." Jason's frustration was evident in his voice.

"A video is a much better idea than wasting time pretending we're an item," she snapped back.

She shook back her hair, and unbuttoned her blouse a couple of buttons. It had been a long day already.

"Okay, a video," he said. "What do you want in it?"

Nice he was asking her instead of telling her. "Ideally, we come up with a winning idea. Then we sell Marty on financing it."

"Sounds good."

"Can you do something about Marty? I'm not comfortable talking to him about this." Especially because he usually made her feel like she was about thirteen years old and hadn't done her homework.

"Sure, Lin," he said in a reassuring tone. "I'll handle Marty."

"Without telling him he's out of it?"

"I'll break it to him gently that he's an old fart."

"Jason," she said in a warning tone.

"Kidding. Lighten up, will you? I'll tell him we're planning a YouTube video and that we will dine out at some gossip hole to discuss it."

"Tactful of you." Marty could believe they were following his dictum, sort of. Meanwhile, they weren't jamming YouTube down his throat, reminding him that the Internet and its cadre of younger people now drove the media.

They agreed to come up with their ideas within the next two days before attending a media meet-and-greet where they could be seen and could discuss the plan.

What an insane day. As she finally put on her preferred nightwear, a girly nightgown, she thought back to all that had happened. Marty had offered them a show of their own. Wow. Jason had kissed her, not once, but twice. Double wow. They were going to pretend to date, on their terms, and do a video together. Squee.

She would be running in several directions at once for the foreseeable future. The new show, the old show, her other shows. Better start looking for some video ideas. Her mother's foundation, shouldn't forget that. She must check the AP wire and other feeds for news alerts relevant to tomorrow's shows.

Decide what angle to pitch to get that second media spot featuring her plus Mom and Magda. Then maybe some sleep.

#

In his apartment, Jason covered the same mental territory while he worked out with weights. Late night was about the only time he could grab for exercise after a brief morning run. He had to compete visually with other men in the media, so exercise was mandatory. Much as he always disliked the reps at the beginning, within a few minutes, he felt a sense of well-being. The reps also chilled him out so he could sleep.

The boring exercises gave him time to think clearly. He'd let his excitement and enthusiasm run away with him a couple of times today. Oh, he'd held it together while they were meeting with Marty. He'd been professional, showing the right mix of eagerness and gratitude. Afterwards, he couldn't contain himself and he hadn't wanted to.

His next step up had happened at last. He could parley this duet show into his launching pad for the big time. He knew it. He had the talent. He'd built the following. He was ready. The network had recognized him without him having to negotiate. Which meant the step after this one would be his game entirely.

Who better to share the excitement with than Lin? Damn shame someone had rattled the door handle of the file room. Linley had been as hot as he was. They would have been having sex in another thirty seconds. There was something about her. The way she looked, the glow of her skin, her scent, the whole combo. He'd gone beyond merely being interested in the sex. He wanted her. Maybe she had her crazy side, but he didn't care.

He could deal.

She was acting elusive. She wouldn't even come out tonight to talk because he'd kissed her again in the elevator. Didn't she understand? Neither of them could talk openly about their big break to anyone else. She had to be feeling the same intense excitement. He had felt it when he kissed her. It had felt good. He was glad he'd kissed her. Given a chance, he'd do it again. And more.

Chapter 20

Dorothy drove into town for her substitute hair appointment. She carefully parked her car at the end of the public lot to avoid hitting anyone else with her boat of a Buick, and then headed for the main street on which all the shops faced. When she got to the sidewalk fronting the main street, she looked up and down and could not find the hair salon. She started walking east, past the grocery and the post office. Surely the salon was over here?

No. It did not appear to be. Or maybe she had missed it, simply passed it by as she was walking? She had reached the end of the prettied-up section with all the flower boxes and benches and fancy streetlights with little seasonal flags on them. The salon was part of this downtown. She must have missed it. She turned around and retraced her steps. After she passed the public parking lot, she slowed a bit because by now her feet were getting a little tired and she still had not found what she was looking for. She passed many handsome shops, but none of them was what she wanted.

She reached the other end of the downtown restoration

section. A fancy name for throwing up a few pots of flowers, some benches, and some antique-look streetlamps. At least the trashcans looked clean with their extravagant ironwork exteriors. Frank Lloyd Wright's Chicago style had come back into fashion. The benches were ironwork in the same squared style. Her feet were a little tired. She sat down on a bench for a bit of a rest.

After a while, she heard a bark. She startled. Had she dozed off? There was a dear little dog, a wire-hair fox terrier. Like the one she had given Greta's son long ago. Why was she thinking about Greta? What was she doing sitting on a bench in town?

The dog came up to her and sniffed excitedly, barking.

"Yappie, behave," a man called. "Or you go back on the leash."

Of course. Yappie. Her little neighbor dog. She petted him.

Bruce Wicklow looked at her, obviously puzzled. "We're just coming from the town park. I thought I'd check out the local landmarks. Are you waiting for someone, Dorothy?"

Oh, dear. Best put a good face on it. "Not exactly. I have a hair appointment. I was a little early so I decided to sit out here."

"I think the hair salon is on the other side of the street, a few blocks down," he said.

She didn't like the odd look he was giving her. She stood. "I'll head there now."

"Please let Yappie and me escort you." He offered his arm.

She accepted gracefully, and they put Yappie on the leash since they were walking toward the more populous part of the main street.

They had a lovely chat. She was only five minutes late for the girl. Bruce even tied Yappie up and came into the salon with her and spoke to the salon owner before he said goodbye.

When her hair was done, the owner insisted on seeing her to her car. "You were my first client, after all. You deserve concierge service," the woman said, smiling. Her name wasn't coming to Dorothy just at the moment. Yet she was certain they had known each other for a comfortable long time.

Once she was in her car, Betty—that was her name, of course—said, "Now you be careful driving home, Dorothy. Remember to turn left at the first light."

She nodded to her old friend, "Of course, dear." She didn't see what Betty's fuss was about. She was perfectly capable of driving home. Although right now, the landscape looked very unfamiliar. There were so many new houses. They seemed to have sprung up like mushrooms after a rainy spell. Here was a whole new community of homes. She didn't live there. She lived by the beach. She should find the road to the beach.

Was this her road? She drove down a twisty lane populated with postwar houses. Her house was old, too. Like her. This was tiring. She could use a rest. She'd been driving and driving. Now she was back in the middle of town. How had she managed that?

Then a little flash came to her. Turn here. Of course. Ah, there was a familiar sight, the town park with its little lake. She must take the left turn. Not right.

It was a nice day for a drive. She passed a lot of new houses. When had all these houses been built? They seemed to have sprung up like mushrooms after a rainy spell. Now she took the turnoff here.

Ah, at last, there was her own house. When had she painted

it yellow? Such a cheery color, but quite a daring one, too, for this conservative community. Well, she liked to shake things up.

It was good to be at her own home, where everything was familiar. She parked the car and opened the door. She was exhausted. She had gotten a little confused in town. Maybe she would stick to ordering taxis from now on.

#

Bruce peeked through his curtains and saw Dorothy had finally arrived at her house. If she had been any longer, he would have gone looking for her. He and Yappie had found her obviously lost. She'd been dignified and clever about hiding her confusion, but he'd seen through it. His ex-mother-in-law, now passed away, had dementia in her later years and used to get lost near her home. That was before they caught on. A couple of times, he and Carol had to go find her. He knew the drill.

Why did some families get struck by this plague and others escape? Aunt Nora was completely together. Except for her obsession about his parents. Uncle Joe had been mentally all there until his death, too. There was no way of predicting what his own later years would be like since he knew nothing about his blood father's family. If Dorothy did know something about Roger Dietrich, he'd better ask her soon before forgetting became a way of life for her.

He ought to call Pam and insist she make some arrangements. That day they'd first met, she hadn't taken up the idea of a plan for her mother's care. Maybe Pam was the kind of person who didn't like other people's suggestions. For Dorothy's sake, he hoped not. The gallant old lady shouldn't have to depend on chance help. Although he'd found the salon owner to be cooperative when he'd suggested she walk Dorothy to her car. Betty was her name. Nice woman. Attractive with her red hair and generous curves. He might have found her more interesting if he wasn't sure Pam was the right woman for him.

They said men were impulsive, that when they met a woman for the first time, they often declared she was the one. That's how he felt about Pam. It was a surprise. His relationship with Carol had developed in a much slower manner. After finding some things in common, they'd eventually realized they wanted a future together.

It had worked for a long time. Even now, he wasn't sure what exactly had gone wrong. Whatever spark there had been at first had been smothered by all the work of raising their children and running a home. By the constant pressure of employment. There always were many reasons to be somewhere other than their home. In the later years, his conference schedule and Carol's as an educator consultant had started to send them away from home several weekends a month. This went on for a long time before they finally realized there was no home left. Just a place to do laundry and sleep. It was a sad realization after so many years together, but it was a relief not to have to try to mesh his schedule with Carol's.

Strangely, when it was over, the first thing he had done was pare back his traveling schedule dramatically. He had switched to writing books, which kept him at home most of the time. He didn't do science conferences anymore. He got his new scientific information on the web. He'd done exactly one short media tour for his publisher, and only under pressure after the book had hit the best-seller list. Television and a little radio thrown in for good measure did help sales. Most of the time now, he simply stayed home, as he had never done with Carol, who herself was seldom home. Pam struck him as the kind of woman who liked to stay home. Restful.

#

Pam was feeling anything but restful as she grappled with calling Magda to tell her about the money. It was so difficult to initiate a phone call. She didn't know why. She had always felt shy about phoning. Yet Magda was someone she had seen nearly every day for years. There shouldn't be any hesitation.

"I have good news," she started.

"We have our jobs back?" Magda asked. Obviously, that's where her mind was. No surprise.

"I don't think that's possible. The company is bankrupt."

"Ah, I must find the new job. I have been looking every day. Nothing." The edge of Magda's accent was heavier as she said the words, signaling her discouragement. Hopefully Pam's news would perk her up.

"Something good has come of that television appearance in which I mentioned you and Marc. Many people have sent you money in care of the show."

"Oh, Lord be praised!"

"I don't know the total," she said, careful this time to err on the cautious side, "but with luck, it will add up to enough to keep Marc at Harvard until the foundation can help."

Magda's gratitude turned to tears. When she'd managed to stop sobbing, they agreed on possible times to meet to collect the windfall.

"Magda, the money is a gift. It doesn't affect your unemployment compensation and you don't have to report it on your income taxes because you did nothing to earn it." She'd called her lawyer to be sure.

"How wonderful, how blessed the people of this country are. How generous and kind." Magda said a heartfelt goodbye.

It was the truth. People opened their hearts and gave what they could spare. She had felt good reporting such welcome news to Magda. She wanted to give other people the same hope and happiness. She must make this foundation a success. If it meant ignoring her dislike of the telephone, and even speaking in public, then she'd make herself perform those tasks. She had to see this through.

To that end, she consulted the clock and then cast aside her usual trepidation about contacting her daughter. Just a quick call.

Linley didn't sound impatient when she picked up, just busy.

"Hi, Mom, what's up?"

"Dear, I have the days and times when Magda could come get the gift money."

"Could you email them? I'm kind of pressed right now."

"Oh. Of course. I will. Have a good day, dear. Sorry to interrupt." She put a good face on being told bluntly her daughter had no time to speak to her. It could have been worse, but there still was an ache because Linley didn't automatically want to make time to talk to her.

She ought to get used to emailing instead of trying to make

personal contact. It wasn't as if she didn't know how to. She had sent plenty of emails at the office. She had been operating on an old-fashioned paradigm it was more polite to call someone. Maybe sometimes that was true. She wouldn't have wanted to miss Magda's joy on hearing the good news today.

Bothering her very busy daughter was a mistake. Or interrupting anybody else who had work to do. If she wanted to take the world by storm on behalf of the deserving, maybe she should get out of her twentieth-century mindset.

After she'd carefully composed and sent her email, she felt as if she had conquered something important. It had been silly of her to think every communication had to be a phone call. Especially when she hated calling. Maybe she'd even learn how to text. Or Twitter. Tweet. Whatever.

How ironic that in the midst of congratulating herself for not using the phone, she got a call. From Bruce.

"Hello," she said in a tentative voice. Another reason to switch to email. Then nobody could hear her hesitation.

"Pam, glad I caught you. I want to tell you what happened this afternoon. Do you have a few minutes?"

"Of course," she said. What could possibly have gone wrong? Why was he calling?

"You know that public park on the edge of town? Of Glenvale Village, that is?"

"Yes." Where was this leading?

"Yappie and I were returning from exploring the town park when we found your mother sitting on a sidewalk bench. She said she was waiting for her hair appointment, but she was way on the other side of town. I'm pretty sure she had gotten confused about where the salon was."

"Why do you think that?"

"Because it looked as if she'd been sitting there a while and was worn out. She was napping before Yappie barked his hello."

"It's an odd place for a nap, but she probably was about to stir herself and go to the salon," Pam said. Bruce had gotten the wind up for no reason.

"Maybe she would have. Maybe not. Anyway, I escorted her there, and I got the salon owner, Betty, to make sure to usher Dorothy back to her car afterwards. By my calculations, even assuming your mother drives like most old people, a good ten miles under the speed limit, she got lost on the way home. It was two hours before she drove up next door."

"She probably went grocery shopping." As she said it, she remembered her mother had her groceries delivered.

"She didn't have any packages with her. Plus, she looked completely exhausted when she got out of her car."

"You said she made it home okay," she protested. "You're wrong about my mother. She's one of the most together, focused, competent women alive. She probably got tired and sat down to wait for her appointment, as she told you."

"Don't you understand? Dorothy is faking it. She didn't even recognize Yappie or me at first."

"No way." He was talking nonsense. Not Dorothy. "Why do you think such a thing?"

"I could see the blank expression in her eyes. She was out of it."

He was wrong. He had to be. Her mother was fine. "Now I see why you're a writer. You're very imaginative."

"That's low. I am not seeing what isn't there." There was outrage in his voice. He continued, speaking each word distinctly. "I'm trying to warn you. Your mother needs help. She needs someone to make sure she doesn't sit on public benches because she's lost or drive around for hours because she can't find the way home."

"You mean it kindly, but I think you're mistaken," Pam said firmly. He was seeing trouble where there was none. Dorothy was the same strong person she'd always been. "My mother is able to take care of herself."

"You're in denial. Or maybe you don't care." He sounded frustrated. "I thought you were a concerned, loving daughter. My mistake."

He said a curt "Good bye."

She burst into tears. He wasn't fair. Of course she loved her mother.

This was why she didn't date. Who needed a domineering male around to dictate what to think and how to behave? She'd like to smack him. The nerve. Telling her she was in denial. Then as good as hanging up on her. What gave him the right? So what if two nights ago, he had made her groan with pleasure as he kissed his way up her back?

All she wanted was a quiet life. No drama. She didn't need a new romance or a new man. She definitely didn't need someone saying her mother was losing her marbles. Although maybe she'd better call Alexander and consult with him. She hadn't seen much of her mother until lately. Her brother saw Dorothy frequently until he moved out of state. Why did he have to move? Was their mother now Pam's responsibility? They hadn't discussed it. He'd announced his plans and gone. How could he do that to them all? Men could be so annoying.

Right now, Bruce topped her list. She and he had not made any firm plans for the next few weeks since he knew she had to be near the city to deal with initiating her foundation. Now, she guessed, their personal relationship was over. Good riddance. He was a nosy neighbor, bent on interfering in their lives.

True, he was handsomer than most nosy neighbors. A great kisser. A pleasant lover. He still was an interloper. She was better off ignoring him from now on.

#

Bruce hung up the phone before he let his big mouth run away with him any more. Too late. The damage had been done. Pam had her back up over this. She was in full-blown denial. Damn her, why wouldn't she listen? Dorothy needed a companion. He'd seen the piles of papers in the dining room and the other spots around the house the other day. The old girl was giving it a game try, but life was getting to be too much for her. That's what happened when the formerly super-competent started to slow down. Dorothy had been a real go-getter by all accounts. Betty practically revered her.

Pam had as much as told him to get the hell out of their family business. He ought to, but he needed Dorothy. He needed her to be healthy, and to be willing and able to talk to him about the past. As for Pam, her stubbornness didn't detract from her appeal. If anything, it proved she didn't have ice running in her veins despite her demure presentation. He already knew that from their times in bed. She could be a fiery partner, not only responsive, but taking the lead, too. His body's immediate reaction to his thoughts reminded him that he'd better think of something else. He and Pam might be on the outs for a while.

He'd keep a more careful eye on Dorothy. Damn Pam for being so stubborn.

#

Dorothy put her keys and her purse on the hall table as she always did. She must have been out a long time. She was exhausted and hungry. How silly of her. She should have ordered a sustaining entree at lunch instead of a salad. She didn't need to diet anymore. No, wait. She'd gone to get her hair done, not to lunch with the girls. She should be able to keep track of a life as simple as hers was now.

Food. That's what she needed. Then a rest. She always did better after a rest. She shuffled into the kitchen and opened the icebox. Icebox, that's what she had called a refrigerator when she was young, because the ice man used to come around the neighborhood and use his giant metal tongs and place a huge piece of ice in the box over the cooler. Had he come once a week? She didn't remember anymore.

Ah, there was one of the pre-made meals she had taken to ordering from the deli. No cooking involved. She'd always hated to cook. As soon as Malcolm began to make any kind of money, she'd hired a housekeeper. Dear old Nancy had died a few years ago. Finding a replacement hadn't worked out. She had never been good at languages, and she had a hard time communicating with the two successive women she had tried. Plus, they didn't know how to cook the food she liked. Perhaps she had been too fussy, but she hadn't tried again. She made do quite nicely with what the local stores delivered. Alexander came over once a month with a batch of meals his wife had cooked up. Although he hadn't come around lately. Oh, that's right. He'd moved to North Carolina. Or South Carolina, she'd forgotten which.

Chapter 21

Linley was at her cubicle late the next evening. She had already put in long hours, but she still hadn't thought of a video hook that would entice the general public to watch their new program. On Jason's show, he and she continued to cultivate a businesslike yet feisty image. What would make their offshoot more attractive? Bits of her and Jason getting scrappy with each other? Those could easily get too personal. Because of that nutso email about becoming a media item, she suspected that was the core of Marty's plan. Evidently, her effort to educate herself about journalism had not impressed Marty with her inquiring mind. Instead, he'd thought of her as a pretty young blonde who could be a visual foil for Jason. Marty was shrewd enough to notice the chemistry between them. Seeing potential possibilities was his job, even if he'd gone for a tacky sexual attraction publicity concept.

She'd received the okay for a tiny segment on the *Today Show*. It was a coup, considering other big companies had tossed out thousands of workers by now and Magda's plight was one of many sad stories. This time, she warned her mom in advance that she would not have time to entertain her after the early call.

The next morning, Linley watched as Magda played her part, looking suitably miserable and yet uplifted and determined when she was handed the pile of letters containing checks. Linley had been the one who'd had the idea of letting Magda and Pam have a desk so they could open every envelope, photocopy each one and each check, to make sure they kept proper track of the gifts. They did footage of the two women working on the pile, which Linley narrated with some on-camera time, too. Magda's rapt, reverent expression conveyed volumes. Then Matt interviewed the women live. Magda brokenly expressed her gratitude. "My son may stay in university. I will work. Soon I will find the job. This is America. God bless the wonderful land."

Matt had turned to her mother next.

"Pam, I understand you're trying to do more to help people caught in catastrophic job loss situations."

Her mother had straightened her back and responded with a pleasant, hopeful attitude. "That's right, Matt, I've started the Bright Side Foundation, a charity that will seek donations to help displaced workers like Magda who do qualify for unemployment pay, but who need additional, immediate assistance."

Matt pointed at the piles of envelopes. "Looks like the public wants to help."

"People have warm hearts. As Magda said, this is a wonderful country. I'm also going to approach financial executives who took enormous bonuses and see if any of them can spare something for the workers they've left in such a bad way."

"Are you expecting a positive response from these billionaires with their private jets?" he asked in a skeptical manner.

"I believe every person wants to be thought of as a good, decent human being," Pam said it with firm conviction. "A donation is proof of good intentions." She looked almost like a crusader for a second. Like Grandma Dorothy.

Matt ended the piece with a reminder to check the Bright Side website for contact info if people wanted to donate to Pam's new foundation.

Linley hadn't thought her mother had it in her. Was she actually intending to confront her old bosses and wring money out of them? This was all big talk for now. Pam hadn't done much yet. Still, Linley was impressed. Her mother had never shown so much initiative in the public sphere before.

Pam surprised her again by giving her a piece of paper and asking if Linley could round up the contact information for the financial executives listed.

"Sure, Mom. I've probably got most of it already at my desk." Then she gave in to the inevitable with as good a grace as she could, and made the expected offer.

"Would you and Magda like to come upstairs while I grab it? We can give Magda a tour, too."

"Oh, no, dear. Just email me. We have more letters to process." Pam said they intended to get to the bank right away, to set up an account for Magda and deposit all the gift money.

"Okay. I'll send you the contact info. And Magda, congratulations."

To Linley's surprise, Magda stopped looking at envelopes, and leaped up and gave her a hug.

"Your mother is the angel from heaven," Magda said. "Respect always." The short, stocky woman with her heavy eyebrows managed to look quite fierce.

As Linley left, the two older women returned to their counting.

Returning upstairs to her cramped little cubicle, a far cry from the lavish *Today Show* quarters, she wondered if Magda had been saying she respected Pam, or telling Linley she ought to respect Pam.

At least her mother hadn't been clingy this time around. Hadn't demanded Linley take time out of her busy schedule to entertain her. Linley was used to her mother wanting something from her. Not overtly, of course, but there was an underlying begging attitude. It brought out Linley's worst, most perverse desire not to respond to her mother's desperation.

This time, Pam had only wanted names and phone numbers. Maybe their relationship had progressed to something more adult than mother and child. Which would be good, because she was a grown woman now, and Pam had never quite acted as if she believed that.

Accepting the gift of the condo was different. That was from her father. She missed her dad. He had always spoiled her, giving her everything she asked for, complimenting her looks and her achievements in school. He was the one to whom she had confided her ambition to become a media personality. He had encouraged her, and overridden her mother's concerns. Before his death, Linley had been hired in her first media spot. He'd had reason to be proud of her. She missed him so much. She wished he could be around to see her big moment.

Come to think of it, she hadn't told her mother about the new show.

#

Pam and Magda had needed hours to count all the money and record all the vital information from each giver. Some people gave anonymously, which made her own secret addition of a postal money order to the pile no big thing. Except for the dollar amount, which was as much as she could safely spare.

Then there was the triumphant trip to Magda's bank, with that nice young man from the studio as their bodyguard. Magda was so happy she was floating. They had to constantly remind her of where they were walking. The money had added up to enough to pay her portion for the entire first year. She was saved. Even in this tough economy, Magda would get another job before next year. She had grit. She had dared to leave her homeland and come to a new country. Magda would soon find her feet again. Until she did, she'd help Pam with the foundation.

Afterwards, they had said goodbye to their escort. Then the two former coworkers parted at the subway.

"You'll be okay now. You're strong, and Marc will be a big success at Harvard," Pam said, patting her shoulder.

"You are the good woman," Magda replied, tears in her eyes. "God will reward you." They hugged.

The first chapter in Pam's new life was over.

Pam took the commuter train home and started thinking about her next step. Magda's happy ending had been a windfall. Finding big money to fund the foundation would be harder, but

Pam would see this through. It was an important, worthy cause and she received a selfish benefit from it. The work gave her a reason to wake up with enthusiasm every morning. For the first time in years, her days felt exciting and full of promise. Spending so much time learning and planning, she'd been sleeping more soundly too, a nice extra. Of course, there were moments she couldn't get to sleep because her mind churned fearfully about her upcoming interviews with CEOs.

She had seen a new light in Linley's eyes today. Could it be that simply by nerving herself to make the effort to help people, she was on track to win back her daughter's long-absent respect and affection? Oh, if only that could be true.

She should call Dorothy and brag. See if her mother had gotten up early to watch the show. Linley had said she would call her grandmother to alert her.

As soon as she got home, she called on the landline. It had better sound than the cell phone, and never dropped a call, either. The phone rang and rang, and finally Dorothy answered in a breathless tone.

"Hi, Mom. Did I wake you?" It was two p.m. Had Dorothy been napping because she'd been up early?

"No, of course not." Her voice was stronger now. "Don't be silly, Pamela."

"Did you watch us on TV again?"

"Yes, and you looked straight into the camera. That was good. The audience takes it to mean you are honest."

"I'm glad. If I go on some program by myself to pitch the foundation, I'll want the viewers to trust me."

"They will, dear," her mother assured her, but in a distracted tone of voice. There was some noise and interruption, and then Dorothy came back on the line. "It's time for me to go walking with Yappie and that nice young man next door."

Was he truly nice? Why was he spending so much time with her mother, anyway? Dorothy was a fascinating person, of course. Perhaps Bruce simply missed his family and his friends, and wanted company.

"You mean Bruce? You're still going on that daily walk together?"

"Why not?" her mother's voice came through rather sharply as if to ask why Pam was daring to question her.

"I...uh...I, oh, forget it," she said, backing down. "Enjoy your walk, Mom."

"I shall. Bruce is here now. He says hello. He wants to know when you're coming out here again."

Oh, dear. Trust her mother to put her in an awkward spot.

"I'm not sure. I'll be busy starting the foundation."

"You'll have weekends off," Dorothy said in her usual magisterial manner. She launched into a lecture about how charities built slowly and weekend events rested on the shoulders of volunteers, which Pam did not yet have beyond Magda and Harper. It took time to build an organization. She concluded by pressing Pam to come out that weekend. "We can strategize together."

Pam didn't see any way of refusing to see her mother, so she agreed and hung up. After all, Alexander had moved away. The rest of Dorothy's children couldn't ignore their mother. At least, she couldn't. Even though at the moment she certainly did not want to encounter Bruce. Which would be inevitable if she went

251

to the beach house.

No time to fret over that. She should check her email for the info from Linley, and get started with more calls to set up appointments.

#

Knowing her brother Alexander spent his afternoons on the golf course, she waited until evening to call him. They had to talk about Dorothy's future. Alexander raved over their new life in North Carolina, and all the new friends they had made. Turned out there were many transplants from the New York area.

"You've moved to another version of New York South?"

"Looks like it. Edie is thrilled."

After enough time had been spent on catching up, she had to ask her question. "Alexander, why haven't we got a family plan for taking care of our mother as she gets older?"

When he seemed to hem and haw, she pressed harder. "You lived nearest to her for years. You saw her more often than any of us."

He sighed. "Edie tells me we moved south because I didn't want to see Mom decline."

"That's why you left the state?" she asked, shocked.

"Maybe." He rushed to explain. "Pammy, Mom and I have been real close. It's a struggle to be far from her now. But there's a part of me that's relieved not to be around to see her go downhill."

"How can you be relieved if you've left your elderly mother all alone way out on Long Island?"

"She's not alone. She's got good friends."

"Her friends are old, too. They can't look after her welfare."

"I did my share. It's someone else's turn. Probably yours."

"I live a hundred miles away, hardly next door."

"You could sell your house and move in with her."

"You're kidding. She thinks I'm weak and stupid. Living with her would be hell."

He said nothing.

"Alexander, we need a plan. You didn't consult any of us. That's not right."

"What's wrong with moving in with her? You don't have anything keeping you in Ardsley. You're not working in the city anymore, either."

"How did you learn about that?"

"I call Mom every day. She told me you got canned."

Ooh, she wanted to hit something. "Yet you didn't even call me after the company collapsed to ask how I was doing. Thanks much, big brother."

"Look, quit whining. You're not hurting for money. And Mom is fine. She'll probably live to be a hundred."

"What's our plan if she can't handle her financial affairs? What if she gets dementia? What if she takes a fall and breaks her hip?"

"Then you move in with her and take care of things."

She let out an exasperated breath. "Don't think I am going to let you do this to me, Alexander. These aren't Victorian times, when unmarried daughters had to sacrifice their lives to nurse their elderly parents."

"Okay, make a plan, but leave me out of it. It's someone else's turn." His voice was determined. "There's enough money to hire a nurse companion. The real issue is someone has to keep watch on the nurse companion. I can't do it. I've had enough."

With that she had to be satisfied. Her phone calls to her two other siblings, Christine in Chicago and Neil in Santa Fe, were even less satisfactory. They were full of vague offers of help but no concrete ideas other than to hire a companion some day. That wasn't a plan, even if it was one leg of a potential plan.

She wasn't even sure why she was getting worked up over this. She'd been angry with Bruce for suggesting Dorothy needed assistance. She'd been suspicious of him befriending her mother, too. Come to think of it, she still was. Oh, he wasn't likely to be a con artist. She'd Googled him and found nothing negative. He was the real Bruce Wicklow, too. Google images had provided publicity photos from his book tour.

Maybe it was because she sensed there was more going on out at the beach. She didn't want to take on the additional work of finding out what it was. She had her hands full with the nonprofit. Although, since by maternal decree she was about to go out there for the weekend, she guessed she'd learn more despite herself.

She'd have to call Alexander another time and apologize for whining to him and then accusing him of running away. The truth was he and his wife had carried all the responsibility for their mother for many years. He had provided companionship and a place for holiday gatherings so the work was taken off Dorothy's shoulders. Of course, he and Dorothy got along well. Dorothy considered him a success. Whereas she thought Pam was an oversensitive weakling, and told her so far too often. Not as much lately, though.

#

Bruce paced his deck and thought up ways he might cajole Pam into talking to him when they met again this weekend. Or perhaps he should go on the offensive and insist she talk to him. She was a sensible woman. Once he explained more, he was sure she would get off her high horse and listen to reason. He doubted she would deny the evidence in front of her face, starting with those piles of unopened mail in Dorothy's dining room.

He tossed a toy for Yappie, who eagerly sprang to retrieve it. He was fun to have around, good company. Bruce was glad he had found Yappie, even if his main purpose in getting the dog was to cozy up to Dorothy. Aunt Nora had reminded him Dorothy was the one who had given him a puppy for his fourth birthday. Of course he had been too young for a puppy, but his mother hadn't minded, according to Nora. Greta had wanted to give her little boy a companion. He had probably cried more over Puppy's eventual death than he did over his parents'.

Yappie had not returned the toy this time, his way of indicating he was tired of retrieving. Bruce sat on one of the deck chairs under the umbrella. Yappie came and nestled at his feet, resting his head on Bruce's left shoe. Good dog.

Strange how life was. He'd come full circle, depending on a dog for his companionship. Things could be worse, but he wanted more. Pam must be soothed, talked out of her snit, whatever it took. She was what he wanted. In bed and out.

Chapter 22

Pam sent Sarah a digital photo of the Chanel suit. Sarah called her up and raved.

"I've got to come see it in person. I want to feel it."

"You can try it on, too," she offered. "I suspect it'll be too big for you. Back in the day, women were more rounded."

"Chanel, girl. It's a classic. I'm coming right over."

Of course it took Sarah a couple hours since she lived in Manhattan. To Pam's surprise, her friend arrived with a large piece of soft luggage. When she unzipped it, Pam saw it was an elaborate shoe carrier.

"Christian Louboutin, Jimmy Choo, Manolo Blahnik, Prada, take your pick. We're still the same shoe size, just like we were in college. But first, let me see the Chanel."

Pam led the way to her bedroom closet and opened the garment bag.

Sarah touched the pink suit with reverence. "Oh, this is beautiful. How marvelous. Look at the detail work. Look at the seaming. Exquisite bouclé. It's in perfect condition."

"I didn't realize you had an interest in vintage clothing,"

Pam remarked.

Sarah laughed. "I never thought there was any point in talking to you about clothes, since you're the girl who wore loafers and bargain store blouses to work on Wall Street."

"I guess I have to care now. My mother says it's very important to dress rich when trying to extract money from rich men."

"She's right. Look what I brought you. Shoes to go with. You have to wear good shoes. The secretaries always look at your shoes, and they're the key to getting in to see the boss."

Sarah, bless her, had also brought a simple black dress with a boat neck, suitable for knocking on doors and setting up important appointments.

"Wear this with gold or diamonds. Nothing else."

Pam was outfitted for the battles to come, with her mother and her best friend as her armorers. She hoped she could do them proud.

#

Expensive designer clothing truly made a difference when she was bearding the lions in their dens. She was treated with far more courtesy than her usual self-effacing personality merited. Which made her feed good. Which helped when she had to listen politely to the self-absorbed, self-satisfied men she was trying to flatter and guilt into donating large chunks of money.

She tried hard to maintain her calm during her interview with Frank Cox, an appointment she'd managed to get very quickly, almost too quickly to suit her. She didn't have her patter down yet. Perhaps he had agreed to see her immediately because he was so thoroughly hated these days no one else wanted to talk to him. She laughed inwardly at her cynical notion. How her interests were changing. Before, she'd never have bothered to consider what executives did with their time, or how they thought.

He had a huge corner office in a posh executive suite, but she knew for a fact he did nothing all day. No one called him. His name was anathema in the banking community since he had single-handedly dragged his company into bankruptcy. The terms of his golden parachute gave him this office high in a building now two-thirds empty solely because of him.

They were seated in a sitting room section of the vast office, drinking tea. Cox was in a club chair, she perched on the couch. She wore the pink Chanel suit.

Cox had started with the moral hazard of giving unemployed people charity. Then he wandered into a rant about the cost of workers being very high.

She paid respectful attention, allowing none of her distaste to show. She let him run on. Now, he was denying that displaced workers should rely on charity.

"We have to cut operating costs to shore up the bottom line."

That didn't apply to already laid-off workers, but it was probably taken verbatim from his last speech before he was ousted. He had fired twenty-five thousand low-paid workers, then awarded himself a thirty million dollar bonus. She struggled to keep her expression pleasant and blandly accepting. She knew she had to wait for him to give her an opening. Ah, there it was. He wanted to know why she planned to help workers.

"The purpose of this charity is to help displaced workers before they get over their heads, Mr. Cox. Sometimes it only takes a little bit of cash to keep an entire lifestyle going until the worker finds another good job. This is short-term help, kind of like a bridge loan."

He nodded. He understood loans. He had leveraged his company with them until he'd destroyed it.

"I wish you well, of course, but I don't see where the valued added is in this for me," he said.

Now she had him.

"Sir, the public wants heroes. You could be one." She stared at him solemnly. "Your name could be a beacon of hope to the many people who are suffering economically in these tough times. By associating your name with this charity, by committing substantial funding to it, you will gain deserved prestige in the community. And you will do a world of good."

He visibly preened. She explained how his multimillion dollar ongoing commitment to the Bright Side Foundation would be picked up as news. The larger his gift was, the more news it would receive.

The hook was set. Now all she had to do was reel him in, as she had seen her mother do many times. These self-important men lived on flattery.

"People will praise your name for this," she began, wondering why God didn't strike her dead for her lies.

Within a half an hour, he had authorized his secretary to transfer a half a million dollars to the Bright Side Foundation, with a promise for a half million more during the next year. Pam hid her shock over the realization he had so much cash readily available in a bank account. Now that he'd done his part to destabilize the stock market, maybe he was keeping all his wealth as cash.

She kept her game face on, channeling Dorothy's most patrician, self-assured style. "This is wonderful of you. I will make sure the world knows about your amazing generosity. Your name will go down in history as a great benefactor of humanity."

She made many more fulsome expressions of gratitude. In truth, she was sincerely thankful he had chosen to donate. Not only had he made her day, but she had made his. The publicity his donation would generate would do something to restore his tarnished reputation. She left him to his dreams of renewed glory and went with his secretary to arrange the fund transfer details.

Pam could see the woman was eyeing her Chanel suit. She fought the urge to confess she was playing dress-up in her mother's clothes. Thank goodness Sarah had brought her the designer shoes as well. Ordinary shoes would have been a dead giveaway. As Dorothy always said, you had to have money to get money. Her mother was right as usual.

Her second interview that week did not go as well. She was led to an executive suite in the same building in which she had worked for many years. The very same building she'd thought never to enter again. The executive was the former head of her own company, Charles Saunders, the man who had put her out on the street along with Magda and thousands more. He recognized her name, but not from her long employment at Menahl.

"Are you related to Linley Ridgeway, the girl on that stock market show on cable, *Hot Tracks*?" he asked, with a frown.

"She's my daughter," she replied proudly.

"She ripped me a new one when they interviewed me two weeks ago. I'm not giving you a cent," he said with vindictive pleasure.

A nasty man. The former Pam would have apologetically skulked off at this point, but there was too much at stake. She dug in her heels and did her best to turn the tables on him.

"I'm sorry to hear that," she said, in as sincere a tone of voice as she could muster. "You'll be missing a golden opportunity." She widened her eyes and leaned forward confidingly. "In one simple step, you can fix your public image, take a tax deduction, and help thousands of your own former employees."

He didn't react to that feeler, so she tried a slightly different tack. The employee gossip pipeline had claimed he desperately wanted to go into politics.

"I suspect you know that influential politicians are careful not to associate with public figures who have tarnished reputations," she offered.

His smug hostility began to fade into a frown.

"You're proud of being a strong figure, a take-no-prisoners business leader, am I right?"

He nodded his head impatiently. "Get to your point, girlie."

Girlie?

"Politicians who might have major regulatory positions to award will be able to consider you for those spots only if you repair your image. They'll get heat from their constituents otherwise. When you're at your confirmation hearings, you can

261

point to your efforts to help the workers who lost their jobs during your watch. Donating to the Bright Side Foundation is an opportunity for you to stop being vilified as a public bad guy. By openly associating yourself with a high-profile charity that will actively seek to aid displaced workers, you can navigate a serious political stumbling block. It's a solid gold recommendation for your future. You can win the support you want."

Because she suspected there was no limit to his self-absorption, she tried a new line of flattery. "Your former employees still care about you. If you help them, they will bless your name and put you in their prayers."

"Not likely," he harrumphed, but she could sense he had softened.

She wasted a lot of time with Saunders trying to get a sizeable donation. She had not left empty-handed, but Saunders had only given her a check in the five figures. He was mistaken if he thought she could restore his public reputation with such a small contribution.

She wouldn't give up. If she succeeded with more of his peers, Saunders's competitive urges might take over. She'd keep him informed about her pledge drive. Maybe drop him a note about Mr. Cox's contribution once it was in the foundation's bank account.

She was proud she had given as good as she got. There was still hope Saunders would come around to her point of view. Plus, she had learned so much. It was unlikely she would be talking to any man quite as personally hostile as this one had been. She had a feeling her suit of armor had kept at bay some of his worst qualities. Thank goodness.

Her mother's designer clothing had given her ironclad self-confidence when she'd needed it. She had felt invulnerable. No longer was she the simple backroom worker with a sweater on her chair because the office was often too cold. No longer was she the mindless cog in the machine. She had woken up. Although she did not respect Saunders, she supposed she owed him a debt of gratitude. She had finally been forced to act as a bigger version of herself. She liked that person. A lot.

She hardly recognized herself in the mirrorlike glass walls of the building's lobby. This soignée woman with the designer suit and shoes, the soft leather briefcase, the subtle makeup and jewelry, was an altogether much more polished package than the usual Pam Ridgeway. Her obscenely expensive designer shoes were remarkably comfortable. She glanced down at them. This new role wasn't easy, but she could get used to some aspects.

She must have absorbed a lot of her mother's teachings over the years to be so effective and wily with these men. Her mother's sharp eye for an opponent had translated into Pam feeling an intuitive sense of each man's weakness. For the one man, it was his vanity. For the other, his greed. It helped to have done her homework, and to have had Linley's notes on each man's reputation. The Bright Side Foundation already had substantial cash to show for her efforts, with more promised. The promise alone would generate more donations from people who wanted to be allied with Mr. Cox, who wanted their names listed on the same page with his name as a contributor. Whether anyone wanted to be near Charles Saunders was still an open question. She intended that he pay heavily to sweeten his name.

Thank goodness her mother had bullied her into taking the Chanel suit. It had made all the difference in her confidence level. Especially when confronting that unrepentant toad who had made billions off her hard work and the work of others, and then let them all lose their security. She was surprised she hadn't surged up from her seat and slapped him.

The funny thing was how well she was channeling Jackie Kennedy while wearing the Chanel suit. There had been a museum show dedicated to her a few years ago. At it, Pam had seen the letters the First Lady had written to convince powerful men to donate large amounts of money or priceless items. It was surprising how simple the letters were, appealing without subtlety to the men's egotism. Pam had followed that exact prescription when claiming a donation to the Bright Side Foundation would cause the public to bless this man's name. These fatuous men wanted to believe that they could be vicious and beloved at the same time. Soon each man would write his memoirs, recalling his glory days of firing huge numbers of employees, and driving up the company's share price, and his own performance bonus. History might or might not contradict them. Meanwhile, she would get as much of their money as she could. Their donations would bring her foundation free publicity, and help launch it. She had to be careful to make sure that these men didn't get their names too well associated with it, though, or try to claim that they were instrumental in the charity's efficacy.

As for finding people worthy of receiving help, it was almost too easy. They would find her, no doubt. She'd need assistance sorting them out. Employees. Oh, she had plans.

Right now, she had to return to her other identity, that of a middle-aged woman whose mother could still act as a puppet master, and who had demanded her presence at her home this weekend.

Chapter 23

Jason and Linley were in a conference room at the studio, talking over the ad for their new show. Neutral territory. He'd gotten a batch of files together for a possible clip show. They'd already hashed over and rejected a dozen concepts.

Finally, he suggested, "How about a retrospective, a 'When Jason was hired, he came on strong,' and then show me supposedly younger, with a stupid wig and bad hair and bad clothes, arguing with the guy auditioning me. Then switch to me now, arguing until the producer tells the cameraman to cut to a commercial."

"Then do the same for me," Linley said, enthusiasm lighting her eyes. "There I am, wearing nineties hair or something to suggest youth and inexperience, and a college T-shirt. The same thing happens. We both argue with the guys conducting the employment audition. We won't let them shut us up. Then a voiceover that we were a pair made for each other in heaven— or hell.

"I like it," she said. "Let's run it by Marty tomorrow. Good night." She gathered up her notes to toss in her bag.

"Wait a minute. You're going home? We finally got the idea." He looked at her as if she was being annoying. She was.

"Yeah, well. I've had a long day and I'm done. See you."

"Wait, Linley. Let's go out to dinner and talk about it some more."

"Nope. That's Marty's fantasy, not mine," she said. Her own fantasy had them in bed, but she wasn't telling Jason. He'd hop on that idea in a minute.

#

The next day, they argued again, but nobody minded. They were doing a sample episode in a new set, debating the world price of oil and what Americans could do about it.

"We shouldn't be dependent on oil produced by nations that hate us and want us dead," Jason said.

He'd said that previously on the other show. Now, Linley had the go-ahead to argue with him.

"You're wrong about our oil suppliers," she said, no compromise in her tone. "Canada is the single biggest source of our imported oil, Jason," she replied. "Look at this chart." She threw up a list of major oil suppliers to the U.S.

"You're missing the point, Linley. If you add Saudi Arabia and Venezuela together, they total more. Both countries have anti-democratic political systems."

She rolled her eyes. "We import more oil from Mexico than we do from Venezuela. Mexico likes us so much, all its citizens try to come here to live," she said provocatively, hoping he'd fall into her trap.

He sidestepped. "Nice try, but you won't drag me into an

immigration debate. We're talking about oil." He waved his hand to dismiss the topic.

"Ignore the truth, Jason, but you're being a bigot. Saudi Arabia is our firm ally."

Jason raised an eyebrow. "You've drunk the Kool-Aid. We're on track to need more and more oil. We can't continue in that direction, especially with anti-American regimes."

"You're dead wrong," she said, showing exasperation. "They're not anti-American."

And they were off, threading every comment with a put-down of the other's stance. Doing exactly the opposite of acting courteous and collegial, in fact.

Marty came up to them afterwards.

"Good, good. This is exactly what I want. Let's get in some experts for each of your positions. We want more ammunition on each side."

"Then we fight to a standstill?" Jason asked.

"Maybe," Marty allowed. "Do you two ever agree on anything?"

Jason blinked. He answered at random. "Occasionally. Right, Linley?"

She'd bet his mind was where it shouldn't be, remembering that night last year.

"We both agree we like pizza," she said brightly. She wanted to appear alert and happy and cooperative in front of Marty. Although she was sure he saw right through her compliant act. Her basic acerbity always peeped through when she was around Jason. Come to think of it, that mean streak of hers was what Marty was rewarding with this show. It also was useful in fending off the comments of her fellow panelists, now that Marty had broken the news about their new pairing.

"I knew you had something going with Jason," Ernie said, stopping by her cubicle a few minutes later.

"Oh, right," she scoffed, relieved that now he took it to be professional, not personal. "How'd you guess?"

"You two never agree on anything. But you're always looking at each other."

Uh-oh. Ernie was more aware than she had thought. Time to brazen it out.

"You need to know what the enemy is doing," she replied, adding a conniving smile. Would Ernie buy it?

"Yeah, guess so," he agreed. Seeing he couldn't get a rise out of her, he gave up and walked on.

Did Jason look at her all the time? She kept track of him, for sure. She'd tried to be surreptitious, but obviously had not succeeded. Ernie said Jason looked at her. Maybe Jason was more interested in her than he wanted to admit.

Then Jason strolled by. Her cubicle was an outer one, basically next to a hallway. She looked up, and he looked in at her at the same moment.

"We made a good start today," he said, stopping near her as she sat contemplating a financial chart.

She leaned back to look at him as she asked, "Do you think we can last?" It was a double-edged question, referencing everything that had gone between them previously, and everything they both lusted for now but were attempting to hold off taking from each other.

Jason acknowledged the implied question, but spoke as

cautiously as she had. Cubicle walls were an illusion. They knew others were listening.

"If there's a basic philosophical divide, we'll naturally hold opposing views. On whatever issue comes up," he added.

What was his view of a non-romance? A backward-growing relationship that seemed to be getting closer and closer as each day passed? There was something tremendously intimate about the two of them being on this show, alone. Even with six other people physically in the studio helping produce it and the wide world watching on air.

"Lunch?" he asked.

It probably wasn't wise, but now people would assume they were planning their show. "Okay."

Jason flashed his million-watt smile and she found she was smiling back. Then he recalled himself. "Meet you at noon." He continued on his way.

Whew. That was too good. What if someone had walked by and seen them grinning at each other like lovesick fools? Lovesick? She ought to email him to cancel lunch. She even started to compose it. She closed the document without saving. She'd go to lunch with Jason if she wanted to, the rest of the world be damned.

Chapter 24

Pam arrived at the beach house feeling good about herself, better than in a long time. Although she was confused about what, if anything, she felt about Bruce.

His phone call had made her so angry. His claim that her mother had dementia. How could it be true?

They had seemed to be building something, but then she had drawn back emotionally. He'd never put much of himself out there to begin with. She wondered if he even realized their lovemaking didn't have much spark because they were both keeping emotion far out of it. She would ignore her doubts unless he wanted to talk about their relationship, though. It was not her first priority at the moment. Enjoying physical closeness again was her objective for now.

Did her mother have any more power outfits hiding in her closet? Why didn't Pam remember her mother wearing the Chanel suit? Wasn't she paying any attention years ago? Or had Dorothy only worn it at a time when Pam wasn't around? She remembered the lessons on strategy over family dinners long ago. Dorothy would tell Malcolm her latest plan, and he would critique it carefully and render his opinion based on his many years of working in a competitive male environment. Although Malcolm never took part in any of Dorothy's protests and actions, his advice was invaluable. His experience, added to Dorothy's shrewd understanding of people and her brassy courage, made a strong combination.

"Hi, Mom," she called as she went inside. The front door had been unlocked as usual. Her mother was sitting in what was her favorite room these days, the sunroom. She didn't appear to be doing anything. She was cocooned in the padded wicker chair.

What a great change from the Dorothy of old. Before, she would have been surrounded by press releases, papers of all sorts, and magazines and newsletters. Her Rolodex and a pad and pen would have been at hand on the nearby table. Plus the phone, which she would be using constantly to call her troops or hector some unsuspecting public official. She had been so successful at it over the years that one phone call from her often would effect an immediate policy change. The person Dorothy pressured knew she would follow through with the maximum adverse publicity. It wasn't worth the risk.

That was all over now, and yet her mother didn't seem to miss it. She seldom referred to her career as an activist. She'd had a retirement party two years ago when she'd turned eighty-five, and that was that. She'd handed the reins to others and hadn't been involved in any public affairs since.

Was Bruce correct? Was her mother now experiencing memory deficits? There had been no evidence of it during her recent visits. Except for asking about jerk chicken at that restaurant. Her mother always made perfect sense on the phone.

"How are you?" she asked. "Bruce told me he found you a little confused in town the other day when you went in for your hair appointment. What happened?"

Her mother looked at her blankly. "I haven't the faintest idea what you're talking about. I haven't left the house all week."

"But Bruce said—"

"You misunderstood." Her mother's brisk tone made it clear she was not going to waste any more time on the topic. "Now tell me why you're back so soon."

"You're the one who wanted me to come, remember?" How strange. Her mother had insisted Pam come visit this weekend. This was disorienting. For now, she would ask about something else.

"Do you have any other designer clothes I could borrow?"

"Oh, of course. Come along." Dorothy rose in her usual commanding manner and bustled to her bedroom and the walk-in closet Pam was beginning to think was an Aladdin's treasure cave.

"The Chanel suit you lent me was amazing, Mom. It gave me confidence. I got a five hundred thousand dollar donation and a commitment for five hundred thousand more from Frank Cox. I even had an interview with Charles Saunders, the man who fired everybody where I used to work."

"Did you get a donation from him, too?"

"A tiny one. Only twenty thousand dollars. I have high hopes he'll kick in more at a later date."

"That's not good enough, Pamela," her mother said. "You have to close the deal at the first meeting. You may never get more than one chance with each person or company."

Couldn't her mother just celebrate her success with her? Be happy with whatever Pam had managed to achieve? Instead of being critical because she hadn't done a lot more?

"I did the best I could. He started off mad at me because of Linley."

"Why?"

"Apparently she raked him over the coals on her television program."

"Good for her," her mother said.

"In this case, I tend to agree with you. He's a bad man."

"Still, a bad man's money spends like anyone else's."

"I'm hoping so. I personally think he'll come around. I'm going to send him a follow-up letter."

Dorothy shook her head. "That won't do it."

Pam's face fell.

Dorothy patted her on the shoulder. "We'll let it be for now." She zipped open another garment bag and carefully pulled out a black dress.

Pam was inclined to dwell on her mother's criticism. Her shoulders had hunched defensively even before Dorothy patted her. The sight of the dress completely chased those feelings away.

"Ohhh." The classic little black dress. It was sophisticated, draped, and meant for a woman with a perfect figure. Which Pam did not have.

"Dior," Dorothy said.

Pam turned from admiring the dress to stare at her mother. "Where did you get these? I don't remember you wearing them."

"Your father knew someone in the garment trade. I was able to get couture at a steep discount."

Of course. Her mother would never have paid full price. That was admitting she was a tourist, not a real New Yorker.

"This isn't as forgiving a cut as the suit. I don't know if it will fit."

"Nonsense. If I could wear it, you can."

Pam took off her casual suburban pants and top. She'd removed her jacket when she came inside. She looked for a back zipper on the Dior. There was none.

"Here. There's a side zipper," Dorothy said, "under the arm, where it isn't noticeable."

With her mother's help, she wiggled into the dress. It was snug, but it fit correctly around the key curves. When she looked at herself in the mirror, she saw a sophisticated woman. She could imagine how a string of good pearls or some diamond stud earrings would complete the look. And a pair of Sarah's delicately made shoes. Which she should be buying for herself from now on.

"I admit it. I'm sold." This dress would be effective ammunition in her battle to wrest money out of corporate fat cats.

"Might as well have the pearls to go with it," her mother said, and opened a drawer. She pulled out a jeweler's box and offered it to Pam.

"Go on. Open it."

Pam tentatively reached out. Inside the box was a double string of cream colored pearls. Real. "Oh, I couldn't," she said.

"You need them to complete the Dior." Dorothy said,

impatient at Pam's hesitation. "Go on. Take them."

"I'll return them," Pam said.

"Don't bother. I have no more use for them."

"If you're sure…"

After that, she tried on everything in her mother's closet. Dorothy was specific about which garments Pam should wear in the city, which were strictly for the outlying suburbs. Dorothy never mentioned the boroughs. To her New York was Manhattan.

After their hour of playing with clothes, her mother was tired. Pam took a look in the refrigerator, and found the pickings tonight were slim. Of course. Tomorrow was the day the local deli restocked. She didn't feel like making a meal of leftovers, or going to a restaurant when she'd driven so far today.

"How about we order some Chinese takeout? I'm not in the mood to cook."

"That sounds delightful."

Dorothy opened a drawer, and Pam found a stack of menus inside, but none for a Chinese restaurant.

"Oh, dear. I guess we could order Italian instead," Pam said.

"No, I'd like Chinese," Dorothy said. "Go next door and borrow a menu."

"I wouldn't want to bother Bruce," she replied. She wasn't ready to confront him.

"Nonsense." Dorothy gave Pam an exasperated look, telegraphing her impatience with Pam's too-sensitive feelings. Dorothy might not know what had passed between Pam and Bruce, but Pam's reluctance made Dorothy all the more determined to insist Pam do as she'd told her. Dorothy had always been that way. She had no truck with playing to the overly sensitive feelings of her youngest child.

"Go on, ask him. Invite him to dinner, too. If you're going to be mulish, I'd enjoy some additional company, Pamela."

Pam winced at the way Dorothy pronounced her full name. So much for a more peaceful relationship.

Her feet dragged as she obeyed, but she eventually covered the distance to Bruce's deck. Bruce looked pleased on finding her knocking on his door.

"Pam. Are you here for the weekend?"

"Yes. We want to order in Chinese food. Do you have a menu?" She tried to keep her words curt, even though something inside had immediately softened on seeing him.

"Come on in. I'll get it." He motioned her in. He didn't attempt to kiss her. He must have sensed her still-cool feelings toward him. She followed him. He had a pile of menus by the kitchen phone.

"Let me order it. Seems like I owe you ladies a meal, anyway. Why don't you bring Dorothy over here? I'll even spring for real plates. Later, you and I can talk."

Oh, he was clever. Without committing himself, he was luring her in again. She could have refused on Dorothy's behalf, although there was no genuine reason to. Dorothy would enjoy being Bruce's guest. Part of Pam wanted to be with Bruce despite everything.

"All right. I'll find out what she wants." She gave him a rather harried look and departed with the menu.

Bruce was cleaning up his umbrella table and chairs as she returned. "Okay if we eat out here?"

She handed him the marked up menu and nodded. There was plenty of sunlight left and it was warm out.

"It's Friday night. Figure an hour for delivery."

It was raining a little when Bruce phoned that the food had arrived. They scurried across the back deck to his kitchen door. Pam breathed a secret sigh of relief as he ushered them into his dining room. Dorothy would never have said anything, but she thought of kitchens as where the help ate.

Dorothy remarked, "These furnishings look familiar."

"They should. I'm renting from your old neighbors." At Pam's enquiring look, he shrugged. "I'd never lived near a beach before and wasn't sure if I'd like it. Thought I'd give it a try before buying."

"Sensible," Dorothy said. "I've seen many people buy homes here who imagined they would enjoy the ocean. It takes a certain kind of person. Some do not last long."

"Oh, Mom," Pam said. "You're not exactly roughing it on the frontier here anymore."

Although the houses along this stretch of beach were not ostentatious, they weren't affordable to people of modest means. The locals whose families had lived in the area for many decades or even centuries weren't foolish enough to live directly on the ocean. Being on the beach required constant major repairs, and only rich people could afford them.

Before her mother could crush her with a counter-argument, Bruce deflected her with a question.

"You've had hurricanes and rogue high tides?"

"We have indeed, young man," Dorothy replied, and launched into tales of past storms.

Later, Dorothy ostentatiously said goodnight and insisted on going home on her own. "The rain has stopped. I'm not likely to get lost walking fifty feet," she joked, pointing at the well-marked path between his deck and her side door that led into her kitchen.

Bruce and Pam's eyes met as each remembered the source of their quarrel, Dorothy's recent adventure in town. He cleared his throat. Pam stared at her feet. At the continued silence, Dorothy gave them a briefly baffled look and left.

When Pam moved to follow her mother, Bruce said, "We need to talk."

"I don't want to hear more of your wild notions." She spoke quietly, as he did, so her mother wouldn't hear as she walked away.

"I apologize about my phone call."

"For which part? Claiming my mother has Alzheimer's or hanging up on me?" She nearly hissed the last words.

As she made to leave again, he moved to get between her and the door, then obviously thought better of it. He paused only inches from her. Pam's breathing accelerated. Because he was so close? Or because she was angry at him? Their bodies were nearly touching. If either of them moved a little, they could be embracing. Her heart started to pound. She looked up into his face and saw his thoughts had followed hers. His eyes were focused on her lips.

She dragged herself back from the precipice. "Bruce," she whispered.

"What?" He sounded distracted.

"I'm leaving now."

"You are?" She could feel his warm breath on her ear. Oh, this was not good. Then his arms surrounded and enfolded her. Her breasts settled against his chest, sending a tingle down inside her body to the part where she wanted more of him.

She forced herself to step out of his embrace. "If we keep on this way, we won't talk."

"Would that be so terrible?" he asked.

"You're wrong about my mother."

Bruce gave her a disappointed look and then made a frustrated turn around his kitchen before saying, "Okay, don't believe me. But be on the alert for the signs."

She sighed. "I do believe you care about her and are sincere."

#

If only that were completely true. He squirmed inwardly, knowing he was keeping something important from Pam and knowing he would eventually pay for doing so. But not now.

"Will you come back later, after your mother retires for the night?" he asked. He couldn't keep his voice from sounding hopeful. Pam gazed at him, wide-eyed. He didn't like that she still seemed poised for flight.

"Uh…it's been a long day," she practically stuttered.

He cocked his head. "No?"

She rushed into speech. "It's—" she paused, obviously searching for the right words, "I think maybe we got ahead of ourselves. We don't know each other very well yet."

"We'll talk. Anything else is up to you," he promised.

She nodded at last. "All right." Then she scuttled off.

He wondered if she would return after all.

Chapter 25

Pam did not return to Bruce that night. She wasn't sure why. Had his notion that her mother was declining mentally soured her on their relationship? No. He meant well. He happened to be wrong, that was all. She was over being angry at him for his mistake.

Something else was happening. Pam felt she was changing, getting stronger. She didn't want to be confused in the midst of such change by a relationship with a man.

Sex was overrated. Or maybe the truth was she had no great interest in sex that wasn't a celebration of deep emotions. She and Bruce hardly knew each other, and he had never offered any significant insights into what made him tick. She hadn't confided much herself, either. They had been too distracted by their immediate sexual attraction. Just like this evening. A mistake to go down that road without knowing the whole man.

She called him. "I'm sorry," she whispered, when he picked up. "I've had a long day and I'm going to sleep now."

"I'm sorry, too," he replied, but didn't try to argue with her. Of course after that, she couldn't sleep for hours.

The next morning, she was up bright and early, and her mind wasn't on Bruce. Her immediate goal was to tackle the piles of mail and papers in the dining room. Her mother had claimed she would get to them, but the stacks kept getting taller. Surely, with Pam's help, Dorothy could go through it all and they could have the dining room in usable shape again?

Breakfast went fine, but when Pam broached the subject of the mail, things went downhill. "No, I do not want to go over all those papers today, Pamela. I have better things to do with my time." Dorothy spoke in her usual decisive tone.

"Like what? What else is on your schedule? I'm here and I can help you. Let's do it."

They went around and around. Dorothy finally said, "This is not your house, Pamela, and I have not given you the right to interfere in my affairs. I am perfectly capable of handling them myself." Then she stalked away to the sunroom and sat in her favorite chair. She turned her face to the water and seemed to ignore Pam from then on. Pam was left with a choice of carrying the battle to an extreme, or subsiding. She shut up.

She wandered around for a few minutes, fussing with the furniture, straightening and neatening. Then Dorothy seemed to doze off.

Why should Pam take her mother's refusal as law? Pam wasn't a child. She quietly picked up a batch of unopened mail and retired upstairs to her bedroom. Maybe if her mother could not see her, and didn't have to do anything about the mail herself, it wouldn't cause further strife.

Oh, lord. The top letter was from the power commission. Because of nonpayment, the electricity would be cut off on Monday.

She couldn't approach her mother, especially considering her recent attitude. Dorothy would snap at her. She picked up the phone and called the power company, hoping someone was there on a weekend.

"We need your mother's permission before we can discuss her account with you," the customer service rep said.

"I can't get that right now," she replied. What to do? She explained the situation. "I don't know what's going on. My mother is very elderly. Maybe she forgot to pay this bill."

The rep was sympathetic, but adamant she could not discuss the details of the account without Dorothy's permission. She suggested Pam could get a power of attorney.

"I can't get a power of attorney over a weekend. What can I do now, today? I don't want you to shut off the lights."

"Why don't you pay it yourself?"

"How much does she...ah, let me rephrase that. How much should I pay today to keep the power on for the next month?"

The rep named a figure of several hundred dollars, explaining it was the equivalent to three month's bills under ordinary circumstances. She also suggested Pam set up automatic bill paying. "If you mother has regular income and direct deposit, you can schedule a payment automatically every month."

She got more details from the rep, then pulled out one of her credit cards from her purse to make an immediate payment by phone. The rep kindly waived the usual service charge, and even said that Pam should call and ask for her specifically by name once she obtained her mother's power of attorney.

"You're a good daughter," the phone rep said. "I hope

everything works out for you."

Pam hung up with the feeling she had averted a major disaster. Now she was afraid to look at what the next envelopes held. She was beginning to get an idea of what they must be.

After an hour, she found things were not quite as bad as she'd imagined. Her mother was from the generation that seldom used credit cards. There were no horrific statements from Mastercard or Visa with outstanding balances subjected to usurious finance charges and penalties. At least, not in this pile.

Dorothy was behind on important payments, not the least of which were the annual real estate taxes. They were late, but the house hadn't been sold at tax auction yet. Yet. Pam shuddered. What if she hadn't come out here this weekend?

She heard the kitchen doorbell ring and roused herself. Dorothy had heard it too, and was already there, accepting the weekly food delivery from the young woman. The girl was well trained. She went straight to the refrigerator and pulled out all the old food and replaced it with the new. Then she examined the leftovers.

"I'll take this little bit of chicken," she said to Dorothy. "It's still good, but rather dry."

Dorothy agreed. "Please get rid of it."

That was why there was no old, moldy food in the fridge. The delivery girl cleaned it out each week. It took an extra five minutes, but the girl knew the drill. She efficiently checked all the prior week's containers. Seeing Pam had come in, she explained. "We always remove the expired food. That way, your mom can't get sick by eating spoiled potato salad. Some people don't notice the sell by dates."

Her mother meanwhile was writing out a check, which she handed the girl, along with a nice cash tip. Ah, that was why there was no overdue food bill in the stack Pam had reviewed. They said goodbye to the girl, who even took the spoiled food with her.

Dorothy was in good humor again. "Now we can have lunch."

"Great idea." Maybe once her mother had a meal in her, she would be approachable about her finances. Or maybe Pam should postpone that talk. First, she should go through more of those now ominous-seeming stacks of mail in the dining room. Then she should call Alexander and ask him what to do.

She had thought she would cut this weekend short. Now, she wanted more time, time in which to quietly go through everything. She was certain she couldn't do it while Dorothy was in the same room with her.

Dorothy ate a good meal, then got ready for her walk with Bruce and Yappie. Pam merely waved to him from farther inside the house when he came by. Once her mother was busy with the dog, Pam tore into the piles.

There were a stack of late notices from the power company, including a summary of the charges which indicated Dorothy hadn't paid the bill in at least three months. Three months ago. That's when Alexander moved away. It had to mean something.

As she dug further, she found the gas was supposed to have been turned off a few weeks ago. When the gas company arrived to manually shut it, Dorothy must have paid off the entire bill with a check on the spot.

The newspaper bills had piled up, but it looked as if possibly the agent had come by personally to collect a check. There was a letter from him saying he would be by next month to pick up the next payment in person. Decent of him, and not surprising. Dorothy had generously helped many local small business people get their start. She'd ridden banks to enforce fair lending laws, and hectored real estate agents into leasing properties to retail beginners, and more.

Here was the water bill. In arrears, of course. Dorothy was lucky. She still had sixty days before the water would be shut off.

Pam could no longer dodge the truth. All these letters had been unopened. She had hard evidence her mother had not attended to the business of her life for at least several months, unless prompted by a personal encounter. Why not? Had Alexander handled everything for her in recent years? If so, how could he have just moved away without alerting anyone and arranging for her financial care? Was Dorothy merely lacking in motivation? Or was it something more complicated?

Could it be dementia, as Bruce had intimated?

She realized tears were dripping down her cheeks. Her super-competent, commanding terror of a mother. What was happening?

The signs had all been there, but she hadn't wanted to admit the truth. The mother she grew up with would never have had piles of papers cluttering her dining room, or unread newspapers and magazines. That woman would not have sat doing nothing for hours at a time, as Dorothy now did in the sunroom much of the day. There had been a fundamental change. Pam had seen it, but she had refused to believe what the change meant. Her mother was getting past it.

She had to talk to Alexander. At this hour, all she got was his wife.

"Edie, did you notice signs of dementia in Mom in the last year?"

"I'm not sure I'd recognize them," her sister-in-law said with her usual air of uncertainty. "I've never known anyone who had it."

"Neither have I. Until now. I'm not sure myself if that's what has happened. I've heard that what is often taken for senility in elderly people is actually depression and malnutrition." She was reaching hard into her small store of knowledge about the problems of the elderly. Why didn't she know more?

"Isn't Dorothy eating?"

"Yes, she eats. Please, have Alexander call as soon as he comes in."

Then she called her sister. There was an unbridgeable age gap between them. Christine had been born five years before Pam, and they'd had very little to do with each other as children, except for some enforced babysitting when Christine was in her teens. Christine had openly resented that their mother had not paid her for the chore. Sometimes it seemed to Pam that Christine still bore a grudge. They'd never developed a good relationship as adults. While each was busy with their own lives, and Dorothy was doing fine, it hadn't mattered much.

The conversation didn't go well. "No, I don't know anything about Mother's financial affairs. Nor her health, for that matter." She brushed off Pam's effort to engage her. "I'm extremely busy with my law practice. And with my son. I have no time for this. You don't have a career, or even a job now, I hear. Can't you handle it?"

"Don't you care about our mother?" It was a cruel question to ask her sister, but she couldn't keep the words from bursting out of her mouth.

"My feelings for our mother are my own business. It's not for you to question whether I care. Anyway, I can't do anything for her long distance. You're the one who lives nearby. You don't have the heavy responsibilities I carry. You're the ideal one to handle Mother."

She wondered if Christine could hear how utterly selfish she sounded. True, Christine and her husband bore a major burden. One of their sons was bipolar and had been caught in several major messes which had taken all Christine's lawyer know-how and connections to smooth over. Their son still wasn't a functioning adult and probably never would be.

"How about if we need money? Christine? If Mother needs money, can you kick in something?"

"Ask me when you know for sure. I can't deal with this now." Christine said a curt goodbye and hung up.

That was happening to her a lot these days. What with all the executive offices she had called that had basically told her to drop dead, and then Bruce getting mad at her, and—

Bruce. Oh, heavens. He had been right. He had seen the signs and recognized them. She hadn't. She owed him an apology. Maybe she should ask him for help, too, because right now she was at sea.

The noise of their return floated up from downstairs. She left the papers every which way on her bed and went down to the sunroom to greet them.

Chapter 26

Dorothy had invited Bruce in.

"Ah, Pamela, there you are. Would you get us some iced tea? It was hot outside and I promised this young man he could have some."

Bruce was smiling at Pam. Then, as Dorothy gestured for him to take a seat on the wicker couch, his eyes alit on the framed photo of Dorothy's old friend, Greta.

"That's my mother," he exclaimed. He reached down and picked up the frame, and stared at the old photo of the pretty young woman. "Why do you have her photo displayed?"

"You're Greta's son," Dorothy said, surprised. "No wonder you looked familiar."

Her face seemed to whiten, and she nearly stumbled as she sank abruptly into her favorite chair. After a few seconds, she said, "Yes, I can see her in you. The shape of the forehead, and your chin."

"You knew my mother." Bruce appeared nearly overcome. "She died when I was four. I hardly knew her. Please, tell me everything you remember about her," he begged.

"It's a long story, boy," Dorothy said, sighing. "Pamela, where's that iced tea?" Pam scurried off to the kitchen and poured three tall glasses, slammed them onto a tray with some cookies and napkins, and rushed back. It looked as if neither of the other two had said a word since she'd left the room. They were recovering from the shock.

"You must have known my mother well to have her photo displayed after all these years. Tell me everything you know about her. Please," he added in a voice rough with emotion.

Yet there had been something off in Bruce's air of surprise. He'd been shocked to see the photo, Pam was sure of that. Not the rest. Still, he seemed almost desperate and that came across as completely sincere.

"It's a sad story, young man, are you sure you want to hear it?" Dorothy asked.

He nodded. "Yes. Yes, I do."

Dorothy took a sip of her tea. She seemed to be looking back across the years. Finally, she began, "Greta was a good friend of mine during the war—World War II, you know. We both came from the same neighborhood on the West Side, went to the same high school, knew each other's families. Most of us worked in the war effort. She and I worked in the same place."

"Yes, we've all heard about Rosie the Riveter," he said, impatience in his tone.

"Greta wasn't a factory girl, nor was I. She worked in a nice clean office as a clerk, like many girls. Mostly typing."

She took another sip of her tea. She grimaced. "It was boring work, but then most women's work back then was. Office work didn't even have the excitement of being different during wartime. It was more of the same drudgery. Greta had too much spunk to put in the long hours required during wartime and then do nothing else. So she volunteered at the USO dances."

Bruce winced.

Dorothy saw it and said in a quelling tone of voice, "Get your mind out of the gutter. It was respectable. The girls danced with the boys and that's all. They weren't prostitutes."

Bruce slowly nodded.

She continued. "Lots of boys convinced girls to marry them. Roger, your father, was one of those boys."

Bruce spoke. "Aunt Nora never said much about either of them."

"Nora, of course." Dorothy nodded, as if that explained why Bruce was asking questions. "She was Greta's much younger sister, too young to be part of Greta's social circle. She would not know any of the details. Greta and Roger made a secret marriage, like many during wartime. Greta never told anyone except me until after the war was over."

"Wouldn't her family have known?" Pam asked. "Didn't most young unmarried women still live with their parents back then?"

Dorothy nodded. "Greta did, indeed. They cooked up an elopement. Roger couldn't get permission to marry from his CO, who was under orders to discourage impulsive weddings. Instead, Roger arranged a weekend pass. Meanwhile, Greta told her parents she was staying with my family for the weekend because she and I were going to a party. They eloped to Elkton, Maryland, and returned home two days later."

"They didn't get caught?"

"No, which was a miracle because Greta didn't tip me off about the elopement until after they came back. She was determined to marry Roger, and she didn't ask anyone's advice or permission. He shipped out the very next week."

"What happened after the war?"

"Roger came home, of course," she replied. "They started wearing their wedding rings, told her family, and set up housekeeping. She was fired from her job because she was married. With the men back, women weren't supposed to work anymore. She had you soon after."

"What a tough world it was for women," Pam commented, mostly to herself.

"Don't waste any tears for Greta's lost career as a clerical worker," Dorothy said. "It was dull stuff. We women wanted to get back to home life, which at least had some variety every day and only one boss to please."

She took a breath. "Now where was I? Oh, after the war. Greta and Roger got a tiny house in Ronkonkoma, a cottage, really. It had two small rooms on the main floor, plus a kitchen and bathroom, and two tiny bedrooms upstairs. The stairs were very steep."

Dorothy stopped talking. At first, Bruce made no move. When Dorothy didn't resume speaking, he reminded her of where she was in her story.

"They were living in the tiny house…"

"Oh. Yes." Dorothy shook off her daydream state and resumed. "One day, I got a call from Nora. Greta had taken a bad fall down those stairs and died. Roger was overcome with grief. A couple of weeks later, he cracked up his car and was killed. Your aunt and uncle stepped in to raise you. A sad story, but a happy ending for you, I think," she finished. "You were happy with your aunt and uncle's family?"

"Sure. Of course." It was clear Bruce's attention was hardly on what he was saying. Bruce stared at Dorothy, searching her face. No one spoke.

Finally, he sighed and said in a sad tone, "Dorothy, please tell me the truth. Aunt Nora told me what little she knows."

"What do you mean?" Pam asked.

Bruce didn't spare her a glance. "Later," he said, in a low tone. "Please, Dorothy," he urged, fastening his insistent gaze on her. "I have to know. Please, tell me."

His eyes were locked with Dorothy's. She appeared to be struggling with some emotion. Dorothy sighed. A lone tear began to leak out of one eye. Pam couldn't remember seeing her mother cry. Ever.

"He killed her, son."

Pam gasped, but they both ignored her.

Bruce set his teeth. "Aunt Nora said that. How do you know for sure? How do you know?"

Dorothy had never been the type of woman who liked being pushed into a corner. Or verbally hounded. Predictably, she lashed out. "Because I made him admit it."

Bruce released his breath.

Dorothy had more to say. "He pushed her around for five long years and got away with it. She claimed the bruises and black eyes were all because she was clumsy. Clumsy, hah. She was a graceful woman."

She made an angry gesture with her hands. "He isolated her

from her friends and family. He kept her a virtual prisoner in that house. When I gave you the dog for your fourth birthday, she begged me not to stay that afternoon. Not even to share the birthday cake I'd brought. The next day, I came back and she had a bruise on her face."

Bruce's face had an ashen cast. He nodded. "I always remembered that day. The slap he gave her. It's one of my most vivid memories. I even remembered you, Dorothy."

Dorothy smiled sadly. "You look like Greta. No wonder I've been thinking about her a lot lately."

"What did he—what did my father tell you about my mother's death?"

Dorothy had begun to look pale herself. The strain of talking about her old friend was showing on her face.

Pam intervened. It was too much for her mother. "Can't you see she's exhausted?"

"I need to know," Bruce said.

"Come back tomorrow, then."

"No," Dorothy's voice had regained its strength. "Tomorrow, I might not remember. Today I do."

Pam cast her a stricken glance. Was Dorothy aware that she had mental deficits?

Dorothy nodded, "I'm not the only one who suspects I'm having trouble with my memory, I see. It must be now, today."

She straightened in her chair. "Your aunt was hysterical at the funeral. After Joe pulled her off Roger, and we calmed her down, I promised her I would get justice for Greta. I went to Roger's home and confronted him. I took a gun with me." Once more her voice seemed to be echoing far off days.

"He was already drunk. Cocky. I told him he was a murderer. He laughed at me, dared me to prove it. I claimed I had a letter from Greta in which she had confessed every horrible thing he had done to her. How she was in fear for her life."

She smiled. It wasn't a nice smile. "There was no such letter, of course. I convinced him that it was only a matter of time before I made the letter public."

Dorothy fell silent. No one spoke.

She took up the tale again. "In those days, no one enforced laws against wife beaters. That's what abusers were called. He would not have gone to jail, but wife beating was considered low-class behavior. Roger was trying to rise in his career as an engineer. If a credible story circulated about him as a wife beater and a possible murderer, the scandal would have finished him.

"I convinced Roger I would destroy him. He resisted me for a while, and then he crumpled. He started sobbing, saying that ever since the war, he'd had these dreadful headaches and flashbacks. When he had them, he wasn't in control of himself. Maybe he'd knocked Greta around. He claimed he hadn't meant to."

Dorothy sneered. "I was supposed to find this confession sympathetic. Today he would have said he had post traumatic stress disorder. Nice excuse for hitting a woman." Dorothy's voice held trenchant disgust.

"What did you do?" Pam asked, apprehensive.

"I laughed at him. I said I knew he threw Greta down the stairs deliberately and I was going to ruin him. He kept denying it. He claimed she fell entirely on her own."

Bruce let out a curse.

"I'd had enough. I told him I should shoot him dead but that would be too good for him. If he did not turn himself in to the authorities in two weeks, I would send the letter to the newspaper. He saw I meant it. Then I left."

She smiled that tough smile again. "I called him every night for the next two weeks. He learned I would not back down or forget about it. Then one night, he told me to come over and take little Bruce. That was the night he crashed his car."

"I ran over to the house and found you all alone with your puppy. His suicide note was on the kitchen table. In it, he said he was sorry he had accidentally killed Greta. He wished you a good life. Justice was finally served.

"The police called, with the news that Roger was dead. They asked who I was, and said an officer would arrive soon. I turned on the gas stove and burned the suicide note. You and I were playing dominoes when they arrived. They could smell the scent of the fire in the air, but I had quickly put a candle in a cupcake I'd brought you, and they couldn't prove anything else had happened.

"I told them about Nora and Joe, who came right over and took you. Then I went home."

"You never told Aunt Nora about the note?" Bruce sounded skeptical.

"No. It was better if she didn't know your father was responsible for Greta's death. Then you never would, either."

"What an amazing story," he said. The creases in his face were much more pronounced than usual. He looked suddenly older.

Dorothy inclined her head.

Bruce stood and paced the length of the sunroom. Then he turned around and sent Dorothy a penetrating look. "Did it happen that way? I doubt it. My father wasn't a murderer."

Dorothy's head snapped up and her gaze pierced him. She frowned. "You don't believe me?"

"I believe some of it."

"How can you say that?" Pam asked, outraged. Dorothy Duncan always spoke the truth.

Bruce turned to her. "Your mother is a talented actress, that's why. Aunt Nora told me Dorothy promised she would make sure my father died. He did die. But then why did she destroy the note? If a suicide note ever existed."

Dorothy heaved herself up and then swayed. Pam rushed to support her.

"I've said all I'm going to, young man," Dorothy said. "Be satisfied. Nothing I say will bring back either of your parents."

She walked toward her bedroom suite, assisted by Pam, who could feel the trembling in her mother's body. Pam cast an angry look over her shoulder at Bruce. How dare he contradict Dorothy? Her mother never lied.

She helped settle her mother in for a nap on the chaise in her large, airy bedroom.

"Poor Greta," Dorothy said. Her voice shook with remembered emotion. "She was such a striking, wonderful girl, Pamela. So full of life. I still miss her."

"What a shame," Pam said, wanting to make Dorothy comfortable quickly. Pam intended to go back to the sunroom and confront Bruce. She mumbled soothing words as she tucked an afghan around her mother's legs. "Can you rest now?"

Dorothy threw her a tart look. "Of course. I'm strong. Don't worry about me."

Despite her protests, the tragedy from nearly sixty years ago still had the power to pain Dorothy. If only Bruce had not forced open the door to the past.

Chapter 27

When Pam returned to the sunroom, she found Bruce waiting near the door to the patio. Traitor.

Her first words were cool. "I'm surprised you're still here."

Bruce's expression changed. Evidently her tone had stung. Good. She continued, rising anger in her voice. "Did you think I would ignore that you hurt my mother? You rented the house next door to gain her confidence, didn't you?"

"Yes."

Her jaw dropped at his open admission. "You deliberately made up to a vulnerable old woman, reviving her memories of a painful time in her life. That's low."

Bruce winced, but he didn't show any other sign of remorse.

"Was anything you told us about yourself true?" Pam asked, an edge of contempt in her tone.

He cursed under his breath. "Get off your high horse, Pam. I haven't lied."

He must have known she didn't want him to touch her, for he didn't try.

"You made love to me merely to get closer to Dorothy,

didn't you?" She tried to keep the pain out of her voice, tried to keep her spine straight under the blow of realizing she'd been used, too.

"No, Pam." His expression softened. "I swear it."

He moved closer to her but she backed away. "Don't touch me."

Bruce's expression turned hurt, even righteous. "Whatever you believe about my intentions toward Dorothy, what you and I have together is real."

His eyes searched her face hopefully, but Pam wouldn't give him the satisfaction of seeing how fraught her emotions were. The revelation of his secret agenda had changed everything. She couldn't trust him now.

"Please leave," she said. "I suggest you cancel your rental and go home. I won't allow you to harass my mother further."

"I have no intention of harassing Dorothy," Bruce replied, angry now. "I like her. I just want the truth."

"She told you what happened. You're in denial," Pam said, her anger rising again. How dare he call her mother a liar?

"Her story has holes you could drive a truck through." He looked frustrated. "Can't you see?"

"Go away." By this time, they were both standing on the patio.

"Fine. I'll go now, but my lease runs several more months. I'm not leaving here without the truth."

"I can call the police."

Bruce's look of condescension was galling. "Your dear mother probably won't even remember telling me this fine story today."

"That's not true." She was furious with him now.

"Now who's in denial?" he asked, giving her a look that held pity. He whistled for Yappie, who had been sitting calmly on the patio the whole time, and the two sauntered off.

How dare he abuse her mother's hospitality and trust? Pam had been a fool to think he might care for her. What a laugh. He'd courted her to get closer to Dorothy. The sex was a bonus. No wonder she hadn't felt right with him. He was completely insincere. She'd thought she was the disaffected one, the one who was out of tune with him emotionally. He'd been lying to her the entire time.

Oh, lord. She'd had sex with him multiple times. Thank goodness they'd used condoms. At least she didn't have to worry about getting a disease from that sneaky, lying seducer. He'd seduced her, and she'd let him, but all the time his real agenda was Dorothy. Pam's emotions were merely collateral damage to Bruce.

Once he was safely gone, she burst into tears.

#

Dorothy was up and about a half hour later, showing no ill effects from the traumatic story she had told. Or from Bruce calling her a liar. He hadn't used that word exactly, but he might as well have.

What derailed Dorothy from fretting over long-dead Greta and Roger—or Bruce, alive and annoying next door—was her discovery that Pam had the bills open on her bed. Dorothy must have come upstairs to find her.

"Pamela, what have you been doing?" she asked, standing in

301

the doorway. Dorothy used the stentorian tone of voice familiar from when Pam was a guilty little girl who had done something wrong.

Pam had to fight off her automatic response of being cowed by her mother. "I started sorting the unopened mail."

"Were these letters addressed to you? No? Then you shouldn't have opened them."

"Mother, please," she protested. "They were about to turn off the electricity. I called barely in time to stop them."

"What are you talking about?"

"I found this notice that the power would be turned off on Monday." Pam explained, picking it up.

"Let me see that," her mother demanded.

Pam handed it over.

Dorothy glanced at the notice. "Obviously, there's been a misunderstanding. If you wouldn't jump in the middle and confuse everything, I could easily get to the bottom of the situation."

"I didn't. Mother, I'm trying to help you."

"I don't need your help, Pamela. I'm perfectly able to handle my own affairs."

"I'm sorry, but—"

"Pamela," her mother said in that drawn-out, censorious way she had. "Don't interfere. You're ignorant about financial dealings."

"I've run a household," Pam said. "Paying utility bills on time isn't complex finance."

Dorothy ignored Pam's protest. "Let's say no more about it." She gathered up the papers from the bed.

"Wait. The water bill," Pam said in an urgent tone. "It's overdue, too."

"No more. I'll handle my own business," Dorothy said.

She took the papers downstairs. Instead of depositing them on the dining room table, which Pam hoped would happen, her mother continued to her suite. She put the bills on her desk there. It was piled with unopened mail also.

Pam's heart sank. There was more she needed to investigate, but Dorothy would not let her youngest and officially least competent daughter have open access to her financial situation. Pam had lost her chance. She had approached the delicate issue of her mother's failing competence all wrong, by grabbing her private papers. No wonder Dorothy was outraged. Apparently, Pam's clever negotiating skills were limited to egotistical CEO types.

What should she do now? Call Alexander to mediate? Try again later with her mother? As she dutifully followed Dorothy through the house to the sunroom, they passed the dining room again. Pam's hands ached to go through another pile, and delve into the mystery of her mother's situation, but Dorothy was too strong, too intimidating to openly disobey. Pam dared not call down her mother's ire on her head again. Surely she'd have another opportunity to search the papers before she left tomorrow afternoon.

Oh, what a mess. Bruce a betrayer. Her mother still her old stubborn self, but possibly in the first stages of dementia. She, hoping to build a new life for herself, now doubting she had the stamina even to deal with her life as it now was.

Chapter 28

Linley and Jason argued over lunch. Not only had they argued earlier about what to order, but now they were arguing about the menu. It was their third lunch together this week. The novelty hadn't worn off. Linley enjoyed pulling Jason's chain about every decision he made, whether for the new show or for pizza at lunch. If he was against it, she was for it.

"How can you eat that greasy, white-carb-laden poison?" he asked. His plate held a virtuous serving of white fish, no sauce. Somehow, he had made it seem like a manly man decision.

"I like cheese. I like tomatoes. I like bread. Together, they're great," she said with satisfaction after she'd polished off her second piece. Of course, she would be eating a very light dinner, but Jason didn't need to know that. She enjoyed sounding like she'd never heard of the food pyramid.

"What are you, a magic eater?"

"I can eat anything and I do. Why do you care?"

At her challenge, he looked intent. "I'm trying to puzzle you out. Every time I think I have, you're different again."

"You're never going to get me, Jason," she replied,

attempting to look serene.

"Yes, I am," he replied, bending a dark look on her that made her nerves sizzle with anticipation.

Neither of them mentioned that one night last year. They had found magic in bed together. Would they dare to try it again?

On Monday the first show went well. Live TV was no novelty to either of them, but the argument format kept them on edge. Marty was pleased. They'd get ratings and reviews beyond tweets, maybe within a few minutes on a couple of the influential blogs. Jason retreated to his office to await the verdict of that transplanted college kid blogger who now worked for the *Wall Street Journal*.

Linley went to the ladies room to calm her shaky nerves. Being alone with Jason for a half hour on television had been too stimulating. Especially since he looked straight at her the whole thirty minutes. She'd done okay during their brainstorming and tryout sessions. Now, when it was real, their chemistry as they spent a half hour disagreeing with each other was shattering. She'd gotten so aroused she'd actually thought about jumping him during one of the commercial breaks, in full view of the crew and the observers.

She was losing it. She wanted him badly, wanted to feel his powerful arms around her, wanted him pressing into her, wanted him kissing her. Kissing, oh god. He kept taunting her with mentions of licking. She wanted to lick him. She suspected he wanted to lick her, too.

She wrung the wetness out of a paper towel and patted the nape of her neck, which had no makeup to mess up. She needed to cool off.

Another woman came into the ladies room. "Nice show," she said.

"Thanks," she replied. Time to move on. She couldn't let her coworker see her standing there minute after minute.

As she approached her cube, Marty stepped into the hall. When he saw her, he motioned her into Jason's office.

"The reviews are in. The kid likes it. The others do, too." Marty was exultant.

She read the blog, which called her "the heartthrob of cable financial arguments."

"Now I'm a heartthrob," she said, taking a bow. It was a great review. She was on her way.

"How about me? The 'finance hunk' who is 'sure to draw drooling female fans.' He's calling me a piece of meat," Jason complained.

"A choice cut, don't forget," Marty said, as Linley smirked. "Now we'll pick up more viewers. More ads. Good job. Go celebrate."

After he left, Jason smiled at her, a sly smile. "Want to go to my place for a private party?"

"Marty wants us to go out and be seen, be an item," she demurred. Not that she intended to. Even that was inherently dangerous. Not because of gossip, once they'd gotten the word out that Marty was pushing a fake romance. No one at the station would rag on them because they spent a lot of time together now. The problem was their carefully crafted walls were cracking. The chemistry between them was real and gaining power.

"Come home with me tonight, Lin," he asked, "You know what I want."

"I can't believe you said that. We have to keep our battle stances to make the show work." She started for the door.

He backed into it, closing it with his body and blocking her. Sealing them in the privacy of his office. "You're a feisty chick— a woman with a strong sense of herself. You'll still fight me on the show even if you lick me all over in bed."

Lick. He'd been thinking the same thing she had. The image he conjured up of them mutually licking got to her. She fought it down.

"No way. I'm not jeopardizing my career for some mattress time with you." She gestured at him. "Step aside."

He moved. As she passed him, he murmured, "I know you want me." There was no hint he'd been put off by her forceful rejection.

"You must be deaf."

"You want me as much as I want you, Lin. The only difference between us is I'm not in denial."

He moved closer. He didn't touch her or overwhelm her physically as he had done before. He didn't even invade her space. He stared at her intently, daring her to keep lying about what was between them.

She wanted to sway and fall into his arms. She wanted him to hold her against his broad chest, not capitalizing on her weakness, but treasuring it. She wanted to have super hot sex with him, no holds barred. For hours and hours. She wanted him to peel off her jacket, push the straps of her camisole down, and put his lips on the peaks of her breasts. For starters.

Instead, she kept her poker face, and spoke as coldly as she could. "Let's keep our minds on business, shall we?"

She walked away, trying to make it look as if she was cool and calm. Her emotions were a wreck. She wanted him. She didn't deny it to herself, but she had to hold him off. She had to exercise a kind of control over herself she'd never needed before.

For years she'd felt free to hook up with guys on a whim. Everybody did it. They practiced safe sex, and used condoms, and there were no consequences except the occasional hurt feeling. How ironic was it that now what she feared most about getting involved with Jason were consequences? Emotional consequences?

#

Jason watched Linley walk away and wondered what the hell had come over him lately. Every time he was near her, he wanted her. He wanted to claim her openly as his. It was building to a dangerous level. Even he knew he was getting crazy. Trust Linley to tell him to his face.

They'd come a long way since that first night. They knew each other now. They had worked together for months and now they were partners, a situation that threw them together even more than before. Yet, she was more elusive.

He rubbed his neck and returned to his desk. Comments were being added to the blog and the twitter feed about their show. They had a good start, but that was all. They shouldn't take it as a sure thing.

This was the moment for him to push his visibility any way

he could, not obsess over getting Linley to come home with him. Yet Linley was all he could think about. He wanted to host a late night talk show, but his thoughts kept circling back to Linley. How to find a moment to make love to her here at the studio. How to convince her to give him another shot. How to coax her to come to his place—and stay there forever. He wanted to sex her up. He'd take his time. He'd lock them both in his bedroom for an entire week if he could. After a few days, they'd send out for her favorite pizza and he'd suck sauce off her nipples. Or anywhere else she'd let him.

He shifted to ease the discomfort of his massive hard on from thinking about her. He had to stop this. He read another tweet.

"Jason and Linley are sweet. They're obviously in love and dying to jump each other."

In love? He'd never felt this way before and he didn't much like it. It didn't suit his macho image of the emotionally free bachelor guy, the man who could get any woman and selected only a few, with no emotions involved. Now he was a mess who had lost all interest in other women. Was he in love? Was that why he wasn't sleeping at night? Why he kept thinking about Lin?

He stood. Maybe he could catch her before she left. They had to talk.

Linley was already on the street when Jason called her name. She turned and saw him coming after her.

"What's up?"

"You and me. Let's go somewhere we can talk."

Chapter 29

On Sunday, Pam was torn. She couldn't do much more about her mother's financial situation on a weekend, and she had promised to babysit her grandchildren all this week, starting later today. She needed to go, but she worried she should stay.

She had reviewed all she could of her mother's finances by dint of setting her alarm for two a.m. She had dragged herself awake, sneaked down to the dining room, and grabbed all the remaining mail. Then she'd retreated to her bedroom and locked the door. She'd spent the rest of the night reading every piece of mail. It had all been unopened.

Things weren't as bad as she'd feared. Most bills had only recently begun to be in arrears. As if everything had been fine and then suddenly it all went bad. The piles of newspapers and magazines were older. They'd been the first sign, but no one had recognized it, not even Alexander.

She hadn't been able to talk to Alexander about it last evening. When he'd called her back, he'd called the house landline. Naturally, Dorothy wanted to talk to him. There was no way to have a private conversation.

Her mother seemed to have plenty of money with which to pay her bills. In fact, there was a lot of extra cash sitting in her checking account, where she received most of her income through direct deposit. Much of it was from pensions that weren't affected by the stock market, thank goodness. The financial meltdown wasn't over yet.

She had health coverage through more than one source, and that was another can of worms. Dorothy took no medications that Pam knew of. She presented as healthy. Yet shouldn't she be seen by a doctor who could diagnose whether she was showing signs of dementia? It could be malnutrition, after all. Or depression, although Dorothy certainly did not seem depressed. Her positive attitude still was her dominant trait.

Hard to believe her mother had ever owned a gun. She'd never seen her with one. They'd never had any guns in the house, surely? How believable was the tale Dorothy had told Bruce yesterday? It certainly had been very detailed.

Pam packed as she thought about Bruce. She'd been so outraged by his deception, and then by his open disbelief, that she had tamped down her own incredulity at some parts of her mother's story. What was the truth? What had happened between Dorothy and Roger all those years ago? If her mother was lying, why? She couldn't have shot Bruce's father. He died in a car crash and an autopsy would have revealed a bullet wound. If they'd bothered with an autopsy. If there was enough body left after the car crashed. She shuddered.

When Jeff died, he'd fallen to the sidewalk in Manhattan. Good Samaritans had made sure his wallet remained on him, which meant she was contacted immediately. She'd had to officially identify him because he'd died on a public street. Not one of her happier memories, although they'd been kind. There had been an autopsy because a man in good health didn't usually drop dead. But Jeff had.

Dorothy's tale of threatening Roger Dietrich with public exposure was plausible. Her mother's usual mode of operation was to vilify her opponent via a community campaign. She was the master of such tactics. Carrying a gun, making a personal threat, didn't sound like her mother, although the part about publicizing Greta's letter was typical Dorothy.

If the letter had ever existed. Dorothy might have been bluffing Roger Dietrich. If there was a letter, where would it be now? Surely she would have kept it? In her safe deposit box at the bank? In some drawer in her bedroom? Where?

During breakfast, Pam remarked, "You don't appear any worse for the wear this morning."

"Aside from getting older, I feel fine, Pamela." Dorothy seemed to have completely put behind her the confrontation with Bruce yesterday. Or had she forgotten it?

Pam spent the morning preparing two other bedrooms for her grandchildren's visit next weekend. This was a big house and could hold plenty of guests. Dorothy now didn't much bother with the upstairs rooms since there was a convenient master suite on the main floor. It was just Pam's ill luck her mother had made the trip upstairs yesterday and caught her in the act. Dorothy mostly spent her time in the sunroom, ignoring the other parts of the house. Certainly the kitchen.

Pam intended to cook some goodies with the children. Callie never seemed to want them in her own showplace kitchen. That was her choice. It was a grandmother's privilege to expose the children to something new.

Oh, she had lots of ideas to entertain the children if they'd let her. During the school week, she would follow the strict routine Callie had set down for their lives in their own home. Here at the beach, they could all be free.

Before she left, though, she broached the idea of her mother seeing her doctor.

"Why would I want to see a doctor? I'm as healthy as a horse." Dorothy replied.

"Everyone should see a doctor at least once a year for a routine checkup."

"That's nonsense, Pamela. It was dreamed up by the medical establishment to make doctors rich."

"Mom, you shouldn't neglect your health. Please consider what's in your best interest."

"I'm fine. I don't need any doctor to tell me that. Or you."

That was Dorothy's final word. Pam had made no headway with her mother on that score and she hadn't tried again on the bills. She wanted to investigate the situation first.

She stayed nearby when Bruce came over with his dog. At least he had the good sense not to attempt to talk to Dorothy about his parents today. Pam didn't trust his motive in continuing to treat her mother like a friend. She didn't speak to him directly. Although he glanced at her as if to gauge her mood, he didn't attempt to talk to her, either.

The day was well launched and it was time for her to leave. She put the beautiful Dior dress in her car, and the pearls, and carefully secreted the stack of bills she wanted to take action on in her large tote bag. This time around, Dorothy didn't go out to the car with her. They said their goodbyes in the sunroom. Her last act was to remind her mother about her next visit.

"Now remember, I'm spending all of this week at Steve's house, and then bringing the children here on Friday night. We'll have two nights here and leave on Sunday afternoon. Steve and Callie are returning Sunday night."

Dorothy nodded, but looked impatient.

"I'll call you before we arrive, to remind you," Pam added.

"Pamela, I am perfectly capable of remembering you will be back here next weekend. Please don't act as if I am in my dotage. My brain works fine." Dorothy's tone of voice became waspish.

Pam nodded compliantly. She wasn't sure of anything. For now, she'd have to hope for the best.

When she went out to the car the final time, Bruce was waiting for her, his hands shoved in a tan windbreaker, and that unruly dark curl lying on his forehead.

"I couldn't let you leave without trying to straighten things out between us," he said with a dogged air.

She sighed. Did she need this now? Did she even care? Their relationship might mean more to Bruce than it did to her. "It's okay, Bruce. We can agree to disagree."

"That's not good enough, Pam. We had something. I want it back." He looked frustrated.

"How can I know if you are sincere?" she asked. Had it all been an act? Did he want a convenient source for no-strings sex? Was he trying to soften her up again only to get at her mother's memories? "How can I trust you?" she asked.

Bruce wasn't happy with her questions, she could tell. The

old Pam might have said anything to smooth over a problem rather than confront it. But she wasn't quite the old Pam anymore. She waited for Bruce to answer.

Finally Bruce said, "I promise I won't ask Dorothy anything more about my parents until you're here again to referee, how's that?"

Bruce's offer bespoke his acknowledgment he had crossed an ethical line yesterday. It was a generous promise, considering how desperately he seemed to want to know details from the past.

She nodded. "I'll hold you to it. I'm bringing my grandchildren here next weekend. Probably we'll all be too busy for any more stories about the past."

Bruce looked disappointed, even taken aback. "Grandchildren?"

"Max and Molly. They're eight and six, and quite charming," she smiled. "You don't have grandchildren yet?"

"No. I've got the gay daughter, remember?" he said. "Sometimes it takes longer to find a mate."

"Right. Sorry." After her awkward gaffe, she turned to place her purse on the car seat. "Time for me to go."

"Drive carefully, Pam. I'll miss you." Bruce said.

What could she say? Would she miss him? She had no idea. She settled for a bland comment. "I'll be back Friday afternoon."

She got behind the wheel quickly and started the car. Bruce stood there and watched her leave. What a mess. She had been impetuous, getting involved with Bruce too quickly and too intimately. A mistake when she knew nothing about him. Now she had reason to doubt everything he'd ever said to her.

Bruce's secret agenda still hit Pam on the raw. How could he have abused her trust that way? Why had she been so easy to fool? She'd trained herself to notice when a high-powered executive was telling her lies, but she still couldn't recognize when a man she'd had sex with was pulling the wool over her eyes. Bruce had been so plausible, so casual and friendly. Pam had been an easy target. It hurt to think she'd been used.

Even if Bruce had been honest and open about everything, was she at the right place in her life for a love affair? She had too much on her plate, starting the nonprofit and now dealing with whatever was up with her mother.

Chapter 30

Five days later, Pam was more than ready for a weekend. A week with her over-scheduled grandchildren was fun in theory, but hard work in reality. She'd forgotten how children felt it was necessary to negotiate every moment of the day.

"I don't want milk. I want soda," Max whined on Friday afternoon at snack time.

"Honey, there's not a drop of soda in this house," she replied.

"You cut my sandwiches funny. Mommy always cuts them different," Molly said. She looked to be revving up to reject her sandwich.

"I'm grandma. I do everything a little differently," she said with a smile. Trying to soothe the children was getting tougher. They had held up well, but with the school week over, they both were ragged from the pain of being separated from their parents.

"Hurry up and finish your snacks. It's time to go to the beach, to Great-grandma's house."

"Does she have a dog?" Max asked hopefully. He'd asked for a dog forever, but Callie thought they brought in germs. There were no pets in this excessively clean house.

"The dog next door comes over to visit every day," Pam said.

"Oh, boy!"

Of course, now Molly wanted something for herself. "Does she have a kitty cat?"

"No, I'm afraid not, dear. Maybe we can find one when we walk on the beach."

Molly looked a little disappointed, but not too much. Max's open enthusiasm was beginning to infect her.

"Are we going swimming?" Max's eyes were wider than she'd seen them all week.

"It's too cold for swimming, but we can play in the water and build sand castles and look for shells."

"Yay! Let's go visit. Can we go right now?"

"As soon as you finish up and brush your teeth. Each of you pick a toy or game you'd like to bring with you."

She'd already packed their clothes. While the children ran off to their rooms, she made an extra effort to clean the kitchen. Although she suspected Callie would take one look on her return and gasp in horror. That girl could intuit dirt.

On the long drive out to the beach, Pam announced it was necessary to take a break at an ice cream shop. The children whooped. They grew even more enthusiastic once they realized she was not going to tell them which flavors they must order, or even which sizes. She asked for an empty container from the store, planning ahead to a few minutes later in the car, when Molly inevitably said, "I'm all full, Grandma. I can't finish my cone."

Luckily, Max wasn't into teasing his little sister at that

moment. The container was passed back to her granddaughter without any negative comments, and the half-finished cone was deposited inside.

"How about you, Max? Had enough?"

"Yes. I finished mine. Mom doesn't let us have cones before dinner," he said.

"Dinner could be awhile. We have to wait until Great-grandma decides what she wants, and then order it from a restaurant."

"Doesn't Great-grandma cook?" he asked, wonder in his tone. Callie usually cooked all her family's meals.

"Not if she can help it," she smiled, taking the turnoff from the expressway. "It's a privilege of age."

"What's a privilege mean, Nana?" Molly asked.

She had forgotten how many questions children always had.

"It means that my mom is retired. Do you know what retired is?"

"I know, I know," Max yelled. "Retired is when you're old, like thirty, and you have to live on cat food." He said it triumphantly.

"Oh, dear. Maybe some retirees do. My mother lives on nice restaurant takeout," she finished up, chuckling. Cat food indeed.

Fielding the children's questions made the trip go by faster. Steve's home was a long drive from her mother's beach house, but they arrived before they all got too worn out. As soon as she'd turned off the engine, Max and Molly undid their seatbelts eagerly and ran for the house. "Great-grandma! Granny!" they cried, "We're here."

She followed at a more sedate pace, bringing some of the luggage. She set it inside the door and went to check on her mother.

Dorothy sat in her favorite seat in the sunroom. She had an arm around each child as they stood on either side of her. She listened intently to the tale of their recent doings.

They seemed quite happy to be chatting with their great-grandmother. How surprising they felt comfortable with Dorothy, considering how seldom they saw her. Or maybe that was why?

After a few minutes, when the children had started to run down, they heard a dog bark. Bruce was coming across the patio, with Yappie by his side. The children ran outside.

"Doggie!" Molly said, wide-eyed. Max was a little shyer. He looked to Pam, who had followed, for direction.

"Yes, this is the friendly dog I told you about. Ask Mr. Wicklow if you may pet him."

Bruce smiled at the children, who were looking extremely eager, but a little scared. "Yappie loves everybody. Go ahead."

Max put a tentative hand on Yappie's head. Yappie immediately licked Max's hand, shocking the boy. Mollie started giggling and held out her hand to the little dog.

"Now me! Now me!"

Dorothy came outside, greeted Bruce, and ensconced herself at the patio table, smiling benignly at the children as they played with Yappie.

"How have you been all week, Pam?" Bruce asked. "I've been wearing Dorothy out with our daily walks, but otherwise I've had my nose to the grindstone."

His way of telling her he had kept his promise. In her absence, he hadn't tried to coax Dorothy into more talk of his parents' deaths. Evidently he planned to ignore the rift between them. She wasn't ready to forget, but with the children here, she could hardly be openly hostile. Of course he was taking advantage of the children's presence, of Max's eagerness to pet the dog, and of Molly's to do whatever her big brother did. It was understandable. They brought joyful noise wherever they went. Bruce lived here all alone except for Yappie.

"We've been busy," she replied. Then she couldn't help adding, "I'm glad you had a productive week."

"Oh, I didn't say I got any writing done. I was too distracted to write much. I did try," he said, acknowledging he'd had other things on his mind.

Belatedly, she introduced the children, who displayed the good manners Callie had drilled into them. Max even held out his hand to shake.

Dorothy spoke up. "Now don't you wear that dog out with too much petting." Then she turned to Pam.

"We'd better order dinner. You should take these children for a walk before it gets too dark. Otherwise they'll never settle down."

Somehow, Bruce was in the picture again as the adults realized the children weren't going to want to be separated from their new animal friend quickly. Dorothy invited Bruce to dinner and he accepted.

"You're a brave man," Pam said, not fighting it.

Bruce smiled at her. "How could I leave you all alone with these wild things?" he teased.

She slipped back inside and retrieved the handful of takeout menus from the kitchen.

"What's your pleasure, Mom?" she asked Dorothy.

"How about Italian? Usually, children like spaghetti."

They put in the order, and Dorothy insisted on waiting in the house for the delivery. "You all go on for a walk. I've had mine."

Bruce, Pam, and the children and Yappie set out for the beach.

"I'm sorry you got roped into this," she said to Bruce as they walked along. Yappie ran to and from the water, almost touching the incoming tide. The children whooped and tried to keep up with his zigzag path.

"I'm enjoying it," he said.

"So am I, but I'll be glad when my grandma week is over. The children wear me out, and I do have other concerns besides babysitting."

"Have you found a new job?"

"Not employment. I've started my nonprofit, and I'm in the process of publicizing it and finding big donors."

"You talked about it before. I didn't know you'd gone through with your idea."

#

Bruce hadn't realized Pam had anything else major going on in her life. This might explain why she wasn't interested in listening to him about Dorothy's memory problem.

He asked questions and was further intrigued by how complicated Pam's plans were. She'd ventured far out on a limb, far from the safety of being a clerical worker at an investment bank or a stay-at-home mom. It made him wonder if he'd gotten the wrong idea about her all along. He'd thought she was the housewife type, someone who would be content with a quiet life and make no waves in it. Maybe that wasn't true. She sounded eager. It clearly was the most important thing on her mind. Something he should consider.

Meanwhile, Pam blithely continued to describe her efforts to corral big shots from the world of finance as major donors and publicity bases for her charity. He wondered if she knew how animated her face, indeed her entire posture was when she described her foundation. She looked beautiful.

The kids of course kept asking questions and running to and fro. There wasn't an opportunity for deep conversation.

The walk took longer than expected. It was hard to turn the excited children back toward Dorothy's house soon enough. Naturally, by the time they neared it again, even Max's legs were tired, and Bruce was carrying Molly.

"Well, at last," Dorothy said, greeting them from the sunroom's French doors. "I was wondering if I should eat alone."

"I think we overdid it," Pam admitted to her mother as the weary band trooped in, leaving Yappie outside. Bruce explained the dog was guarding them.

"It's getting a little cool to be dining outside, I'm afraid," Bruce said.

"We'll use the dining room," Dorothy said with her usual air of certainty.

They looked across at the room, with its table still piled with newspapers and magazines. Bruce put Molly in a wicker chair and Max flopped down beside her.

"Okay," Bruce said easily. "We can clean this up in a jiffy."

Pam waited for Dorothy to tell Bruce not to touch anything. It didn't happen. Dorothy merely nodded her assent. Seeing that, Pam sprang into action.

"There's string in the kitchen drawer to tie the papers. I'll get it." She practically raced into the kitchen to gather up the twine and some scissors, eager to openly declutter the dining room at last.

She and Bruce made short work of stacking and tying up the newspapers. Then he took the heavy bundles out to the trash area where the recycle bin resided. The newspapers were all from the past three months. She had intended to do something about them soon. She'd even gone online this week and investigated the local recycling collection service. It was a relief to get the job done without her mother being angry at her.

Within a few minutes, they had the whole table cleared. She'd tied up many magazines, only saving a handful in case they could prove useful for entertaining Max and Molly.

Who by now had recovered from their walk and were ready to help. Finding Max at her elbow, she asked him to put the few remaining magazines in the living room. As he did, she turned to his sister.

"Molly, if I show you the silverware drawer, can you set the table?"

"Yes, I can."

"No, she can't. She's too little and gets confused," Max said.

"Then you be a good big brother and help your sister,"

Dorothy directed as Pam opened the top drawer of the server to reveal the flatware.

Bruce was finally done with taking out the recycling. Dorothy had pulled out a tablecloth and the pads she'd had custom made to protect the table. She and Pam laid them and the tablecloth. Then Max and Molly raced around the table, putting silverware at places while Bruce retrieved the cartons of Italian food from the kitchen. Pam procured china plates and serving dishes from the breakfront.

Dorothy looked around the table, now set with china and silver, napkins, and even a centerpiece of a few fruits Pam had put in a basket. "This is very nice. It's a shame Malcolm can't be with us, but he has to work late."

Pam let that hang in the air. Her father had died nearly forty years ago. Bruce looked puzzled, then comprehending. The children ignored their great-grandmother's odd statement.

They spent a happy half hour eating and enjoying the children. Then Max and Molly were excused to play with the toys they'd brought in their backpacks. Callie, of course, did not allow them to play video games.

"Nice kids," Bruce said after they had done as they were told and gone to the living room to play.

"My daughter-in-law, Callie, is a stickler for good manners and rules."

"So is your mother," Dorothy pronounced.

They lingered over the meal a while longer, but then Bruce demonstrated his recall of being a father by excusing himself. "I'll say thank you and goodnight. They're going to crash soon. You'll want to get them bathed and into bed."

She glanced over in time to see Molly rubbing her eyes. "True," she smiled.

He said his goodnights and left. The children were so tired they didn't even try to keep Yappie. Dorothy insisted everybody help get the food cleared off the table. Then she put herself in charge of refrigerating the leftovers and sent Pam and the children upstairs.

"Time to pick out your bedrooms and get bathed."

"All right, let's go," Pam said, leading them into the hall. "Each of you take your backpack with you," she directed. She shepherded them up the stairs. Molly was dragging her feet, looking tired. As expected, Max wanted the biggest room, the one her brothers always took. It had two beds and old sports memorabilia. The next bedroom was frillier, created to please her elder sister, Christine. Not that anything ever had. It made little Molly smile. Then Pam showed both children her bedroom, to reassure them she would be nearby.

Soon each child had gotten the surface dirt cleaned off and was outfitted in pajamas. They all trooped downstairs one more time for a last drink of water and to kiss Dorothy goodnight.

"You little rascals," she said, pleased at the attention. She hugged and kissed each child in turn.

Pam tucked the children in bed. Max was a bit old for a story so she left him with a book and the promise she'd check on him in case he couldn't sleep. Then she read a picture book to Molly, who was asleep before it ended.

Pam soon descended to the main floor to reconnoiter with her mother and be sure the leftovers had made it into the refrigerator. It was as well she checked. Dorothy had put the food in the freezer, not the fridge. Easy to remedy, but why had she done that? Not that it mattered terribly.

Pam went out the kitchen door to get her luggage from the car. Light poured from a side window of Bruce's house. It shone from his living room, which faced the water. Did she wish she was with him right now? Or upstairs, in his bed with him again? She wasn't sure. Too many people had told her she should get on with her life. She should find another man, they said. When she had found him, she had plunged into a physical affair too quickly. She'd been so flummoxed by her attraction to Bruce she'd taken him at face value. She hadn't dreamed he could be lying to them all about who and what he was.

He'd claimed he never lied, merely omitted some key bits of information, but his long-ago connection with Dorothy had changed everything. Dorothy didn't seem to hold it against Bruce for coming here with the hidden agenda of coaxing her to tell old secrets. She'd only gotten her dander up when Bruce questioned the details of her story. Was that because she hated to be doubted, or because she was prevaricating about her confrontation with Roger Dietrich so many years ago?

They ought to learn more about Bruce from someone reliable. Doubtless her mother's attorney could recommend a good private eye. Investigating Bruce was a melodramatic step, but Dorothy was at a fragile time of life. Pam didn't want any more surprises. She must make sure he wasn't likely to take further advantage of her mother. If she'd had a moment to herself in the past week, she would have already set a background check in motion. There were only so many hours in a day, and her grandchildren seemed to fill them all.

She found Dorothy flipping through the magazines Max had placed on a side table in the living room. "*Arizona Highways*. A beautiful magazine. I only subscribe because my sister loved it. She went to college in Arizona," Dorothy said, as if she hadn't told Pam this a thousand times.

Pam plopped down on the couch next to the table, and picked up the top magazine. "It's got pretty pictures. I thought we could have Max and Molly cut some out to paste and color if the weather turns sour. Or in the unlikely situation that they get tired of the beach."

Dorothy made a sound of derision. "They'll be too tired. In all my years here, I've never had a child visit who got bored enough to do an art project."

"We'll run them up and down the beach so many times they'll need naps each day," Pam said. She was happy they'd cleaned up the mess of the dining room, but didn't dare say so. No need to remind her mother of their fight over the mail. The mail Pam had stolen. At least the dining room was usable again, returned to its former glory. She had even placed a beautiful crystal bowl in the center after dinner. Tomorrow she'd put some flowers in it.

Maybe sometime she could suggest her mother reduce the number of her subscriptions, so the backup of magazines wouldn't happen again. None of the newspapers had been read, either. That subscription ought to be canceled.

Instead, she basked in the moments of peace with the mother whose active lifestyle had always intimidated her. Dorothy wasn't even criticizing her as much as she always had.

The next two days passed swiftly, with plenty of laughter and fun for all. There was one disturbing moment when Bruce cornered Pam on the patio and kissed her. She'd automatically kissed him back before pushing away angrily.

"What are you doing?" she cried, although some of her anger was at herself for responding. No wonder he thought she was a pushover.

"Trying to communicate without words that I am a man you can trust," he said.

"Attempting to manipulate me with sex, you mean." He'd succeeded, too, until she regained her senses.

The children were already running down the steps to the beach after Yappie. Dorothy, who had gone into her suite for a moment to retrieve a sweater, stepped outside then, ready to take her daily walk with Bruce.

"I'm a simple kind of guy," Bruce said. "What you see is what you get."

"I see ulterior motives," was her icy reply.

Bruce's face fell. "Can we talk this out? Please?"

"Not now," she said. "I have to keep an eye on the children." She followed them down the path to the beach, leaving Bruce to escort Dorothy.

Pam's thoughts roiled. Did he think a few kisses would wipe out his lies? Or had he assumed that because she hadn't caused any scenes in front of her grandchildren that all was forgiven? Her body clearly did not care about Bruce's ethics, but her mind and heart did.

The next afternoon, the visit drew to a close. "I hate to leave," Pam said. "We've had such a good time." She and her mother stood on the patio watching Max and Molly take a last short romp on the sandy area just below their steps.

Dorothy said, "Steve looks undergrown for being ten years old. Have you checked with a doctor about him?"

"That's not Steve. That's his son, Max. He's only eight. Those are Steve's children, my grandchildren." She cocked her head in enquiry as she looked at her mother. Had Dorothy mistaken them?

"Oh, of course," Dorothy said.

"Max looks a lot like Steve," Pam offered, automatically smoothing over the gaffe. Then she did a mental double take. When during the weekend had her mother addressed the children by name? Only once, immediately after they had been introduced to Bruce. Had Dorothy spent the entire weekend thinking these were Pam's children?

That couldn't be. It was merely a flash, because so many children in the family had played on this beach. For a second, her mother must have confused this moment with some other beach visit from long ago.

Dorothy nodded. "Of course."

She said that phrase a lot lately. Was her mother being very clever? Covering up with polite nothings when memory drew a blank?

"Now, Pamela, don't let up on your foundation project. Your initial success is nothing to coast on."

That was more like it.

"Mom, I plan to make the Bright Side Foundation a big success."

Later, driving the children to their home, she thought about her mother's second of confusion. Was this what Bruce had noticed? That Dorothy was a little unsure of who was whom these days? Especially if she hadn't known the person for a long time, as she knew her own daughter?

Chapter 31

Linley rejected Jason's attempt to get her to dine with him. She knew what he wanted. The same as what she wanted. They couldn't have it. She stuck to that mantra throughout the next two weeks as their show got into its stride and became more secure. Amazingly, they found topics to argue about every single day.

They never ran out, because their points of view were so different. Tweeters and bloggers kept commenting on what a conservative she was, how tough she was on the ordinary citizen. She and Jason incorporated the comments into the show.

"Here's an email from Average Joe in Indiana. He thinks you're way too hard on the average citizen, Linley." Jason had the devil in his eyes as he said it.

Linley faced the camera. "Average Joe, do you owe the American average of nine thousand dollars in credit card and other non-secured debt?"

"He doesn't say that."

"If he's representing the average citizen, Joe is in debt and he doesn't do anything to save for a rainy day. Joe, it's raining.

What are you going to do now?"

Jason winced dramatically. "That's harsh. How could Joe or any other person have anticipated the mortgage crisis or the collapse of major financial institutions?"

She shook her head. "You don't get it. Everyone experiences troubles. That's why we're supposed to save for a rainy day. Because they happen."

"Come on, Linley, you're being too tough on Joe. He couldn't know that real estate would take a massive nosedive."

She cocked her head and let an expression of disbelief settle on her face. "Did you listen to what you just said? All financial bubbles pop. It's an immutable law of money."

"Now you've got Joe ready to hang himself," Jason said. "What do you suggest he do?"

She rolled her eyes. "It's obvious, Jason. Stop using credit."

"Get real," Jason acted disgusted. "The entire American economy is based on every one of us being consumers. You're completely unrealistic about all the temptations out there for the average person."

Linley pretended to take offense. "Oh, really? Then answer this. Should an alcoholic cruise bars?"

"Of course not." Jason acted puzzled and impatient. "What's your point?"

"It's the same principle with money," she said heatedly. "If you're short of money, don't go where you're likely to spend."

She swung to face the camera again. "Joe, if you're listening, take your credit cards out of your wallet and leave them at home."

"Your idea isn't new. It won't work," Jason said.

"Don't be a nay-sayer," she said. "Joe, how about trying what I've suggested? Email us in a couple of weeks and tell us how you're doing."

Once the show had ended, she said, "That was too easy."

Jason said, "I'm right and you're wrong. Nothing's going to stop people using credit and debt as their way of life." His tone was passionate.

Marty interrupted. "Save it for another broadcast. Come to my office, you two."

They walked out of Marty's office five minutes later, both reeling. Their show had hit big numbers. Salaries had been more than doubled. Linley was getting an office. Jason was getting an assistant and an audition to host a late night television show for their network.

Jason took her arm in the hall and said in a deadly whisper, "If you don't come to my office right now, I'm going to call Barbara Walters and have phone sex with her."

She looked up at him. Jason was so happy he was blazing, and he wanted to be with her in his moment of triumph. She let him drag her into his office. She let him close and lock the door, and then turn off the lights, so their movements wouldn't be visible through the windows. She let him back her up against the door. His face was rigid with passion.

"Yes or no? This is it, Lin. Now or never."

Something inside her loosened and relaxed, even as the rest of her tensed up with the longing for sexual release. She started to deliberately unbutton her blouse, all the while staring directly into his eyes.

"Yes."

Their coupling was awkward and intense. They groped at pieces of flesh still robed in clothing. They fought to get access to each other. Jason lifted her skirt, pulled down her underwear, and impaled her against the door. She grabbed his back and held on desperately. They caressed each other fiercely as they pressed their hips against each other with manic intensity. In seconds, they both came.

They didn't separate. Her knees wanted to buckle, but Jason's strong arms held her upright. He held her against his chest as if she was precious, the way she'd once imagined.

This was more. This had to be more. She knew it. He was much more than a pretty man from a casual hookup. If only he would say something. Admit that this was more than sex. Then she could admit it, too.

"I want to be with you openly from now on." His voice sounded deeper all of a sudden. "Move in with me. Marry me. Whatever you want."

Whoa. Marriage? Exponentially different. She hadn't thought past a relationship. "I—I want to be with you, too, but I don't know about the rest." She should be relieved. Ecstatic. Instead, she was fretting about her career again.

"We have to be together," he insisted.

Making a commitment was scarier than she'd imagined. "It could mess everything up for the show," she said.

"Nah. What's the worst that could happen? We'd be angrier with each other on air. The viewers would eat it up."

"What if we get so lovey-dovey we can't fight anymore?"

Jason smiled. It was a clear, happy smile. "Let's find out."

They were still joined intimately, and suddenly Jason was

moving inside her again. Thought fled. She offered herself up to him blindly, moving as he urged, gasping with pleasure at every shift. This time was slower, intense in a different way. She couldn't seem to catch her breath. Then she lost it entirely. When she could think again, she was lying on the floor with Jason. He had her firmly pressed against him from head to toe.

Time passed. She could hear the sounds of people leaving for the day. Finally, she spoke. "We'll need to go by my place so I can get some of my things."

His arm tightened. He let out a long breath, then turned so they looked each other in the eye. "You're going to marry me," he promised.

#

She didn't remember how they got themselves together enough to leave the studio. She was sure they must have looked like the besotted idiots they were. She didn't care. At her apartment, she started to gather underwear from her dresser, but found Jason behind her. His embrace made her forget what she was doing. They made love on her bed, this time hurling off all their clothes as they kissed and caressed each other to completion.

Hours later, Jason again asked her to marry him. She didn't say yes, but she didn't say no. The night passed with more lovemaking and a few stretches of sleep.

Finally, morning came. They both had shows to report to. She sighed. He gathered her in his arms. "It's not the end. It's the beginning."

Chapter 32

Steve and Callie arrived home on schedule. They were both smiling and lightly tanned. They ran to the children and scooped them into their arms, crying, "We missed you so much."

Max and Molly squirmed with delight. They talked mile a minute about their weekend at the beach.

"Great-grandma almost has a dog. His name is Yappie," Molly said.

"Is that so?" Steve smiled, ruffling her hair.

Callie had already begun fussing over her children, neatening their hair, straightening their clothes, and more. They stood it well. Callie's love was in every touch. "You've been eating right? You brushed your teeth every day?"

Molly nodded, but continued her dog theme. "He lives next door, with Nana's boyfriend, Mr. Bruce," she said.

"Does Nana have a boyfriend?" Steve teased, looking at his mother in inquiry.

"He's Dorothy's neighbor," Pam demurred.

"He kissed you. I saw him," Max spoke up. "Isn't he your

boyfriend, Nana?"

Steve raised an eyebrow but soon diverted the children to the presents they had brought from Tahiti.

Later, as Pam was getting ready to leave, Steve asked, "Do you really have a boyfriend, Mom?"

"Oh, maybe. I'm not sure I can trust him." She quickly laid out the story of Greta, and Bruce's secrecy about his identity.

Steve's open, pleasant face showed his shock. "Grandma with a gun? I don't believe it."

"It's puzzling," she replied. "I need to hear the story again. Bruce wants to, too." She explained more of the situation, including her plan to investigate Bruce.

"Do the children have it wrong, then? This Bruce is not a new love affair for you?"

"His intentions toward my mother concern me more," she said, not wanting to talk about her intimacy with Bruce.

"You would have found some evidence of foul play by now. You know. Big checks written to him, or whatever."

It was on the tip of her tongue to tell Steve what she had discovered about her mother's finances. She decided not to burden her son with that information.

He continued, "Get the detective. To be sure. I'll help pay for one. The soonest I can bring everybody out for a weekend is a month from now."

"I'm going again in a few days."

By now they were walking to her car. "Thanks for taking care of the kids, Mom." He looked rested and happy.

#

Finally returned to Ardsley, Pam looked around her home as if it was an alien place. She had lived in this house a long time, but it no longer represented her life. Should she get an apartment in the city? Or move out to be with her mother and protect her from questionable men like Bruce? If she did, would she be a making a big mistake, submerging her life into her mother's? Could she stomach living with her mother? They had only recently begun to be more at peace with each other. Dorothy still fussed at her and called her a fool. For her part, she still cringed over some of Dorothy's pronouncements and habits.

Living together might be hellish. Why was she even thinking of it? Because her mother's grasp on her life appeared to be diminishing?

Did Pam have a martyr complex? Dorothy didn't need a savior, nor was she helpless. Dorothy had always been one of the least helpless people she'd ever known. Other girls had envied her having such a cool mom. Pam had found her mother difficult to live up to and resented being associated with such a superwoman. People expected Pam to be a rabble rouser, too. Not the shy, retiring type she was.

What did she owe her mother in her declining years? What could she reasonably give, and still have something left for herself?

#

Bruce wondered what his next step should be. He felt under obligation not to pester Dorothy when she was alone, much as he wanted her to retell the story of his parents' last days. Given what he believed about her increasing mental deterioration, it wasn't ethical to ask for more without someone there to protect her interests. He'd already put himself on incredibly shaky ground with Pam. He didn't want to blow it altogether. Then she might refuse to speak to him again, and deny him any access to Dorothy despite his boast she couldn't. Not his finest moment. He'd been daring enough to keep up their daily walks, but if Pam became adamant or sicced the law on him, he'd have to desist, and he'd lose Pam. If he hadn't lost her already. They needed to talk.

What if Dorothy did have a gun that night? What if she shot his father two weeks later and orchestrated the car crash? She wouldn't have had to do more than wing him, probably. Enough to even the odds between a hulking male in his prime and a slender female. Why had Nora told him? Had his father murdered his mother?

Dorothy was not someone he believed. Talk about an unreliable narrator. She bent facts to suit her notions. Her tale had sounded like a Joan Crawford movie melodrama, not something real. Had Dorothy killed his father? Even if she admitted to cold-blooded murder, what could he do about it? He couldn't call the cops and order them to lock up an eighty-seven-year-old woman who was a pillar in her community. He'd be run out of town on a rail.

What did he want?

Justice. The truth.

Pam, if he could get her. She was proving elusive, and that was entirely his fault. They'd had something. He wanted it back, and he wanted it to grow. Despite her recently started effort to be like her mother and raise money for a cause, Pam was far too soft to take to it with the gusto her mother was famed for. Pam took to making love with plenty of gusto. He'd like her in his bed again, but he'd have to win back her trust. She'd made that clear.

Chapter 33

Linley and Jason still simmered with repressed desire, and they snapped at each other and disagreed with each other as violently as before. Now they went home after a long day at the studio and released their desire in fierce lovemaking that went on into the night.

After one such marathon, it was nearly midnight when Jason and she finally were eating a light dinner. He wore athletic shorts only, and she had donned his dress shirt with the sleeves rolled up.

"You look sexy, babe. Come here," he said.

She shook her head. "I'm starving. I need to keep up my strength."

Then she sat in his lap anyway with her plate of sushi. She fed him and herself a few bites. He shifted her on his lap so her legs were wrapped around his waist. He began to undo the buttons of his shirt, exposing her breasts.

"Jason, I'm hungry." She sighed.

"So am I," he said. He latched onto one of her nipples and sucked at it fiercely. She almost dropped the plate. After he had paid proper attention to one nipple, he switched to the other. His large hands sought her bare waist under the shirt. She shivered as they closed around her.

"Put the plate down," he said, in a low voice, releasing her nipple and staring up into her face. She knew he was going to have her again in a few seconds. They were already entangled. He looked determined and focused. She liked that. She ditched the plate on the table.

Chapter 34

A week later, Pam returned to the beach house. The detective had worked quickly. His report had cleared Bruce of any shadow of criminal intent. He was exactly who he'd said, no more, no less. He was Roger and Greta Dietrich's orphaned son, who had been taken in by Greta's younger sister, Nora Wicklow. Nora was now a widow of eighty. Roger Dietrich had died in a one-car crash. No autopsy had been performed. Greta had died two weeks earlier, the cause listed as a domestic mishap. The detective had checked with the local police, but had not found anyone alive who remembered the case.

Pam had been busy that week, too. She had visited two more executives and sent out a press release regarding her biggest donation so far. She had also called her old friend, Harper Hastings. Harper was currently unmarried, unemployed, and bored, something rich women did not enjoy as much as the working class imagined. She willingly took on the mission of brainstorming a strategy to enhance the Bright Side Foundation's donation base and its social visibility. She also approved of Pam's classic Dior dress and said Pam looked smashing in it.

Pam felt pretty good about herself at the moment. Despite how difficult it was to confront executives and ask them for money, she wasn't backing down. Sometimes she shuddered with nerves in the nearest ladies' room before or after her interviews. But she persisted. Facing the smug, self-absorbed men in their fancy offices got easier each time.

The selling proposition her mother had detailed, that of getting in on the ground floor of a new charity, worked powerful magic. Men who started the interviews cold and bored soon understood that Pam was offering them an opportunity to achieve what money alone had not yet brought them: Fame. Social power. A chance at a legacy.

Every time Pam walked out of an executive office holding a check for the Bright Side Foundation, her belief in herself grew. She almost began to enjoy the challenge.

She was making progress on other fronts. Although she hadn't put her house on the market yet, she had spent many hours going through more stored items, and she'd made a series of large donations to local resale charities. It was time-consuming to target the right item to the right charity, but she didn't mind. She wanted everything to be used and useful, not junk for the landfill.

She was considering what she wanted to do with the rest of her life. That was the big one. Also what she ought to do, which might be substantially different. She spent a lot of time thinking about what she owed her mother and what would be right for her mother's future. That involved a long phone call with Alexander, which did not go well at first.

"Why didn't you tell me you've been helping Mother with her bills all this time?" she had accused.

"You didn't want to know, for one thing. For another, you didn't want to know," he said.

"Have I been that selfish?"

"Yes. You all have. Christine is a total self-absorbed bitch. Her excuse is her effed-up kid, but that's just her excuse."

"What about Neil?"

"Useless. He's a money-grubbing asshole who thinks of no one but himself."

"Okay, we're all terrible. Level with me about what's happening."

"Mom's getting a bit vague, that's all. I went over on the first of the month and we'd do all our bills together. She's perfectly capable. That way I made sure she did them, and I saw that no one was scamming her. That's the big fear with older people, scams."

"Were you the one who thought of the weekly deli delivery?"

"Set it up a couple of years ago. Mom hates to cook, we all know that."

"It works well. Especially because they take away all the old food, too."

"I arranged that. She's paying extra for the service, but it's worth it."

"Has she seen a doctor? The man who is renting next door, Bruce, told me he bumped into Mom in town, apparently confused about where the hairdresser's salon was. He also claimed Mom took so long to drive home he was sure she got lost on the way back."

Alexander cursed.

There was a pause. Then he spoke again, slowly. "There's no way of proving it. Mom's too clever to admit a fault."

"You're right," she said. She'd had firsthand experience this past weekend, she explained. "It wasn't until she called her great-grandson by my son's name that I realized she didn't know who he was. She never calls anyone by name. Except me."

"Then it's always 'Pam-e-la,' in that awful tone," he said and laughed.

"Too true." Pam's rueful laugh was a little ragged.

Alexander said, "Get her to a doctor and have him test her for dementia or Alzheimer's. Or anything else that might be wrong. This could be something else, you know. Small strokes, maybe."

"Then what?"

"That's going to be up to you. Don't worry. Whatever you choose, the family can afford to pay for it. A very good quality assisted living situation. Or an at-home live-in companion. Or whatever. If necessary, I'll go to Chicago and shake down Christine myself to make sure she pays her share. We can send Neil a bill. He'll pay it."

Pam was encouraged by her talk with Alexander. He made it sound as if taking care of their mother was something she could handle. She'd never thought about it before. She had always assumed she would take care of Jeff or he would take care of her. She hadn't even thought about the unfairness of expecting Alexander to look after their mother. He had been the obvious choice because he lived near her and they were so close, but it still wasn't fair. When he had taken the geographical cure, he'd been within his rights. Now it was up to her. She was less afraid than previously. Her recent visits to Dorothy had gone smoothly most of the time.

Before she returned to the beach, she should talk to Linley. Linley had been completely incommunicado lately. The new television show, which paired her with the emcee, Jason, was a treat to watch. Pam hadn't missed an episode. It was obvious Linley and Jason were in love. They even argued like lovers.

Finally, she got Linley on the phone. "I want to see you before I go out to the beach again. When can we meet?"

Linley sounded taken aback at Pam's forcefulness. "I'm busy right now," she claimed.

"This is important, dear. Name some time tomorrow or the next day when we can get together and talk." Her words sounded rather brusque and commanding, an attitude she hadn't projected at Linley in many years. To her surprise, her daughter reacted obediently.

"Okay. Tomorrow at two-thirty. We can go to a coffee shop to talk. They'll be empty."

The next day, Pam had just come from one of her hard case interviews so she was dolled up in her Chanel suit and the whole nine yards. Linley looked impressed.

"Is that Chanel?"

"From your grandmother's closet," she said. "She's the reason I wanted to talk to you."

It wasn't easy to get the words out, but she explained there was some question about Dorothy's competence to handle her affairs unassisted.

Linley looked pole-axed. "Not Grandma. She's so strong. It can't be."

"We don't know for sure," Pam consoled, seeing Linley's vulnerable side for once. Then she broke the news about Bruce's story.

Linley was astonished. "You mean this man deliberately rented the house next door to cozy up to Grandma?"

"He even got a cute dog to soften her up. It worked, too. They're friends now. They take a daily beach walk."

"Is he after her money? Does he want to fleece her?"

"Something worse, I'm afraid," she said. She told about Dorothy's confession.

"Grandma had a gun?" Linley looked amazed and disbelieving.

"That's what every person who knows her has said. Me, Alexander, Sarah, Steve."

"So Grandma claimed at first that this woman—Greta, right?—died accidentally. Then Grandma changed her story and said she'd forced Greta's husband, Roger, to admit he pushed this Greta around?"

"More than that. Classic abuser tactics. Isolation, mysterious bruises, and then the accidental death that was the result."

At Linley's continued look of shock, Pam continued. "I'll protect her interests. Not from Bruce—whom incidentally I had investigated and he's not a scam artist. He apparently doesn't mean to cause her any harm. I want to shield her from her painful memories."

"What if Grandma actually killed this man?"

Pam shook her head. "Very unlikely."

"If she can't remember what happened, and she's the only witness," Linley worked it out, "then the police wouldn't be involved?"

"That's right, dear. Even if the gun story is true, there's nothing Bruce can do about it with no evidence."

"Then Grandma is safe."

Pam nodded. "Bruce says he only wants to know for his own peace of mind." She shrugged. "Maybe that's true."

Then Pam switched topics and regaled Linley with a summary of her achievements with the foundation. "I'm telling you this because if you see any opportunities for the Bright Side Foundation to get any publicity, I want you to let me know. Either I or Harper will follow up on them. Magda is keeping an eye on email if that's all you have time for."

"Okay, but you should take care of Grandma first."

"You can help with that, dear. Why don't you schedule a weekend visit with her?" she asked.

Linley squirmed. "I'm…I'm kind of busy right now."

"As are we all. Steve is taking his family out there next month." Pam said it knowing Linley was fiercely competitive with Steve. Always had been. "Surely you're not busy all the time?" she asked.

Linley blushed slightly.

Ah, it must mean she and Jason were an item now. "Why don't you and Jason come out in two weeks?" Pam added.

"Me and…" Linley paled.

From her reaction, Linley was remembering how during her teenage years, she'd called Pam "psychic mom."

"Please don't try to tell me you hadn't noticed your on-air chemistry or done something about it by now," Pam said with asperity. "You always leaped right into sexual involvements in the past, ignoring any advice to go slowly."

Linley actually flushed red. "Okay. You're right. I never used to listen."

"So, you and Jason?" Pam prodded.

"We're seeing each other," she said in a low tone of voice.

Linley resembled her sulky teenage self of years ago. Since she had admitted to the relationship with Jason, Pam did not press her further.

"That's nice, dear. Bring him with you when you visit. He'll want to meet Dorothy sometime."

At that remark, Linley got a rather wicked smile on her face. "That could be fun."

#

Two weeks later, Pam had gone back and forth to Ardsley too often. She had even moved a pile of her clothes to her mother's house for convenience. She was about ready to ask her children which pieces of family furniture they'd like, if any. Then she was putting the house up for sale, terrible real estate market or not. She was done. Her memories of Jeff were with her wherever she went. She didn't need a shrine to him. As for employment, she was never going back to being a cog in a machine again. No more plodding through life like a robot.

She looked for a small place in the outer reaches of Queens or the west edge of Suffolk County. She'd still need somewhere to live and to keep her car. A long phone talk with Sarah had convinced her not to give up her life to her mother.

"It's a stupid, martyr-like thing to do. Your mother doesn't want or need you stomping all over her life," Sarah said.

"The books say there should be moderation, but how else

351

can I supervise her?"

"Move closer. Call and visit often. Hire a caregiver." Sarah said. "There are a million strategies you haven't tried yet. Throwing up your new project and effectively shutting down your own life is not on the list. Especially since your family has plenty of money to pay for help."

"True."

"You don't need to be her caregiver. You can supervise whoever does it."

Sarah continued, "All you need is a Long Island Railroad station conveniently nearby, so you can get into the city. You can live anywhere on the island."

"Then I could continue to develop my foundation while keeping watch over Mom," she said, relieved to realize it would be practical to have her own separate home. She was just finding her life again. She didn't want to give it up.

"Sarah, you're the best," she said.

"Of course I am."

#

Pam asked repeatedly, but Dorothy refused to see a doctor. Her memory seemed just fine when it came to remembering that Pam was nagging her.

"Pamela, you're beating a dead horse," Dorothy said, her voice firm. "I have no intention of seeing a doctor."

"But Mom—"

"That's enough." Dorothy went to sit in her favorite wicker chair in the sunroom, leaving Pam standing in the dining room, frustrated.

What could she do? Her mother still thought of Pam as ineffectual and shy, what she'd been as a teenager. The weakling daughter, the one who held back. Dorothy didn't think Pam had anything useful to say. Pam had changed over the years and taken a massive leap forward recently, too. But her mother couldn't see it.

Dorothy respected Alexander. Pam checked the clock on the living room mantel. After five o'clock. He should be home from golf by now. She picked up the landline phone on the stand in the corner of the room and dialed. Dorothy still had a pastel pink telephone with a dial.

"What's up?" Alexander answered.

"It's me," Pam said. "Will you please tell Mom she should see a doctor?"

"Why do you need me to? Tell her yourself."

Pam heaved an impatient breath. "I've been telling her 'til I'm blue in the face. She won't listen to me."

"O-kay," he said, drawling the word. "I get it."

Pam turned and called toward the sunroom. "Mom, Alexander's on the phone. He'd like to talk to you."

"Oh, how nice," Dorothy said, rising from her chair and quickly walking through to the living room. Pam held out the old-fashioned wired phone to her mother.

Dorothy spoke into the receiver. The affection she had for her younger son was clear in her voice. Pam gazed out at the water, wondering if she could ever get through to Dorothy that her youngest daughter wasn't a total incompetent.

"All right, dear. If you think I should," Dorothy said into the phone. "Yes, I'll let you know what the doctor says. Absolutely."

After a few more words, Dorothy put the phone back on the receiver. "Alexander wants you to make an appointment with my doctor."

"Wonderful," Pan said, heaving a sigh of relief Dorothy had finally consented.

Dorothy gave her a look. "You don't have to act as if making a doctor appointment is difficult."

"I'm not—I didn't mean—oh, forget it," Pam said, frustrated again. "I'll call the doctor's office right away."

Why did any of her three siblings think it would be a good idea for Pam to move in with Dorothy? Living with her would be hell.

Chapter 35

The doctor diagnosed Dorothy with mild dementia. He prescribed the current Alzheimer's medication to combat it and slow it down. He told Pam that was all they could do. Dorothy seemed not to take in what he said.

"See, that wasn't such a big deal, was it?" Pam said to her mother after they had picked up the prescription. They were lunching in a restaurant in town. It was a pretty cottage renovated into a tearoom. Probably a little too precious for her mother's taste, but it suited her own.

"I don't like doctors, never did," Dorothy said. "I especially hated them since they let Malcolm drop dead on the sidewalk."

Pam winced. "No, Mom, that was Jeff, my husband." She shook her head. "Dad died of a heart attack in your house."

"That's what I said. Doctors let our husbands, both of them, die long before their time," Dorothy said in an aggrieved yet still authoritative manner.

Sustained conversation with her mother was proving difficult in a new way. Before, Dorothy had nagged her constantly. Today, she seemed unable to keep on topic. Perhaps the outing had made her tired. Or perhaps it was not being in her own home that made it hard to focus?

Their meal arrived. After eating something Dorothy seemed more together. Pam was grateful, noting it for the future. She should make sure her mother ate regularly. The doctor had warned her that the medications dimmed appetite substantially. "You'll have to remind your mother to eat."

Chapter 36

Linley thought it was funny that Jason was so particular about what clothes to bring for their weekend at her grandmother's house.

"Pack khakis. It's no big deal."

"Hey, I've never been to a beach house. I grew up in the hinterlands of Pennsylvania, remember?" he said in his defense.

"Are you nervous about meeting my family?" she asked.

"I want them to approve of me."

"Grandma already likes you. She watches our shows. She told me you were hot."

"What about your mother?"

"You met her already. She's a pushover," she said. "Honestly, Jason, why do you care?"

"I want them to approve of our marriage," he said.

He took her breath away. He'd said it that first day. He kept saying it. She hadn't agreed, but Jason was a stubborn guy, and he kept bringing it up. He talked about where they'd live after they married. Whether they should buy a new co-op together. He asked her if she wanted to have babies someday. That took her breath away. He even asked about her dream wedding. The time of year, the venue, whether she wanted to wear a fancy white gown.

Now she said, "I thought we agreed to hold off on that."

"No, you want to chicken out of committing to me," he said, impatiently. "You're still pretending at the studio we don't live together."

"Meanwhile, you've been going behind my back and calling me your fiancée," she said, angry all over again since the first time Ernie had said it.

"You're going to marry me. Of course you're my fiancée," he insisted.

"Not if you annoy me so much I refuse."

At that, he turned and caught her up in his arms and planted a major kiss on her willing lips. Her stubborn back took a few seconds to yield. Then she plastered her body against his, fiercely kissing him. After a while, Jason raised his head, clearly satisfied with her response.

"When do you want to get married?"

"Ohhh." She banged out of the bedroom, only half pretending to be annoyed at how he had outmaneuvered her. When he kissed her like that, she melted. She'd thought it would fade after the first few days. In the past, the appeal of most other guys had dimmed quickly. Not Jason's sexy charm. He said and did the most outrageous things, and then all he had to do was kiss her and she was distracted. She wanted him as desperately now as she had three months ago. Only now, she could have him every night.

Did she want to marry him? Did she want to marry any man?

She didn't intend to be a doormat wife like her mother. She didn't want to make a mistake and end up divorced, either. No "starter marriage" for her. How could she be sure Jason was the right man? He was so wrapped up in his ambition.

As was she. Did they have the right to marry when they couldn't give much attention to a relationship?

There wasn't any other man she wanted more. In fact, there never had been. Loving Jason had taken her to a new level of caring for the first time in her adult life. She'd given him a hard time, but he'd hung in, anyway. Jason didn't want to be the boss of her, either. He was too busy trying to figure out how to be a hit with the public. That meant she was on her own when it came to her ambitions. She could try what she wanted and he wouldn't interfere, although he wasn't available to help much at this point, either.

Did he care enough? For that matter, did she? How committed did a person have to be to have a successful marriage? Especially when they were media people, well-known faces who got lots of offers? The more famous they became, the more likely it was that other people would try to grab at them and their fame.

She struggled with her thoughts all the way out to the beach. She and Jason had rented a car. Neither of them bothered owning one in Manhattan. Who wanted to throw away a fortune on garage space? He'd let her drive since she knew the way. Also because he wasn't a total macho pig with his ego tied up in who was at the wheel.

The weather had already turned, but that made the beach even more romantic. It was deserted. Any crowds were long gone. There was a sense of the beach having seen great drama and then having been abandoned.

Her mother and grandmother must have been watching for them. They came out of the house as soon as they parked. She was struck by how healthy and happy her mother looked. She'd never noticed before. How strange that she hadn't.

There was dear Grandma Dorothy. Daddy's mother had died young, but Grandma Dorothy was hale and hearty.

Why was she noticing the health of her relatives all of a sudden?

#

When Linley raced to embrace her relatives, Jason saw she skipped her mother to go for her grandmother first. According to what she'd let drop, she didn't think much of her mother but she idolized her retired activist grandmother. He had checked out Dorothy on the net and learned as much as he could about her. She'd done a lot of good for people and never taken anything more than a thank you for her trouble. One of a dying breed.

"Hello, Jason, nice to see you again," Pam Ridgeway said, offering her hand to fill in the awkward moment when her daughter chose to embrace her grandmother. "We met briefly a few months ago."

"I remember. I hope we'll be seeing each other often in the future, Mrs. Ridgeway," he replied.

She raised an eyebrow at his comment, then smiled. "Oh, call me Pam. Everybody does. Except for my mother. I'm always Pamela to her." She turned to Linley and Dorothy Duncan.

"Mother, this is Linley's young man, Jason Egan."

After more handshaking, Pam urged them inside. "You both might as well bring in your things now. We're going to have our afternoon snack break in a few minutes," she added.

Pam sent them upstairs on their own to pick their accommodations. She explained where her bedroom and Dorothy's were, so they could infer where they'd have the most privacy. "Take as much space as you want. Or as little," she said, smiling knowingly. Linley must have told her about them. Good. His future mother-in-law was okay with him already.

He looked into several rooms before he found what had obviously been a shared boys' bedroom. It still was filled with trophies and sports memorabilia. "These twin beds pose a tactical challenge, but being on this side of the house will give us the most privacy," he said.

"Why would we need privacy?" Linley asked with a saucy smile.

Jason happily rose to the challenge. He lifted her off her feet and put her on the nearest bed, then followed her down and started kissing various of her body parts. She couldn't help groaning.

"Aha. See? Noise leak," he gloated.

"Ooh, I'll make you pay for that," she said, smiling. Her talented tongue made short work of his sangfroid. He started groaning, too.

"Woman, you don't play fair." He flipped them over onto the hard wooden floor, where the scatter rug was little cushion. That knocked the wind out of both of them enough to stop their hijinks.

Then he escaped. Oh lord, she was magnificent. She was the woman he'd always wanted. She had to say she was his. Not only for now, but for the future. Maybe her mother and grandmother could help him convince her. Speaking of them, he'd better get downstairs and encourage them to think good thoughts. Not the obvious, that he and Linley could hardly keep their hands off each other.

#

Downstairs, Dorothy was waiting in the sunroom for Pamela to bring some refreshment. The couple who had just arrived puzzled her. Linley, of course, she recognized. Her granddaughter. Who was that handsome man with her? He looked familiar. Oh, wait. He was on television, too. Jason, that was his name. He worked with Linley. How interesting that he was here visiting with her. Were they friends, or was it more?

"Pamela, are those two young people engaged?" she wanted to know.

The young man arrived downstairs just at that moment. "I'd like to marry Lin, but so far, she hasn't said yes officially." He smiled at both women. Dorothy was sitting in her usual chair. Pam was setting a tray of drinks on the nearby coffee table.

She straightened up. "You've proposed?"

"Not formally," he admitted.

Dorothy laughed. "Then don't raise our hopes, boy." She turned to Pam. "Men always anticipate a sure thing."

Pam had gestured to a seat, and Jason took it, lolling on the couch comfortably.

"Can you blame me? Life is risky for us men. We have to do

all the asking and inviting."

Both women smiled at him.

#

Pam enjoyed a few minutes chatting with Jason before Bruce arrived and introductions were made. Bruce had formed a habit of coming in after the usual afternoon walk and hanging around during snack time. Pam hadn't tried to fight it once she'd realized Dorothy ate better if he was there to distract her. They still hadn't had that talk he wanted.

Pam had made snack time into something like a British high tea, hoping to tempt her mother into eating heartily after her main exercise of the day gave her a little appetite. The medicine Dorothy was taking had reduced her sense of being hungry, just as the doctor had predicted. Pam wanted to be sure Dorothy ate well at least once a day.

"Bruce, Jason is Linley's friend and—I guess you'd call it a co-anchor or something?—from the television network."

The men shook hands, sizing each other up. Pam had the impression Bruce viewed Jason with disfavor. Until Linley came downstairs. Jason's eyes lit up and he eagerly walked to meet her, telegraphing where his romantic interest lay. Then Bruce seemed to relax.

Pam made an excuse to accompany Bruce outside when he left. When they were on the patio, safely out of earshot, she asked, "Were you bristling at Jason?"

"What if I was?"

"Why?"

"Because I thought he might be interested in you," he said,

the relief obvious in his tone. He placed his hands on her shoulders and looked into her doubting eyes. "You may not want to hear this, but I care about you. I get jealous of any other man who might look at you."

"Each week, in the city, I have interviews with captains of industry. Are you jealous of them, too?"

"Don't," he said. "I've walked the line you insisted on. You know I want you."

"You want my mother's memories unlocked," she said with sudden bitterness, "To get at them, you're willing to distract me with sex."

"Were you distracted?" he said, with hope in his voice. "Because I admit I was. I never expected to fall so hard so fast."

"Liar."

"No. It's the truth. Believe me."

"I'm going in now," she said. She wasn't willing to argue about what was between them, not with company nearby, but his seeming sincerity had affected her despite herself.

Inside, Dorothy was regaling Jason and Linley with stories from her golden days. Dorothy was letter-perfect on those stories. According to the books the doctor had recommended, older memories remained sharp long after newer ones got vague or could not be stored effectively in the deteriorating brain. If that was what was happening with her mother. They were trying the medicine merely as a precaution.

Everything went smoothly that evening. They went to a nearby restaurant for dinner, and as usual, Dorothy was treated as visiting royalty. Not only were they given a prominent table, but many people came up to speak to her. A few did double takes, recognizing Linley and Jason from television, but Dorothy was the star of the evening.

The next morning, Pam was up early and made coffee. Dorothy was still sleeping in when Jason came downstairs and passed through the kitchen for a cup. He was dressed for a run in jogging shorts, a loose white T-shirt, and sneakers.

"It's a half-mile east to the old pier, if you want to keep track of your distance," she offered. "Or two miles to Glenvale Village on the road."

"I'll try the beach," Jason said. "Thanks for the coffee."

Pam smiled. It was pleasant to do for a man occasionally. "Biscuits in half an hour."

"Great." With a wave, he let himself out the kitchen door and took off down the path to the beach. Yappie barked once to say he'd noticed Jason.

Pam busied herself with cooking, enjoying the sunlight coming through the kitchen windows. It looked to be a beautiful day. She was setting the dining room table when Dorothy came out of her bedroom. "Biscuits in five, Mom."

"Splendid. I'll finish here. You go do your magic in the kitchen." To Dorothy, any real cooking was like an arcane art.

Pam was pulling the biscuits, perfectly golden, out of the oven when she heard her mother's voice raised in anger.

She dropped everything and ran into the dining room. Dorothy was at the doorway, barring Jason's motion further into the house. He'd come in the patio door.

"I repeat. Who are you, young man? What makes you think you have the right to enter my home?"

Jason was taken aback. Clearly, he was floundering for an answer.

"Mom, this is Linley's fiancé, Jason, remember? He's a weekend guest." Pam spoke in a soothing voice.

"Pamela, Linley is a little girl. She's too young to be engaged," her mother insisted. Her voice began to rise again. "Call the police."

Jason looked confused and stymied. He kept still, making no gestures.

"Grandma, what's the matter?" Linley came tearing down the stairs.

"Who is this strange man?" Dorothy asked.

"Don't you recognize Jason? He's on my TV show with me." Linley put her arm around Jason and hugged him. He hugged her back, but kept his eyes on Dorothy.

"Linley?" Dorothy suddenly looked confused, at a loss. She didn't seem to recognize Linley. "Linley is a little girl. You're not Linley."

Pam swiftly moved to put her hand on her mother's arm. "Linley is all grown up, Mom. Remember? She's a television star."

Dorothy's face registered a look of panic and then comprehension. "Oh. Of course."

Pam coaxed her to her favorite wicker chair. "Why don't you sit down for a while? Look at the water. When breakfast is ready, I'll call you."

"All right," Dorothy said. She looked shaken. She cast Jason a confused glance.

Pam motioned for him to leave the room. "It's all right, Mother."

Dorothy wasn't listening. She had lapsed into some internal monologue Pam could not penetrate. Pam left her in the sunroom and herded her daughter and Jason out of Dorothy's line of vision, into the kitchen. They looked shell-shocked.

"I'm sorry that happened. I had hoped all would be smooth sailing this weekend." Pam bustled about, covering the biscuits with a cloth and turning off the oven.

"You said Grandma had only a little bit of memory loss," Linley accused.

"She has occasionally blanked on recognizing someone. It was always a minor thing that she covered smoothly. I presume this is because her sense of time is getting confused."

"Don't you know?"

"I took her to the doctor," Pam replied. "He said he didn't think she has Alzheimer's." Unspoken was the knowledge that Dorothy's behavior a minute ago, so different from her usual demeanor, looked awfully like that dreaded disease. Perhaps the doctor was wrong.

She turned to Jason. "I'm sorry. I hope you understand that my mother meant nothing just now."

Jason had gotten over his surprise. "It's my fault. I should have said something to reassure her. I drew a blank."

Linley muttered, "It can't be Alzheimer's. It can't."

"Maybe it isn't," Pam shrugged. "We'll have to be careful from now on. We don't want Dorothy calling the police on you, Jason."

Linley's accusation seemed to come out of nowhere. "You've let Grandma get run down, and now you're trying to justify your neglect by saying she has that awful disease."

"Don't go off half-cocked, Lin," Jason urged. Then he seemed to take a mental step back. "Look, this is family business. I'll leave and let you two talk."

"No, stay," Linley said. "Tell me what has been going on," she demanded of Pam.

"All right." Pam recited the entire tale Bruce had related to her about Dorothy's hair appointment. She added what she had discovered about the finances.

"Your uncle Alexander helped her for a long time. After he moved away, she stopped paying attention to her bills. They were about to turn off the power a couple of weeks ago when I discovered all this."

"No." Linley's face showed her shock.

"I'm afraid so. In other respects, your grandmother has been very clever. She can still write a check, and she keeps calendars everywhere to remind her of her few appointments. When she's confused around people, she carefully doesn't say their names in case she makes a mistake. She agrees with what others say instead of admitting she doesn't know what they're talking about."

Pam tried to speak calmly and not voice the sadness she felt. "What happened this morning is new. She has never shown any overt confusion or anger before. That could be indicative of Alzheimer's, not merely dementia. She might have it after all."

Linley looked liked she'd taken a punch.

Pam continued. "I've been reading up on Alzheimer's. Personality change is the first sign. Until today, she has been positive and calm."

"You took her to the wrong doctor. Can't you do anything right?"

"I'm sorry, Linley. I've done my best. The doctor said—I'm sorry—"

"Don't say that again," Linley interrupted, gaining speed and volume as she spoke. "This is your fault. You neglected her, leaving it all up to Uncle Alexander. You've been a zombie since Dad died, not that you were much before. You should be taking care of Grandma. Not letting bad things happen to her."

Jason looked shocked, but said nothing.

Linley continued her tirade. "As for your stupid Bright Side Foundation, don't think it's any big deal. I've seen plenty of foundations go nowhere. Your little project is no excuse for neglecting Grandma. You'd better dump it right now and move in to take care of her."

Linley slammed out the kitchen door and headed in the direction of the beach.

Jason looked after her in concern. He began to follow her, but Pam held him back with a touch on his arm.

"I wouldn't. Her tantrums burn out a lot faster alone."

Her warning obviously made him uncomfortable. Pam was fighting with a much stronger feeling, the sense of having been publicly flogged. Her daughter's scorn had humiliated her, and worse, in front of a near stranger. The scorn was nothing new. Being treated so badly in front of this man was. Pam could not resist a warning. "If you want to marry her, these scenes will become familiar."

Jason looked at Pam seriously. "I love her. Despite the drama. She went off on me a few months ago. We got past that."

"Did she?" Pam fought back the tears. "Linley has been putting me down like this since she was fourteen years old. It doesn't get better. I'm tired of it, but I'm her mother. That relationship can never end no matter how estranged she is from me. I will love her until I die. If you marry, will you get tired of Linley's tantrums when she isn't perfect enough to suit herself?

"That's what it is, you know. I used to think she hated me. Now I've realized she hates the female frailty I represent. She despises me because she fears she might be tempted to make compromises in life."

She roused herself. "Why am I saying these things to you? You say you want to marry Linley. I shouldn't be painting a negative picture of her." She wondered if he had thought through how complicated being married to Linley might be. Perhaps her daughter would never change. She had gotten into the bad habit of blowing up at people. Linley might destroy her hopes of a successful media career if she wasn't careful. Her lack of maturity hurt Pam personally, but also made her worry for Linley's sake. When would her child grow up at last?

"I love Linley," Pam said. "I don't want her to suffer because she has never learned to control herself. If you let her tantrums go by, you'll be enabling her as I used to. No more. I've finally found my spine."

Pam demonstrated what she said when Linley returned a half hour later through the patio door. Pam rose from her seat in the sunroom and put a hand out to stop Linley from walking by her. "Stop for a minute. I have something to say."

"I'm not going to apologize—" Linley began, obviously still angry. Pam's hand was unusually firm on her shoulder.

"I said stop," Pam repeated sharply in an authoritative tone of voice she hadn't aimed at Linley in a decade.

Linley's expression showed how stunned she was. Pam led her daughter into the nearby dining room, where Dorothy could not hear them.

"Now, listen. I have let you get away with your tantrums for years, hoping you would grow out of them. You haven't. No more. Don't say another nasty word to me. I can live my life without your completely mistaken judgments on it."

Pam kept her voice low as she continued. "You're welcome to stay here the rest of the weekend if you can stop trying to blame me for everything wrong with the world. If not, then please leave now. Your bad attitude will not help your grandmother."

Linley looked dumbfounded. She was used to Pam cringing and begging for her love, not criticizing her. "You're just saying that because you don't know what to do…" Linley began in the same tone of voice she'd used in the kitchen.

Pam raised her palm. "Enough. If you can't stop pouring out poison, then go pack."

"You can't make me leave," Linley shouted. "This is Grandma's house, not yours."

Pam cast her a steely look. "Be quiet. Don't disturb Grandma. Grow up, Linley. This isn't about you." Then Pam walked away from Linley without a backward glance.

#

Brunch in the dining room went smoothly, but with someone missing. Linley was sulking upstairs somewhere, Pam assumed. Jason was obviously embarrassed to be left alone with Linley's family, but he held his peace. Pam assumed his loyalty was to her daughter. Dorothy was completely recovered from her earlier confusion. An hour in her favorite sunroom chair had restored her. She chatted with Jason as if she knew him. Another instance of Dorothy putting on a good act? Possibly.

Pam tried to help Dorothy keep her hold on the present. She reminded her who Jason was, underlining that he and Linley worked together. "You've seen them on television together many times, Mom." She also repeated "Mom" as much as possible, to remind her mother who she was, too. Pam wasn't taking any more chances today.

Was her mother's condition declining rapidly? Only a couple of months ago, Dorothy had been capable of making all her appointments, making friends with Bruce next door, and, except for what came in the mail, taking care of her financial affairs. That was a big exception, but still. Now, Dorothy seemed to visibly fluctuate.

A few minutes later, Linley appeared downstairs with her luggage.

Pam braced herself for another scene.

"I'm going home. I'll wait for you in the car, Jason," Linley announced. She kissed Dorothy and sent Pam a hostile glare before sweeping out the front door.

Jason stood up abruptly. "Excuse me." He went upstairs, presumably to pack.

"It was nice to have company for such a long visit, but we'll be fine on our own now," Dorothy said. She calmly buttered her toast.

Pam trembled, hardly paying attention. She'd finally done it. Laid down the law with her rebellious daughter and made it stick. It felt good. Scary, but good. If it meant Linley left early, and in a snit, so be it.

Chapter 37

"Slow down," Jason said. They were on the Long Island Expressway and Linley was speeding like a maniac, passing cars with mere inches to spare. "I happen to like being alive."

She accelerated even more, not looking at him. Her expression was furious.

"Ah, I get it," he said, as if he was talking to himself. "No one tells Linley what to do."

She made a sound of protest, but didn't slow down.

She hadn't killed anyone yet, but Jason wasn't willing to take his chances.

"Slow down." He made his voice commanding. Would he have to stomp on the brake himself? Grab the wheel? Even slap her? She was trying to kill them.

Linley made no sign she heard him, but she slowed down to the speed limit exactly. It was a calculated insult, but he didn't care.

"Take the next exit," he said. She promptly wove the car through four lanes of traffic, cutting others off, eliciting angry honking as she left the expressway with a screech of the tires.

Then she let the car drift to a stop on the access road. Jason reached over and turned the ignition key to off and pulled it out. He pocketed it and got out of the car. Leaning against the front fender, he took a deep breath. Then he went around to the driver's door and yanked it open.

"Out," he ordered.

Inside the car, Linley gave him an angry, sulky look. He didn't melt. She started sobbing. Jason let her.

"Get out, Lin," he repeated.

Finally, she looked up at him with a childlike expression of disbelief. "I won't."

"You've got five seconds."

"It's my rental, not yours."

"Out."

He started counting aloud. Still she wouldn't budge. At five, he pulled her up from the seat, and forcibly removed her from the car. He frog-marched her to the passenger side, and put her in the seat.

He started the car and guided it back on the expressway. She began sobbing. After twenty minutes of tears, to which Jason would not allow himself to respond, Linley spoke.

"I could have killed us. I'm a monster."

"No, you're a spoiled brat who needs to grow up," Jason replied. "Your ego is outraged because your mother dared speak up for herself. You were willing to kill us both to escape the feeling of being chastised by her. Even though you deserved it."

"She never did before. Daddy always stopped her," Linley's mouth snapped shut. Then she said, slowly, "My father stopped my mother from disciplining me when they both knew I deserved it. He let me say mean things to her. He encouraged me to be spoiled and nasty to her." She sagged against the car door.

Jason willed himself not to respond sympathetically. "You take some time to think this all through," he finally said. He couldn't put what he felt into words. Despite her seeming remorse, was she a hopeless psycho? Driving like a maniac put Linley's angry moments in a whole different light. Was he being an alarmist? Who knew?

Tears dripped down her face, and she made an occasional whimper. He should have felt sorry for her. Maybe he did. Mostly he was relieved to be alive. Now to get them safely to Manhattan.

#

Jason dropped Linley off at her condo, saying he'd be back in an hour. "I'll pack all the things you left at my place. We've got to take a break."

She nodded and went inside.

An hour later, he returned with three trash bags filled with her clothes and personal items. He rang her bell and delivered the bags himself.

"I'm sorry it had to end this way," he said when she came to the door. She accepted the trash bags and the keys to the rental.

Jason waited for her to speak, but she said nothing. Her face didn't give her feelings away.

"See you at work," he finally muttered.

She said nothing, just stared at him.

He turned to walk away. It had been a wonderful dream, but had turned into a nightmare.

Chapter 38

Pam was still mentally reliving the disastrous scenes with Linley when Bruce arrived hours later with Yappie. Dorothy went out to the patio to play with the little dog. Bruce and she exchanged a few words and then he came in to speak to Pam.

"Where are your houseguests? I was thinking maybe we could try going for a sail."

"They left," she said, shuddering at the thought of being cooped up with Linley in a small boat. Not her idea of a good time.

Perhaps she shouldn't have confided, but something about Bruce always made her go the extra mile. She told him what had happened that morning. "Linley didn't take Dorothy's mental condition well. Even though I warned her in advance, seeing it for herself was tough."

"Is she one of those people who's afraid to be around people who are ill?" he asked.

"I think she was overcome by the enormity of it. My mother has always been the strong leader of the family. The idea she's losing her hold on reality isn't a pleasant one. Linley didn't have the weeks I did to absorb the brutal truth."

"Which you also denied at first," he reminded her.

"Thank goodness you found Mom that day in town. I'm sorry I didn't want to believe she was confused."

"Apology accepted. Now maybe you could work on believing me when I say I have never meant your mother any harm," Bruce replied.

"I've thought about it," she said.

"What can I do to convince you?"

"Promise you won't ask Dorothy again about Greta."

He looked shocked. "That's a lot to ask."

Pam nodded. "Promise me."

He threaded the fingers of one hand through his hair, and walked around the room, clearly flummoxed by her demand. He looked over at her. "I can't promise that. I came here to get the truth from Dorothy."

"She told you the truth as she sees it." Pam didn't soften her tone.

"Did she?" Bruce looked unconvinced.

Pam said, "I don't really care. I'm sorry if that hurts your feelings."

"No, I understand. You want to protect your mother." He came and stood in front of her. "You mean a lot to me. Okay, I promise."

Something loosened in her chest. "Thank you."

"May I kiss you now?" he asked, a somewhat sad expression on his face.

"Yes."

His hand stroked her cheek. He leaned over and kissed her.

Pam closed her eyes in bliss. They hadn't kissed in weeks. Oh, it was so good. She'd forgotten how wonderful Bruce's touch was.

"Do you believe I'm an honorable man now?" he asked. He kissed her again.

"What?" She was in a fog of feelings.

"Do you believe me?" he persisted even as he distracted her brain from operating. He kissed her eyes, her nose, her ears, and then her lips again. She moved into his arms, which tightened around her.

Minutes or seconds later, she didn't know which, they drew apart. She sighed happily.

"Tonight?" he asked. His hands framed her face gently. She nodded her head, looking him in the eye. She would sneak out like an adolescent, after her mother was asleep, and go to Bruce's bed. Her body hummed in anticipation.

#

The day stretched on. While Dorothy was napping, Pam called Sarah and updated her.

"The doctor claimed Mom doesn't have Alzheimer's. Her personality hasn't changed, she doesn't have night terrors, and she doesn't wander. But you should have seen her when she didn't recognize Linley's boyfriend. Mom freaked out."

"That's not like her."

"You're right. She was screeching. I think he scared her. Why? He's obviously a nice, respectable young man. He's good looking, he was wearing an ordinary pair of shorts for running. He didn't look like a home invader. How could Mom have mistaken him for a dangerous stranger? Let alone one who somehow was threatening?"

"It sounds heavy."

"It was. Then I had a screaming match with Linley."

"What was her problem? As if I can't guess."

Pam felt she ought to defend Linley. "It wasn't about her, precisely. It was about her reaction to Mom's condition."

"Really?" Sarah conveyed a world of cynical doubt in one word.

"I think she was freaking out about the idea her grandmother may have Alzheimer's. She started blaming me. Said I neglected Mom. But I haven't, Sarah, I swear," she protested.

"Of course not. When's the last time Linley visited Dorothy?"

"I don't know." She couldn't help defending her daughter a little. "No one expects young people to pay attention to their elderly relatives."

"Sure, cut Linley a break. How about cutting yourself one, too?"

"Okay, I will. None of this is my fault. My mother and I never got along well in the past, so we haven't spent much time together until recently. My mother is a very clever woman. She hid the signs of her decline in cognition very well."

"I believe you. My ex hid the signs of his extramarital screwing around for years before I caught on." Sarah said it lightly. At the time, a decade ago, she had been devastated. When Sarah swore she would never marry again, Pam believed her.

"Anyway, it was a very dramatic morning," Pam said.

"Are you going to have sex with Bruce tonight?"

"Wow, get right to the point, Sarah, don't beat around the bush."

"He's still interested, right?"

"Yes."

"You've had him investigated? He's on the up-and-up?"

"Yes."

"So why not enjoy the free ride?"

"No need to be crude."

"Why not? Bruce is the perfect distraction from all this angst. He's convenient, and there are no strings. Enjoy him."

"I do, but I feel guilty," Pam admitted. What could she say? He was using her to be close to Dorothy and she was using him for sex? Her emotions might be involved, but she had retreated from exploring that aspect of their relationship. The sex was enough. When he tried to talk about their relationship, she fended him off.

"Sarah, can we talk about something cheerier?"

"Okay. How's your nonprofit coming?"

"Pretty well, considering how distracted I've been lately. Harper has a lot of experience on the charity circuit and she's keeping everything moving."

"Any more donations?"

"Yes. I got ten thousand dollars and a promise of ninety thousand more from a man connected to the former head of accounting at Bernie Madoff's company. He's probably a crook, but his check didn't bounce."

"I'm amazed you can bear to talk to these sleazes."

"I've turned over a new leaf. Or you could say I'm

channeling my mother."

"You're also expressing yourself more cynically. Have you noticed?"

"I feel different. I'm not in a rut anymore."

"Good. Too bad it took the imminent collapse of the entire Wall Street banking system to jog you out of your apathy."

Pam chuckled. Sarah's dry wit was bracing.

#

After Dorothy woke up, she started talking about the past. At first, Pam was obliging. Then she started to get uncomfortable. Dorothy was talking about Greta.

"Mom, you told me this before," Pam protested. Today wasn't a great day for Dorothy to be upsetting herself with thoughts of her long-dead and possibly murdered friend.

Dorothy was as stubborn as she had always been. "Hush, Pamela, I'm trying to tell you something important. Something that happened before you were born.

"I confronted Roger at his house after the funeral. I wanted justice for Greta. He was already drunk. Miserable. I saw he had been looking at photos of her, and crying.

"I told him he was a murderer. I pulled out my gun, the gun I'd borrowed from a boy who had seen service."

"Roger laughed at me. 'I'd murder myself before I'd hurt Greta.'

"I called him a liar.

"'Sure, I killed her,' he finally admitted. 'By marrying her.'"

"I must have looked puzzled.

He pulled two tear-stained pages off the table and handed

them to me.

"It was a diary-style letter written by Greta. I recognized her handwriting. She wrote in a rambling way about how boring and frustrating her life was, how she liked to do crazy things to liven it up. While Roger was having fun all day at work, she'd try to walk the top of a fence, or slide down the banister on the stairs."

"To add drama to her day, she'd let her friends and relatives see her bruises, and tell outlandish, fake tales of how she'd gotten them. It was a game for her. She had created a melodrama. She knew her sister and I had both fallen for it.

"I accused Roger of forging the letter. He laughed at me and then tears fell from his eyes.

"'Do you really want to know how Greta died?' he asked me. 'The truth?'

"As much as I didn't want to believe anything he said, I nodded.

"'That night, she was up to her usual tricks. She'd had a couple beers—oh, you didn't know she drank now, did you? To you, she was this perfect angel. She took up drinking after the kid was born. She was a quick drunk. One or two beers and she was seriously lit. Then she liked to take risks. This time, she wanted to ride the banister, but not sitting on it. Oh, no. That wouldn't have been risky enough. She wanted to stand on it.'

"Roger took another drink himself. I didn't know whether to believe him or not. Then he continued. 'I was already in bed. The kid was sound asleep. Then I heard Greta banging around, coming up the stairs. She'd had a third beer, she shouted at me. She finally felt free. I dragged myself out of bed, and there she was, standing on the banister, at the top of the stairwell, drunk and crazy. She claimed her life was so boring, she might as well be dead. Then she lost control of her feet and fell.' He covered his face with his hands.

"'The fall killed her?'

"'Yes,' he insisted. 'But already, people are whispering about me. I know what they're saying. That I was bad to her. Not true. I loved her and I killed her by marrying her. Greta played games, and she went too far. Now I and the kid have to pay. You coming here trying to avenge her is proof my name is mud now. I haven't got a chance.'

"Then he looked at me and said, 'Don't worry. I'm checking out real soon.'"

Dorothy said, "The scandal, the whispering, would have ruined his life. He knew it. He was convinced it already had.

"I didn't need to threaten him. He was a beaten man. He was grieving for Greta as I was. I urged him to sober up and consider his young child. I went home."

"What happened next?" Pam asked, apprehensive.

"Two weeks later, I got a call from Roger. He asked me to come get his son. He was going on a long trip, alone. I arrived at the house only half an hour later. The smell of burning was in the air. I could see a corner of what he had burned. It was Greta's letter. Another paper was open on the table. Roger's will, giving his son into Nora's custody.

"The boy was sitting at the bottom of the stairs, hugging his puppy. The puppy I gave him. He asked me if I was there to take him to his new mommy. A few minutes later, the police arrived, and told us the news about Roger. They saw the will and assumed he had killed himself out of grief for Greta. Which of course they hushed up and said was an accidental death so there was some life insurance for little Bruce. I called Nora to come get him."

"That's an amazing story," Pam said. "Very different from what you told Bruce and me several weeks ago. Then, you said Roger killed Greta."

"Sometimes, I only remember what I believed before I confronted him. Roger felt guilty for trapping Greta into a life she hated. Even he admitted that. Later, I realized that perhaps I had caused some of the double tragedy by threatening Roger directly. I'd brought home the truth of what the world thought of him."

"But you didn't tell Greta's sister?"

"Greta's letter went up in smoke. I had no way to prove Roger's innocence to her. She didn't want to believe that Roger was blameless in Greta's death, although I did try to tell her. I finally decided I would let it lie. If Nora wanted to hold onto the idea that everything was Roger's fault, as long as she never took it out on the boy, it didn't matter."

Dorothy sighed, looking every year of her age. "Nora was a lot younger than Greta and had always admired her. She couldn't bear to think of her sister as an unbalanced daredevil. I, on the other hand, had seen some of Greta's stunts during the war. Much as I preferred Roger as a villain, his supposed abuse of Greta had never jibed with her personality. She wasn't the submissive or fearful type. His story made more sense. I decided I believed it."

"You always claimed you were motivated to become an

activist by a tragedy. I thought you meant something different," Pam said.

"It was a tragedy," Dorothy insisted. "Oh, Roger was no angel. He probably did knock her around a little, but that would hardly subdue Greta's fiery spirit. No, Greta felt fatally constricted by the societal role she was forced into after the war. Something in her twisted. She turned her frustrated energy against herself."

Dorothy shifted in her chair, sitting more upright.

"What I took from Greta's sad end was we women had a lot of energy despite all the babies and homemaking, and we needed to use it constructively, or we'd end up crazy and hurting ourselves and others."

Pam understood at last. Probably her mother had said bits of this before, but Pam had not been listening then. Now that she had finally broken out of her supposedly safe rut—or more correctly, been thrown out—Pam did have some understanding of the importance of finding meaningful work, a way to contribute. Linley had scoffed at her nonprofit, but it was a lifeline, a way at last of having a personal presence in the world. Something Pam had been afraid of when she was young. The fear was gone now. She might have twenty-five more good years to live, years in which she would be healthy. She could do something genuinely useful with her extra time on the planet. As her mother had.

Dorothy retired to bed early. Pam took the opportunity to go next door.

Bruce was happy to see her. He moved to take her into his arms, but she held him off.

"I've got another version of your parents' story. Mom just told me." She repeated everything her mother had said.

Bruce was stunned. "Wow. How could Aunt Nora have been so wrong? What kind of crazy woman was my mother?"

"Mom said she was a daring and adventurous person who found her peacetime life too constricting. She livened it up by acting like a reckless kid."

Bruce nodded. "This version is more credible than the tale your mother spun of holding a gun on my dad. He'd seen action in the war. He could have disarmed her easily."

"I hadn't thought of that," she said, struck. "Do you believe this new account?"

Bruce smiled ruefully. "I think so. Or maybe we wait for the next version from your redoubtable mother."

"You think she might tell us another?"

"Why not? Dorothy seems to be a creative woman. The second story is the mirror version of the first. Instead of my father being unhappy with his peacetime role, it's my mother."

"You're right." How disappointing if the mystery still had not been solved.

Bruce shrugged. "She's circling back to the past as if it's unfinished in her mind. Why else did she have my mother's photo on display?"

"She saw your resemblance to Greta, and it nudged her memory."

"Every time she sees me, she probably gets that same nudge. All we have to do is wait for her to talk about those days again."

"Then you'll pick the version that pleases you the most? They're all pretty miserable. I think my mother feels guilty.

Confronting your father may have caused him to kill himself. That's why she tells it differently each time."

Bruce's expression was sober. "There's enough blame to go around for everybody involved. Even Aunt Nora, whose freak-out at the funeral motivated Dorothy to threaten my father. Bottom line, both my parents died. Nothing changes that essential truth. I'm old enough to know we don't always get a happy ending."

Pam's hand was on his arm in a consoling gesture. She moved it up to cup his cheek gently. "I'm sorry." She reached up and kissed him.

His arms came around her.

#

Pam went back to Ardsley the next day. She and Bruce had made love the night before, the first time in weeks. It had been very pleasant. That was all. She wasn't in love with Bruce. Maybe she never would be in love again. Or perhaps love at her age was so different from young love she did not recognize it.

Bruce might not be in love with her either, although she got the feeling he thought he was. He was the most decent of the men she met these days. The corporate scumbags she solicited for donations were something else.

As she pulled into her driveway, she mentally ticked off some of the tasks ahead for this week. Starting the lengthy process of finding the right help for her mother. More efforts to build the foundation. Some key changes in her own living situation. There was satisfaction in knowing she could handle everything.

Chapter 39

Six months later, Pam had made substantial progress, including selling her house. On a crisp spring day, she showed Sarah around her new condo in Melville, an affluent Long Island suburb.

"I'm about as near to the city as before, but now I'm far enough out on the Island that visiting Mom isn't a huge trek. There's tons of nearby shopping. Look at my big balcony." She led Sarah outside to a generous terrace, screened on both sides so it was private. They were on the tenth floor. The skyline went on for miles.

"This would be a million dollar view in Manhattan," Sarah said. "You have so much space." She admired the large rooms and the high ceilings, plus the Palladian windows letting in so much light.

"New furniture, too."

Sarah approved. "You've started a new life."

"I've let go of my past. Symbolically, at least."

They relaxed in comfortable chairs in the sunlit living room. "What do your children think about your move?" Sarah asked.

"They're still shocked, especially at how fast it happened."

"You kept the money from the sale, I hope? You didn't give it to them?"

Pam answered Sarah's last question with a shake of her head. "I kept what was left after purchasing this place outright. Now I won't need a paying job. I can concentrate on my foundation."

Sarah eyed Pam critically. "I can see you've already spent some of your profit on yourself. Your hair is done and you're dressing more upscale."

"You noticed." Pam preened a little. Her casual at-home outfit of chrome yellow slacks and top was from a high-end ready-to-wear designer. "It's spillover from needing to present myself carefully to solicit donations. Look." She held out her hands, showing off professionally manicured fingernails. "Legitimate business expense," she giggled.

Sarah laughed. "You've made amazing improvements to your life since the Menahl disaster. I'm proud of you."

Pam smiled. "Thanks."

"Time for the elephant in the room," Sarah said. "How's your mother doing?"

Pam took a deep breath. "All things considered, pretty well." She explained about the professional organizer she'd hired to visit Dorothy several times a week, to help with her social life and her new habit of not reading her mail.

"That's an unconventional choice of a home helper."

"She only needs light oversight for now."

"My aunt went through this, so I've heard a lot from my cousin about how dementia goes. Eventually, you'll need a fulltime companion or housekeeper to oversee regular physical therapy visits and nursing care."

Pam sighed. "Arranging it all takes time." She brightened. "Bruce decided to extend his lease, so he's still next door. He keeps an eye out for Mom and they still take their daily walks."

"Going to marry him?"

Pam shrugged, her fingers playing with a crystal paperweight on the table next to her.

Sarah stood. "Yeah, why bother? Keep it to sex and the occasional dinner out." She smoothed her sharp-looking pantsuit. "Speaking of which, let's go find a restaurant."

#

Two months later, Pam was still searching for a full-time housekeeper, slash companion, slash practical nurse when she got a phone call from Magda. Although they kept in touch by email about Bright Side Foundation business, they seldom talked directly.

"How are you, dear? How is your son?" Pam asked.

"Harvard is wonderful university. Marc so happy."

Magda asked in turn how Pam was, and somehow, Pam ended up telling her former coworker about Dorothy.

"You need housekeeper. I can be housekeeper."

"What? You're a trained financial professional and you're looking for a paying job and you're already donating lots of time to the foundation."

Magda laughed. "Pusher paper," she said, as usual getting the idiom backwards. She coughed her smoker's cough and continued. "No jobs. I look. Every day. Stan no job. He married. Me, I need job."

"But…but would you be happy being a housekeeper out there at the beach? It's isolated compared to the city," Pam said.

"Keep house for husband. Keep house for your mama. Email for rest."

Could it be that simple? Pam and Magda decided on a tryout. Why not? They'd worked in the same office together for five years. Except for that last day when she set the documents on fire—under considerable pressure of emotion—Magda had been levelheaded. Magda was a trustworthy person. She had a good heart. Now they had to find out if Magda would enjoy living out on the beach, and more significantly, if Dorothy would tolerate having her as a housekeeper.

There was plenty of money to hire help. Even the recent financial meltdown hadn't significantly touched the large resources available. Malcolm Duncan had known too many stockbrokers to trust all his savings to them, and Dorothy had continued the tradition of diversifying her assets.

Alexander helped with the initial steps. He flew up from North Carolina to be there on the day when Pam took Dorothy to see the lawyer to have a power of attorney drawn up.

"Where have you been lately?" Dorothy scolded her son.

"I'm living in North Carolina now."

"That's very disobliging of you," she harrumphed.

He smiled, and hugged her. "Mom, my wife threatened to leave me unless we got away from the harsh winters up here."

He nodded at Pam. "Little sis is going to take care of all your business affairs from now on. I'll oversee what she does, I promise."

Dorothy looked mollified. She still thought of Pam as a

lightweight and she always would. Her brain did not process much new information about her family anymore. It was a wall Pam had to work around. She struggled not to break down when she thought of what inevitably would happen. The slow wreck of her mother's wonderful mind. Pam pasted a smile on her face and tried to deal with today and tomorrow only.

"Come on, you two. We're off to see the lawyer," she said.

Alexander led the way to his large rental car and helped Dorothy into the spacious front passenger seat, while Pam climbed in the back.

"I hear you have a boyfriend," he said, as he drove.

"Who told you?"

"What's his name? Bruce?"

"Yes," she replied, wondering where this was leading.

"When I called Mom the other night, she said you were off with Brooooooce," he dragged out the name to two syllables in falsetto.

Alexander continued to tease her all the way to the attorney's office. Her brother was okay with Pam taking control of their mother's life. He thought most of Pam's ideas were good. Unsaid was his determination not to be around to see their mother deteriorate day by day. Pam ought to be angry at him for leaving the state without even warning her about what he was doing. He had evaded the issue, thinking Dorothy was all right living alone for a while. How could he have known the situation would change so rapidly?

Surprisingly, Dorothy did not put up a fuss at the lawyer's office. She agreed to the power of attorney, and at the lawyer's urging also updated her will, and enacted a durable medical power of attorney naming Pam, as well as a living will.

"Any more thorough, and he would have taken a blood sample," Dorothy remarked as they left.

"Being thorough was the idea, Mom," Alexander said. "Now you're set."

To ride off into the sunset of her life. The truth was painful. Their mother was losing her mental acuity. If she stayed physically healthy, they could look forward to Dorothy eventually being a shadow of her former self mentally. Which was worse, to die in the next year or two, when she could still recognize her children? Or to drag it out for another decade? Dorothy had often stated she would not live to be ninety because no one from her side of the family ever had. Yet, Dorothy had always been an exceptional woman. She might beat the family odds.

Pam shivered. Alexander put his arm around her. She looked at him and saw her own sadness reflected in his eyes. He was putting on a good show, but he felt the same pain she did. This was the beginning of the end.

Back home after a lavish restaurant lunch, they settled Dorothy in the sunroom, and then Pam and Alexander walked into the kitchen to discuss details of how they would handle day-to-day and emergencies.

"It's a good thing your friend is starting as housekeeper next week, but meanwhile, take Mom's car keys," he warned.

Pam sighed. "I don't think she has used the car since that day Bruce thought she got lost."

It had been painful to call Dorothy's best friend locally and explain she would be arriving and leaving by cab from now on.

Adele Watson had said, "I suspected Dorothy was getting a bit vague. I didn't know Alexander had moved away. I'm glad you're taking over."

"I hope you don't mind me asking, but how is your own situation, Mrs. Watson?" Pam asked.

"You don't have to worry about me, dear. My youngest grandson lives with me." She laughed. "He couldn't afford an apartment so I let him live here rent free."

They agreed as long as both of the elderly friends enjoyed lunching together, Dorothy would be reminded of her regular date and sent over in a cab.

"I do love Dorothy," Adele Watson said.

Pam also made a special visit to the local taxi company. She explained the kind of help she needed from the drivers.

The company owner was eager to be of service. "She helped me start this business, you know," Celia Jones said. She was a sixtyish bottle blonde. A reminiscent smile touched her world-weary face. "I'd had a devastating divorce, and Dorothy got me back on my feet. She forced the local bank to lend to me, citing the Fair Credit Act that banks weren't honoring yet. I owe her a lot."

They set up a billing plan, and Pam insisted on paying a retainer. "I'm sure my mother would want to do it this way," she said, when Celia offered to let Dorothy run a monthly tab.

Pam gave everyone her cell phone number. She even made herself learn how to set it on vibrate only, and how to retrieve and send text messages and email. Drifting out of touch with today's new communication technology was an affectation she could no longer indulge, not now that she had important business to conduct.

Alexander stayed for a few days, visiting old friends. Bruce came over and Pam introduced Alexander to him. The men got along well, but since Pam had no marital plans, it hardly mattered. She soon returned home to Melville. She and Bruce had not taken their relationship beyond the casual, and currently it looked as if they never would. That was all right, though. They had sex whenever it was convenient, which was enough for her. For him too, she suspected, despite his hints at an emotional attachment. They never made any extravagant declarations or promises. That was fine with Pam. She had plenty to keep her occupied in the city. Bruce's extension his lease of the house next door was some kind of a commitment on his part, but Pam did not care to confront him about his intentions. They enjoyed each other's company, and that was enough for her at this point in her life. Maybe in a few years, once her foundation was on solid ground, she would think about being a wife again. Or maybe never.

Dorothy had not volunteered another story about Greta. She had even put away the framed photograph. Perhaps by telling the second story, Dorothy had exorcised whatever unhappy feelings she'd had about Greta's death. Maybe there would not be another version.

Pam heard nothing from Linley, not that she expected to. The holidays had passed without any mother-daughter contact whatsoever, although Steve and Callie had invited both Linley and Pam to their home. Linley hadn't come, and Pam had stopped begging for Linley's attention. Of course, she worried about her daughter, but she could see her on television every day. She set the DVR to record Linley's shows and watched them later. Linley had not looked happy immediately after the disastrous beach visit. The zest had gone out of her performance with Jason. Thus it came as no shock when their new show was not renewed after one short season. Jason's promotion to his own night-time talk show was the ostensible reason. In the avalanche of publicity about him surrounding his new show, there wasn't one word about a fiancée. The relationship might have ended, possibly badly. Something else she couldn't talk to Linley about.

#

Dorothy enjoyed looking out at the water. It was always different, but always the same. As the noise in her head had gotten louder, she'd found the water calmed her and helped her think clearly. Her children took care of her finances now. That was a relief. Pamela was a good child. How ironic. The two children she'd had the least time for when they were young were the most solicitous of her now. Alexander and Pamela had gotten the short end of the stick when it came to maternal attention. By the time she'd had them, she had been immersed in her causes, plus busy with Christine's and Neil's activities.

Christine had been a daughter to be proud of, making good grades and being popular and winning scholarships. She'd never needed anyone. She was a cat who walked by herself. She left and never looked back. Neil, another star achiever, found the perfect wife and changed his loyalty so completely to her and her family that he barely acknowledged his blood family anymore.

She didn't blame her children for living their own lives. For many years, she'd kept so busy, she hardly missed them. Her world had narrowed only recently. She'd decided to give up driving. She did not want to get lost on the road. It wasn't that she was afraid, precisely. She just wanted to live out her remaining time with as much dignity as she could. So no more driving. She'd have to tell Pamela to sell the car.

Pamela was a good child. How ironic. The two children she'd had the least time for when they were young were the most solicitous of her now. Alexander and Pamela. She'd seen both of them recently. Difficult to keep names and dates and places in her head today. It was calming to look out at the water. It was always different, and always the same.

Chapter 40

A year had passed since Linley had her blowup with her mother and then with Jason. Much had changed. He had moved on to his dream job as a night-time talk show host. It had happened at the right moment, since their on-air chemistry had completely vanished after that disastrous trip to the beach. They'd tried to fake it on the show. Paradoxically, considering how angry she often was, she didn't have the fire for arguing anymore. Especially because she finally had realized she loved Jason, when it was too late. It wasn't only sex she wanted and needed from him, or a leg up for her career, or even the pleasure of having somebody to be with. It was Jason himself.

She'd thrown their love away by being an immature, self-absorbed brat. She couldn't win Jason back again. She had used up all the second chances he'd given her. His cold shoulder to her since that weekend at the beach had been absolute.

She stayed with the panel show, eventually graduating to a secure segment on a more broad-based finance program. It wasn't quite what her ambitions had forecast for her, but then, she wasn't quite the same person anymore.

Intensive therapy focused on anger management had cleared up personal issues she'd never faced before. She hadn't even realized she had issues. When she was wailing to Caitlin about the breakup with Jason, her friend pushed her to get therapy.

"You need to see a shrink."

They were seated in a tiny restaurant, having a nonalcoholic Sunday brunch about a month after the traumatic event. Caitlin had declined the mimosas on the menu without any visible struggle.

Linley shook her head. "I don't have mental problems."

"Same know-it-all Linley as usual," Caitlin said, with an air of impatience Linley had never seen from her friend before. "Seeing a shrink helped me stop being a drunken slut. It could help you, too."

"I'm not the one who…" Linley started to deny, but Caitlin interrupted her.

"No more unfunny jokes about me waking up in bed with two men. That experience was not a laugh riot."

When Linley tried to speak, Caitlin held up her hand.

"I've forgiven you. We're talking about you, not me. My psychologist says if you keep having the same problems, you are the cause of them."

"I don't know what happens to me. I see red and I just go off."

"You yell at people."

Linley didn't refute the accusation.

Caitlin continued, "I love you, but you have an anger problem. Get some help?"

Linley sighed. She considered her waffles glumly. "I used to think I never made mistakes."

"I know. I let you be my friend in spite of your superiority complex." Caitlin smiled to take the sting out of her criticism. Caitlin had never said such frank words to Linley before. That she thought them was a revelation.

"So if I want a different outcome, I need to find out what the underlying issue is?" Linley asked.

"Yep. For me, it was simple. You know I had a crap time as a teenager. As an adult, I wanted to drink in as much fun as possible. The operative word being drink," she said ruefully. "The shrink helped me see I had gone beyond the fun stage into self-harm."

"People get stuck, repeating something that used to work for them, that's the concept?"

"Anger must have been an effective weapon for you in the past. You say it's been the cause of your recent troubles. A mental health professional can help you get un-stuck."

Linley had put the name of Caitlin's shrink in her phone, and then surprised herself by calling for an appointment. The therapist had seen through Linley's façade right away to the chip on her shoulder. There was a lot of work to do, she said. Linley had collapsed with relief. Then the therapist had made Linley work. It had turned her attitude around.

Linley discovered she'd been carrying over classic hostile teenager behavior into adulthood. Along the way, she'd convinced herself she was perfect. She'd looked down on others, never giving anyone the benefit of the doubt. Especially her mother.

Once she'd gotten deep enough into therapy to realize how

rotten she'd been to her mother for years, the issue of mending fences arose. It hadn't been easy to face up to calling Pam and asking to meet with her. Pam showed no emotion during the phone call. There was no clue to her feelings. Linley's heart sank. Maybe it was too late.

Linley chose a neutral venue, a quiet midtown restaurant on a weekday after the lunch rush. Pam arrived in a fashionable dress, wearing designer shoes and carrying a designer bag. She looked utterly confident. Linley didn't know whether to embrace her or not.

Pam didn't hesitate. She leaned in to give Linley a quick kiss on the check. Almost an impersonal touch, but meaningful considering they hadn't seen each other or talked in months.

"Hello, dear. It's been a long time."

"Hi, Mom."

They sat in a booth, facing each other. Her mother looked sophisticated. Distinguished. Heads had turned as she'd walked in.

"How's the foundation?" Linley was finding it difficult to get to the point. Maybe she wasn't ready after all.

Pam looked at her with a knowing expression. "You of all people could research exactly how the Bright Side Foundation is doing. I'm sure you had some other reason for wanting to talk to me."

"You're right." Linley gave a dry, half-laugh with no humor in it. "That's something I've seldom said to you."

Pam made no comment.

Linley took a deep breath. "I want to apologize. For everything. For all those years of being a know-it-all, selfish princess."

Her mother said nothing.

"For acting as if all you did for our family was worthless."

The final words were hard to say. She opened her mouth, but nothing came out.

Her mother helped her. "And?"

"For blaming you for what's happening to Grandma Dorothy." The last words came out in a rush.

Pam nodded. "That is a very complete apology. I accept it."

"Thank you," she said, relieved, but still feeling small.

Her mother leaned forward and covered her hand with her own. Her expression was earnest. "It's my turn to apologize, for letting you get away with being spoiled. I took the easy route to family peace. We both have paid for my mistake."

Tears sprang to Linley's eyes. "You have nothing to apologize for, Mom. You did your best."

"Maybe," Pam shrugged. "I tried to make our family life as ideal as possible. Perhaps I should have debated with you about a woman's contribution to a home and a family. That was not my way."

"Dad and I were lucky to have you."

Pam sighed. "I'd like to think so. That I didn't waste all those years. Bruce won't be that lucky. I have no ambitions of being the little hausfrau all over again."

"Bruce?"

"My boyfriend, lover, regular hookup," Pam said, "whatever you call them these days. You met him at Dorothy's."

"I thought he was just a neighbor trying to worm his way into Grandma's confidence." Linley shook her head. "I didn't realize you were…seeing him."

Pam raised an eyebrow.

Linley's shock subsided as she struggled to find an adequate response. This was a test. Had the therapy made a difference, or would this news make her freak out again?

They both were silent for a minute. Pam withdrew her hands and sat back, waiting. Still with that smile on her face. Daring Linley to make a big bratty deal of her mommy having a sex life. The therapist had warned this could happen.

Linley took a long, shaky breath. She spoke slowly. "I think I'm okay with that."

"Good." Her mother's smile widened.

"I've been seeing a therapist," Linley said. "Working on my anger issues."

"You're doing fine, dear."

Suddenly, Linley saw the love that always was in her mother's eyes. Her own eyes spilled over with tears. "Mom, I'd like to start again."

"You're my daughter. You can always start again."

Linley leaped up from the table and ran around it to hug Pam, sobbing.

"There, there," her mother soothed. "It's all right, dear."

"But I hurt you. And Jason dumped me. And I love him."

Pam moved over and made room for Linley to sit next to her on the banquette. Pam kept an arm around her as Linley poured out the whole story about Jason. Pam made sympathetic comments, or squeezed her, and finally took her napkin and dried Linley's tears.

"Such a sad little girl," her mother said.

"I'm different now, Mom, believe me," she said.

"We won't look back. We'll look forward," her mother said, still in comforting mode.

"But I love him."

In the past, Pam might have trotted out a platitude, but now she frowned in consideration. "What does your therapist say?"

"That Jason is done with me. But I still want him."

"The relationship feels unfinished to you?"

"Yes."

"Making amends can be powerful."

"And then he'll forgive me? Like you forgave me?" she asked.

"Mothers are different." Pam smiled, with a hint of sadness in her expression. "Other people don't always give you another chance. You have to forgive yourself if they won't, so you can put it behind you."

Linley thought it over. "I guess you and the shrink are right. I can't go back."

There was a world-weary smile on her mother's face, an expression Linley had never noticed before. "Only forward."

"Get on with my life."

At her mother's nod, Linley gave a choked laugh. "I hate you both." But she smiled.

Pam chuckled.

After that, the conversation flowed freely. Linley brought up her frequent phone calls with Dorothy. "Grandma Dorothy sounds like her old self on the phone. When I see her, she's very different. She's confused."

"She can fake it more easily on the phone because there are fewer distractions."

"She's getting worse, isn't she?"

"Yes, despite the fact that she's taking the standard dementia medicines. She doesn't show any more signs of classic Alzheimer's, which is wonderful."

"I've been researching the disease," Linley said. "What you mean is she hasn't suffered a personality change for the worse."

"Right. Your grandmother is still the same person. Just missing some pieces."

"It's not fair."

Her mother didn't answer. She didn't try to make it right for her spoiled princess, or sugarcoat the truth. Life was imperfect, and her mother accepted that. Now it was up to Linley to live as if she did, too.

From then on, Linley made the effort to keep communication open with her mother. They now called or emailed regularly. Pam even texted occasionally. They weren't best buds, dishing about every date, but their long estrangement was over.

She sensed she was the one doing the running. Her mother was busy now, with her foundation, with Grandma Dorothy's affairs, and with that hunky over-the-hill science writer next door, Bruce. She wondered why they didn't get married. Her mother never said anything against her father, but the fact that she didn't marry again spoke volumes. Maybe her father hadn't been such a perfect husband after all.

Linley hoped her new attitude was changing people's minds about her. It extended beyond family. She was ashamed of how unkind she had been to Caitlin in the past. Now, Linley was beginning to feel a compassion for other people she had never felt before.

Even her opinion of the silly consumers who ran up their credit cards had mellowed. She didn't despise them anymore. She had sympathy for their weaknesses. They were fooling themselves, that was all. Eventually, they'd have to face the truth, as she'd had to.

Her mother was doing well. Her foundation was a moderate success, getting regular mention in the press as she convinced one big name after another to make peace with his conscience. Ironic that corporate greed was the bedrock of the foundation's donors. That alone made for a good story, giving the foundation additional press.

Her grandmother was doing fine, too, with that lady from her mother's old job, Magda, as her housekeeper-companion. Although Dorothy was increasingly divorced from reality.

Linley hadn't gotten involved with any new men, and she hadn't hooked up with any either. Ernie had wanted to hook up, but she'd said no. She was too busy working on her interior life to seek out men or sex. The memory of intimacy with Jason was too strong.

Perhaps she hadn't completely given up hope that some day, she and Jason might reconcile. Meanwhile, her therapist had suggested, same as her mother had, she should forgive herself for screwing up her love affair with Jason.

It had been true love, but she'd never recognized it until it was over. She hoped one day she'd find another man who made such a deep connection with her. There was plenty of time. She'd been in a big hurry before. Her immaturity had insisted she deserved to have it all before she was thirty, whether she was ready or not.

Today was an ironic day. Her first personal finance book was coming out, and her new publicist had managed to get her on Jason's late night show. The angle was that they used to work together. The cable network was about to launch her new show, *Money 101*. They'd combined calling in some PR favors with the book launch.

She was nervous in the green room, checking her appearance endlessly. Not too much makeup, but not too little. No bright red cocktail dress, no showing off her assets like a starlet. Instead, a smoothly flowing medium blue number that merely hinted at her curves. Sophisticated, yet not severe.

How she looked was okay. It was how she felt. She hadn't seen Jason even to bump into in the halls in months because their shows were scheduled at very different times of day.

He was now the big deal he'd always wanted to be. She'd seen his show. It fit him like a glove. He was having a ball, obviously. Had he changed? She knew she had, but would he see that? There was always the possibility he had agreed to have her on the show to skewer her in front of a live audience.

She had time to fret, because she wasn't the first guest. That was a movie star who was guaranteed to interest a lot of women, and some men. He bantered about his new movie, they showed a clip, and then he was gone. He was too important to stick around.

Next came a comedian. Jason made short work of him.

Then it was her turn. She walked out carefully, with a smile pasted on her face. Jason stood up to greet her, which she expected, but then he leaped over his desk and embraced her.

The audience went wild. He kissed her lightly and they

screamed. Then he personally led her to the guest chair.

"Linley and I used to be an item," he joked to the audience. "We had a regular date on WFWF every afternoon."

He was being playful. Okay, she could do that. She smiled, struggling to conceal her shock. "That's right. We argued about money on national television. Every day."

"It was almost like being married, but without any privileges, if you know what I mean," he replied, wiggling his eyebrows. The audience roared.

That set the tone. They bantered about being old enemies, about his rise and her slower ascent, about her new book, which he held up, and about her new TV show. They smiled the entire time. They made a cute impression. Old buddies and sparring partners. Now friends.

When the segment ended for a commercial, Jason's smile switched off. He stood up and motioned for her to do the same. He told the audience. "I'm going to walk her out. She's that important now." He ushered her off the set, muttering a warning, "Don't forget we're still miked."

When they got behind the curtain where the audience couldn't see them anymore, he suddenly whirled her around and kissed her. Passionately. His lips possessed hers and his tongue thrust into her mouth. Electricity arced between them. It was still there, all of it. Nothing had changed. She returned his kisses until they had to break for air. Then she backed away from him, knowing he could see the fear and pain in her eyes.

His own expression showed shock. He touched the mic on his lapel, to remind her not to speak. Then, with one finger, he caressed her lower lip.

"Goodbye," he said. He turned and went back through the curtain.

Maybe this was closure.

No. No way would she accept that, not when he still wanted her. She'd go after him and get him back.

Starting tomorrow.

A Note from the Author

Thank you for reading *A Daughter's a Daughter*. If you liked this book, please tell your friends, and consider reviewing it wherever you prefer to post reviews.

If you'd like to be notified when a new story is coming out, please go to my website, www.irenevartanoff.com, and sign up for my mailing list. I'll only send you information about new releases. I promise no sharing and no spam.

Acknowledgments

My thanks to authors Loretta Ellingsworth and Janet Mullany, who read this story in manuscript and made several key suggestions for improving it.

Made in the USA
Middletown, DE
16 March 2018